A Little Child Shall Lead Them

LaVonne Snowden

Unless otherwise noted, all Scripture quotations are taken from the King James Version of the Bible.

A Little Child Shall Lead Them
ISBN 0-9667234-2-2

13150 SE 32nd Street
Bellevue, WA 98005

Dedication

To my mother, Mable Ruth Maddeford, who is
responsible for my beautiful book, as she
nagged and fussed for me to start writing.
I always retorted, "Mother, if you wanted me
to write, why didn't you send me to school?"

To my wonderful family: my beloved husband,
Powell; and our four precious children,
Patsy, Joy, Jerry, and Bill. I love you all.

Acknowledgements

Thank you to Linda Lowenstein and Sylvia Tacker
for typing the first pages of this manuscript
and to Elizabeth Sherman for her help
in publishing this book.

Contents

Note to the Reader

I am LaVonne Snowden, age eighty-three. I live in an elegant retirement home now, but my life started out in dire poverty, surviving the dust bowl in the Ozarks during the Great Depression. When I was six, my brother was seven, and my sister was four, our father walked down the road and left us. I guess the reason the picture is so vivid is that my mother was crying and begging him not to go. We never heard from or saw him again. My mother looked for him all her life. In those years we lived in our car, tents, and when I was thirteen, we lived in a hay barn.

When I was just a teenager in 1933, I borrowed a friend's wedding gown and eloped with my sweetheart. We spent sixty-two glorious years and had four beautiful children together before he passed away a few years ago. When I was twenty and he was twenty-seven, we met Jesus and entered a glorious life we didn't know was out there. I have been a Bible teacher, a counselor, and yes, even a preacher. Although this is not a religious book, I have included many quotes from the Bible.

With only six years of schooling, I educated myself with hundreds of books. In fact, the first time I saw a public library, all those books were like bricks of gold to me! So you see, it seems only right that I should write a book. I have written this book for forty years in my heart, but have written it physically the last six years.

My story is about life in the little town of Paw Paw in the Ozark Mountains. It revolves around the General Store where the men of the town gather on the porch to sit, whittle, chew 'baccy, and read the Paw Paw Times. They are the town's conscience, the Baptist Church is its anchor, and the grave beside the front porch of the county's richest man is one of its mysteries.

All my characters are based on real people, and the stories are based on actual events in my life. These are heady, exhilarating, passionate people. The sexual overtures and acts of passion are portrayed as the sweetest of pleasures as God intended them. My book is humorous, filled with the banter and witticism only found in the Ozarks of the 1930s. And the people had a deep spiritual faith that was necessary in the face of starvation, want, and fear during the Great Depression.

Of course, my joy is being published before I die.

LaVonne Snowden
Fall 2001

The hand of the LORD was upon me,
and carried me out in the spirit of the LORD,
and set me down in the midst of the valley
which was full of bones, and caused me to pass
by them round about: and, behold, there were
very many in the open valley; and, lo,
they were very dry. And he said unto me,
Son of man, can these bones live?
And I answered, O LORD GOD, thou knowest.

Then said he unto me, Prophesy unto the wind,
prophesy, son of man, and say to the wind,
Thus saith the LORD GOD; Come from the four winds,
O breath, and breathe upon these slain, that they may live.
So I prophesied as he commanded me,
and the breath came into them,
and they lived, and stood up upon their feet,
an exceeding great army.

EZEKIEL 37: 1-3, 9-10

Preface

The Sound of the Depression

Out in the distance, unseen and unknown, was a huge black noisome cloud gathering strength and momentum to establish a foothold in the tiny town of Paw Paw. It crept in slowly; mute, like a phantom in a vast desert of silence. The residents of Paw Paw never noticed it at first. Before two years had passed, wanton and unfettered, it would penetrate every home in town and all the surrounding regions. All would see, hear, taste, and even smell the death of the Great Depression of the thirties.

Without doubt, the Depression and the drought had clasped hands together. There were clouds without water that even failed to drop the dew of the night. It was as though the God of the Universe had bound up the water in thick clouds and refused to release their silvery moisture. Heaven itself seemed to mock and laugh at earth's calamity and despair. The blazing sun burned on, sending a cruel message of want and disaster. The trees in the fruit orchards turned ugly and barren. Row upon row they stood like sentinels guarding white sepulchers. The smallest gust of wind would rustle their dead leaves and flutter them to the ground. Paw Paw's residents who were the breadwinners of the family shivered and trembled at the new terror they were encountering. How long could it last? It might be years; no one knew.

It first started out quite innocently. The sawmill cut its production down to four days a week. The men on the porch agreed that they could all get along on less pay. However, they were a little startled when the next month they were cut down to three days a week. Every family that worked at the mill discussed this topic around the supper table at night. The children were alarmed at the seriousness of the talking between their fathers and mothers. Some children thought that they were the cause of the unrest in the home, so many of them quit their squabbling and fussing. Others wore looks of apprehension.

It was less than a month later when the final blow came.

It was a Monday morning. Mr. Russell Walker, the owner of the sawmill, came out of his office and addressed all the men. "Now men, this hurts me as much as it does you, but my back is against the wall. I had to close the mill last night. I met with my lawyer and several other prominent businessmen in Whippoorwill, and we can't see any hope in sight. We are in the worst drought we have ever seen here in our neck of the woods. One person thinks this is only the beginning of what will come later. Our nation is being caught up in this nightmarish Depression. There is no place to run to; many have already tried that. I have no buyer for the stockpile of lumber, so I leave that to you. You can pick up your checks in the office. I hope and pray that our God we serve will bless you in these trying times."

In the area around Paw Paw, there were many creeks, streams, and living springs that had flowed unhindered through the years. The water had been slowly ebbing away, and they now lay dormant and stagnant with an eerie silence. All the wells, except for Plenty Well—the well that was inspired by a vision—dried up. Dead things formed as the life-giving water ebbed away. Many kinds of fish that had lingered too long in their favorite swimming hole gulped convulsively as they were caught in the muddy brackish mire.

The parched earth from the receding waters developed into mud flats. Then these too dried up leaving big cracks that tapered down and formed hollow curly cups begging, to no avail, for a drop of moisture from the heavens. As the water receded, big white stones in the creek beds lay bald and naked, adorned only with black rings and bracelets of the mud. Was there a melancholy painter lurking in the background with a brush and palette of ebony paint?

Big Morgan Creek was the last to disappear. Everyday one or two of the men on the porch would follow the dry creek bed. Nowhere in any of the stories that the sages handed down were there tales of Big Morgan going dry.

The children started to play games in the dry creek bed, but they soon gave it up because of the eerie silence. They seemed puzzled and confused about where the water had gone.

At first glance, the look of all the men that sat on the porch at the General Store merged into one. Their faces were weathered, drawn, and pinched. There was a wounded look in their eyes. They were unshaven with wild limp hair creeping out from the ragged brims of their straw hats. They all wore bib overalls. The legs were generally too long and had to be rolled up around their rough shoe tops. Every rolled cuff, which they hadn't bothered to shake out, was filled with the white grayish dust from the road. A somber dark mantle of worry hovered over each one, while a river of fear flowed in their bellies.

Almost unbelievably, when one man crossed his legs, the others could see that he had resoled his shoes with a piece of worn-out automobile tire. He explained, "You just fit your shoe on a shoe-last, cut the rubber tire to fit your sole, and nail it on. I will admit it's a mite uncomfortable, but it works. Maybe in time I can buy a new pair of shoes, who knows."

The men had quit looking to the heavens for a cloud that might produce some rain. Their mirth and laughter had ceased. Current events of each day, family situations, tales of bygone years were seldom mentioned. If they did speak about something, it was in a disheartened murmur, almost a whisper. In all this trouble, the men gathered closer together, and the bickering and arguing ceased. Neighbor took neighbor when they walked through their fields, inspecting dried grasses, which in the past had always been green. Now the fruits of their labors lay wearied and lifeless.

Before the drought, everyone had filled their barns, sheds, cellars, and larders to overflowing. The woods and fields yielded wild berries of every kind, theirs for the picking. Wild greens, tubs of them, were canned by the women. Smokehouses hung with bacon, hams, and beef, which had been cured over smoking fires and salted down for keeping. Dried corn, beans, peas, and fruit of every kind were stored. The housewives and grandmothers filled their cellars with countless quarts of vegetables, meats, fruit, juices, pickles, jellies, and jams. If a neighbor would happen by, the lady of the house always took them to the cellar to view the shelves of their sweet labor of love. Cabbages, apples, and pears were buried in the straw in the ground so they wouldn't freeze. When needed they would be uncovered layer by layer.

Some of the women folk who were lazy, flitting away the days and not taking advantage of a bountiful harvest, had children who seemed to be a mite skinny when spring rolled around.

During this drought time, many of the men still dared to plow their fields and plant their seed. But the fierce hot winds would blow the good topsoil away making their efforts futile. These dust storms hid the sunshine from view for days at a time. Many of these men had to borrow money from the bank for their early spring plantings. In the past, these loans would be paid back out of the first yield of harvest. This was a time and a place when only a man's word and handshake would be needed for a business transaction. There was no first harvest and with their loans unpaid, they felt shame and guilt.

Families tried to seal the cracks in windows with rags, but that didn't keep the dust and sand out of their houses.

One of the strange phenomenons of those dark days of drought and Depression was the action of the animals. They all had an uncanny knowledge of what was happening with the weather. The horses, cows, and pigs would turn their tails and backs to the hot winds to protect their eyes. The chickens and other fowl stood with their feathers and wings stretched out all awry, trying to catch a puff of wind that might venture by.

There was a sound to the Depression. All the men heard it, but none could explain it. It was the sound of a silent town weeping silent tears.

Who is this that cometh out of the wilderness
like pillars of smoke
perfumed with myrrh and frankincense,
with all powders of the merchant?

SONG OF SOLOMON 3:6

Chapter 1

A Big Pink Rose That Landed in a Ditch Beside a Road

Everyone in the little town of Paw Paw knew that little Jimmy Simpson would be the first to see her, which was just the way it was, no explaining why.

Jimmy had told his mother he was going to hunt for a rabbit or two for their supper that night, but so far he hadn't had any luck. Not even one fat little rabbit. He was tired, so he hunkered down, resting his back against the trunk of a big oak tree, his rifle across his knees. The sun filtered through the leaves and gave a dappled, speckled look to the shiny barrel of his gun. By his side sat a rust-colored hound dog. The dog's liquid brown eyes worshiped his beloved master. Jimmy Simpson had an expression on his face of a young boy who believed that God was seated on His throne in heaven and all was right with the world.

He gazed down the road out of Paw Paw which was straight as far as you could see. It was then that she appeared on the horizon. At first, she looked like a stick-man with a head, arms, and legs like a child would draw on his first day at school. The next thing Jimmy noticed was that she didn't just walk. She marched military style, which was a triumph in itself as she carried a big suitcase and a large valise of some sort. In spite of these loads, she held her head high, without looking around.

By now Jimmy could see her plainly, but she couldn't see

him even though he was just a stone's throw away. She was dressed in black—black dress, black hose, black shoes—and she wore a black hat with a big pink rose on the brim.

Then suddenly she stopped. Was she tired, he wondered? She set her burdens down and appeared as though trying to make a decision. While she was still, Jimmy studied her. She was a tiny, elfin, delicate woman, what the men on the porch would call puny. Nevertheless, Paw Paw would soon learn that the word delicate would not describe the sprightly, brisk, rather Victorian young lady who had not one ounce of fat on her body. Her eyes were grayish blue. She had one finger beside her rather peaked nose, and her forehead was wrinkled in thought as she tried to think her problem through. Her face would have been lovely if she hadn't so desperately tried to look unattractive.

Evidently, she had come to a decision, for in a whit she took off her hat, yanked the big pink rose off, and blithely threw it into the ditch beside the road. In doing this puzzling action, her hair tumbled down her back in lustrous tawny waves. She appeared to panic a little when this happened and furtively looked to see if someone was near. Satisfied that she was undetected, she leaned over, gathered her hair in her hands, and pulled it up into a tight bun on her head. When several strands escaped this bondage, she repeated this drama over again. She had a faint smile on her face and looked pleased as she patted and felt her hair. With a firm hand she placed her hat back onto her head, picked up her heavy burden again, and at a fast clip headed for Paw Paw's General Store.

Jimmy's eyes were riveted on this pantomime unfolding before him. His breath quickened and like a seesaw raced down his spine. Who was she? Where did she come from? What was the reason of her coming to Paw Paw? Jimmy often said that Paw Paw was the end of nowhere. Now the bigger question was, Why was he so captivated by her? Why this mysterious feeling? It seemed to be almost a spiritual bond or fetters lacing them together by the love of God. "Strange indeed," Jimmy murmured.

Suddenly, Jimmy's questions came to a halt. There sitting beside a big bush sat two little gray rabbits, looking at Jimmy eye-to-eye, wrinkling their little wet noses. As if on command, they both started to thump their left foot on the ground. In wonder, Jimmy picked up his gun and started home. This was not the day to shoot sweet little rabbits.

The men on the porch stopped talking when they saw her coming. Usually they would have sized her up, commented, expressed their opinion about her and whether she brought good news or ill repute to Paw Paw. This kind of harangue would continue until the person set their foot on the first step of the stairs of the porch of the General Store. In the way they stepped up those stairs, the men judged that person's age, health, and freedom from ailment. If they held to the wobbling banister, they needed some help, and one of the men—if not all—would give them assistance. However, this stranger was different.

They didn't comment about her, about who she was, where she came from, or why she had come to Paw Paw. They sat motionless, glued to their chairs.

The woman planted her feet dead center of the stairs, carried her burdens up with her, and didn't touch the wobbling banister once. She set her load down on the porch and said directly to them, "Good afternoon gentlemen. My name is Miss Idy Crandall, and I have moved to your fair town of Paw Paw."

By much slothfulness, the building decayeth;
and through idleness of the hands
the house droppeth through.

ECCLESIASTES 10:18

Chapter 2

The General Store

To be honest the old, gray, weather-beaten store was hag-like and ugly. All the nails that kept the building up were loose and rusty, and it was badly in need of a few coats of paint. In fact, the older men who sat on its porch every day declared that they had neglected to paint it when it was built. There were rough-hewn pillars supporting the old porch. Every other pillar had warped upward, while the ones between were slowly returning to the earth from whence they had come. This gave the appearance of ups and downs, like the waves of the sea.

All of this had happened gradually over the years, so no one in Paw Paw ever noticed. If perchance a stranger happened by the General Store, which was seldom indeed, they would be too polite to say anything. But they would look with alarm at this precariously positioned porch. When they entered the store, they would be careful to step on the higher warped boards, as one never knew when the lower boards might collapse.

The porch served one purpose: to accommodate all the men in the vicinity. And, of course, every man who came to sit there brought his hound dog. Each dog adored his master. When any man moved, his dog moved. There were some occasional dogfights, but generally that required too much vim and vigor. The dogs displayed energy by lifting one eyelid from time to time, then going back to sleep.

There were six cane-back chairs on the porch. One had caved in a while back. So, after much pro and con, the decision was made to throw all of them onto the nearest woodpile. Then someone with a very inventive and clever mind—Old Mr. Plenty declared over and over that it was his mother, Hilda—rescued the men's bottoms with the idea of reweaving the chairs with old inner-tube strips.

The wonder of these rubber seats was the fact that they stretched and fit the concaves of everyone's personal seating capacity. However, by frequent use some of these had broken over the years, so the chairs had taken on the same appearance as the wavy floor of the General Store's porch. Old Mr. Plenty declared that one time he sat down too heavily and when he went to get up, one of the strips jumped up and slapped him.

Two long, crude benches sat against the wall of the store to support the men's backs. If perchance a problem arose in Paw Paw that took more than six men to solve, the benches gave the extra men a place to sit. The men knew that their wives and children would do their evening chores. No worries there.

The little town of Paw Paw was named thus because of the big groves of pawpaw trees that had once surrounded the area. Through the years, they had been cut down and carted away for progress and for practical reasons. The pawpaw fruit was edible only if one was on the verge of starvation. One lone tree was left for posterity, and it stood beside the sign that read "Welcome to Paw Paw."

There were no qualms about yanking the trees up because this was fertile soil. They could plant something else or just leave this vast acreage as grazing land for cattle. Although there were many rocks, it would grow almost anything that was planted. The men that sat on the porch of the General Store declared that one could pick up a rock, drop a seed in its place, and lay the rock down again on the seed, and you could still look forward to harvesting a bountiful crop. Many of the newcomers would look askance at this description, but the men continued to vouch that it was the truth.

The men on the porch dispensed their wisdom in different ways to different people. If their visitor appeared rather prosperous, they got the "seed and the rock and bountiful harvest" story. However, if they came dragging their heels and looking cast down, they would be told of one or two violent feuds to scare them away.

At first glance, it was clear that the town of Paw Paw was not planned but just a hit-and-miss conglomeration of various buildings. For sure, the General Store was the largest, and it had erupted smack dab between four well-traveled roads.

Two of the roads were well traveled, especially the one to Whippoorwill. When the citizens had to do big business and make major purchases, they went there. The other main road led to big farms, ranches, and the upper crust of society. This road branched out to a big clutter of woebegone log houses whose logs also were sagging and returning to God's good earth. Fred Pinkham would sigh, "Yes indeed, that area is where the poor call others poor. And, sad to say, the Good Book tells us that the poor will always be among us."

Another road was in fairly good shape and was built near the time of the others. "This road was a failure," Tom Curry explained. "It don't go nowhere; it just peters out like a sudden halt." Jimmy was sitting on the porch with the men when they were talking about the roads, and he butted into the conversation. "Fred, the right word for that is epilogue."

Otis Simpson hadn't noticed that his son was there. Testy and irritated he said, "Jimmy, you get yourself home and do your chores! That word of yours sounds a little racy and off-color to me."

Jimmy left murmuring, "I wish I could learn to just keep my big mouth shut!"

Tom Curry related a story Granny Octavia had told him. "She said that one lone man made that road and when he got so far, there wasn't anywhere to go, so he just laid down and died. She said she didn't know whether he was a praying man or not, but she thought it was a sad story indeedy." Tom looked pensive, lost in thought, "Maybe someday we'll know who he is, if and when we get to heaven. Oh yes, my friends, Granny also said that when we get there, we'll be surprised to see people we didn't think would make it and some will not be there that we were sure would make it. And many will be shocked to see any of us there."

They all laughed hilariously.

The other roads were mere cow paths. They had free range for livestock, and one day while looking in that direction, Amos gave a gasp, "Boys, here comes two white-faced cows, meandering down the road. I do believe they are Luddy's that he bought last week at the farm auction." He jumped off the porch and looked at their new brands. "Sure enough, they are Luddy's," he said. He waved his hand to his comrades, picked up a long stick, and yelled at the top of his lungs to help drive them home. He was a good neighbor, for sure.

Between the four roads, other structures were built around the General Store. There were a few misgivings and complaints, as they didn't build in a square but a circle. That, of course, caused many a chuckle from the men on the porch. They named it "Circle Square." Once again, visitors were bewildered by these descriptive comments.

Just across the road from the General Store was the telephone exchange. Maggie Jenkins skillfully ran the party lines. When she got the job, she had a little front window taken out and a big one put in its place. That way she could always see who came and went to the General Store. She was also provided with a world of information from the men who sat on the porch. Often wives would call her and ask her to send their husbands home, and she would shout their various messages from the door.

The little white Baptist church sat in the sight of the men on the porch also. Sometimes it was a beehive of activity for the women. Paw Paw boasted that they had the largest one-room schoolhouse thereabouts. Otis said on various occasions, "Our men seem to be very prolific in Paw Paw, so we had to build a big school house."

The men would grow testy and peevish when Otis would use one of those unfamiliar words that they didn't know. His answer was always the same. "It is one of my brilliant son Jimmy's words."

There were a few empty buildings in town just waiting for a bank, a doctor, or a five-and-ten-cent store. They all knew those would come eventually, so they calmly bided their time.

No one remembered how long Luke and Jossie Chadwick had owned the General Store, but Fred Pinkham remarked, "However long it's been, it's been too long." No matter how hard the residents tried to like them, it was all in vain. Both of them were "weighed in the balance and found wanting." The minister of the Baptist church quoted this Bible scripture when he saw Jossie put a finger on the scales as she weighed some cheese for him. "A false balance is an abomination to the Lord." Many of the residents tried going to Whippoorwill to do their shopping, but that kinda slacked off as the trip proved they never saved very much.

On the first day of spring a warm and contented sun shone down in Paw Paw. All were happy, as they had just endured a harsh winter. The men gathered quite early on the porch to celebrate the day. Suddenly their peace was disturbed by Jossie yelling at Luke in the store, "Luke, it's time to paint this store!"

Amos drawled, "Well boys, this proves that spring has arrived when Jossie starts to scream at Luke to paint the store. Of course, we have heard her all winter, quarreling and clamoring, but in some way she raises her voice one octave higher in the spring when she wants Luke to paint the store." Oh yes, they all agreed at this profound wisdom of Amos' while the cry and clamor continued from Jossie to her husband.

"Luke, I want you to get busy on this project. And, oh yes, we have enough paint in the back of the store for the job. You were so taken in by that paint salesman last year, you bought all those cans of paint and we've not sold a one of them! I still think you were bewitched by his pretty wife. And you must have noticed, your old cronies sitting on the porch are not about to paint their own houses. All of the men in our community, and this includes you, seem to have been born with a 'don't care' spirit. Luke Chadwick, are you listening to me?"

Now Luke was a "figure-upper," not to be confused with a "fixer-upper." He was always "figuring" on doing some project later in the day, and then he'd figure it was too late in the afternoon to begin it. He had a list hanging on the inside of the cupboard door so that when he went to get a cup for his coffee, there it was, staring him in the face. To avoid this, he usually used his dirty cup, but this morning he had to get a clean one, and there on the inside of the cabinet door was his old list. He studied it for a moment and was very surprised, for even though it was yellow with age, barely readable, with time-worn crackling edges, there on the bottom line was "Paint the Store." What good fortune that was! He needed to do several other things first before he could begin painting. He figured he wouldn't have to paint the store for quite some time. Luke was saved from doing anything on the list by the bell on the screen door; a customer had come in the store. "Sweet bell," he murmured.

One of the things all the men on the porch had in common was their chewing of tobacco. They religiously practiced aiming at one certain target. It had one time gotten to some of their wives' ears, via the grapevine, that wagers had been made on their crack shots of amber juices. They all vehemently denied that accusation though.

And one and all would be whittling. Some of the men, who had a little talent, would create little toys for their children, but the others just whittled for the sake of whittling—this occupation not a wife could understand. All the lovely and patient wives called the men on the porch a "perch of mocking birds." Some proclaimed them "people who think twice before saying nothing."

Down in the valley was Paw Paw's Big Morgan Creek, rushing down like a silver road hustling and bustling from its fountainhead. Its water was clear as crystal, and it tried to make everyone believe it was a river. In places where big rocks jutted out, there were white caps from its raging foam. It had a never-ending source of fish, and the men in the community kept trotlines across the water for all to use. The rules of this system said that the man who took the first fish must put bait on the line, so others could reap from the teeming silver hoard that abounded in Big Morgan Creek.

All the men from Eden's Garden are prone to exaggerate the length of the fish they have caught. The Paw Pawites were no different. In fact, this was the first conversation of the day. However, before they could get scales to weigh them and the yardstick for their length, the fish landed in a pan of cornmeal, then in a skillet of smoking hot grease. Jimmy Simpson declared those fish would make one's taste buds to rise up and walk.

Then a tragedy happened. No one in Paw Paw or in Whippoorwill could understand how such a thing could occur.

Luke and Jossie Chadwick had closed the store and gone to Whippoorwill on some kind of business. When they were returning to town, the horse and buggy went over the cliff at the sharp, horseshoe turn in the road. The buggy was found turned upside down. The horse escaped but not the Chadwicks. They were killed instantly. The news spread far and near, but for all the publicity, there were very few who came for the funeral. Several commented that there wasn't a tear shed or even any cheeks dampened.

However, the greatest tragedy was the loss of the General Store. Who would run it? They didn't have to worry long for as soon as the funeral was over, a lawyer from yon side of Whippoorwill appeared on the porch of the store. The word had spread via the grapevine, so a goodly crowd had gathered to hear what was going to be done about the store.

"People of Paw Paw, I am Daniel Peterson, a lawyer for the Chadwicks. I have some very good news for you. The Chadwicks must have had a premonition of what was going to happen, as the day of the accident they came to my office and had a will drawn up. Now, as you all know I'm sure, they had no children, but Mr. Chadwick has a nephew in Chicago. They never met him and never made contact with him, but they left everything to him. He was, of course, shocked by my letter to him but replied instantly that he would come as soon as he could pack and get a few things taken care of. He said he could be here within a week to ten days. I shall keep in touch daily if something is needed.

"Now, about the store and its merchandise. The Chadwicks said in their will that if anything happened to them, they wanted Jimmy Simpson to take over its operation. He will be in charge until the new owner arrives. And he is to be well paid for this work."

The lawyer looked at his paper. "Oh yes, Luke's nephew is named Jacob Johnson. Now, can anyone tell me where I can find this Jimmy Simpson?"

There were a few embarrassed coughs and some shuffling of feet as Jimmy stepped up to him.

The lawyer looked quite puzzled. "Are you the Jimmy Simpson the Chadwicks meant?"

"Yes sir, I am he. And I am well qualified for this job. If you would want any references, just ask the men here."

Flustered and confused, he sought help. "All of you men here, do you think this young man can do this responsible task?"

They agreed almost in one voice, "Mr. Peterson, he can handle it."

Therefore, Mr. Peterson took Jimmy into the store where they ironed out various duties that needed to be done until Jacob Johnson arrived. Mr. Peterson finally left for

Whippoorwill, shaking his head in disbelief. "This kid is fated for something real big. I shall keep my ears and eyes wide open to what it will be."

The townspeople returned to their homes, thinking that wonders would never cease in Paw Paw.

Precious in the sight of the LORD is the death of his saints.

PSALM 116:15

Chapter 3

Train Up a Child in the Way He Should Go

Growing up in Chicago, young Jacob Johnson couldn't remember when he first started to play the piano and sing. It was always with him, and in some mysterious way, it dwelt within him. His mother told him that when he was a small boy, she had had a little wooden box that sat on the piano bench, so he could reach the keys. Every moment they could spare, they played and sang together. He went to sleep every night and awakened every morning, hearing her playing and singing in her golden angel voice.

He had inquired through the years about his father. When she spoke of him, her countenance took on a radiant glow. "Dear Son, I loved him so much and I still do. I have pursued every hint, every shadow of where he might be. In every crowd of people, I still seek his face. He never knew the joy that he had a son, a replica of himself." She always held him close to her and kissed him when he asked about his father.

Jacob was finishing his last year of high school and he was working part-time at a feed store. He nagged and pestered his mother to let him quit school and work full-time, as they desperately needed the money. She would firmly reply, "Jacob, you are not quitting school, and that is final. I am determined for you to finish high school. We know you can't go to college, there seems no way for that, but you must have that high-school diploma."

The months dragged on before his graduation, and he began to notice his mother wasn't well. She looked so frail and fragile, and he often found her in bed when he came in from work. She always declared, "Jacob there is nothing wrong with me except I am a little tired at times. I think I'm getting lazy, and I must snap out of this."

Without asking his mother, Jacob went to see a doctor whose office was near his school and asked him to come to the house to see her. He came the next day. His mother was still declaring, "Doctor, I am not ill. I just have a son who worries needlessly."

The doctor gave his mother a lengthy examination and his findings weren't good. As he left, he didn't give Jacob any hope—his mother never expected any. He left her some pills for when she had pain.

Jacob missed many days of school to care for his mother. Finally, he went to the principal at school and told him of his mother's illness. They arranged for him to come to school once a week, to pick up his lessons, and do them at home.

Jacob had to keep his job, as that was the only income they had. One day he had to go to school for his final tests and right after those had to rush to his job. When he got home, he was exhausted, discouraged from his grueling day at school and having to work longer hours at his job. However, his mother seemed a trifle better.

Every night before they went to bed, he would play and sing to her. She lay in her bed, and her face would glow upon hearing her talented son's playing and singing.

One time, Jacob sat down at the piano and recklessly began to dash out some ugly erratic notes. Then he felt his mother's soft hands touch his shoulders. "Jacob, my son, did you know that the spirit of a man is the candle of the Lord? Never allow yourself to be the one to extinguish this flame. The world will attempt to blow out this inward candle. And abstain from things that war against men's souls. And also, my beloved son, never doubt in the dark what God has told you in the light."

Day after day his mother dropped her treasures, her gems of advice, and they found a soft resting place in his heart. "I shall keep them and guard them all my life," he whispered to her. And indeed, many times all through his life, he had to reach and touch them, when he failed miserably in living in his mother's quiet serenity.

Finally, after much distress and many painful months, Jacob got his diploma as his mother insisted. He never stayed for the graduation ceremonies but hurried home to her. He was exuberant and excited when he handed it to her. Her face glowed with happiness as she read of his accomplishments in the last year. Even though he was so overburdened with caring for her, working, and his school studies, he had done it. She wept for her son, for the heavy burdens he had to bear and him being so young. "Jacob, my son, would you please sing my favorite song until I can go back to sleep again. I am so tired."

In reverence and homage, he began playing and singing. "I come to the garden alone, while the dew is still on the roses." This was the last song that Jacob would play and sing to her in this earthly realm.

Jacob was so exhausted he didn't realize that he had fallen asleep with his head lying on the piano keys. He awakened in alarm and rushed to his mother's bed. Angels and cherubim had wafted his beloved mother to heaven's portals, her eternal home in a garden of roses, and she was still smiling at her son's playing and singing.

Young Jacob had to do another painful thing after his mother's death; he had to sell her piano to pay for her funeral expenses. He thought he would be devastated and overwhelmed with sorrow when he walked into the room and saw the empty void left against the wall. Strange indeed, he felt the opposite. He felt her presence with a warming glow, as he smelled the essence of her broken alabaster box. Jacob opened the door and, still feeling her presence, stepped out. Then he gently closed it behind him, knowing his future rested in the palm of His hand.

I went down into the garden of nuts
to see the fruits of the valley,
and to see whether the vine flourished,
and the pomegranates budded.

SONG OF SOLOMON 6:11

Chapter 4

A Man and His Piano

Young Jacob Johnson had a small amount of money left from the selling of his mother's piano. He knew he needed some transportation to look for a job; luckily for him he found a small truck within his means and bought it.

Music was such a force in his life he was compelled to look for a job in that area first. When he was just a child, he remembered going through the run-down, dilapidated part of Chicago where he had seen a sign, "Piano and Organs." He got in his truck and went to see if he could find it. He drove by it twice before he recognized the place. The ravages of time had taken its toll on the little sign. Jacob had to turn his head sideways so he could read it, as it hung recklessly askew, getting ready to plummet down upon an unsuspecting citizen.

In spite of the bedraggled, unkempt look of the building, Jacob decided to go in. Any other young man seeking work would have run away at breakneck speed.

The door at one time had been painted a silver gray. Its corners revealed that. But around the doorknob, the bare wood lay exposed with deep worn grooves made by countless hands through many years.

Gently and softly, Jacob pushed the door open and walked in. There was no need for a tinkling bell to announce a customer. If the shrieking and squeaking of the door, which Jacob perceived had never been oiled in its lifetime, did not awaken the old man who sat near the door, all other attempts would fail.

Jacob was standing on a piece of ragged carpet. One corner had been lifted up and a mess of dirt and shavings of wood had been hastily swept under it. Leaning against a counter was a stub of a broom. The culprit who had used it was sleeping on a big, badly worn rocking chair.

Well nigh merging together were an old man and a huge dog, which lay beside its master with one eye open, observing Jacob. Clamor issued forth in an unsteady rhythm from the old man's snoring. Jacob thought at one time he had breathed his last and jumped to shake him, but luckily, the old fellow caught his breath in the nick of time.

He had a huge, white, grizzled head of hair, and Jacob wondered if it had ever been combed. His hair continued down over his ears, traveled under his nose in a mustache, and ended in a long hairy beard. The mustache had been parted down the middle and each end was waxed and twiddled into perfect curly circles. Strangely, he had parted his beard in the same way and tweaked it into two big circles. This task would have taken continuous action indeed. Jacob stared at the four round circles that almost hid his face.

He had on two sweaters. Both were buttoned up wrongly. In fact, they both were intertwined with one another. He looked all zigzag and gave the observer a dizzy effect. He had on bib overalls, but over them, he wore a pair of pants, which at one time had been white. Now they were overrun by the soil of yesteryears. Jacob wondered why the pants hadn't been worn under the overalls.

He had on a pair of sheepskin-lined house shoes, but somehow the sheep wool had traveled up to the outside of them. Therefore, that left the old gentleman walking on a very thin sole of leather.

The big dog opened his other eye, looked up at his master, then back at Jacob again. Then the dog gave a violent shudder and flopped his long ears across his master's face to awaken him. Seeing Jacob, the old man jumped to his feet, mumbling of not getting any sleep the night before.

"Do come in. Do come in, young man. My name is Willy Cedar, and this is my only living relative," he said, pointing to the dog. "His name is Mr. Debacle. You know, my good man, these are perilous times. One must have a guard dog nearby."

Jacob was bewildered, indeed, as he saw Mr. Willy's big, blue twinkling eyes laughing up at him out of a maze of wrinkles on his rosy pink face.

"Mr. Cedar, my name is Jacob Johnson. And just why I'm here I don't know, but I am looking for a job." At this, Jacob surveyed the big room. Absolute chaos surrounded them. Jacob quickly looked back lest the old man would notice his intake of breath at the appalling spectacle before them.

Mr. Willy pushed Mr. Debacle from the chair. "Do sit down, Jacob," he said with a shy forgiving smile as he motioned with his hand and gave a small bow.

Jacob sat down and immediately Mr. Debacle climbed up beside him and promptly went back to sleep with his head on Jacob's lap. Unconsciously Jacob started to rub Mr. Debacle's head and ears. Mr. Debacle knew another master had moved into his world.

While this love relationship was going on between a dog and a new master, Mr. Willy was throwing articles from the other lone chair: a few soiled garments, an empty box of crackers, and a bright red apple. He seemed startled at seeing the apple, and after giving it a few shines on his sleeve, he laid it up on the counter beside the stub of the broom.

After the formal introductions and getting acquainted were finished and Mr. Willy's task of much ado was completed, he sat down in the emptied chair. Jacob leaned his head on the back of his chair and experienced an untroubled inner peace. He knew what his mother would say, "Jacob, a true friend is one that you can sit in silence with and dare to be yourself."

He didn't know how long he sat, but he knew it was for a time, so he wasn't startled when Mr. Willy broke the silence.

"Dear Jacob, our world evolves, emerges, and unfolds by the transforming power of music and singing. This is true in every culture, no matter how far away and how crude. Most of the time, it speaks better than we do. In my worldly journeys, I have found that music speaks all languages fluently. God, from the beginning, has used playing and singing to keep us in touch with the deity. Did you know that playing music and singing could put demons and evil spirits to flight? Oh yes, dear boy."

"So, my dear Jacob, you want to learn how to build pianos and organs?"

Jacob had not said this was what he wanted to do, but if there had been any qualms or uncertainties in his thoughts and dreams, Mr. Willy had begun to settle them.

Jacob still had his head leaning on the back of his chair with his eyes closed.

Mr. Willy continued, "Do you want to build the best in the world, or do you want to settle for the mediocre, the ordinary? The ordinary will make you lots of money, maybe make you rich. However, be careful and aware, the best can put you on a street corner with a tin cup in your hand. This is not just a profession; it is more like an obsession. If one is not careful, it could become your mistress."

From somewhere Jacob heard the whispering words: "Do you take this woman?"

"As you strive for the mastery, I have found one must reach up one hand to God and the other hand to man. You must have an ear tuned up to God's heavenly portals and the other one around us mortals. Only then can you be satisfied in the making of pianos."

As Jacob listened to Mr. Willy, he heard his mother's voice again, so woven, so intertwined with this man that they spoke as one. Jacob felt such comfort and kinship as he bared his soul to him. He told him all about his mother, the wonder of her, her death, and the pain that he felt for the one who had reared him alone. He told of his father leaving before he was born and how his mother had diligently searched for him but never found evidence of where he had gone.

Jacob got to his feet. He was so overcome emotionally that he paced back and forth. He had to hesitate at times to push aside the rubbish on the floor. When he finally quit pacing and headed back to his chair, Mr. Debacle moved and gave him room to sit down again. Jacob bowed his head in his hands for a minute and then raised his eyes to meet Mr. Willy's. In almost a whisper, he said, "I have had dreams, both asleep and awake, that I could build pianos and organs. And that I take my music into places where children and adults have not had the opportunity to enter the magical kingdom of music. I would lead them beyond folk songs, which are very good, but I could introduce them to operas, symphonies, concerts, and the worshiping hymns of the church. Perhaps, I could teach fathers and their sons to build pianos and organs for churches, schools, wherever the people gather to enrich their lives."

"Jacob, my son, come with me." Mr. Willy opened a door at the end of the room. "This is my sanctuary, my holy refuge to escape the rigors and harshness of the world outside my door." Mr. Willy pulled off the covering white sheets. There on an elevated platform sat a piano and an organ.

Jacob stood spellbound, captivated.

As the sun came in through a window, it reflected off this vision of splendor. Jacob could hardly breathe. In awe, he sat down on the piano bench and started to play. In some magical way, he became a part of this masterpiece; they merged together as one.

Oh yes, it was unavoidable, even predestined, that Jacob was touching the sublime and the divine that Mr. Willy was teaching him.

Jesus said, "Ye hath not chosen me but I have chosen you and ordained you, that ye should go and bring forth fruit and that fruit shall remain, and whatsoever ye shall ask of the Father, in my name, He will give it to you."

In the finality of the day, when the old clock on the wall chimed the midnight hour with the sound of silver bells, Jacob arose from the piano and started for the door. Mr. Willy and Mr. Debacle were sound asleep on the old dilapidated chair. Jacob touched Mr. Willy on the shoulder, whispering, "I'll be back in the morning."

Jacob looked startled when they both, dog and man, were smiling!

Jacob had no way to know that he would be stepping through this door for the next five years.

Every man should eat and drink and
enjoy the good of all his labour.
It is the gift of God.

ECCLESIASTES 3:13

Chapter 5

Jacob's Foundation

Eager and excited, Jacob arose with a smile early that next morning for his first day of work for Mr. Willy and Mr. Debacle. As he opened the door of the shop, Mr. Debacle almost knocked him down by leaping up and putting his big feet on his chest. Then the dog gave him a slobbering kiss and flopped his enormous ears across his face. From the back of the shop, a wild and furious dust cloud billowed out into the air and all over Jacob, which sent him into a fit of coughing. Mr. Willy, abashed and embarrassed, explained, "I was just tidying up a mite before our sweet pupil and protégé arrived." Then he set his little stub of a broom against the counter and smiled at Jacob. This morning's greeting was likened to a three-ring circus with Mr. Debacle's frenzied, wild hello and Mr. Willy bowing and smiling.

"Sit down, sit down, my dear boy. One must put first things first, you know." He sat down in the chair that he had emptied the day before, and Jacob sat in Mr. Willy's big chair. Finally, Jacob was seated and the lesson began. Angels and cherubim stood quietly by and watched the scene unfold before them, and Jacob moved his soul and spirit into Mr. Willy and Mr. Debacle's dwelling. Only his body went back to his little house to sleep.

A pattern began that would continue for almost five years. Mr. Willy poured them both a cup of hot tea and taught Jacob a lesson with a spiritual point of view. "My dear Jacob, there is a portion of God's deity that is housed in our bodies. Someone said it's like a candle or an inward flame, a lamp that the enemy tries to blow out but is not successful. Our Lord builds our foundation and every man makes his choice of how he builds thereon. Some will use gold, silver, and precious stones; others build with wood, hay, and stubble. Tell me, dear Jacob, whose work shall stand?"

Without waiting for Jacob to answer, Mr. Willy jumped up, clapping his hands. "It is now time for Jacob to start to build, to mold, to bring into being his first piano, which shall emerge from God's own heart."

Jacob and Mr. Debacle jumped up at the same time. Mr. Debacle started barking and running around in circles trying to catch his tail as Mr. Willy handed Jacob his first tool. "Now, my dear boy, do not get in a hurry, or you might strike the wrong key or wrong chord, in more ways than one, in building your beauteous masterpiece. It starts like this. First, one starts with a tiny bud in building pianos or in building one's life. Next comes the blossoming, then the unfolding. Finally, the fruits, the jewel that you have brought into being, ripen for the public eye to desire and treasure. We don't create any fair-to-middling product here."

"My dear boy, I have traveled the world over (many years ago as you readily can guess), and I do confess to obtaining most of my knowledge, working in music shops. I learned how to obtain the best materials in the world by observing, watching, and hungering for the finest. Oh, yes, the mastery, the complexities, the intricacy that you must know." Mr. Willy's voice came in a low whisper, "But, Jacob, my dear son, I believe the best comes only from within a man."

They always had buyers from far and near to buy their pianos and organs, so they always had enough money to last them until the next one sold. The only problem that Jacob had to endure was Mr. Willy's "spiritual leadings." All the buyers had to pass a certain test before Mr. Willy would let them buy a piano or an organ. One day, Jacob complained about the practice.

"Oh, my dear son, you are a novice. You are making swift progress, better than anyone I ever knew, but we must remember to try the spirits to see if they are of God. We don't want to place a part of your soul and spirit—the part that enables you to create, and yes, give birth to your treasures—with someone who would put it into a drunken saloon do we?"

Jacob halfway agreed with him. "So that is why we barely get out of a pauper's existence," he muttered peevishly.

Then came the morning when Jacob arose and looked outside to see the snow of all snows blanketing the city of Chicago. He felt elated. "This will be the perfect time for me to relax, read, or just go back to bed," he muttered to himself. He fixed himself a little breakfast then crawled back into bed to snooze a mite longer. He took to counting the sheep as they jumped over the fence. Still he was wide-awake. He had to admit he was lonely to go back to Mr. Willy and Mr. Debacle.

The snowplows had already cleared the street, but he had to shovel the snow from his driveway. That accomplished, he got into his truck only to find that it wouldn't start. He did everything he knew to do, without success. Throwing up his hands in disgusted resignation, he stalked out into the deep snow and headed for Mr. Willy and Mr. Debacle's.

Adding insult to injury, the snow was banked halfway up the shop's door. Jacob struggled to contain himself, but after much ado, Mr. Willy finally opened an upper window and threw him down a shovel. Jacob began furiously shoveling the snow away from the door. At long last, with much huffing and puffing, he was able to squeeze his body through. When he collapsed in the big chair, Mr. Willy and Mr. Debacle stood before him, their eyes smiling a lovely welcome.

Jacob grimly said, "Oh yes, you can both smile because you don't know what I had to endure to get here!" Then he began to speak with grave deliberation of his morning thus far.

When he finished he leaned back in the chair.

Mr. Willy leaned down and whispered into Mr. Debacle's enormous ear, "Mr. Debacle, we must be very careful of our protégé's sudden outbursts of temper today."

Mr. Willy signaled and to Jacob's amazement, Mr. Debacle started barking and running in circles, trying to catch his tail. Mr. Willy's smile was a mite bigger than the one he wore routinely every day.

The weeks, the months, and the years rushed by, and Jacob had become the very finest in his profession. He knew when he had accomplished the superior, the unequaled, when he first began to play his finished product. Yet, lately this accomplishment didn't satisfy him as it had in the past. He had met a few young people and would go out at night to different places of pleasure, but he didn't find the thing he thirsted for.

One morning, when Mr. Willy had finished his lesson, Jacob began to tell him of the vacancy in his life. "Mr. Willy, I need something more in my life than just building the finest pianos and organs. Maybe I want the beggarly elements of the world: money, wealth, possessions, a house, a fine car, and success by earthly standards. A beautiful wife, children, maybe even to leave Chicago and go to some exciting places."

"Oh Jacob, we can have heavenly treasures in our earthly realm. I made my mistake years ago of not taking a wife and having children. I realize now the joys I have missed just by having you in my life. God is in the business of answering our prayers. It all depends on one's heart. God looks at the heart; man at outward appearances. Our happiness, our joy, depends on living by God's Principles. You can find them in Matthew 5, 6, and 7."

Lately Jacob had been watching Mr. Willy's and Mr. Debacle's health fail. Now they were never out of bed when he came to work every morning. Their smiles never diminished though. Jacob would get their meals from the café nearby, but now they refused to eat them all, even with his caring and coaxing. Evenings he would put them into their little bed, play the piano, and sing until they went to sleep.

Then one day a letter came. It read:

Mr. Jacob Johnson,

I am a lawyer in the town of Whippoorwill and am handling the estate of Luke Chadwick, your mother's brother. He left a will and deeded you the General Store in Paw Paw, which is a little town nearby.

In surveying the store, it appears fully stocked with non-perishable items at this time. It has living quarters in the back and side of the store.

I do not know if you understand what a general store means to a small community, but it is needful. These stores carry far more than just food. They carry farm supplies, cattle feed, and such. You might call it a station. The outlying areas of Paw Paw have a larger population than the town. Those folks bring their farm produce, milk, cream, and eggs to sell to this General Store.

The store itself is in dire need of repair, but there is a large building behind the store that is almost new. I think the former owner intended it to house hay, feed, farming implements, and various supplies for the farmers.

If you don't want to locate here, I will try to sell the store for you. I think it can be sold rather quickly, as the people need it very badly.

Let me know of your plans immediately.

I am your servant here,

Daniel Peterson

Jacob made a mad dash to Mr. Willy's, who seemed to gain strength at the reading of the letter. Mr. Debacle tried to run in circles after his tail but couldn't make it. All day, they read and reread the letter, reading between the lines very carefully.

Mr. Willy was excited by the letter. "Jacob, you need to go. I feel that this is in the plan for your life. I have noticed you don't have the drive of reaching out for your goals anymore. You have already reached one, because I'm sure, I'm positive, there isn't anyone who could create a better piano or organ than you could. Now you must move on to fulfill the other dreams and visions you have. Someone said that a dreamer is one who sees the dawn before the rest of the world. You must take this gift that has been bestowed upon you out into the world where people hunger."

Jacob ceased his pacing back and forth across the room. "Now Mr. Willy, I will not go unless you and Mr. Debacle come with me. Did you think I would go without you? Who do you think I am? You are my father, the father I never had. So, there is no reason to discuss this any further; when I go you both will go with me, or I shall not go."

All the rest of the day they laid their plans. Jacob wrote a letter to the lawyer in Whippoorwill and told him that they would be coming as soon as they could arrange to leave. He was so exuberant and enthusiastic about their leaving. He was glad to have his friend's steady hand, as together they decided what they should take with them and what they should leave behind.

"Jacob, I am convinced that you should buy your lumber from here and order extra supplies of everything you need for building your pianos and organs. We are going to an out-of-the-way place where you might not be able to buy the essentials, the necessary nuts and bolts, so to speak."

Jacob started laughing hilariously, which started Mr. Debacle to try to catch his tail again. "Mr. Willy, I'm glad you are able to keep me from cloud kissing!"

Together they made lists of all the things they might need. They discussed the size of the wooden crates needed to ship pianos by rail and even what kind of special box they would need for Mr. Debacle. Mr. Willy was worried about that and said, "We need to call the railroad depot to find out what we will need for him. Now Jacob, we must put him in a car where we can take turns staying with him."

As the day slowly gathered to an end, a bright, orange-crimson sunset burst through the open door and the two dusty windows. Mr. Willy whispered, "Why look Jacob, God has lighted His glorious, spectacular lamp in heaven just for us."

Jacob was consumed with haste to leave Chicago forever. He ordered his lumber, all of his stock, supplies, and implements to ship by train to Paw Paw. He left the sale of his house to his local bank; he found a buyer for his small truck who allowed him to use it until he left.

It was dark when he reached home. He had intended to see Mr. Willy before he went to bed but felt he might already be asleep. Exhausted and drained from his strenuous day, he fell across his bed. It was daylight when he awakened. He didn't take time to shave or change his clothes, for he felt a foreboding uneasiness as he rushed to the shop. Jacob opened the door and stepped through. He leaned his body against the door and closed his eyes. "Yea, though I walk through the valley of the shadow of death, I will fear no evil for Thou art with me, Thy rod and Thy staff will comfort me."

Oh yes, Mr. Willy had arrived safely through his shadow and was sitting down before a piano made of gold. He was singing with the angels a song that mere mortals had never sung. Who was the lady standing by Mr. Willy and singing? Oh yes, of course, it was his mother; he recognized her gentle voice.

In Mr. Willy's small bed, Mr. Debacle had decided to leave with his master. A sweet touch of gentle fragrance filled the room. Jacob remembered the scripture Mr. Willy read just a few mornings ago, "The wolf also shall dwell with the lamb, and a lion shall lie down with the child."

"Then, my Lord, maybe You can allow Mr. Debacle to slip in with Mr. Willy in some way."

Then Jacob noticed that one of Mr. Debacle's enormous

ears was slapped across his master's face, as if to say, "Wake up, Mr. Willy! We have a new customer, one that I have never seen before. It looks like an angel from heaven. Could it be?"

Jacob went to the bank where Mr. Willy had an account. The bank had several small businesses it serviced and was the same bank that was going to sell Jacob's home for him.

The banker greeted him. "Do come into my office, Mr. Johnson. Please, sit down. We were all saddened at Mr. Willy's passing. We know he was like a father to you. He left a will saying that everything was to go to you. He was always saying he had no living relatives except you and Mr. Debacle. Now since you are leaving town, do you want me to sell his shop and send the money to your lawyer in Whippoorwill? In addition, I will give you a certified check now as Mr. Willy has left quite a little savings in your name."

Jacob was almost speechless at his inheritance. As he prepared to leave the bank, the banker gave him a letter from his old friend.

Jacob went back to the shop, almost empty now except for the love and sweetness that filled to overflowing all the rooms. Jacob sat down beside the little bed and read his letter.

> My Dear Beloved Jacob,
>
> Do not grieve for me. I have no words to use in telling you of the joy and happiness that you have bestowed upon me. You have made life worthwhile, you know. All I have is thine. Go to your new home; fulfill your dreams of music. All I ask of you is that you build according to the foundation that I left for you.
>
> Your loving father

Jacob made himself an altar with boxes of piano keys and knelt down beside them. He was fulfilling the spiritual wish of Mr. Willy. Then he arose and began his new journey.

"What must be, shall be," he murmured.

Who is she that looketh forth as the morning,
fair as the moon, clear as the sun,
and terrible as an army with banners?

SONG OF SOLOMON 6:10

Chapter 6

The Kiss

When Clara Meade first saw Jacob Johnson, he was standing in the doorway with an air of boredom and indifference. He was aloof, removed, even annoyed from what he saw in the crowd of people. He wasn't overly handsome but had a dignified bearing about him. He radiated power and strength that appeared to be held in check in some way. He was taller than the men who surrounded him. He had dark brown hair that was a little longer than was the custom. It curled down over his collar. His dark brown eyes were electric as he scanned the crowd before him.

Jacob had turned in the door to leave the dance when he caught a glimpse of her hair against the dark attire of the men. It was a blushing red with glints of gold. It was held up at the sides by jeweled combs, and then it fell down her back in radiant disarray. Why had she not pinned it up on her head as the rest of the ladies had chosen to do, he wondered. As she turned, he saw her face. It was a pale, translucent ivory that was common with red hair. Her green eyes sparkled and danced around the room. Jacob was overwhelmed by her beauty.

She had on an elegant, black dress that barely covered her knees, almost flaunting her perfect legs. Her only jewelry was a string of pearls that graced her flawless neck. Everything about her reeked of wealth. She bore an aura of calm assurance that the world belonged to her and it was there for her taking.

Shocked indeed, by his own bold and brazen actions, Jacob recklessly touched her dancing partner on the shoulder and took Clara into his arms. The man stared at him with mouth agape.

There was no need for Jacob to say anything, as he skillfully guided her through the door. Clara got her shawl, Jacob put it around her shoulders, and they walked out into the darkness. Jacob led her to his small truck and helped her in. He went to the other side and slipped behind the wheel. Then he spoke.

Though these were his first words to her, she already knew how his voice would sound.

"Do you want me to kiss you first before I ask where you live?"

She turned her face to him. He held it in both hands and softly, gently kissed her mouth. A violent cluster of stars fell from the heavens above, and they all settled on Clara and Jacob's receptive hearts. Clara knew she was going to marry him; it was just a matter of time.

She gave him the directions to her home. He knew the area; it was where the rich and powerful had their magnificent, stately homes. As he stopped his truck in her driveway, Clara looked at him with merriment in her eyes. "This is the first time I was ever kissed by a man before I knew his name. I will admit that isn't necessary; in fact, that could be the reason I'm so impressed. There could develop serious consequences from a man who hasn't done a lot of kissing." Jacob was glad it was dark, so she couldn't see his face flushed with embarrassment.

Abruptly, Jacob started the truck. He didn't get out to walk her to her door. As she left, she provocatively sang out, "My name is Clara Meade, my darling, tell me your name." Jacob never answered her as he sped down the street.

Jacob was fuming, near to anger, even rage, at her. He drove his truck wildly home. How dare she criticize his total lack of finesse in the art of kissing? How could anyone doubt that kiss? Why, it fairly made the world stop turning! He made it home finally, without a mishap. He got out and started to his door. He hesitated for a moment, muttering, "Mr. Willy, you were right. I will make music my mistress." Then looking heavenward again added, "Thank you, my friend, wherever you are."

He entered his little house and slammed the door so hard that it fairly shook on its foundation. Vigorously wiping his hands of all the female gender, he stumbled into bed. Jacob was exhausted but spent a restless night thinking of Clara, her striking beauty, her violent red hair, and her sparkling green eyes. His heart went a winging as he not only saw her, but also felt the aura of her of loveliness, like a caress, surrounding him.

Morning found him sitting on the side of the bed muttering, "Why, I am a fool, stupid fool." In some sixth sense, Jacob knew that she would come to him with a beckoning of his finger. Oh yes, he was mad. The pompous, arrogant fool was mad. Mr. Willy would have used the word "cockamamie" fool. He got up from the bed, shook himself, and relentlessly erased her out of his mind. Unwavering, he slammed the door again, and again the little house shook. Jacob had numerous errands to do before he could leave Chicago forever.

It was almost dark when he returned home that evening. He wasn't surprised to see Clara sitting in her car waiting for him. She got out and took hold of his hand. Without a word, they entered his small house. He leaned his back against the door and closed his eyes. She knew what he was thinking. It had taken her all day to make the decision to come here tonight. In some mysterious way, she knew the die had been cast.

Finally, he smiled at her. "Clara, Clara, why have you come here tonight? How did you know where I lived?"

"Well, my darling, you are dealing with a formidable and determined young lady. All I had to do was call that friend of yours that invited you to the dance last night." Seeing Jacob's consternation, she laughed and added, "And, I might as well tell you now that I am going to marry you. Therefore, we don't need to play those little games that lovers always do. But thinking of them would be fun, I think."

Clara rose from the sofa and walked to him. She knew he was stunned by her shameless words. She put her arms around his stiff and rigid body, and it grew soft and yielding to the magnetism between them.

Suddenly, Jacob roughly and hungrily pulled her close to him. In this aching and want of her, he began kissing her glorious red hair, her eyes, brows, and finally her mouth as a surging torrent of love wrapped itself around them. Jacob whispered hoarsely, "Oh, my darling, why did you come here tonight? You know this can never be."

Abruptly, without saying anything, Jacob let go of Clara, strode to the kitchen, and made a pot of coffee. Clara silently stood in the doorway and watched him. He leaned over the counter, his shoulders slumped over his hands that barely held him up. Clara felt rather than heard a whisper. "This must come to an end."

Jacob, with a note of resignation and composure, straightened up and filled both their cups with coffee. "Dear Clara, come and sit down." He sat her on one side of the table and he sat opposite her. "This must be settled with us looking at each other."

"Clara, I know you realize that I love you. However, we must understand there could never be a marriage between us. We don't even know one another. I am leaving Chicago in a few days and going to Lord only knows where. You know nothing of my world, and for certain I know nothing of yours."

Hastily Clara interrupted Jacob with a passionate plea. "Oh, my love, there is no need for you to leave Chicago. We can live here. My father has powerful influence everywhere. Why, you can choose any job you would like to do. Oh, I wish you knew how much I love you. You have torn up my world in just a few hours."

In this outburst, she got up and stood in front of him, thinking he would take her in his arms again. Instead, he put his hands on her shoulder and firmly sat her down.

"Clara, listen to me please. There is no way for us. I just hope you can understand, as for sure, I don't completely, but I must go. And that's final."

Jacob got to his feet, clasped his hands together on the back of his head and began pacing back and forth across the little kitchen. Despair and a feeling of hopelessness was in every step. A silence likened to a shadow penetrated the little room. He wanted to tell her of the driving force in his soul and why he must go. But he was reluctant to tell her of his dreams of building pianos and organs, of teaching music and singing, of the joy and peace he had experienced these last five years with Mr. Willy. And how he felt the physical calling, but more important, the spiritual realm he had moved into with the help of his teacher. Was this the trying or examining of the spirits Mr. Willy had tried to teach him? What was this shadow in his little kitchen?

Jacob didn't linger for the answer to his question. "Clara, my love, I can imagine with towns called Whippoorwill and Paw Paw, a person can guess they would be in a wilderness." Jacob continued, "I feel an intense emotion, a challenge, to go there and see for myself. I want to find a place that I can say belongs to me. I have already written to Mr. Peterson, the lawyer handling my uncle's estate, and told him that I was coming in a few days, just as soon as I can get my affairs in order."

"Then you don't love me the way I love you. Why don't you just say so?" Clara pleaded.

"I will tell you what we can do; we can correspond to each other. There is a lot to write about, as we surely don't know much except our kissing." They both laughed at this.

"Oh Jacob, you make it wound so nice, our separation. I

know what will happen. You will fall in love with a little hillbilly girl and marry her." Clara started to cry and sob, so Jacob had to console her by swearing his love for her would never cease.

"Clara, our love can surely stand a few months of separation. If it can't endure that, it is very shallow indeed."

It was past midnight, and they were still bickering and quarreling. Of course, this would lead them into a passionate love scene. Then there would be more accusations of one another, then more lovemaking. Finally, Clara realized he wouldn't stay, so, in tears, she slammed the door and headed for home. Again, the little house shook for a third time that day.

After Clara left, Jacob, still trembling with emotion, went back to the kitchen and poured himself another cup of coffee. He sat down in the chair Clara had used. He could smell her sweet perfume, so he got up and moved to the other chair. He had to put her out of his mind, if it was possible. His gentle counselor, Mr. Willy, had not fully prepared him for this surging power of love. A kind of love that could hold a man captive in its wake. Perhaps Mr. Willy had not tasted this sweet ecstasy of God, this passion, and this fervor that could take first place in a man's heart. Maybe he hadn't stopped long enough in his journeys over the world. He had remarked one day, "If a man is not careful, he could make his music and singing his mistress." He often said, "One must be practical, realistic, show good judgment." One of his favorites was "look before you leap."

"I must come down to earth, have more control over this obsession that is possessing me. This is insane for me to revel in this newfound love."

Jacob folded his arms on the table and rested his head. "Oh, Mr. Willy, my mentor, my teacher, yes, yes, my father, how I wish I could talk to you now."

All night long, he wrestled with this warm beast of desire and aching passion. What had she done to him? He got up and sat on his bed. Why hadn't Mr. Willy prepared him for this kind of obsession that couldn't be quieted or quenched, this kind of love that could make a man helpless? Aloud he spoke to himself, "This is crazy, you know, so get up and load your equipment onto the train and leave for Paw Paw today. That way you won't see her again and be tempted with her loveliness and beauty. That way you won't be tormented with the fire she has created in your body, heart, and soul."

He hurriedly packed his clothes and other belongings and raced to the train to see that his precious cargo was crated so it wouldn't be damaged. He left his truck with the ticket agency to be picked up by the new owner. Racing, he got onto the train and found a seat. He was exhausted after this hectic, frantic job was completed.

The train began its furious groaning and clanging as it pulled out from Chicago, heading for the world beyond. He leaned his head back to sleep a little while, but there she was taking control of him. She had bewitched him, cast an enchanting spell over him. What could he do?

"I will write her a letter, maybe two or three, on this trip," he murmured to himself. Luckily, he had a pen and tablet in his valise. Still shaking with excitement, he began his labor of love. Then, with his pen poised to write, his body became rigid, unmoving; he dare not breathe, as he heard her coming down the aisle. Then Clara, the love of his life, sat down beside him. Without speaking, he laid his pen aside and tenderly, lovingly took her in his arms. It was as though she had always been with him.

And, strange indeed, the big train changed its course and soared skyward and into heaven itself.

And they had a king over them,
which is the angel of the bottomless pit, . . .
One woe is past; and, behold,
there come two woes more hereafter.

REVELATION 9:11-12

Chapter 7

Clara's Trip to the Bottomless Pit

On the first leg of their journey to Paw Paw, Jacob and Clara basked in the rapture of their joyous love. They had no time to get involved with any of their fellow travelers, but the male passengers walking by were quietly envious of their happiness and lovemaking. Clara kept telling Jacob that they would never see these people again, so with that kind of encouragement, Jacob showed a bold, undaunted side of himself he didn't know he had.

The closer they got to Whippoorwill, the more wild and untamed the region and terrain became. The trees and the foliage grew up almost to the railroad tracks. They crossed many beautiful rivers and lakes, but to Clara's eyes this vast boundless growth seemed primeval, untamed, a howling wilderness, which made her a little uneasy and apprehensive. Not Jacob. At every click of the wheels on the train, his excitement and enthusiasm grew. "Oh, my darling, look at all this timber. Do you suppose it is virgin; untouched by man?"

"Jacob, I doubt if any of our forefathers ever trekked this route in their journey westward. If they had, they would have stopped here for certain, as this is the end of the world."

Jacob appeared bold and undaunted, even lion-hearted as the train rushed on following its torturous course toward the town of Whippoorwill.

Clara's first glimpse of the town was indeed earthshaking.

Her view was through a pall of dust stirred up by the men riding horses, horse-drawn wagons, disreputable trucks and cars. There were several boys wrestling, playing pranks, and romping with dogs. She was soon to learn that it hadn't rained for some time, but she also learned that when the rains came, the dust would turn to mud. What she was tempted to say about this first impression was best buried in the sea of God's forgetfulness.

Jacob was running hither and yon, getting their luggage into the depot. He lovingly helped her into the depot too. "Honey, do you think you could stay here for a little while? I need to go see my lawyer and tell him we have arrived. And I have to get us some sort of transportation to take us on to Paw Paw."

Shaking with excitement, he never gave her time to answer, but did give her a very meaningful kiss as he rushed out the door.

Clara looked out the door at Whippoorwill. Stunned indeed, her mouth stood agape and her eyes stared in disbelief. "And they say Paw Paw is worse than this," she muttered.

Suddenly two cows meandered around the side of the depot and started in her direction. With her heart pounding in terror, she slammed the door and ran to the ticket master yelling, "What does this mean? Cattle running wild down the street."

The man, calm and polite, said, "Ma'am, we have free range in this county. That means that every man must put his brand on his livestock, and then they are allowed to roam the range freely. If and when he needs to find them, he is able to identify which ones belong to him by that brand."

Hot tears coursed down her lovely face and mingled with the dust of the town. She never even bothered to wipe the dust from the bench as she sat down again.

Her waiting was short-lived, as a rattletrap truck came to a screeching halt outside the depot door. After two exploding backfires, which terrorized her, clouds of dust bellowed out behind the truck. Then Jacob and the driver walked unruffled through the dust to her. "Clara, my dear, I want you to meet Whitey Garrison. He is going to take us to Paw Paw."

Bewildered and nauseated by the sight of the man, Clara closed her eyes and shook his sweaty, soiled hand.

Jacob's face was glowing with excitement as he grabbed their baggage and put it in the back of the truck. Then he helped the benumbed Clara into the cab. He pulled her close to himself and gave her a little love pinch with a knowing smile. Clara responded with a hard pinch of her own, and her smile was mirthless. Jacob was a mite startled, but he knew she was exhausted so paid her no mind.

Clara was squeezed tight against Mr. Garrison's body, which was very damp and oozing with sweat. She wondered how long it had been since he had had a bath.

He had on a pair of blue bib overalls and a soiled blue shirt, and every few minutes he spat a gob of tobacco juice out his window. Somehow he always managed to leave a few speckles on his fierce-looking beard, which resembled an eagle's nest. And another drop or two would slowly cascade down the inside of his door. Mesmerized, Clara watched as they slowly came to rest on a big stain on the floor that must have grown through the years. Still in bewilderment, Clara saw big drops of sweat on Mr. Garrison's brow uniting in strength and traveling to the end of his large, red nose where they hung, suspended in midair. Amazed at her reasoning and reflection, she thought of Adam and Eve being driven from the Garden of Eden. Adam to spend the rest of his life earning his living by the sweat of his brow, and poor Eve spending her time having babies. Weak and forlorn, Clara thought the end had come when Whitey pulled out a big red handkerchief from his back pocket, proceeded to catch the driblets of sweat at the end of his nose and brow, and then spread the tainted object to dry across the panel in front of her eyes.

Why was everything liquid concerning this man?

Whitey saw a car behind them and sped up. Clara bravely voiced, "Mr. Garrison, would you please slow down. I feel very faint."

"Oh yes, my lady," he graciously and kindly responded as he slowed the truck down.

The car behind them sped up and passed them in a flurry cloud of dust and sand that billowed through the window. Not realizing what she was doing, Clara snatched the red handkerchief and covered her face with it.

"Remember Miss," Whitey asserted, "you asked for this."

Clara sank into the state of oblivion, a never-never land, with Mr. Garrison's red handkerchief still covering her face.

They drove up the slight hill, and there before their eyes lay the little town of Paw Paw and the General Store that now belonged to Jacob. It was surrounded by several misplaced sheds and buildings arranged in a big circle with no order whatsoever. Just before they got to the store, the unexplainable, unthinkable happened. The truck backfired with two more loud explosions and then stopped.

Instead of Jacob helping with the truck, he made a mad dash in the direction of the General Store. Clara sat mute and numb as she watched Jacob gallivant around his "estate."

Mr. Garrison tried to get the truck started again but with no luck. He turned to her and said, "Miss Clara, you will have to walk the rest of the way, as I don't know how long I will be fixing this." Then he took their baggage out of the back of the truck and set it under one lone tree nearby.

Trembling, Clara got out of the truck, walked to their baggage, and sat down in utter despair. Just above her head was a billboard, of sorts, that read: "This is the last Paw Paw tree. It was left, so future generations would know why we named our town Paw Paw."

Suddenly, Clara heard some unusual animal sounds on the other side of the tree. She forgot all of her weariness and leaped to her feet ready to take flight toward the store. She had heard if a person was in dire straights, they could rally around and summon an unknown strength to save themselves.

Then stealthily, furtively, she looked around the tree. A huge sow lay on her side, and nine little piglets were squealing, grunting, and fighting for the best place to dine. The mother pig was looking up at her. Clara was startled by a thought: Did mama pigs ever smile? Then wonder of wonders, she was tempted to see if they were branded.

Oh yes, for sure, she was out of her mind. Soon she would hear everyone say she had gone around the bend.

Then courageously, halfway between rashness and cowardice, she arose, held her shoulders erect, grabbed two of the largest bags, and started for the General Store. "Yes, this experience I shall always remember. Alas, I shall never forget it."

My God, my God, why hast thou forsaken me?
why art thou so far from helping me,
and from the words of my roaring?
O my God, I cry in the daytime,
but thou hearest not; and in the night season,
and am not silent.

PSALM 22:1-2

Chapter 8

Broken Dreams

Jacob was in back of the store, inspecting the big new building. He was in a frenzy of excitement in his inheritance. This was exactly what he needed for building his pianos and organs. Suddenly, he was quickly brought back to earth by Clara's frantic screaming.

He rushed back through the store and found her standing on the porch, shaking and crying loudly. "Jacob, what are you doing? Have you lost your mind, leaving me alone with that uncivilized man and these wild beasts roaming around?"

Jacob tried to take her in his arms and console her in her fright, but she never gave him a chance. She turned and angrily stomped into the store.

By this time Whitey Garrison had gotten his truck started again, unloaded the rest of the baggage onto the porch, and left in a cloud of dust. As Jacob carried the luggage into the store, his excitement took wing and flew away.

He found Clara standing with her hands on her hips in the little apartment in back of the store. It was sparsely furnished and was in dire need of repair. After seeing her glowering expression, he said, "Clara, my darling, we'll go back to Whippoorwill tomorrow and buy all new furnishings, paint, and some rugs for the floor. What do you think of that idea?"

In her anger, she didn't answer him.

Jacob cleaned off the little table in the kitchen, then went into the store. He got a can of meat, a tin of crackers, and some canned peaches for their supper.

Clara finally settled down, as they both ate hungrily.

Jacob talked enthusiastically, ignoring her deadly silence. Then he cleaned up after their supper.

Clara went into the store, brought back new sheets and pillowcases, and made the bed. She tossed one of the pillows onto to the weary, old sofa. Then, as if she were performing in a play, she methodically removed her outer clothes and lay down crossways on the bed, leaving no room for Jacob. She promptly went to sleep; Jacob, fully dressed, lay down on the sofa with his eyes wide open, wondering.

Eerie noiseless feet crept into the small bedroom and in some uncanny way, carried an evil spirit that penetrated every corner of the room. Was this a sign, a foreshadowing of things to come? Was there such a thing as dead air? Jacob found himself trying to measure out each breath, so there would be enough for the next.

Then Jacob heard Mr. Willy whisper, "Jacob, there is just a silken thread between love and hate, so we must take heed and not let this frail bondage be severed. It is said that the heart is a fetterless thing, like a wave of the ocean or a bird on the wing. Jacob, from the heart, the seat of our passions, the essence of our being emerges our soul for all the world to see."

Jacob wept for Mr. Willy, he wept for Clara, and he wept for himself.

So God created man in his own image,
in the image of God created he him;
male and female created he them.

GENESIS 1:27

Chapter 9

Albert Peabody's Conversion

Albert J. Peabody had just driven by the men on the porch in his black hack. He gave them a wave, a "Good morning, friends," then hurried on his way. This gave the men fuel for talking about him and the many things good and bad that lay at his door. In summing him up, they figured there were far more bad things about him than good. However, he was rich and maybe that counted for something.

The men that sat on the porch of the General Store had talked before on this particular subject but never came to any agreement that was satisfactory. Albert driving by reminded them of it again. Amos was the first to break the silence, "Mr. Plenty, since you have joined us this morning, I will broach this subject with you as you might shed a light on it. Why did God make so many ugly people when He could have made more pretty ones?"

Mr. Plenty gave a long sigh. "Now, my friends, that is one of the mysteries in the Good Book, but I think I can come up with one reason. When God created this world and everything in it, I think He stated five times that it was *good*. But when He created man, He looked him over and said that he was *very good*. Mind you, He only used the words *very good* that one time. You know when I was in school, our teacher always read a verse from the Bible to us every morning and also said a short prayer. Then we started our lessons. Therefore, we were pretty much schooled in the Bible, and I was very adept, as you all know.

"Now getting back to pretty people and homely ones. If God had jumped the gun and made women more beautiful than they are, men never would go out and work. Now when you go home, read this for yourselves. God told Adam, 'You are to dress and take care of the garden.' But no, Adam had to stay home with Eve all day, and that's when he ate the apple."

The men marveled at Mr. Plenty's oratory.

Albert Peabody wore a black hat, a black suit, drove a black hack, and had a black horse named Agatha. Agatha was as skinny as her master and her back callused from the many flicks of the buggy whip he laid on her when he was in a hurry, and that was all the time. Everyone near or far did agree that Albert was spindly, lean, and down right scrawny. The men on the porch said he had a countenance that verged on the same description. The men were too kind to call him ugly, so they used the softer word homely. The women folks, especially if they were members of the Baptist Church, used the term ill-favored. The men also used the word tightwad and the ladies used quite thrifty to describe him. This was the reason he had never married. In dry humor one day, he told the men on the porch that when a man says, "I do," he immediately lets his new wife have half of his wealth.

Albert had a full head of hair that circled his head but had no hair on top. This caused him to waste a lot of time in his grooming preparations, as he would pull quite a swath of hair from one side and arrange it across his scalp. The bad thing about this procedure was that if a strong whiff of wind happened by, it would lift it almost straight up. He had never heard anyone say it, but it did look like a big rooster's comb. Someone had told him to spread the white of an egg on the bare spot so that when it dried it would secure the hair. Therefore, every morning, he had to waste the white of an egg, but he used the yoke for his breakfast. "Very thrifty," he'd say with a smile.

On the west side of Paw Paw was a large ravine with Big Morgan Creek flowing down the middle of it. On each side of the creek were two landmarks made of huge white stones engraved with the name Peabody. These marked the middle of Peabody acreage, and all could see he would never worry about water for his ranch and livestock.

The land above and on either side of the ravine was flat. One side was a lush green pasture, which was used for the one hundred head of big, white-faced cattle that dotted the horizon. The other side was used for farming: grain for the cattle; tobacco; and all kinds of vegetables for drying, canning, and fresh food for the table. Beyond these huge gardens were fruit orchards. The yield from these trees was almost Biblical in proportion.

Albert Peabody might have been small of stature, but he was a man of strength in organizing his ranch. He had sharecroppers in the area, and they were given one-half of their production with the other half going to Albert. Several did complain that he shouldn't receive half of their earnings, but Albert didn't pay them no mind.

The men on the porch had tried in vain to find more information of how Albert had obtained his vast holdings. It was whispered that years ago he had obtained his first hundred acres in a card game. He won it from the nephew of an old, weak-minded lady who signed over her land. Both she and her nephew were dead now, so there was no way to find the truth. Other shady land deals and dubious shenanigans were pursued, but they also led to a dead end. All the men's efforts were stymied in some way, but they did prove to be popular topics, which they complained of quite often.

It came like a bolt out of the blue when Albert Peabody got the old-time religion. Miss Idy delivered this information to the men on the porch in person.

She arrived at the porch breathless and stopped in front of the men. "Well gentlemen, I will tell you what has happened, as I know none of you men were at the Wednesday night prayer meeting. After a lengthy prayer, Albert Peabody stepped up to the podium and told of his conversion. He didn't spare himself in his confession of being a sinner, in fact, readily admitted the fact. Bravely he related how he was out walking over his vast acreage and gloating over his good fortune. Tiring of this, he went into the house and sat by a little antique table. On it lay his mother's worn Bible. He opened it up, and his eyes were riveted to the passages he read. The congregation sat in rapt attention as he quoted them from memory: 'Thy pastures are clothed with flocks; the valleys also are covered over with corn. They shout for joy, they also sing.' And, 'Sing, O ye heavens; for the Lord hath done it: shout ye lower parts of the earth: break forth into singing, ye mountains, O forest, and every tree.'

"Then he said, 'I have repented to the Lord all my sins and mistakes, and He has forgiven me, and I hope the members of this church will forgive me too!'

"Well, to top this, he began quoting Zacchaeus, who was converted in a tree. When he came down to the ground, he said, 'Master, half of my goods I will give to the poor. If I have taken anything by false accusation, I will restore four-fold.'

"Overcome by this confession, we all gave him the right hand of fellowship. I am sure he will be our next preacher; he not only knows the Scriptures, but also has a wonderful gift of oratorical speaking. I hope this testimony will have a big effect on you men and that you will decide to come to church more often."

Then Miss Idy clicked her heels, went into the store, and slammed the door after her.

What was going to happen next in Paw Paw? The men on the porch were left speechless, and that was a miracle by itself.

Shortly after her visit, Miss Idy's prediction came true when Albert became the Reverend Albert Peabody of Paw Paw's Baptist church.

For we brought nothing into the world,
and it is certain we can carry nothing out.

1 Timothy 6:7

Chapter 10

Filthy Lucre

Jimmy Simpson. If a person just stood back and surveyed him, they would say he looked very ordinary, much like any other boy. Just run of the mill. He was tall and lean, with arms, hands, and feet growing faster than the rest of his body, and always had a hungry look in his eyes.

But, there the similarity to all other boys ended. No matter what Jimmy was doing, he had a built-on smile on his face. He had mischievous, dancing, black eyes, which were always alert for excitement of any form. He had a thatch of unruly hair that appeared to never be combed, and he looked like he should be seated in a barber chair.

Jimmy had observed, as far back as he could remember, that one could get along better by being charming and courteous and by using flattering remarks, which always contained a grain of truth.

He planned his day when he opened his eyes in the morning by asking himself this question: "How can I make this day better for me?" This attitude didn't always work out, but it was not for the lack of trying.

The Simpson house was on a hill on the north side of Paw Paw. When Jimmy arose early in the morning and walked out onto the front porch, he could see all over the little town. He knew every person far and wide. If a newcomer moved in, he made it his business to get to know them as quickly as possible. One never knew what might come from the new folks. Perchance they would have more money to spread around than the current inhabitants of Paw Paw who surely didn't have much.

He struggled with two things in his young life. The first was money. Rev. Peabody called it "filthy lucre" in one of his sermons, which puzzled Jimmy because he knew the Reverend himself loved it so much. The second thing he struggled with was knowledge—especially about the birds and the bees.

He desperately wanted to hear and know the things that were discussed by his dad and the men on the porch at the General Store. He felt this information would be vital to his happiness some day.

There were several thorns in his flesh that he had to deal with in his quest for money and his thirst for knowledge.

School was one. The hours spent in school were the best hours suited to gainful employment in his frenzied way of life. He knew there was no way to stop going to school. There would be a death in the family, and it would be his if he tried that. Plus, he did agree that he needed that book learning as he planned to be the richest man in Paw Paw. So all his work and his schemes had to be arranged around his school hours.

His teacher was taken aback and left wondering by his uncanny ability to excel in every study. She had even overheard one of his buddies call him the "top dog." In his spare time, when he was too bored to study along with the lessons, Jimmy wrote poetry. It was mostly about the people he knew. Sometimes the poems were funny; other times they were just plain outrageous.

Jimmy was a delivery boy. He delivered for all the old people who couldn't get to the store. He also delivered for the harried new mother who was trying to take care of a new baby while her two-year-old was having a tantrum and her three other children were crying for something to eat. Jimmy used this time as an opportunity to meet everyone, to study them and their way of life, their tragedies, their sorrows, and their pain. He found out whether they were lonely or if the Lord had blessed them in some unexpected manner. If they had been touched by the joy of a birth of a baby or the death of a loved one. He had a way of extending himself by just laughing when they laughed or weeping when they wept.

Jimmy's life was full indeed, and he used the cleverness he was endowed with to further his efforts to be rich.

Who can find a virtuous woman?
For her price is far above rubies.
She will do him good and not evil
all the days of her life.

PROVERBS 31:10,12

Chapter 11

Tibet Grey Jumped the Broomstick

It was one of those mornings in Paw Paw that was breathtakingly beautiful. The bright morning sun, placid and unruffled, was glancing over the mauve and purple mountains. The golden sun's purpose and intention was to stealthily take over the silvery mist that shrouded the valley where Big Morgan Creek flowed.

The men had just settled into their favorite chairs when down the road, making a big ruckus with dust flying in its wake, a beat up, old ramshackle truck came into view. At one time, it had been red, but time had taken its toll and a ruddy rust color prevailed now.

"Well, I be switched and overcome, to say the least," said Fred Pinkham. "That's our long-lost friend, Tibet Grey."

Tibet had been one of the men who had sat on the porch in times past, but he had moved to Whippoorwill awhile back and the men hadn't heard from him; they had lost touch.

Tibet was a dog lover; he especially loved hound dogs. When he lived in Paw Paw, he was free to hunt every night if he wanted to. He didn't have a wife to nag him to distraction at the mere mention of going hunting. Back then he thought the men on the porch were jealous of him as he was so foot-loose and fancy-free to run his hounds whenever the spirit moved him.

So thinking that, he was very cautious when the men tried to get him wedded off to the weaker sex. His answer was always the same. "Boys, I have not met the lady that I love more than my Miss Henny here." Miss Henny was his favorite hound, and she was always at his feet. He would pat her on her head often. "Yes, for sure, she is my jewel." At his pats and words, Miss Henny always rolled her big, sad, brown eyes up in love to her master.

Then Tibet announced with a sigh, "Now my good buddies, get a hold of your chairs for this catastrophic news. I have jumped the broomstick; I got married!"

The men all sat stunned at hearing this.

Tibet brokenly blurted out his story. "I was in Whippoorwill on a Sunday morning on a stressful business deal. You know I wasn't a church-going man, but I felt a little bad in doing a transaction on Sunday, especially a transaction about a hound dog. I drove out of town a little ways and passed by the Baptist church. I was surprised to see all the people gathered in the yard. Then, lo and behold, I realized it was an all-day meeting and dinner on the ground. Suddenly, I smelled the aroma of fried chicken in the air and I was a goner. You know what I mean? I parked my truck on the far edge of the church, figuring no one would notice me in the crowd. Then I bravely joined the joyful group. And there she stood right in front of my eyes."

Tibet paused for a while to let his words sink in. "She handed me a plate piled high with fried chicken and pickles. Then she handed me another plate filled with two pieces of cake, white and chocolate, one piece of cherry pie, and a piece of wild gooseberry. Now you all know how I love wild gooseberry pie. Then she gave me a flirtatious look with a big smile and whispered, 'I cooked all the food on your plate.'

"Well, one thing led to another, and, well, you know how it is. The gist of it all was I needed to separate the two. Did I love her, or did I love her cooking? Could I love her more than her cooking? So, wantin' to make the right decision, I started going to church. Not that I was converted right then, but I had to size up this love thing. She wasn't such a beauty as to win one of those beauty contests, but she was pleasingly fair of face and she was robust, hearty, and able to do a fair amount of work. And, as I said, she could cook.

"Now I was always aware to take a bath before going to see Ella May because I been told at times I smelled like Miss Henny. That seems mighty strange to me, as I never smelled her even when she slept in my bed. I brought Ella May to my house, which was all topsy-turvy and pretty messed up. I believed that she should see with her eyes wide open where she would live. But I didn't want to scare her completely, so I shut up my dogs in the barn. All except Miss Henny that is. I was afraid she might die of shock, as I have always babied her all her life. Oh yes, she is my jewel." Tibet patted her on the head again.

"As I look back, my eyes were blinded with love. If I had been listening and looking like I should, I would have seen the fervent glint in her eye. She certainly would have heard all the wives comment about me, that she couldn't make a silk purse out of a sow's ear.

"So finally the day arrived for my being wedded up. We were married in the courthouse by the local judge and started out our honeymoon at my house. I was quite overcome by the hugs and kisses she bestowed on me, even when I was driving. I was distracted by this lovemaking but arrived home safely. Laughing, teasing, and kissing each other, we jumped out of my truck. Then the unfortunate happened.

"All the dogs in the barn had escaped somehow and were greeting us by jumping and barking with joy. Somehow I cleared the dogs away. I was breathless and shaking with excitement because I had thought I would perform the lovely custom of carrying Ella May over the threshold. I picked her up in my arms, displaying my manly strength, and started for the door. Then I noticed that Miss Henny was stretched out across the doorway. I was afraid to step over her, as she might decide to get up at the same time, so I had to put Ella May down. This was the first time Miss Henny heard my wrath and unkind words, and she ran and hid under the porch. I turned to pick Ella May up again, and she shoved me aside and stiffly marched into the house."

All was hushed on the porch, as the men tried to think of a way to comfort their old friend.

After sadly sighing, Tibet began again. "Now, my fellow citizens, the worst is yet to come. To my sorrow and grief, Ella May did not like dogs, least of all hound dogs. But she did comfort me a little. It was our wedding night, you know. However, all through the night, I heard my Miss Henny, my jewel, walking back and forth on the porch. She was used to sleeping by my side at night, but there was no way I could get by with that. I just hoped it wouldn't curtail her hunting instincts in any way.

"We slept a little late the next morning, reveling in our newfound love. Still laughing, we started a late breakfast. I fried the ham while she made the biscuits and gravy. I very sweetly told her to make a double portion because we had to feed the hounds. You know all hounds are skinny no matter how much they eat. Anyway, she started making the double portion, but the silence in that kitchen could have been cut with a knife. We sat through breakfast with nary a word spoken. She filled a bowl with all the leftovers, and I carried it outside to the dogs. You all know the ruckus they make when they're fighting for their share of the food. Well, she looked scared I tell you. I guess if one wasn't used to it, maybe any woman would be frightened.

"Well, I work a few days a week at the courthouse and the jail keeping the weeds cut down and doing the odd jobs that seemed to get bigger every day. I was in the kitchen kissing and trying to love up on her before I had to leave, and you know I was doing a great job of this as she clearly responded. Then as I went out on the porch to leave for work, I noticed Miss Henny going back and forth under the porch. She seemed satisfied in some way that delighted me.

"All day long I whistled and sung some of the church hymns I had learned. I was one happy man I want you to know. I went lickety-split for home as soon as I could. From a distance, all looked serene. However, when I got out of my truck, there seemed to be a flood around the house. Every stick of furniture was in the yard, except the stove. Ella May had poured buckets of hot sudsy water throughout the rooms and just swept it out the door. I am telling you, she was strong. I doubt very much if any of us men could do the task she had accomplished. Then, you can't guess what happened. She came out onto the porch and heaped all the hugs and kisses you ever saw on me. I not only trembled with excitement, but I looked carefully around to see if anyone was near to have us arrested for conduct that's off the beaten path.

"She was bright and happy and said, 'Oh, my darling, I'm so glad you're home. I felt like I should tidy the house up a bit. This is still our honeymoon, you know.' Then she smiled coyly up at me and said, 'I guess you'd better help me get this heavy furniture back into the house.'

"Seems she didn't recall how she got it out. Well, we carried the table back into the kitchen, and there on the stove was a big pot of chicken and dumplings simmering. And a huge blackberry cobbler sat on the cupboard. She had picked the berries herself in the thicket nearby.

"Oh, my dear buddies, I wish I could have stopped her, but it was not to be.

"I know you gentlemen have heard of people that took their extra dogs and cats and dropped them off by some farmer's house, thinking they would be taken care of. We know how seldom it works out. They generally die or are killed. If I can recollect, I read that in the big cities, they put them to sleep with some strong medicine.

"I could still smell the wonderful odor of clean sheets even after a glorious night in bed. Ella May was up. I hopped out of bed, and suddenly I heard such screaming and vicious cussin' it would have made a sailor turn pale. Where she learned these words I don't know, as some of them were new to me.

"Her face was livid red and she was shaking violently as she said in a shrieking voice, 'Look under the porch! Look under the porch!'

"So I rushed out and met Miss Henny wagging her tail and frolicking around. Her eyes did sparkle up at me as if she was proud of something. I looked under the porch, and there was eight baby pups. Little replicas of Miss Henny." Again, Tibet sighed. "That is the one fault with Miss Henny. When she has babies, she has babies.

"Well, there was no talking with Ella May. She wouldn't let me touch her or kiss her good-bye. I was late for work so had to leave right away, but when I ran past Miss Henny, I gave her a pat on her head."

Tibet continued. "I know these next scenes should be buried in God's Sea of Forgetfulness, and maybe they will be someday, but I'm afraid this will be indelible in my heart and soul forever. I rushed home as fast as I could, hoping things had calmed down a little.

"Everything was still and peaceful like a holy bush. I got to the back door, and there on the first step lay all eight of the puppies lined up in a row. They had their little tails hanging over the step in exact, precise order. They had been drowned, one after another, in the big rain barrel nearby."

The men sat stupefied and bewildered. Their faces blanched white with fear and only a few moans escaping their lips.

"Well, when I stood looking at this sad sight, out from under the porch came a cautious and frightened little puppy. Ella May had missed him somehow. I picked him up, and he began kissing me with his little wet nose."

At this point Tibet had to get out his handkerchief, blow his nose, and mop up his tears. "So I have him in my truck.

Thought I might give him to someone here in Paw Paw. He's going to be a prize one, I'm sure."

As if in answer to prayer, Jimmy Simpson came down the road from school. Seeing the puppy in the truck seat, he picked it up. It wiggled for joy and started to kiss him. Tibet leaped down the steps. He didn't use the wobbly banister, and they declared later that he never used one of the six steps on the porch either.

"Jimmy, do you want a prize dog? He's a dandy. And I'll tell you something else, this dog will be heard from by and by. He has a good omen about him."

Jimmy held the pup and smiled. "I think I'll call this little runt Goliath. Tibet turned to the men on the porch and with a smirk on his face said, "Well men, I still have three hounds and Miss Henny, of course, and I found a good home for her pup. I guess you could say I'll be leaving Paw Paw a happy man."

The words of the wise are as goads,
and as nails fastened by the masters of assemblies,
which are given from one shepherd.
And further, by these, my son, be admonished:
of making many books there is no end;
and much study is a weariness of the flesh.

ECCLESIASTES 12:11-12

Chapter 12

The Letter

Before Miss Idy ever embarked or set sail on any of her many missions, she always carefully dotted all her i's and crossed all her t's . Over her kitchen table hung a big calendar. Each day had an organized list of activities that would demand her full attention. These lists were further divided by events or people, according to importance.

Today, she would go and spend the day at Paw Paw's one-room schoolhouse. She had never done this before, but she knew they would accept her graciously. She packed her lunch in a little lard bucket, hunted up a poem, and hurried off to school.

She arrived at the ringing of the bell. Every morning, unless it was bitter cold, the children stood in line as Miss Anderson greeted them, then they marched to their desks. All the children and even Miss Anderson looked at her with a bit of alarm and fear. Nevertheless, Miss Anderson said, "Miss Idy, we are happy you have come to visit us. Would you like to sit at my desk?"

"No, thank you, Miss Anderson. I'll take a chair and sit in the back of the room. I don't want the children to be nervous by seeing me."

Her sitting in the back didn't help much as teacher and pupils alike had a few sweaty brows all day.

Before they were dismissed, Miss Idy stood up and said, "I sincerely enjoyed myself today, watching and listening to your performance. Who knows, we may see a future president of the United States coming from this very school." She gave them all one of her rare smiles, and they rushed out the door.

Then, instead of going home, she tripped her way to see the men who sat on the porch of the General Store.

The men on the porch watched her coming down the road. The sun was in their eyes, but that failed to hide her purposeful walk. Amos gamely offered, "I perceive that Miss Idy is quite flustered this afternoon, so we must prepare ourselves for the worst."

Miss Idy climbed the steps to the porch, being careful to not touch the wobbly banister that would betray a weakness on her part, according to the men's reckoning. "Good afternoon, gentlemen. Are we relaxing a bit today?" Without giving them time to answer, she plunged ahead. "I have spent the day visiting in our schoolhouse, watching and listening to our future leaders. I was dismayed that our children weren't learning very much or showing profound knowledge or scholarship ability. They are not "up-to-snuff," as you would say. It is not altogether Miss Anderson's fault, and it is certainly not our children's. But it is vital that we help our children rise to their full potential," she said, raising her voice a few octaves. "What we need in Paw Paw is a library! We need a newspaper too, but a library is the most important. The books the children are using now are disgraceful antiquities from the distant past. There could be literary giants in our school, but we'll never know because all their books are in tatters. Who can learn from rags? Also, I believe some of these tattered pages have wound up as paper airplanes. If we had an investigation, it would lead to Jimmy Simpson, I'm sure."

Otis Simpson gave a gasp at this accusation.

Miss Idy continued, not giving Otis a chance to reply. "The one nice book we have in our homes is the Bible. However, our youth refuse to read it because they cannot grasp the depths that it portrays. When and if they learn to read, we hope they will be able to understand the books and the book of all books, which is the Bible.

"We must teach them that by reading a book and searching for its golden nuggets, they will enter into a world they never knew existed, a world rich in wonderful ideas and even wealth.

"So gentlemen, what do you say about us getting together and trying to get a library and maybe a newspaper here in Paw Paw?" All were silent for a time.

"Miss Idy," Jeremiah cautiously ventured, "it certainly is a great idea, but how would we manage to do these things? We have a meager amount of money in our city public funds. It would be just a drop in the bucket of what we would need."

Fred Pinkham lamely put in his two cents. "Miss Idy, we must be careful about progressing too fast. We don't want our children to get any new-fangled, modern ideas that we can't afford. Neither can we afford a departure from our godly heritage, our ancestry that has been passed from one generation to another. Just looking around us, what do we see? Contentment, happiness, and satisfaction." Fred had begun his speech rather lamely; he finished it the same way.

They all felt that in some vague manner Miss Idy was not satisfied. "Well, I knew some of you men would throw a conniption fit about this betterment and progress for our lovely children and, of course, the adults who need it. Didn't you ever hear that the pen is mightier than the sword? Is this improvement in Paw Paw going to be put aside, laid to rest, tucked away in some dusty pigeon-hole desk? I say absolutely NO! There is a little saying, 'Put this in your pipe and smoke it.' Well, since you don't smoke just take another chaw of your devils' brew, but be careful where you expectorate. Thank you gentlemen."

This time she loudly clicked her heels, gave them a salute, and marched down the road to her house.

Miss Idy hurried home and wrote her friend Jeanette Long. They had shared a room together the last year at school. Jeanette was not so straight-laced as she was, so that was the reason they had gotten into a disastrous situation. One night they had almost slipped through the crack of sin by going with two men on a joy ride. They'd just escaped by the skin of their teeth. They had to walk three miles back to school in the pitch darkness. She shuddered now just recalling it.

My Dear Jeanette,

I hope this little note will find you hearty and well. I want to ask a favor. I am dwelling in a little town called Paw Paw. They have no library or newspaper. Would you please search around and ask some of the people who graduated in journalism if there is anyone who would like to come here and start a newspaper and a library? Maybe a man and wife. I will assure them they would have my undying eternal support. Time is of the essence and most crucial, my dear. Waiting and dilly-dallying is not a virtue that I possess, as you well know.

Love and prayers,
Idy Crandall

She rushed to the post office. She placed her spit on a stamp and finished it off with a loud fist. She didn't want the stamp to get lost from her letter.

And the king spake unto Ashpenaz
the master of his eunuchs,
that he should bring certain of the children of Israel,
and of the king's seed, and of the princes;
children in whom was no blemish,
but well favoured, and skilful in all wisdom,
and cunning in knowledge,
and understanding science,
and such as had ability in them
to stand in the king's palace,
and whom they might teach.

DANIEL 1:3-4

Chapter 13

Jacob's Past, Present, and Future

The dignitaries, the citizenry, and the common laity of Paw Paw—as Jimmy Simpson with his book learning was fond of saying—were jubilant at the latest addition to their population. They had just sailed into town one hot summer afternoon in a beat-up old truck loaded to the hilt with suspicious cargo. The men on the porch, who were immediately aroused from their napping and apathy, looked in a skeptical manner when no one emerged form the truck.

"Well, I'll be hanged," gasped Fred Pinkham. "Why, they are kissing up a storm. And here comes Miss Idy. When she sees them kissing, the fur will fly indeedy."

The occupants finally jumped out of the truck with the glow and radiance of youth. They fairly danced up the stairs to the porch, talking and laughing at the same time, trying to appear sedate in front of the men but failing. Miss Idy just knew these people were in answer to her letter and an answer to her prayers!

"Hello, I'm Timothy Rameth. And this is my lovely wife, Tabitha. We are on our honeymoon, and, as a matter of fact, this is the first time I've introduced her as my wife." Again, the two were overtaken in laughter.

Timothy Rameth was tall and skinny with an unruly thatch of nut-brown hair, bleached blond on top by the rays of the sun. He was badly in need of a haircut. The hair kept falling into his eyes, and he was constantly brushing it back with his fingers, which made it look even more tousled. He was ruggedly handsome, and his hazel eyes fairly laughed with joy.

Tabitha was a tiny lady with a creamy complexion and a brown row of freckles across her nose. It wasn't hard to notice that she had been by Timothy's side as they soaked up the sun together. Her hair was fiery red. She had braided it into two braids and wound them around her head. It made her look like she was wearing a reddish crown. She had dazzling green eyes, and they too smiled when she laughed so charmingly.

The men on the porch were quite taken with the utterly enchanting young couple. Even Miss Idy had a trace of a smile on her face.

Jeremiah jumped to his feet first, shaking the hands of their delightful visitors. "Welcome to Paw Paw. I am Jeremiah Jones and these are my friends hereabouts. And this is Miss Idy, our front-runner in Paw Paw."

Jeremiah was embarrassed as he looked at the front door of the General Store for Clara who, as usual, was fussing and ranting. And they could hear her from outside as she railed on Jacob.

"Jacob, I never saw your like. You haven't cleaned or dusted the back of the store in a year. There were times when we could have made a sale, but no, we couldn't find the article because it was buried back there. You and I should stop right here and have a funeral over everything. One thing wrong with you is that you are exhausted from staying up till midnight in that shop of yours. I can't understand what you do out there every night. And I have wondered why you keep that big lock on the door, never allowing me or the townspeople to see what you are doing. Jacob are you listening to me?"

"Yes Clara, I am listening. How could anyone fail to hear you? I am going to the kitchen now to get my list of things that need to be done."

"Jacob, what are you saying? You will have to talk louder if you want me to hear you." Jacob was in luck as the bell chimed on the screen door as it opened and everyone from the porch came in with peels of laughter and excitement, all talking at the same time.

Jeremiah introduced them. "Jacob and Clara Johnson, owners of our store, this is Timothy and Tabitha Rameth. They are on their honeymoon and decided to stop in our little town.

Clara felt the blood drain from her face, her knees started trembling when Jeremiah introduced Tabitha.

Tabitha. Why, she hadn't heard that name since her own baby Tabitha died and left her all alone.

Jacob took hold of her arm afraid she might fall, but he was visibly shaken too. They were both glad the men on the porch continued their welcoming chatter.

Clara was standing next to Tabitha when Jeremiah loudly declared. "Well, I am a monkey's uncle. Clara, Miss Tabitha, you have the same color of hair. And that isn't all. Everyone look at their eyes. That pretty green color."

Everyone was mystified by their identical resemblance to one another. Even Miss Idy was speechless.

Tabitha was the first to recover from this baffling puzzle. "Well Mrs. Johnson, it appears we are kinfolk for sure, so that gives me the opportunity to hug and kiss you," which she proceeded to do. Overcome with emotion, Clara also encircled Tabitha in her arms.

Jacob looked at the enrapturing drama that was unfolding before him, as he desperately tried to keep his own eyes from overflowing. It all became fresh again to his wounded soul. He remembered the day of thick darkness and gloom, the day of black clouds, which had spread over his mountains, the day of such anguish and pain it had taken away his dignity, his self-esteem.

In this emotionally charged atmosphere, Jacob, in a flashback, remembered there were some happy times when they first arrived in Paw Paw. Those times were centered mostly on getting to know the rather shy, tenderhearted people who all made an effort to live by the Golden Rule and the Ten Commandments. These rules were prominently displayed in the schoolhouse and in the Baptist Church. They were also displayed in the General Store behind the counter. This copy had turned yellow, had crinkled edges, and was barely readable, yet everyone in Paw Paw knew the words and was comforted in the knowing.

Oh yes, Clara had put up a bold front and was all smiles to the townspeople—she knew they were dependent on the store for their livelihood—but toward him, she seemed to glory in his humiliation. There were a few instances when she would bestow her favors on him like a gift to a child, liken to a bit of candy. It was in one of those rare intimate moments that she became what the people of Paw Paw called "in the family way."

Clara never told Jacob about her suspected pregnancy. She just announced that she was going shopping in Whippoorwill. As she left, Jacob cautioned, "Why don't you get someone to go with you? I hate to see you go alone."

As usual, she never answered him as she flitted out the door.

Jacob had an extremely busy day at the store. It was getting dark, Clara hadn't returned home, and Jacob was getting worried.

Then, Clara came in the door and Jacob gave a sigh of relief. Then out of nowhere, she started kissing him. This startled him, as he could not remember when she had ever initiated anything like this, so out the window flew the scolding he had rehearsed. He locked up the store, and Clara began making a light supper.

Jacob was amazed when Clara began singing as she rattled the pots and pans. This was indeed a surprise. "Maybe we should take a little trip together away from the store. Jimmy could tend it," he mused.

Clara poured them both large bowls of soup, and then she buttered two thick slices of Miss Idy's famous yeast bread, which she had brought them the day before. Clara served peaches and cookies for their dessert.

"Well, my dear Clara, it appears that you have had a happy day shopping from the amount of your packages. What did you buy?"

Jacob was once again startled, as smiling mischievously, she said, "I spent a lot of your money. Some things I needed, and some on things I didn't need but just wanted. What do you think of that?"

"Clara, you know I don't mind. Anything you want I would gladly give you, if I could. I am going to bed. I've had a pretty rough day without you to help in the store." As he got up, he daringly kissed her lips. She kissed him back and smiled at him provocatively.

What is going on here? What is happening to Clara tonight? he wondered. Was she really different, or was he trying to read something that wasn't there?

With questions still running around in his head, he went to bed. He left the light on for her but turned his back to it. Then he heard it. It was just a wisp of a sound, then the room became charged. He turned over and there she was in a shimmering satin green gown the color of her eyes. It swirled luminously around her body and her glorious red hair fell like a flame down to her waist. She danced around and around. At each turn, she leaned over and tantalizingly kissed him. Her lips were scarlet red from the lipstick she wore, which was a "no no" in the church.

Then in all this wonder she began singing, "Clara has a secret, Clara has a secret."

Jacob was voiceless and stared wild-eyed at her.

Then, with wild abandon, she gave a leap into his arms, laughing hilariously and singing to the top of her lungs, "Jacob and Clara and God have made a little baby."

Oh yes, that beautiful time when Clara was pregnant, he was amazed at how she reveled in delight and joy at her pregnancy and was eager to tell every lady in the Baptist Church about her coming baby.

Then the dark shadow of death moved into the little General Store and took the only ray of sunshine that had ever glistened there. Oh yes, he remembered where she had sat for over a year in her grief the night he boldly marched into the guest room, threw aside the silver screen, yanked Clara to her feet, carried her to their bedroom, and unmercifully slammed her down on their bed—all the while screaming wildly at her. He remembered the long walk down the hall to his new bedroom.

He opened the door and shut it behind him, knowing full well that he had closed the door to any happiness that might come from Clara, his only love. He felt desolate. Not only had they lost their wee baby, Tabitha, but now they had lost their love too. He dropped his clothes he had carried from their bedroom on the floor. Drained in body, soul, and spirit, feeling like the world had collapsed on his shoulders, he didn't bother to undress but just stretched out on the bed. He was still trembling and shaking from his emotionally charged altercation with Clara.

Where had this anger come from? He had often wanted to vent his anger to her but was fearful he might lose her. Well, he had accomplished the deed in just a few moments.

What had happened to that twenty-three-year-old, brash, impetuous young man? When he first came to Paw Paw, he was full of hopes and dreams. Why, he was a fool, a reckless, harebrained fool, who thought he could make a difference in all of the children and the young in heart. It seemed that everything went wrong from the beginning of coming here, except his love for Clara.

He never tired of watching her and the elegant movements

of her body. She was enchanting; a radiance flowed from her. He remembered his little house in Chicago where their violent love for each other began. No, it had started the first time he saw her, the night he caught a glimpse of her dancing with another man. She danced with emotion; each movement was sheer poetry. That was the night he had rudely and very ungentlemanly taken her in his arms and walked her out into the night with him.

A few days after their arrival in Paw Paw, there came the two big trucks loaded with his precious materials for building his pianos and organs. She never asked or wondered what he was unloading into the big building behind the store. Jacob decided to tell her about his dreams of music and building pianos when she wasn't so angry. However, she was always angry, so year after year he stifled the words in his heart.

Jacob could feel Clara's body and arm around him, yet he continued his darkened haunting memories of their past. He had slept fitfully through that night so long ago.

A troubled and wounded Jacob heard the roosters crowing just as the gold and pinkish tinge of the morning light crept into his new bedroom. A faithless, unbelieving transgressor called Jacob stumbled from his bed and out the door. He unlocked the big shop behind the store, which he called his Holy Sanctuary. It had been his haven of rest since he had moved to Paw Paw. Here, while he communed with his God and built his pianos and organs, he dreamed his dreams, held onto his hopes and aspirations, and waited for the time when all of them would come true, when his God would bring them to fullness and completion.

In fascination, he stared at the breathtaking beauty of the pianos and organs. He had always thought of them as both God's and his creations. Now his God was not with him. Jacob had lost Him somewhere in the shadows of Paw Paw. It would not be blasphemy to bow and pay homage to his jewels, as he called them.

He got the big white sheets out of the chest where he kept

them stored and covered up the pianos and organs, lest the gray dust of Paw Paw settle upon them. As he locked the door of his shop, he wept for the man he had become, he wept for his beloved Clara, he wept for tiny Tabitha, and he wept for his treasures he was leaving behind. He took the key and dropped it into dust, grinding it deep with his shoe.

Then he remembered going in to the store, picking up his swatter, and beginning to swat the flies that were coming in the door.

Suddenly shocked and horrified, Jacob came down to earth from his lengthy haunting memories of his past. What must they think of him? But wait, everyone was still laughing and talking excitedly about plans for a newspaper and a library. In his amazement, he found he still had his arm around Clara. He was startled as she took his hand and pushed her body closer to him. Then from somewhere came a cry. "I shall appoint unto them that mourn, to give unto them beauty for ashes, the oil of joy for weeping, a garment of praise for the spirit of heaviness."

Trembling and shaking in wonderment, he asked himself again what was going on here. That scripture was from the Bible. He must have heard it from Mr. Willy. Was this one of the spiritual revelations he was always talking about? Questions upon questions raced through his mind. Then he felt a shadow lifting and an emotion aroused by something awe-inspiring. Whatever it was, Clara was involved. Why, the two of them were one flesh. Where did that come from? Shaking again, he realized Timothy was standing in the midst of them talking.

Timothy raised his hands, "Now since we all have calmed down a little, I want you to know that we have a mission here. We both graduated from college with degrees in journalism, and we want to start a newspaper here in Paw Paw. We have looked at various places, but this is where we have decided to stay, if you want us. One thing that impressed us very much was the letter we received from your goodwill ambassador,

Miss Idy Crandall." He bowed his head at her. "She wrote quite a letter, I must say. She was very emphatic, forceful, and determined that we come to your town and take a look before we decided where to start our newspaper and library."

"She said to discuss our project we must come to the General Store, talk with the Johnsons and the men that sit on the porch. Then she said something quite puzzling. She said we must be concerned about a grapevine that flourishes on the porch, the local telephone that Maggie Jenkins operates very skillfully. But best of all would be Jimmy Simpson, a boy wonder and outstanding young man. She said we must keep our eyes on him because all will know him soon."

Timothy continued, "A paper will benefit us all, even into the surrounding communities. It will cause new families to move here. Indeed, it will create more jobs, which are sorely needed, as everywhere we look there seem to be many idle men sitting on the porches of general stores.

"This is almost a spiritual thing for us. We both have the same calling." Timothy turned to Tabitha. "Darling, you tell them your dreams."

Tabitha rose and said, "I would like to have one whole page of the paper devoted entirely to our teens. Maybe even younger ones that are soon to enter that stage of life. I'd like them to write letters. To talk to me of their frustrations, their happiness, things that they could do to make Paw Paw a better place to live.

"I would like to start a program, an open discussion of things good and bad. The things they should do to achieve a higher goal for their dreams, visions, and desires. It could be held one night a week, maybe on Saturday evening. Just them and me. However, before I could print anything in the paper about the results of the meeting, I would get their approval. They could use their names in the paper or not. I would like them to know their goals are limitless, endless, and that exciting wonders can unfold before their eyes.

"In this dream of mine, I see authors, journalists, doctors, ministers, dentists, lawyers, musicians, artists, teachers, veterinarians, and maybe politicians and farmers. We must teach our children to be strong in mind, soul, and spirit. We must teach them that they must work in this world but must also include some recreation—ball games, music, and such.

"I shall devote an entire page to what I will call 'What Fell Out of the Wastebasket Today.' This will be a miscellaneous hodgepodge of comments of ways to make life more exciting. It will be filled with letters and ideas from everyone. We shall carefully consider complaints and gripes, give space for a neighbor's kindness, women's thoughts, raising children, recipes, church activities, etc.

"I clearly see and understand our elders, the city fathers, will say we can't do this in a tiny town like Paw Paw, but I believe we can. Therefore, we must sit down and reason together. Build on my dreams and yours. We must have fire in our bones that cannot be quenched. Tim and I have often wondered how many lights have been smothered, how many candles have been snuffed out by not listening to what our children say.

"Our teachers must stress reading and the love of words. We must have books, books, and more books. We must have a library. For now, we must show our children how powerful mere pencils and pens can be by them just writing and reading.

"If we encourage them, the rewards will be endless. I shall be guilty of saying: 'Winning isn't everything, it's the ONLY thing.' My motto shall be: 'A journey out of darkness into the light.' And this shall be said so often that every child shall know it."

Clara's face was pale and colorless, hardly daring to breathe. She was overcome by Tabitha's speech, by her exquisite beauty, and by the tender grace that began somewhere deep within her and overflowed to everyone that sat on the porch. Clara's tears fell unheeded down her face. In reality, they came from the same source of Spirit as Tabitha's beauty and grace.

Jacob boldly asserted, "I don't think there is anyone that does not agree wholeheartedly with you starting a newspaper here in Paw Paw. I will promise you that I will do all I can to make your dreams come true."

The men on the porch looked with amazement at Jacob, as they hadn't ever seen him in a role of leadership, as a take-charge person.

They all agreed with shaking hands, a lot hugging, and everyone talking at the same time.

Timothy, quite shaken himself, stood up. "I think we all have entered into a celebration of love on this porch of the General Store."

Even Miss Idy was finding it hard to not weep openly at this sweet gathering together in Paw Paw.

Before I formed thee in the belly I knew thee;
and before thou camest forth
out of the womb I sanctified thee,
and I ordained thee a prophet unto the nations.

JEREMIAH 1:5

Chapter 14

Tabitha/Tabitha

Hesitantly, Tabitha asked, "Mrs. Johnson, we looked around when we drove into Paw Paw, and we didn't see a hotel or an inn. Is there a place for us to stay until we get our paper project going?"

Clara, who was at her best when entertaining guests, said, "Oh, yes indeed, Tabitha. We have a place here, a guest room for you to stay in. Come this way down the hall, the men are so busy talking they won't miss us."

"When we first arrived here from Chicago, this was a big neglected room, but we cleaned and painted and Jacob put in a big picture window, so one could see out over our little town. The furniture was mine in Chicago. We sent for it, as I thought it would be in keeping with our little town."

Clara opened the door and Tabitha gasped, "This is so lovely." Then she rushed over to the big window. She was overwhelmed by the rapturous, panoramic view that was before her eyes. The hills were dotted with small houses set like gems against the dark green trees; all were veiled with a touch of purple haze. Many little roads and paths led into Paw Paw. Among the green hills were flowering peach, persimmon, and dogwood trees with their sinister message of Christ's crucifixion. Down the center of the valley, guarded by tall stately pine trees, flowed Big Morgan Creek, rushing at random wherever it was wont to go.

Tabitha had a glow of delight on her face as she turned to Clara and, without speaking, took hold of her hand. Neither one was aware of this gesture that spoke with sweet and loving body language.

On a raised pedestal platform was the huge, high, feather bed that presided over and dominated the whole room. The bedspread was an elegant patchwork quilt in a pattern of a flower garden. There were huge bolsters and pillows that were also covered with the same flower garden motif glowing in a riot of color. In the center of the room was a round marble-top table adorned with a lace doily and a vase of dried pussy willows. Some of their velvety, silver catkins had fallen and were gracing the doily. On both sides of the bed were two small matching marble-top tables. There was a small kerosene lamp with an antique match holder on each of them.

A victrola with a huge horn graced another table. The fireplace was ready with wood for lighting and with hand bellows nearby. At the entrance, beside the door, was a hall tree. A big combination of a long mirror with hat rack, umbrella stand, and a tray for calling cards. Wall-to-wall and curled over the pedestal where the bed was resting was a hand-woven rag carpet. It had a pale beige background and carried the bright colors of the flower garden quilt throughout.

Tabitha was left speechless by the elegant, exquisite Victorian period furnishings. "Mrs. Johnson, I have never seen a room so lovely, so beautiful as this."

The two still didn't realize that they were holding hands.

Clara and Tabitha were standing near the corner of the room that was curtained off by a folding screen of silver and gold tapestry. Tabitha was looking at the collection of old books on a shelf.

Clara's mind was somewhere else altogether. It would soon be two years since she had looked behind the screen. She recalled her memory of that bittersweet time when she knew she was going to have a baby. She had been deliriously happy and that so pleased Jacob. "Jacob, what are you doing with my pink satin and velvet ribbons? I have been looking for them," she asked him one day. He shyly took her hand and led her to an empty room behind the store. There it was, a white wicker baby bassinet. She could see the love for her and their baby woven, entwined, as he had plaited the ribbons through the wicker. Oh yes, she clearly remembered reaching up and kissing him. Even though they both were sure she was going to have a baby girl; she whispered in his ear, "I had better check my ribbon supply to see if I have enough blue." She also remembered asking Jacob if he liked the name Tabitha.

"Yes, yes, of course I do," he told her.

"Jacob, someone told me it meant 'ring of gold.' Did you know that?"

She remembered the nights they had lain in each other's arms and how they would fall asleep with their hands feeling her tummy and how Jacob was sure the baby was trying to get out so she could say, "Hello, Mama and Dada."

Jacob didn't know that ere long they both would fall into an abyss with arrows in their hearts. Or that Clara would sink even lower in the darkened chasm and wouldn't know how to come back.

On the first day of spring, at the first light of dawn, Tabitha was born. Clara held her in her arms; what glory that was. Jacob beamed and called her their "tiny minute."

Their joy was soon replaced with stark fear as Clara cried out, "Jacob, Jacob, something's wrong!"

The baby clutched one of Jacob's fingers with her tiny hand as she struggled and hungered for the milk at Clara's breast. How many times did she tug, was it two or three? Clara recalled the sweet pain when tiny Tabitha got the nipple in her mouth, but she couldn't swallow. A drop of milk from her breast, lingered a moment on the tiny mouth. Jacob's "tiny minute" and Clara's "ring of gold" put up a fierce battle to stay with them, but it was all in vain.

She remembered Jacob pleading, "Let me hold her for just a little while." Such piteous, heartbreaking words, but her answer was a hard, cruel stony silence as she clutched her baby to her breast.

"You never got to hold her, dear Jacob. Why was I so blind to your suffering?"

"Then Tabitha left me. Why didn't I say left us? Why was I so selfish? I still hear your whispered anguished words: 'Clara, I too have a wound that cannot heal. Must I cover my pain and grieve alone?'"

With cruel deliberation and purpose, Clara had locked the door against his comfort. In that place of sorrow and grief, Jacob was not allowed to enter. Yes, she knew he would have gladly been with her. They could have shared their Gethsemene together. But she had built a door that he could not open. She was the one who loosed the silver cord that held them together and broke the golden pitcher at the fountain. She used the "tools from Satan" to blame him for bringing her to Paw Paw, away from her home in Chicago. It wasn't true, of course. She had grown to love the people here, their kindness and the simple way of living, but she would never let Jacob know.

Yes, her tears had finally ceased to flow but now they lodged somewhere in an empty void inside of her. Someone had told her that weeping was the silent language used around the world when death came to visit.

For over a year, Clara refused to live a normal life. She wouldn't help in the store, wouldn't cook the meals, and wouldn't do their washing or ironing. She just sat in the corner where her baby's bed was—behind the tapestry—day after day, night after night, for weeks, and even months.

Then came the night when Jacob came behind the screen and yanked her to her feet. Angrily, his face reddened in fury and rage, he said, "You have been sitting here for a year, and now you are getting up and are going to start living a normal life. I don't want you to go behind this screen again. If you do, I won't be responsible for what I might do. You are taking up the normal duties of a wife, except I will never allow you in our bed. That won't be much of a chore for you because you have never been a wife anyway."

He picked her up, carried her to their bed, and dropped her mercilessly onto it. Both of them were screaming and trembling now. "What have I done?" he raged. "Tell me if you can. Why do you heap torture on me and put me through your strange viciousness every day right in front of our neighbors, customers, and, yes, my friends? You have reduced me to a namby-pamby. I have lost my manhood, my dignity. I have stood by and let you manipulate me and deliberately humiliate me. You have put me to shame, and I have allowed you to move me to a coward's corner. How I ever fathered a child is a mystery. It had to be a miracle beyond my understanding." His eyes narrowed with contempt, his voice tinged with hatred and anguish. Pain and grief wavered back and forth in his being.

"I have allowed you to do all this because I love you so. I thought in doing this you might love me again, but now it is all over. There, I have said it finally aloud. Leave. Go back to Chicago. I don't care."

Clara, in fright and terror, did manage one accusation. "If you love me as much as you say, why don't you tell me what is in the building behind the store? And why do you keep a big lock on it? You darkened the windows, what are you doing in there in secret? People think you're crazy."

"Clara, I was going to tell you several times, but I felt such a mysterious, spiritual power not to. Now I know why. You would have taken that from me too. You see, it is my church. You go to the Baptist Church, and I go to my sanctuary in the building behind the store."

With those words, Jacob took his clothes out of the closet, out of the dresser drawers, and moved down the hall to the back bedroom, leaving behind a stunned and dazed Clara.

When Clara returned to the present, she was still standing by the tapestry screen; Tabitha was still at the bookcase of old books, smiling and commenting about them. Clara was glad of that as she was trying desperately to pull herself together after the tattered and torn memories of her baby Tabitha, and yes, Jacob.

She was astonished at her quick change of thoughts. Then, incredibly, she heard the words: "It is time." Time for what? Confused and bewildered, she remembered Reverend Peabody's sermon on Sunday.

The text of his preaching was, "There is a time for everything. A time to weep and a time to laugh, a time to mourn and a time to dance." The Reverend had continued on by asking, "What would you rather do? Would you rather weep than laugh? Would you rather mourn than dance? You are the one to make this decision in your life."

Was this the time to take away the darkened veil and let God's shower of golden sunshine invade the sepulcher that Clara had mentally erected? She answered her own question as with calm, peaceful assurance she moved the silver and gold screen aside. Was it eons ago that she had placed it there?

There was the tiny white wicker bassinet that Jacob had built with the pink satin and velvet ribbons woven throughout. There was the pink satin coverlet and the tiny pink satin pillow with the name "Tabitha" embroidered on it.

Shocked indeed, the adult Tabitha stood motionless, captivated, by what was unfolding before her eyes. Was this one of the reasons they were led to Paw Paw? Why, of course! There was no doubt.

A silent hush enfolded them as an unseen choir began singing a baby's lullaby. Clara sat down on the small rocking chair. Tabitha knelt beside her, put her own red hair next to Clara's red hair, and tears of joy and happiness mingled together out of their matching green eyes. A new mother and her new daughter.

If one were looking at this drama, they would for sure repeat: "A new mother and her new daughter." Oh yes, step-by-step, the Holy Spirit of God had gently guided Clara and Tabitha to this birthing room.

A little child shall lead them.

I have blotted out, as a thick cloud,
thy transgressions, and, as a cloud,
thy sins: return unto me;
for I have redeemed thee.

ISAIAH 44:22

Chapter 15

Revelations in a Swing

Pardon

Pardon? For me?
You don't know my life
The things I've done, the things I've said.
It was I myself who caused it
To all come undone. I was the one.

Grace? You see, my face,
The hardened lines put there
From selfish thoughts,
Defensive acts,
That hurt so many hearts;
And still,
He would impart His grace?

New life? Contentment out of strife?
Too much time has passed
To seek new life.
It's almost over, don't you see?
I fear it's much too late for me.

Love? He loves me still?
Though He knows my past
And all the failures that I've known?
He wants this heart of mine
To call His home?
· Then take it, Lord
Pardon, cleanse, forgive.
Call my heart your dwelling place.
Please come in and live.

AUTHOR UNKNOWN

After supper, Jacob, Timothy, and Tabitha had gone to bed, but there was no sleep for Clara. She was too shaken and charged up by the tumultuous day. What had happened to her she did not know, but she must find out.

She went out onto the back porch and sat down in the swing that Jacob had built for her when they first arrived in Paw Paw. There was a huge lilac bush that through neglect appeared dead. She remembered the sharp words she had used that long-ago day. "Jacob, you get out there at once and cut down that dead lilac tree. It's a big eyesore!"

Jacob had protested, "Why Clara, there is life in that old lilac; I think I can save it."

She had retorted, "If you are that crazy, go ahead and try."

He drastically cut the dead limbs away and put some fertilizer on it. Every day he nursed it back to life, and now its huge purple and lavender blossoms were bursting with their intoxicating sweet essence. Its scented dew dampened her face and seemed to settle down inside her.

Is this where one's spirit rested? Oh, I wish Reverend Peabody would preach more clearly on such things, she mused.

She used her toes to push the swing back and forth. Its every movement whispered peace and contentment to her.

She had come to love this little town and the high social position she held by owning the largest business in the area. And she had come to love the people with their kind and simple ways and the way they showed love for one another.

However, the feeling she felt now was a mystery, an unexplainable, confusing mystery. So step-by-step, she went back to the beginning of the day.

She bowed her head down with shame as she realized that Timothy and Tabitha had been standing outside of the screen door, so they must have heard her wrangling and scolding Jacob. She was yelling at him really. Then the bell on the screen door announced their coming.

Oh yes, it was the bell on the door. That was it! That was what started this confusing day!

Had Jacob put a different bell on the door? Of course not. Jacob didn't do anything that needed to be done. Whenever there was a lull in the store, he spent his time in his shop, in the mysterious "sacred shrine" as she called it. However, there was a difference in that bell; it had a softer, gentler sound like a silver chime. Who was it that said, "A chime is the music nearest to heaven?"

She knew that singing the song, "No Sweeter Song Had 'ere Been Heard" on Sunday morning embraced her in a soothing hush. It erased the pain that was always with her in the grief of losing her baby Tabitha.

Then she remembered the way this morning's wonderful awakening began.

The men on the porch came in with the new customers. An exuberance and eagerness surrounded the two young people, and everyone was talking and laughing at the same time.

When she saw Tabitha, she felt as if she were looking into a mirror.

When Jeremiah introduced them, Clara gasped. Her face turned deathly white, her legs began to tremble, and she felt she was going to faint. Jacob saw her reaction and understood;

he pulled her to himself and put his arm around her waist. She felt his strength, his virtue, and his capacity to love. No matter how much abuse she had heaped upon him, he loved her still. In the magical change that was taking place, she pulled his body closer to her.

Clara pushed the swing a little higher as she reflected on the terrible way she had treated Jacob. "Oh my love, what have I done to you, to us?" she whispered. One by one, she had taken from him the things he valued most and she left him with empty hands. Day by day, week by week, month after month, year after year, she had taken away his dignity, his self-worth. All the things she had admired in him, she had destroyed. She had reduced him to thinking that his most important task was swatting the flies that made their way into the store.

"Oh my darling, can you forgive me? Can you forgive the unholy grievous hurt I have heaped upon you?" She reached for the pillow at the end of the swing, laid her head upon it, and wept in contrition and sorrow. Then, as it had been since the beginning of time, God reached way down and wiped Clara Johnson's tears and pain away.

"I must go to Jacob and reveal to him this mysterious happening in my life," she said. Trembling and smiling in anticipation of what she was about to do, she remembered the night so long ago, the wanton passionate love they had yielded to in Jacob's little house in Chicago. She also remembered the night she revealed to him that they were going to have a baby. She had purchased a silvery green nightgown in Whippoorwill, and that night she put it on and danced around the room in it for him.

What wasted years. It was all her fault. What a terrible person she was.

All at once, Clara gasped and sat bolt upright. "Oh, merciful heaven! Oh, hail and farewell!" Icy fingers raced down her spine as she suddenly realized they had never gotten married when they first arrived in Whippoorwill. They had discussed doing it when they went back to see Jacob's lawyer, but she didn't go with him; she had been too busy being angry.

This was impossible! How could they have forgotten such an important thing? Her eyes widened in terror; her heart was fluttering and performing flip-flops. She started to pray but only a mute, guttural cry came forth.

Her mind rushed back to the unbelievable day they arrived in Whippoorwill. She had been overwhelmed with all the cows, the dogs, the kids, the dust, and sweaty old Whitey Garrison.

Wait! Why, if they never married, they were living in adultery, or was it fornication? What was the difference? She wouldn't dare ask Reverend Peabody, as he would detect her wild anxiety. Maybe it was both. Either way, it was surely blasphemy!

Then she remembered that at church Sunday night, they had sung the song, "Sin Can Never Enter There." She had sung it louder than anyone had, except for maybe Miss Idy. Why, she was a hypocrite pretending to be so sanctimonious and pure as the noonday sun when all along she was a vile sinner. Now she remembered and understood Reverend Peabody's sermon about hypocrisy. His text was aimed at those who pretended to be beautiful outside but inwardly were full of dead men's bones. She remembered being a mite uneasy at such a drastic scripture. Now here she was a full-blown phony, a hypocrite. She and Jacob both were!

The custom of the church was if one had committed a vile sin, and this surely was one of those, you came to the altar and repented. Then the Lord would gladly forgive you and cast your sins into the Sea of Forgetfulness. Reverend Peabody then loudly would declare that the church should do the same. However, in this hour of her travail, she didn't think the church would enter into that Sea of Forgetfulness. Not wholeheartedly anyway. She had heard various comments by the ladies in the Sewing Circle in the past. Sunday night, Reverend Peabody had gone on to say, "He that covereth his sins shall not prosper."

"Oh for goodness sakes, does that mean our store will go down the drain?"

Crying, she lay down again on the swing, trying to calm herself and decided what she needed to do.

Clara quit crying and started to laugh. "Oh heaven forbid, this is no laughing matter," she scolded herself. Then trying to be serious, she started laughing again.

What should she do? It was plain that Jacob hadn't given it a thought either, or he would have told her immediately. She pondered the problem back and forth but realized that nothing could be done until morning.

They would have to tell Timothy and Tabitha that they needed to go to Whippoorwill on an urgent matter. "If this isn't urgent, nothing else is!" she said as she laughed hysterically again.

She gave the swing a big push and its sound changed from soft sweet music to a loud crescendo as she jumped up and ran to her bedroom.

Jacob was still sleeping when Clara awoke. She quietly arose, pulled the curtain aside, and viewed the golden sun as it was beginning to spread its enchantment over the little town of Paw Paw. She was filled with wonder; her load of anger, bitterness, and resentment had taken wings and soared away. God had taken her pain and filled her soul with joy and unspeakable glory. Oh yes, her tiny Tabitha had returned to her in the form of Tabitha Rameth.

"God, You said that a little child shall lead them," she whispered as she went into Jacob's room.

"Now Jacob, you have to wake up and listen. Something that you can hardly believe came to me last night. I am still in shock, and it will be a shock to you as well. Jacob, we are not married. Do you know that?"

"Clara, Clara, what are you trying to say?"

Clara had a hard time keeping sober as she reminded him of that hair-raising day when they arrived in Whippoorwill. Although unhinged herself, she finally convinced Jacob of this unbelievable and outrageous crime they had committed. Then she wept, as no one would understand.

Jacob bolted upright in the bed, gasping pop-eyed. "Why Clara, do you know what this means? We have been living in adultery or fornication. Maybe both!"

"Jacob, I said those very words last night just before I came into your room. I decided it would be best to tell you this morning." She couldn't help herself and laughed aloud at the bewildered, astonished look on his face.

"Clara, we must not take this as a laughing matter. You know how straitlaced and prudish the people are here. Why, we could even be put out of the church for this! The elders, and that includes Miss Idy, could bring charges against us. We could lose the store, as people might not want to buy from us if this were found out. Parents will not allow their children to come into the store. Oh, what a fine kettle of fish we are in!"

Jacob came up with this plan: "We won't tell anyone, as no one would believe it anyway and we could go to jail." Clara started to cry again. Jacob washed her tears away and started to kiss her. Then the serious and humorless Jacob began to laugh uncontrollably. Tears ran down his face.

Clara started to shake him. "Jacob, we must quiet down. Timothy and Tabitha might hear us!" Then she fell down in the bed, trying to restrain and curb her own fit of laughter. Jacob fell beside her and pulled a quilt over their heads. If, perchance, one would be eavesdropping outside their door, they would be alarmed that the staid, dignified Jacob and Clara were planning an elopement.

Thoughtfully, in spite of their panic, they left a note for Timothy and Tabitha, "Make yourselves at home. We'll see you tonight. Call Jimmy Simpson to help run the store."

Sing unto the LORD a new song,
and his praise from the end of the earth,
ye that go down to the sea,
and all that is therein; the isles,
and the inhabitants thereof.

ISAIAH 42:10

Chapter 16

The Golden Key

Jacob and Clara didn't arrive home from their mysterious rendezvous until quite late. Jacob, very innocently, had taken the longer, little-used road back to Paw Paw. Clara had vehemently protested, "Jacob, how will we explain our drastic behavior if someone should happen by?"

"Oh, my darling, no one would fault anyone that was on their honeymoon."

Clara, overcome with laughter, fell into his arms.

Timothy and Tabitha were in the kitchen about to make supper when they arrived home. Bursting through the door, Jacob and Clara grabbed Tabitha and Timothy in loving embraces, and Clara kissed Tabitha in their new relationship. Then Jacob began his practiced speech, which he had rehearsed several times on the way home. He was trying to be droll and sober. "We are very sorry and need your forgiveness for our actions of running away today, but really, it was something that could not wait."

Jacob looked at Clara, which was the wrong thing to do, as she started to smile but then burst into a hysterical, uncontrollable laughing and crying at the same time. She doubled over, verging on the wild side, as Jacob caught her, afraid she would fall face down on the floor.

Timothy and Tabitha stood in the center of the kitchen,

staring in disbelief at their actions. By sheer willpower, Clara got control of herself, but they all cast a wary, cautious eye toward her for the rest of the evening.

Timothy and Tabitha were totally perplexed because they thought there would be an explanation for this strange conduct. A seemingly calm, sedate, placid couple that had gone to bed the same time they did now appeared drastically different, even boisterous, in fact. However, no explanation was forthcoming, and Timothy and Tabitha were too polite to ask any questions.

Finally, things settled down in the Johnson's little kitchen. Clara donned her little apron and tied one on Tabitha. Clara explained, "There is not a housewife in Paw Paw that would dream of not wearing an apron when cooking a meal. It is an unwritten code for every household."

While Tabitha watched in wonder, Clara quickly put the chicken on to fry. When it was crispy brown, she laid it on a platter and made milk gravy from the drippings. She mashed the potatoes, then made hot biscuits. She put just a smidgen of water in a big pot and put in to wilt the wild greens she had gathered the day before. Tabitha by now was amazed at the mysterious dish that would soon be forthcoming.

Clara explained, "When we first came to Paw Paw, the ladies taught me the wonders of wild greens of the field, such a dish is essential to our diets they believe. Eleven varieties grow wild just about everywhere. I think the most wonderful is the Polk-Salet. Its tender stalks are like the asparagus we would buy from the store in the city. And watercress grows in abundance around my little spring."

They gathered around the table for this wonderful country fare.

"Oh, Clara," Jacob remarked, "Jimmy Simpson brought us a jar of honey. He found it in an oak tree. He said he got a tub full, so he's sharing it with everybody. Timothy, there is nothing any better than slapping some wild honey on a hot buttered biscuit."

Oh yes indeed, Jacob was at his best tonight, Clara thought with a smile.

The happy group talked about the people in Paw Paw. Their sweetness, their customs, their established ways of doing things, which were sometimes quite bizarre but always worked. The strong Christian influence that all believed in. And above all, Miss Idy. Clara laughed, "Miss Idy rules this town I want you to know, but you will come to love her."

Jacob butted in, "Now Clara, that only happens now and then." Then Clara and Jacob related all of her accomplishments.

Clara and Tabitha washed the dishes and tidied up the kitchen while the men conversed about the newspaper. Then they all sat around the table again. Suddenly Clara jumped up and said, "Oh, I have a wild gooseberry pie that I forgot about in this busy day." She cast a little wink at Jacob, which, thankfully, the others never noticed.

Clara poured them some hot sassafras tea and explained about the wonderful brew. "There are roots of this abundant bush that grow everywhere. The mothers declare every child needs to drink a lot of it in the springtime, as it thins the blood that has become sluggish from the winter. One can believe that or not, but it is delicious tea to go with a big piece of wild gooseberry pie."

The little kitchen leaped for joy at this little foursome's happiness. There came a lull in the conversation, and Jacob got slowly up, stood before them, and cautiously announced, "My children, if I might take the privilege of calling you that, I know we shall have your newspaper here in Paw Paw. I believe your dreams will come true here; I think it is in the will of God. Your coming to us has filled a need we so desperately searched for; I can truly say that this is the most wonderful day of my life. Today, Clara and I have begun to move away from our 'winter of sorrows.' The arrows of pain in our hearts will tug no more. Tabitha, you have led my dear Clara out of the shadows into the bright sunshine of your love. This love is liken to that between a mother and her daughter."

Jacob turned to the young woman with tears in his eyes, "I thank you, darling Tabitha."

Jacob continued his story. "I have had dreams and hopes all my life. I guess they came from my mother and her passionate love for musical instruments and singing. It was her goal and ambition that I would excel in that realm. She didn't have to wait long. Before I got out of high school, I was seized by the wonder of music. I was apprehended by something that was larger and higher than I was. Then after my mother died, I met a very special man, Mr. Willy Cedar. I knew it was destined that I should go to work with him. For five years, he took me under his wings, taught, and tutored me in the world of music. He would say, 'A man must know when he builds something to leave a portion of himself in it, whatever it is.' Mr. Willy traveled all his life, searching and seeking out secrets from the world of music. Every day he retraced his journeys and he took me with him. Always at the end of a lesson, he would whisper in my ear, 'You are to take this to the children, as a little child shall lead them.'

"One day, as I sat riveted at his feet, drinking in the wealth of this man, he said something wonderful to me. He said, 'When a man is captivated—made a prisoner shall we say—by your music, it is liken to the kingdom of heaven. It is like a treasure hidden in a field which when a man finds it, he hides it again and for the joy of it goes and sells everything he has to purchase that field. It is like a merchant man, seeking expensive pearls, who, when he finds one of great price, goes out and sells all that he has to buy it.' Oh yes, he taught me how to live under God's principles in the earthly kingdom we inhabit.

"I want to insert here about Mr. Debacle, Mr. Willy's dog. At the very start, he included me as his master also. He would always sense when any funny or important thing happened. He would run in circles, trying to catch his tail."

Jacob's little audience laughed at this description of Mr. Debacle.

"I think there is a portion of God's Spirit in each human's heart, and this is not quieted or stilled except by music and singing. Music has always been one way that God speaks to His people. King David, the sweet singer of Israel, was brought before King Saul to play his harp and sing and to drive the evil spirits from his so he could rest. The right kind of music can make a man see with his ears. It can be the speech of angels in the universal language of all men. Tonight, my aspirations, my hopes and dreams are ready to be fulfilled. No more rose-colored promises, no more illusions, no more starry-eyed castle-building in the sand."

Jacob's little group sat spellbound at the gracious words that fell from his mouth. Clara sat transfixed, her face pale by this emotional eloquent outburst from her husband's heart. They all felt a smoldering fire that far too long had lain quenched in his soul and was now being released.

But what did he mean? Timothy and Tabitha looked at Clara inquiringly, but she looked bewildered too. It was plain she knew nothing of what Jacob was saying.

"Come with me," he said. Silently, as if treading on holy ground, they followed Jacob out the back door as he led them to the big building behind the store. They were doubly amazed when he grabbed a shovel nearby and started to dig in the ground in several places. He was rewarded in his search, and he turned to his guests with a big smile as he lifted a rusting key from the soil.

He unlocked the door, stepped inside, and lit two large lamps. He raised the blinds from the windows. Jacob sounded apologetic as he said, "My friends, my lovely wife," he smiled at Clara, "I have but one chair, so you will need to sit on my couch."

The atmosphere of the big room was charged with a feeling of the supernatural as they all sat down. In wonderment and uncertainty, they stared at the white coverings that hid a man's heart and soul.

Like winding cloths for the dead, Jacob pulled the sheets off, one by one, folded them reverently, and revealed his treasure-trove. He turned to Clara and gave a little bow. "My darling wife, where a man's treasure is, you can find his heart also. Because of this day, that has been like no other day in my life, you will be my treasure and I will hold you in my heart forevermore."

There on a raised pedestal, as if they needed to be a little higher than the common things around them, sat two pianos and two organs. Clara, Timothy, and Tabitha gasped for breath at their beauty. From their brilliance, rays of lights caused a prismatic glow to wave from Jacob's works of art. Works fashioned after Jacob's and Mr. Willy's God.

Without a word of explanation, Jacob sat down on the bench at the nearest piano. He began to play the arpeggio. At first, in nearly mute, muffled tones, he rippled the keys. Then he rested. A louder ripple and rested again. Then the rippled soared, escalated upward becoming a storm, a thunder roar, a lightning flash. Then a rain of biblical proportions beat against the door.

The three spectators didn't know that they sat in a rough building erected hastily by some lowly carpenter who had once lived in Paw Paw. It became a concert hall, an opera house, and a cathedral for beholding only the genius, the most gifted of the world. The watchers, in their fancy, saw Jacob on center stage, illuminated by a spotlight that radiated from him. Jacob seemed removed from them. He was lost in God's Spirit. He was hiding his talent on some distant isle, secluded from prying eyes that would, by force if need be, place him among the elite, the renowned.

They saw and heard the majestic eagle soar from its abode on the towering mountain of stone bearing a healing on its giant wings, touching heaven itself.

Then Jacob played a funeral dirge of the lamenting voice of the pale horse of death and its rider racing toward an abyss of shame. Then they heard David singing the Twenty-third Psalm,

"Tho I walk through the valley of the shadow of death, I will fear no harm for Thou art with me, Thy rod and Thy staff they comfort me."

Jacob played a piece that sounded like the comical parts of a clown in a circus, the trumpeting of an elephant, the roar of the shaggy king lion. They saw the trapeze high above them; they looked like tiny children. They saw twelve ballet dancers dancing on tiptoes to the "Waltz of the Sugarplum Fairies."

When Jacob played and sang of King David's psalms of his omnipotent God, the earth shook on its foundations and the hills moved. He bowed the heavens to come down, as he rode upon a cherub and did fly. He flew upon the wings of the wind. Then came the velvety tones of God's amazing grace to all His creations that would dwell with Him forever. Jacob took them on a journey, surging to the ultimate, the crowning crest, then immediately plunging downward. He put them on a seesaw, then a carousel, and a merry-go-round with children screaming in delight.

As Jacob played, he often would sing in a melodious voice. He would begin in a whisper, liken to the rustle of a lady's taffeta ball gown. He held them in suspense, in postponement of what was coming next. Then the thunderous crash of cymbals hurling against ancient cliffs took their breath away.

Clara trembled, a throbbing sensation came from her heart, and icy fingers grasped her throat. Why, she didn't know this man that she had lived with for years, this man she had married just today at all! She had never heard him sing. Maybe he didn't have anything to sing about, living with her. In desperation, she looked at Timothy and Tabitha, but their eyes were intently gazing at Jacob.

Then Jacob in a soft and tender voice began singing a baby's lullaby. Clara knew he was remembering their tiny wee Tabitha, whose death had given them eternal night. Jacob and Clara's tears were falling unhindered but for different reasons. Clara's weeping, as an arrow piercing her wounded heart, was for her and Jacob. For what they had missed, for what they had lost through the years, for the ecstasy, the happiness, the love and, yes, the glory of love that had once belonged to them. She was the one who had violated the law of man and the law of God. This forlorn, desolate shame was hers alone. Clara sat still, her face pale, while even with her eyes closed, tears overflowed and dropped one by one from her lovely face.

Then came a silence. Jacob had ceased to play and sing.

The room was still and hushed. Clara opened her eyes. Jacob was sitting with his hands hanging by his side.

"What is the matter, Jacob?"

"Clara, there is nothing wrong. I am just savoring, drinking in the sweetness of our new life together, my darling." Timothy and Tabitha never heard them speaking. This conversation consisted of a harmony between three hearts that belonged only to Jacob and Clara and their God.

Then from the stillness, without any warning, Jacob took them to a place of worship, a wedding chapel as, like a crash of cymbals, he began playing the "Wedding March." They saw her—a virgin in a white billowing gown, her train of silken ruffles flowing behind her, her face veiled by a silken net. The aisle was covered with pink and white rose petals. She met her groom at a golden altar of love. "Do you take this man? Do you take this woman?"

"Oh yes, yes, my Lord." These holy words had wafted from Eden's Garden.

Jacob slowly got up from the piano bench, walked over and took Clara in his arms and crushed her body into his and kissed her wanting lips. He took the key to his shop and placed it in her hand. Clara's eyes were riveted on the key; it had turned to gold.

My beloved is gone down into his garden,
to the beds of spices, to feed in the gardens,
and to gather lilies.

Song of Solomon 6:2

Chapter 17

A Poem From God Without Words

Every spring a phenomenon occurred in Paw Paw. It had been happening for years untold. What made this even more startling was the fact that it seemed to happen almost overnight.

Straight across from the General Store and Big Morgan Creek were ten acres of fertile soil that lay in a slight slope. This was in view of all the locals, especially the men who sat on the porch, and all those that traveled this road. Every spring this whole acreage was a broad-sweep miracle of colors from its wildflowers. If heavy dew had fallen in the night, then in the early morning God would turn on His glorious sun lamp in heaven and embroider His shower of gold on every flower, leaf, and petal.

Sprays of daisies, columbine, sweet william, golden rod, lady's slipper, and jack-in-the-pulpit grew in profusion. Wild purple violets covered the ground, working and toiling in vain as they tried to reach up to their taller, hoity-toity, colorful neighbors that swayed and danced in the breeze. Blazing orange wild poppies dotted the field like falling confetti, and there were grasses like miller's dream. At the water's edge were profusions of velvety spikes of cattails and pussy willows lying in wait for a tiny gray mouse to come softly tiptoeing by. Every once in a while they were so happy they would shake and dance and scatter their little tufts of cotton that would say

"Hello" to everyone in Paw Paw.

For sure, there were a few people that would start sneezing, weeping, and blowing their noses about this time of year. But they cheerfully put up with it for their fellow man. Granny Myrtle said there wasn't any reason for anyone to brag and tell of the self-sacrifice they endured because of the wildflowers, because there were other weeds and grasses that grew elsewhere in town that caused the same problems.

The men on the porch like nothing better than a mystery. When they would get every day's current events solved to their satisfaction, they would return to the baffling and perplexing question of the immense field of wildflowers. This huge, flowering, ten-acre meadow had been deeded to the town of Paw Paw. But by whom? It was put in the care of the ruling dignitaries, those honorable men with high principles whose conduct was above repute.

The answer to this mystery could have been found in the deed itself, but a fire in Whippoorwill burned the county courthouse down and all the recordings of any transaction were destroyed. So this information was handed down by word of mouth, which was good enough for the ruling body of the men on the porch.

One day the men were gathered early on the porch and barely had time to settle into their best positions for comfort when a car drove slowly up to the store and stopped. A young man bounced out.

"Good morning, gentlemen," he said as he jumped up the steps and shook hands with the men. After some small banter, he announced, "I am Luther Carnahan. I am the photographer for a large magazine in St. Louis. Naturally, I always have my eyes open for any spectacular views or scenes or anything I find of interest in this neck of the woods." Luther smiled broadly, "I went hog-wild over that meadow across the way. In all my journeys, I have never seen anything more beautiful."

Young Luther quit talking for a minute and gazed almost

reverently at this display of God's handiwork. Suddenly, with much ado, he waved his hands in a sweeping motion and said, "Come one, come all, rich man or poor man, and drink in this glorious pageantry from our Creator." Then he sat down with the men and talked and visited with them the better part of the day. Every once in a while, Luther got up and took picture after picture of the meadow. Some up close of a single flower, others with the rail fence in view, and several of the men on the porch. He was excited and delighted with the men's dogs as they lay beside their masters, looking up at them with worshiping eyes.

When it was time for Luther to leave, all the men on the porch followed him to his car. Young Luther and the men were reluctant to say good-bye, as it had been an unforgettable day for them all as they conversed heart to heart, friend to friend. He complimented them on their simple way of life and the lovely surroundings that they were blessed to live in. He said, "This day I have felt closer to God than at anytime in all my life." As he started his car, he said softly, "I am going to call my picture, which I am sure will appear on the front page, 'A Poem From God Without Words.'"

The men on the porch all were trying to keep any tears from being observed. One of them said, "We must be careful when we entertain strangers, for they might be angels unaware." They had no way of knowing what sweetness would emerge from God's Poem.

A few months went by and a bundle of magazines came from St. Louis. On the front of the magazine blazed forth the flowering meadow with the rail fence and Big Morgan Creek. Across the top of the picture were Luther's words "A Poem From God Without Words." The back cover showed the scene of the men sitting on the porch with their dogs beside them. Both of those pictures were framed and hung on the wall of the General Store.

One day, Old Grady Brooker's son, Phillip, brought him to the General Store to get a few commodities and "do a bit of bartering," as he was prone to say. His son dropped him off and left; he knew the men on the porch would help him up the steps. They were all joking and there was much clowning banter as they got him safely into a chair. One man laughed and patted him on the back. "Grady, how old are you now? You been claiming you were a hundred years old, is that so?"

"My yes and more than that!" The old man said proudly. "I don't rightly know much more because the family Bible got burned up with our house. Oh, you young whippersnappers have got everything easy now compared to my younger days."

As usual, the men on the porch sat and listened to the same stories over and over of what he had to endure while growing up, and they all smiled knowing they made Old Grady a happy man by just listening. When he finally ran out of breath, he noticed the big wildflower field across the creek.

"My, my, what a sight to behold. Here I am over one hundred years old, and this is still the purdiest picture in the world, I do say!"

Suddenly one of the men spoke up, "Now Grady, if there is anyone can solve this mystery for us, it would be you. Can you tell us who planted these flowers and who deeded this field to the town?"

"Well, my good friends, you have come to the right source for this information. I can settle your qualms and misgivings right sudden like. Now mind you that I wasn't there when this happened but I got the answer from a very reliable source, my mother-in-law. It came about on thisawise.

"A man moved here from somewhere in Europe and homesteaded all the property hereabouts. He was impressed with this hillside, as it didn't need too much clearing. Well, as the story goes, weeds and grasses came up in the spring, so he burned the whole field and plowed it up. Then he let it lay through the summer. In the fall, he burned it again and plowed it up again. By this time, all the seeds from the weeds and grasses had left his field clear of any residue.

"Then, lo and behold, one day came these large bags of flower seeds from Europe. That man sowed all those seeds that very day. He didn't tell any of his neighboring homesteaders, but come spring, all of his flowers burst open in a field free of weeds. It must have been a sight to behold! Neighbors came to visit the old man just to see the flowers. They said it lifted their spirits so much that when they toiled hard in their own fields with their ordinary crops, their souls sang the praises of God."

Grady took time to rest in his storytelling and fell fast asleep. They shook him awake. "Grady, finish your story."

"Well sir, that fella was growing those flowers, harvesting them, and intending to send them to Europe to make perfume for the ladies. But I heard that he soon passed away while harvesting his petals."

Grady's son returned for his father, but the men on the porch had to tell him that Old Grady Brooker had entered into his own "field of dreams," into heaven itself.

None of the privileged people who had the opportunity to view this wonderful field knew that there would come a day when this sweet poem from God would rescue from hunger and perhaps death itself.

And further, by these, my son, be admonished:
of making many books there is no end;
and much study is a weariness of the flesh.

ECCLESIASTES 12:12

Chapter 18

"Read All About It! Read All About It!"

The old Hines building was a huge enormous eyesore that sat smack dab in the curve of the road near the General Store. It was covered from stem to stern with great squares of old rusty tin that hung loose in haphazard ways. It was in sight of anyone who stood on the porch. Since everyone in Paw Paw had to come to the store once a week or so to do their shopping, many would stop, stare, and complain about its ugliness.

When Timothy and Tabitha Rameth came to Paw Paw, they saw promise in the old building and were eager to buy it. They saw it housing the newspaper they wanted to begin and the library they wanted to establish. Everything seemed perfect except for one thing: no one knew who the owner was.

Miss Idy was not about to let such details get in the way of progress, so she went to the Whippoorwill County Courthouse and checked the tax rolls for the name. After much searching, she found that the acre of land the building sat on had not had its taxes paid in a long time. She couldn't determine who the original owner was, as the record of ownership had been obliterated in the fire long ago, so she and the assessor finally concluded that the back taxes amounted to one hundred dollars. She paid that out of her meager funds and became the new owner of the building. Then she had the assessor draw up a new deed naming Timothy and Tabitha as sole owners of the Hines building.

After this strange transaction, Miss Idy firmly told the man she did not want it noised about by anyone that she had done this. "The Bible says," she reminded him "'don't let your left hand know what your right hand does.'" With these words, Miss Idy clicked her heels, stepped outside, and looked for the mail car.

The mail-car driver frequently gave rides to the townspeople as it made his day less boring to have a little company. Miss Idy felt a warm inner glow in her spirit. She had taken a step of faith. She knew there would now be a newspaper and a library in Paw Paw.

It appeared that everyone in town had at least one finger in the renovating of the old Hines building. They turned the old eyesore into a strutting peacock, which housed the newspaper office, the library, and even a small apartment for Timothy and Tabitha to live. They did all this in a very short time.

Miss Idy had never seen such cooperation of the Paw Paw residents; even the men on the porch worked in a frenzy of excitement. One of the most unbelievable happenings was that Jacob became the boss of this project. It was as if he were a new man. They all watched in admiration as he became the "biggest toad in the pond." Jacob, Timothy, and Miss Idy had their heads together every step of the way.

Everyone coming and going at the General Store lingered and looked with proud eyes at the old Hines building. Across the front of the building were two signs: "Paw Paw Times" and "Paw Paw Library." There was a distance of about twenty feet between the front doors of these establishments. Over the door of the library, a small motto had been carefully and painstakingly painted. It read: "I saw above a sea of hills a solitary planet shine. There was no one near or far to keep the world from being mine." Everyone knew that Jimmy had made it.

The first paper from the Paw Paw Times finally rolled off the press early one Saturday afternoon.

The second page of the newspaper was devoted to getting books for the library. "BOOKS, BOOKS, BOOKS" in big letters was the title of the page.

"We must have books, hundreds of them, to fill the shelves of our new library. Whippoorwill has sent us ten boxes filled with books. Where they found duplicates, they shared them with us. We certainly thank them for this most generous gift.

"Every child and adult can learn all the basic knowledge we need from books; but there is joy, happiness, and glory in just reading. Many proverbs sing the praises of books.

"A garden carried in the pocket"—an Arabian proverb

"The world carried in the hand"—Anonymous

"If one is lonely, a book can be your best friend and companion"—Richard Whitlock

"Books are the compasses and telescopes and sextants and charts which other men have prepared to help us navigate the dangerous seas of human life"—Jess L. Benner

At the end of this page was a note from the editors.

Dear neighbors and friends,

When we came to Paw Paw, you poured out your love to us very generously. In just the few months since we arrived, you have helped us fulfill our dreams of starting a newspaper. To honor you we wanted to establish a library in this wonderful town, and you helped build that too. Thank you all very, very much. We feel blessed.

However, for the good of all, we must ask you for more help. If you have any books, even ones you think might look a little disreputable with wear, please donate them to our new library. We shall teach the children in the area how to help us restore any books in need of repair.

Sincerely,

Timothy and Tabitha Rameth

A man that flattereth his neighbor
spreadeth a net for his feet.

PROVERBS 29:5

Chapter 19

Jimmy's Foot in Big Business

It was Saturday morning and Jimmy Simpson stepped out onto the porch of his home. He surveyed the little town of Paw Paw. There was a bit of dampness in the air from an earlier light rain. However, come rain or shine, nothing could stop Jimmy C. from his appointed task of going to the General Store. Actually, that was true for most people who lived thereabouts. Nothing but the most violent of storms would keep them from going to the store to buy, sell, barter, or just talk.

Jimmy slipped out of the house before his mother could yell for him to check on the twins. He grabbed two biscuits and some bacon from the kitchen on his way out the door.

All the way to the store, the sign of money circled his brain as he tried to figure out how he could make a few more coins that day. As far back as he could remember, he had never failed to make his coffee can a little heavier on a Saturday.

As he walked into the General Store, he was amazed at the people lined up at the counter to pay for their purchases. Some of the customers were fussing and complaining about having to wait so long.

Suddenly, Mrs. Honey Baker, scurrying as usual, came into the store. "Jacob, I want to buy a new pair of dress shoes, and I am in a hurry," she said tartly.

Jacob responded, "Miss Honey, Clara is sick today, and I

have to handle the store by myself. So that bein' the case, you will have to wait your turn at the end of the line."

Immediately a light flickered on in Jimmy's head. "Mr. Johnson, I would be happy to help you today, without any charge of course."

"Well thank you, Jimmy. That's very kind of you, if you think you can do it." Jacob didn't want to face the wrath of Miss Honey, if she had to wait very long.

Jimmy turned to Miss Honey, then, with a slight bow as if in homage, took her arm and led her to the shoes. He sat down carefully. "Now my Miss Honeysuckle Baker, what can I show you today?"

Miss Honey was startled but burst out laughing. "Oh Jimmy, you are a card, for sure, but we all love you anyway."

Jimmy knelt in front of her and took off her shoes. He held her feet just a little longer than was necessary, which delighted her. "You see Jimmy, I have made myself two new dresses, and these old clod-hoppers I'm wearing don't go along with them."

"Right you are, Miss Honeysuckle." They both laughed hilariously again. Jimmy looked up just as staid and strict, old maid Ruby Carson gave them a disapproving look. Jimmy was glad Miss Honey had her back to her. Jimmy, still kneeling at her feet, asked, "What size do we want here?"

"I think I need a seven or seven-and-a-half, but it's been such a long time since I bought a dress shoe."

"Well, I do declare, I would have guessed about a size six; your feet have such a petite and small look about them."

Jimmy brought several pairs for her to look at, but they just didn't fit. Some were too large, some too small. He was almost discouraged when he spotted a shoebox on the highest shelf. Struggling, he finally got it down. There, in tissue paper, was the most beautiful pair of shoes he had ever seen. They were soft, white leather dress shoes trimmed in black patent. Almost reverently, he showed them to her, and without a word, he gently put them on her feet. They fit perfectly.

Jimmy stood up and surveyed them, turning his head at different angles. Then, with sparkling eyes, he said, "Mrs. Honey Baker, these are the shoes for you!"

Miss Honey was shaking with excitement. "But Jimmy do I dare wear a shoe like this? I love them, but what will the church ladies say?"

"Now Miss Honey, I want to talk to you as a grandson. It has been over two years since you lost your husband, your sweetheart, and it's time to get out and go places other than church. However, getting back to the shoes, even I have noticed that skirts are getting shorter every day and ladies' shoes will be getting dressier. And you know, you will be showing more of your lovely legs." Even though they both were blushing, Jimmy went on because he realized he was going to be the winner."And since I have been so bold, I will just go on. I've seen Bernie Little eyeing you at church, and he will love these shoes."

She was flustered, but radiant, as Jimmy put his arm around her and led her to the counter to pay for the shoes. "Jacob, if you and Clara were very smart, you would hire Jimmy here for your salesman," she said.

Jacob was a bit uneasy as he said, "Miss Honey, I will pay him today for his work," a commitment he knew he couldn't withdraw on account of the many people who were standing by listening.

She bid Jimmy good-bye, and he stood at the door and watched her as she fairly skipped down the road to her house.

Jimmy Simpson seemed stunned and beside himself as he began to realize his uncanny ability for selling.

After pocketing the generous amount of money Jacob paid him, he vaulted off the porch and headed toward home. He stopped suddenly, did a turn about-face, and started for the newspaper office to have his business cards printed up.

He knew how they would read: "Jimmy C. Simpson,

President of Simpson Enterprises."

On his way home he shuffled his cards, gloating and basking in their beauty, when he suddenly thought of his parents, why they would be upset about his new name and his business cards. Why, they should be proud of him. Nevertheless, he wanted to play it safe.

The first thing he did in preparation for an encounter he might not win was to use his face in certain ways. He had the ability to display disgust, displeasure, and pain on a moment's notice. He called this his "window dressing."

He always chose suppertime to introduce his clever, cunning schemes. It was an outrageous idea—and it generally was—that instantly put the whole family on the alert.

That night, he walked in the kitchen door with his head bowed to one side in what he called his "dejected hangdog" look. His countenance displayed a suffering martyr wearing a crown of thorns. After seeing all of this, his father became a little testy. "Okay Jimmy, what's this all about? Let's hear what you want, so we can all eat our supper."

"Well, Dad and Mother, I have decided to change my name."

Otis and Maudie were startled and they looked at one another.

"Well, I really just want to add a middle name, and since you didn't think I was important enough to give me one, I gave one to myself. I have chosen the name Chores on account of I'm always called Jimmy-get-your-chores-done. My new name is Jimmy Chores Simpson, but you can call me Jimmy C., if you like," he proudly told them.

"Why Jimmy, you can't do that," his father exclaimed.

"Why can't I Dad?" Is there any law against it?"

Cranky and irritable now, his father added, "Jimmy, this is a little nutty, even for you. Why can't you go through life with just one name? Even if one has a middle name, it's hardly ever used in conversation."

Jimmy replied, "I checked with Timothy and Tabitha at the Paw Paw Times, and they thought it would be a good idea, that it might appear more important and businesslike."

Once again, Maudie and Otis looked at one another, then at their son, and shook their heads in disbelief.

Jimmy, still wearing his woebegone expression, cautiously announced, "Mother, Dad, I might as well tell you. I have had my business cards printed up already." He handed each of them a card. It read: "Jimmy C. Simpson, President of Simpson Enterprises."

Maudie, looking at her son, said, "What is Jimmy Chores planning to do with his lofty, high-falutin' plans here in Paw Paw?" As she spoke these words, she was sorry because she saw how they hurt him. She had pondered and tried to evaluate the wonderful son of hers many times. She knew he was far beyond what is normal for a lad of his age. She also felt there were going to be other "ponders" awaiting her not too many years hence.

But without faith it is impossible to please him:
for he that cometh to God must believe that he is,
and that he is a rewarder of them that diligently seek him.

HEBREWS 11:6

Chapter 20

Reverend Peabody's Walk of Faith

Miss Idy was the one who had started this unlikely romance between Reverend Peabody and Miss Lizzy Davis. It all began after one Sunday morning church service. A pouring-down rain had started, and Miss Idy asked the Reverend to take Miss Lizzy home as she had walked to church. Reverend Peabody grudgingly consented. It was a long way from where he lived, but there wasn't any way to refuse.

This purely innocent gesture got out of hand when he drove his buggy up to the door of the church so that Miss Lizzy wouldn't get too wet. She lost her footing when she stepped up into the buggy, and down she fell in the mud and mire. Of course, Reverend Peabody ran around to aid her, being the gentleman that he was. Poor Miss Lizzy. In the fall her dress had, in some unexplainable way, wound up at her waist, and there in plain sight were her ruffled bloomers. (Later on, the ladies standing in the church door would wonder about the ruffles being on such a destitute and poor young lady). Trying to get Miss Lizzy up, Albert's foot slid out from under him and he fell down beside her. Muttering words that shouldn't be said by a man of the cloth, he got up and got them both into the buggy. Poor Agatha felt the lash of the leather as they hurried to Lizzy's house.

During the entire trip to her home, not a word was spoken between Miss Lizzy and the Reverend. When they arrived, however, Albert, once again being a gentleman, tipped his hat to her and said, "I truly am sorry for everything that's happened. Maybe the next time we meet things will be different."

It took him all afternoon to clean and scrub the mud from his only suit. He went to church; he was glad that Lizzy wasn't there. He cut his sermon short and rushed home exhausted from the ordeal in the mud. He awoke in the middle of the night and sat up straight in the bed. He had been dreaming of a pair of ruffled bloomers. He had a big smile on his face as he thought aloud, "Just wait until tomorrow. This will be a good reason for sparks to fly in Paw Paw." Saying these words, he lay down on his side, smiled smugly, and slept the sleep of the righteous.

Lizzy had her own reaction to the events. Her family laughed at her when they found out why she was so muddy. She saw nothing funny in it at all. But as she started washing her bloomers, she began to chuckle. "What a first impression to leave on the most eligible bachelor in town. I'll probably remain a spinster all my life now, unless the Reverend liked my bloomers." She laughed at the possibility then stopped. "I wonder if that would be so far-fetched. I sure can say that I made an impression on him." She was smiling at her fantasy as she hung her bloomers on the line.

Early the next morning, Reverend Peabody leaped out of bed and flexed his muscles, such as they were, and rushed out to the kitchen to fix his breakfast. He always read a scripture from the Bible every morning; he randomly opened it and there it was!

"Behold I will lay thy stones with beautiful colours, and lay thy foundation with dark blues and purple sapphires. And I will make thy windows of rubies and thy gates of carbuncles shining like a burning stone of garnets, pearl, sparkling gems," Isaiah, Chapter 54.

The Reverend Albert Peabody knew this was ordained from heaven now to fix his old house up for his ladylove Lizzy Davis at this time. If someone would pass by, they would be startled to see a preacher dance a little two-step going out his door.

Oh yes, Reverend Peabody was in love, and he could see clearly his new home with Lizzy and a house full of children. It never occurred to him that they would not be wed. One of the gifts of the Spirit is faith. He was safe in that realm, so he knew Miss Lizzy would marry him.

He quickly ate a little breakfast, then rushed to the barn and harnessed up Agatha. He hitched her to the hack and laid the lash to her. He thought of stopping at the General Store but changed his mind and headed straight for Whippoorwill and Summer's lumberyard.

He bought all of their finished wood and almost all of their glass windows. Startled indeed was Lyle Summers. "What are you going to build, Reverend Peabody?"

"Well, Lyle, I will tell you. I am going to get married, so I need to fix up the place." He had a big smile on his face and a twinkle in his eye.

He looked through Lyle's catalog from Kansas City and ordered a big front door with oval stained glass. Lyle was shaking with excitement at this order, as that made his coffers to shine.

"Well, Lyle, I'm going all out for sure. It seems I've lost my mind, but all I can blame it on is love." Albert opened up the furniture catalog and ordered new furniture for the whole house except for the upstairs bedrooms. "These will be our children's rooms, and I'll let my Lizzy choose them."

Before leaving Whippoorwill he hired three skilled workmen to start renovating his house and even extend some of the rooms.

Many people called Aaron and Betsy Davis, Lizzy's parents, the "poor of the poor." They lived on the outskirts of town and had a passel of kids. They had them so fast and furious that the neighbors couldn't remember their names. Miss Lizzy was their eldest, at twenty-two years.

She had dark blue eyes and an abundance of dark brown

hair, which she always braided and wore in a coil on top of her head. However, by the end of the day, several curls would escape their bondage and frame her pixy, impish face. She had a pert little nose and a Cupid's bow mouth. The men on the porch declared up and down, back and forth that she was always laughing, even when there was nothing to laugh about. Jeremiah said one day, "Miss Lizzy just blooms out like a fresh pink rose."

The Reverend knew the good Lord was smiling down on him. So bursting with confidence, he headed for the Davis house. When he drove into the yard, little faces peered out of every window and door. He was quite taken aback by the number of children but smiled to himself that this was a positive sign of what the future would hold for them.

As he knocked on the door, little questioning eyes surrounded him. When Lizzy appeared at the door, her eyes were questioning too. He had been very brave until now. He opened his mouth to repeat his well-practiced speech, but found to his horror that he had forgotten it. Now, only a strange guttural sound emerged from his throat. Lizzy smiled at him and said, "Good evening, Reverend Peabody, won't you come in?"

Finally, Albert blurted out, "My dear, Miss Lizzy, will you marry me?"

Then his nerves got the best of him, so without waiting for an answer, he turned around and bolted for his buggy.

Laughing hilariously at his predicament, Lizzy called out, "Yes, my dear Albert, I thought you would never ask. Yes. Yes, I will."

The men put down new floors of hardwood. They took out small windows and put big ones in their place. Albert even had them put in a big window in the kitchen so Lizzy could see outside as she washed the dishes or see him coming from work.

They added a porch on two sides of the house—one for a swing they could sit on in the evening, the other for a screened summer kitchen, complete with cookstove. It was for the hot days. Lizzy would be able to cook, and they both could eat in the cool breeze. Albert also put a pump in the kitchen to bring water from the big spring down the hill.

Soon all of Paw Paw had a reason to go out of their way to see what Albert was doing to his house. When they saw it, they were astonished. They stared in wonder at the big, ornate, stained-glass front door, the big brass knocker beside it; at the big fireplace in the living room, which was covered anew with white marble and golden accessories; and at the fireplaces in the bedroom and the kitchen, built for Lizzy's pleasure. The people of the town thought wonders would never cease, and they hashed and rehashed Albert Peabody's generosity to his beloved Lizzy.

During these weeks of building, the only time Albert got to see Lizzy was at church on Sunday and at the Wednesday evening prayer meeting. She refused to go see her new house. "Albert, I don't want to see it until we are married, if you don't mind."

"Of course, my darling, it is all right with me. I'm glad you don't want to see it until it's finished."

Deck thyself now with majesty and excellency;
and array thyself with glory and beauty.

Job 40:10

Chapter 21

Bloomers Trimmed in Red Lace

Sunday night, Albert headed out to pick up his ladylove for the evening service. He gave Agatha a little flick with his whip, and she trotted off. In fact, the old horse sensed something delightful in this journey, so she ran at a fast clip without being urged again.

Miss Lizzy was in the doorway, waiting for her lover. She didn't give him a chance to stop and help her into the hack, as she literally danced down the path, face aglow, and jumped in beside him.

Albert's heart smiled at the sight of her. He expected a little peck of a kiss on his cheek, but no! This time she pressed her lovely lips to his with determined firmness. His heart began to race haphazardly. Did she realize this kiss was different? Probably not, she was so innocent and shy. However, this kiss left him in such a state he dared not look at her. He must be careful not to show all of his emotions at once, as that might frighten her. He vaguely remembered that one young woman who ran back to her parents after being terrified by a too-eager husband. She never did go back to him.

Albert decided that he could wait, so he concentrated on old Agatha's speed. They were halfway to church when Lizzy put her arms around him and gave him another firm kiss, then another, and finally, one so fervent and passionate it was almost his undoing.

This was disturbing to the Reverend and interrupted his thoughts on a very important matter—their marriage.

"My love, this is a serious moment in our lives, and we mustn't take it lightly. I have done a lot of soul searching for quite some time. I thought at times that my love for you was a sin. I was, and am, overwhelmed by a smothering sweet pressure whenever I see you. I have wept at times because of this surging, overpowering love with all its fervor and hunger; and I have prayed to our heavenly Father about it.

"You know, my darling, I didn't know our kind of love existed. But God intended for man to experience this, or He wouldn't have given to our hearts this immortal thirst for one another. I know now, dear one, that it is a marriage made in heaven when another person's needs are as important as your own."

"Oh my dear Albert, don't depend on my prayers to help you. I was enjoying it as much as you, maybe more," she said as she fell into his arms again. "But just to be sure, I think we should get married lickety-split" she teased.

"Albert, I wish you could see your face!"

It was a good thing that Lizzy didn't know what Albert was thinking. Talking to himself he wondered if she really was a virgin. Then he quickly added, "Oh dear God, perish this thought from me."

The rest of the way to church Albert was silent but not Lizzy. She kept teasing him, kissing his neck, and singing little worldly love songs in his ear.

Who was this little girl he had fallen in love with?

Understandably, Reverend Peabody was not in any shape to preach the evening sermon. He told Miss Idy that he didn't feel well and asked her to read some scripture, comment on it, and lead in a few songs. He asked her to be sure to give an altar call; one never knew when someone in the congregation might need to do some serious praying.

The men on the porch referred to Reverend Peabody and

Miss Lizzy's romance as "toadying up." Some called it "spooning;" the elite of Paw Paw called it courting.

The men on the porch were evaluating the pros and cons of the sudden engagement of Reverend Peabody and Miss Lizzy. Jeremiah asserted with a low judicial sound in his voice, "I am a mite doubtful of the May/December marriage. Biblically, I don't think there is nothing wrong in it. At least, when I searched the Bible, I didn't find anything there. I figured the Reverend might have some qualms or second thoughts, but so far I haven't seen a man so happy. He just grins from ear to ear."

"Now Jeremiah," Fred Pinkham said defensively, "in the Old Testament some of those kings had a wife and still had those concubines to choose from. Some of them would have to have been young. You could bet your boots on that!"

"Fred, I agree. We have no answer to this alarming situation. All we ask is proper principles regarding right and wrong in our standard of living in Paw Paw."

"We also agree that everyone loves our delightful Miss Lizzy. But I have noticed she has gotten a little cheeky lately. And she don't walk in an everyday manner. No, she bounces along. Even her laugh is a trifle noisy, and she lets it burst forth for no reason at all. And boys, my little wife went to prayer meeting last Wednesday night, and she caught a glimpse of our Reverend making cow-eyes at Miss Lizzy while they were praying."

Jeremiah again took on his face an "afflicted with sorrow" countenance and asked himself why there was such a big rush to the wedding altar.

It was best for man and beast that they didn't know what Miss Lizzy was doing in Whippoorwill this day. It was happening on this wise.

Lizzy, with her mother's help, scraped up a little money, went to Whippoorwill, and bought some white organdy and lace for her wedding dress. She also bought some white slippers. To her surprise, she had enough money left over to buy some lace and ribbons for two pair of bloomers.

She was looking at the white lace when an impish smile danced across her face. Then she asked the clerk to measure out two yards of gaudy red lace. She leaned over and whispered in his ear, "This is for my new bloomers for my wedding night." The clerk gasped at this disclosure. Paw Paw residents were not prepared for this new wife of the beloved minister.

Miss Lizzy didn't know that Reverend Peabody was in Whippoorwill at the same time she was. He had a close friend named Hubert Clay who had been a judge until he took to preaching. Hubert soon found out that there wasn't much money in preaching. One farmer gave him two live chickens; another gave him a gunnysack of new potatoes and some onions. Several of the little old ladies baked for him. He got apple and cherry pies, and one baked him a wild gooseberry pie. It was such a teat that if he had kept on preaching, that wild gooseberry pie would have been the reason. Instead, he returned to judging.

Reverend Peabody had a hard time locating him. Business was bad and Hubert had to go near and far to find someone who was willing to sue one of their neighbors. The way Albert figured, he and Lizzy would be married by a preacher and a judge. He smiled at his cunning and shrewd decision of choosing both a sinner and a saint.

Rejoice, O young man, in thy youth;
and let thy heart cheer thee in the days of thy youth,
and walk in the ways of thine heart,
and in the sight of thine eyes: but know thou,
that for all these things
God will bring thee into judgment.

ECCLESIASTES 11:9

Chapter 22

The Shivaree and the Hack

It was the custom of the area for the young people to shivaree newlyweds. The would invade the couple's home on their first night together and make a big ruckus by ringing cow bells, banging on pans and buckets, whistling, yelling, and even shooting guns into the air. Sometimes this would go on half the night.

If by chance the couple didn't welcome them into the house with candy and treats, they would take the new husband and throw him into the creek. Then he'd have to walk home soaking wet.

On the ride home from their wedding, Lizzy said, "Albert dear, this news will spread like wildfire. We must stop and buy some candy because the young people will expect it. If we don't, we might suffer the consequences."

Albert defensively spoke, "Lizzy, no one knows that we are married. I am also against these worldly escapades of our youth. You know I have a prominent and esteemed spiritual position to uphold in the Baptist Church and that doesn't include being subjected to a shivaree!"

"I promise you, my darling, I will not be taken from you tonight on our first night together. Oh, just the thought makes me shiver." Albert looked up into heaven as he spoke.

The new Mrs. Peabody wondered if these would be the

famous last words of Reverend Peabody.

It was late afternoon when the Reverend and his new wife, Lizzy, arrived at their new home. Lizzy gave a gasp. "Albert, is this the house we are going to live in? I have never seen a house like this. It's fabulous!"

"Oh yes, my darling, this is your house now," he proudly told her.

The house was painted glistening white. It had four pillars on the front porch that reached up to an upstairs bedroom balcony with lavish ornamental trim.

Albert lifted Lizzy down from the hack, and they walked arm in arm up to the porch. On each side of the stained glass door were two large china pots filled with blooming wildflowers. Albert had hung a note from the front door's brass knocker. He laid it in her hand.

She began reading it aloud. "Enter this door as if the floors within were gold and every wall jewels, all wealth untold."

It was signed, "Your devoted husband."

In awe and wonderment, Albert picked up his wife and carried her across the welcoming threshold.

Before going to bed, Albert checked the locks on the doors and windows. Chuckling to himself he said, "Just let them try to get in." Then rubbing his hands together and stepping a little higher than usual, he did a little two-step as he entered the master bedroom.

There Lizzy stood in her new bloomers with the red lace ruffles. Albert, shivering with anticipation, took her in his arms. She had just yielded to his embrace when the pandemonium broke loose.

The shivareers were hooting and hollering, banging on pots and pans, and some were firing shots into the air. They created bedlam as they marched around the house, pounded on the doors and windows, and rang the doorbell incessantly.

Lizzy began to shake and was on the verge of tears. "Albert,

I told you that this would happen, but, oh no, you wouldn't listen to me." These I-told-you-so words have echoed from every wife from the beginning of time itself. She grabbed a pillow and quilt and went to the front room. There she slammed them on the couch and stretched her little body out as far as she could, covered up her head, and feigned falling right off to sleep.

Sad and forlorn, Albert stood abandoned in the middle of the room, looking at his wife. Suddenly, without any warning, he saw the quilt begin to move and heard hysterical laughter. Then Lizzy tossed back the quilt and ran back to their bed. There on the floor beside their bed were her white bloomers trimmed in garish red lace.

A thought came to Reverend Peabody. "How am I going to cope with and handle this fiery little lady who is now my wife?"

Outside the Peabody home, evil forces were at work at giving birth to a diabolical maneuver. Jimmy C. and a few of his friends sneaked in the big hay and tobacco barn, found some ropes, then quietly pulled Albert's black hack out of the shed.

Some of the boys tied ropes securely around it, while the others climbed up to the barn's peak. Then they gradually pulled the buggy to the top and left it astraddle the barn roof. Silently, they hung the ropes. The boys had planned to hide and watch what the Reverend would do, but they all got sleepy and went home.

Much later, Lizzy told this story.

"I thought for sure Albert would die when he saw his hack up on the barn roof. I ran to hold him up because his face went beet red, then purple, then back and forth between the two colors. He began gasping for breath. I pounded on his back, as he couldn't speak. When he caught his breath, he headed to the General Store, screaming bloody murder."

The men saw him coming and knew something terrible had happened. He screamed, "I am going to the top with this.

I'm going to hire me a detective from Whippoorwill to find the rapscallions, the scoundrels, who done this. But right now I want you to get the word out that I will pay ten dollars reward to whoever brings them to justice."

As the news spread, crowds of people came to the Peabody Ranch. Of course, all the men from the porch of the General Store were there. They gawked and stared at the sight of the hack straddling the roof of the barn. The notables and gentry of Paw Paw scratched their heads and looked on in amazement.

Otis, Jimmy's dad, heard one of the learned men say that whoever accomplished this feat could be qualified as an engineer. He had to restrain and control himself from saying "That's my son!"

Jimmy Simpson and the boys who had done the deed stood quietly back; they didn't dare to give their advice.

Otis took charge of handling the results of this shenanigan. He knew Jimmy was the "bell-ringer" in this prank, and he didn't want him to face the wrath and rage of Reverend Peabody if there was a way to avoid it.

"Reverend Peabody, would you be willing to pay that ten dollar reward to the person who gets your hack down? Even if we do find out who pulled this stunt, and I really don't see too much headway of catching them, you would need a trial. And that would mean court costs. To my way of thinking, it could be an embarrassment to you, and it might not be forgotten by our townspeople for a long time. We must end this now if we can."

Albert was still angrily staring at his hack. "All right, if you think I should, Brother Otis. But someday I will find out who accomplished this devious deed."

Otis asked loudly, "Who will help us figure out a way to undo this evil yet stupendous feat?"

There was a dead silence. No one volunteered.

"I will add here that you will not be confessing guilt by

coming forward but will be patted on the back if you can get it down none the worse for wear. And there is the splendid amount of ten dollars, which is not to be sniffed at.

Cautiously, Jimmy and three other young men went into the barn and got some ropes down. Then they climbed up on the roof and secured the hack. Then to the amazement of all, they gently lowered it to the ground.

There was a happy shout for their cleverness and ingenuity. Everyone knew that Jimmy C. was the ringleader and that, as usual, his cunning brought him gains in the end. Reverend Peabody very reluctantly put the ten dollars into his hand. Jimmy was startled as he thought he heard the Reverend say a word that verged on sacrilege. Oh no, he thought to himself, I must have just imagined it.

Jimmy was proud and happy. And he really liked the idea that his dad had figured it all out. Jimmy thought that if his dad kept at it, he would soon know as much as his son. Then he threw his arm over his dad's shoulder, and they hurried home to their dinner.

Let him kiss me with the kisses of his mouth:
for thy love is better than wine.

Song of Solomon 1:2

Chapter 23

The Constant Love Affair

It was a beautiful day. The tranquility reigned over the Peabody Ranch. Lizzy had cooked ham, hot biscuits, and flour gravy; and Albert had eaten too much, again. She was a wonderful cook and could make even simple food taste like an elegant repast.

"Lizzy, would you like to go out this morning and see what will be yours, if anything should ever happen to me?"

Startled, Lizzy took off her apron and, smiling brightly, grabbed Albert's hand.

Pleased, he took it and shyly realized how much pleasure he enjoyed from this new experience of her holding his hand. They spent the next two hours just looking at the vast acreage.

"Albert, let's run back to the house," she challenged him.

Laughing like a child, he ran after her. She waved her hand for him to hurry and catch her. He knew she had deliberately slowed down for him. When he caught her, they locked in each other's arms and fell down in the tall grass.

Later, they leisurely walked back to the house hand in hand. They started to enter by the front door when Lizzy stopped and looked around. "Albert, I am curious, why did you plant this area beside the porch in a circle?"

Albert looked very sheepish and embarrassed. "Lizzy, I know and you know that I am years older than you. Thank you, my dear, for not talking about it, but according to nature and God Himself, I will die much sooner than you. This is where I want to be buried, beside the roses and plants." Then softly, almost in a whisper, he added, "Darling, I want to hear the footsteps of our children running and playing over me."

Arm in arm, they went into their house. They knew this was a holy moment that needed no words.

At times, Albert would help Lizzy with her various household duties, so she could go out with him while he cared for the livestock and the other endless chores of a big ranch. On those days, she would pack them a picnic lunch to eat under a big tree. Even that would be her undoing. "Now, Reverend Albert, I can plainly see I'm not safe from you anywhere. And you a preacher too! You must have limits on your lovemaking," she teased.

Their lunch always came in second.

One morning, as she was going out to help him cut the weeds in the cornfield, she combed her hair and put it in a bun on top of her head. She put on one of his old straw hats, a pair of his bib overalls, and one of his shirts. Then she ran after him, her sleeves flopping and her pant legs flapping.

"Hey Reverend, slow down a little. Your scarecrow is coming with you. When we get the weeds cut, you can leave me in the cornfield. Then maybe the crows won't eat our corn."

Albert never tired of her childish ways. "Oh no, I can't do that. The crows would just find you so irresistible that they would cart you away!"

Their gardens and cornfield weeds were forgotten.

They had already planned for their first baby, and Lizzy had begun making its tiny garments. Blue things for a baby boy and pink ones for a baby girl. Every night when Albert came home from working on their vast acreage, she would excitedly show him what she had made that day. He would tease her, "Now my little Liz, you must be sure there are more blue ones!"

One day when he mentioned this, he lifted her up and held her close to him. "Oh, my sweetheart, either a little boy or a little girl will be all right with me. How could I not love a little girl, who I'm positive will look just like you?"

At this time of year, the big ranch was very busy and he would often be on the far side of it. He would be too far away to come home for dinner, so Lizzy had to pack it in a tin pail. She never failed to send a little love note along with it. Sometimes they would be funny and other times she would seriously try to convey her love for him. Sometimes there would be a note with just kisses and hugs; sometimes all it had was a big question mark.

Albert loved her notes. He kept them in his pocket and hid them in a little box upstairs. One note read, "What have you got planned for our evening entertainment?" Albert hurried home early that day, so he could answer her note in person.

Lizzy loved to surprise him. Sometimes she would hide behind the kitchen door and jump out into his arms. One time she hid herself in a hay mound, and as he was unharnessing the horses, she leaped up and startled him. However, he wasn't the only one surprised that time; the horses made a big commotion.

"Oh, was this your plan? Well, now I have one for you!" He picked up a little flat board, grabbed hold of her, and began spanking her gently. They both fell back on the mound of hay. The horses were not happy with all the activity, as they had to wait longer for their feeding.

One day as Albert was reading the Bible and making notes for his sermon, Lizzy danced around and around him, teasing and kissing him. He tried to ignore her but finally burst out laughing. All of a sudden, she took his Bible and laid it on the table. Then she jumped astride of him and covered his face with her kisses.

"Now Lizzy, I know we are sinning for sure! In this outrageous conduct, you have taken my Bible from me."

"Oh for pity sake Albert," she said, "Look at the angel watching us; he's grinning from ear to ear."

Unfettered and unrestrained, their love knew no boundaries, no limitation as they explored their new world of delights and wonders. In this miracle of their love, Albert began a transformation. It was like a gentle breeze on his face. The frown lines and wrinkles had melted away. His nervous habits, quirks, and tensions lessened. He had new energy and strength. His sharp features softened and rounded as he gained weight from his lover's cooking. His usually piercing eyes danced and twinkled with wonder, and an inner calm and peace settled on him as he took abode in an enchanted world he never knew existed.

Lizzy, of course, was the reason for the drastic change in the Reverend. Whenever he had to leave her to go to work or to attend to the countless duties on the ranch, she always walked arm in arm with him to the door. One morning she said, "Albert darling, if you have to leave me, this is the way I'm going to always tell you good-bye."

"Oh Lizzy, my little sweetheart. My young and foolish girl. How can you love me so?" He fiercely and passionately pulled her close to him, his rough cheek against her smooth and satiny face. They stood in golden stillness.

"Is this kind of love morally wrong? God forgive me, if You can, but for now, I must humbly bow and worship before my earthly altar that you have given me." Frightened at his words and thoughts, he wondered if this was blasphemy. He turned and hurried out the door, trying to escape his irreverent and sacrilegious utterance!

Albert and Lizzy felt a physical healing in the wonder of their love and happiness. Every day they radiated their joy. They knew no cloudy days.

Lizzy was like a child at a fountain, standing on tiptoe to drink and savor the exquisite nectar of their love.

The men on the porch closely followed the newlyweds.

The first to speak on the subject was Amos. "I'll say one thing, and I do declare it's true, the Reverend is getting handsomer day by day. That weddin' has sure agreed with both of them. Lizzy gets prettier every day. Those big blue eyes of hers just sparkle and flash. I see she has quit wearing those gray colors. I saw her in a pink dress and in a blue one. And I do declare that one day she had on a red one! Of course, it was a dark red. I just hope she don't wear it to church. If she does, all the ladies will start clucking like a bunch of old settin' hens when you take away their eggs."

While Amos was trying to draw a breath, Ray Linda announced, "I had to go to Whippoorwill the other day, and I happened to look through the jewelry store window. There was Albert buying some jewelry for his Lizzy. And, here's more. Just try to recollect back to the Sunday night before his weddin'. Remember how he took his text from the Good Book and read so loud and clear, 'A wife should not be adorned with wearing of gold or precious jewels, but be adorned with a meek and quiet Spirit'? This love bug when it bites a feller, he completely loses the things that he believes in. If Lizzy wears the jewelry to church, he is going to be in a tight spot, yes indeed. He better hunt up a scripture from the Good Book to explain this drastic deed, as all them strict Baptist ladies will jump on him like a chicken on a june bug if they see any jewelry on her except her wedding ring."

They all said, "Amen."

Let us not therefore judge one another any more:
but judge this rather, that no man put a stumblingblock
or an occasion to fall in his brother's way.

ROMANS 14:13

Chapter 24

The Poem

Again, bedlam and pandemonium swept through the little town of Paw Paw. It was noised about that even in Whippoorwill it caused a little ruckus. The mystery of this scandalous conduct never came from the grapevine on the porch of the General Store but had come from the Paw Paw Times.

The men had gathered that afternoon after they had attended to their various duties at home. Otis sighed, "Boys, the paper will be here at any time, and as usual it will be covered front to back with the escapades of our teenagers' disgraceful conduct."

Before they had time to comment on this further, Jimmy C. Simpson came into view, yelling at every step, "Extra! Extra! Read all about it! Extra! Extra! Read all about how our esteemed and distinguished Reverend Albert and Lizzy Peabody have deviated from the path of virtue."

Otis grabbed the paper and read aloud. "This news was received by mail in the form of a poem which is printed in full in the "What Fell Out of the Wastebasket Today" column. In light of the fact that this scandal may be brought before an open church meeting, we wanted to give the Peabody's a chance to clear the slander that threatens to blacken their name and that of the Baptist Church. So, late last night one of our reporters tried to find the Peabodys but was unsuccessful."

"He did find Miss Idy Crandall, a credible witness for sure. Miss Idy has been elected deaconess and spokesperson for the Baptist Church. She had won this honored position by an overwhelming landslide. In fact, there was only one dissenting vote. All of Paw Paw has wondered who this could be; as of today, it remains a mystery. Someone ventured forth that it was Miss Idy herself that had put the no vote in the hat that night."

Otis turned to the section and read the poem aloud to his buddies.

To begin this shocking story, Reverend Peabody thought of it—not Miss Lizzy.
He pled, "There is no one in this wide world that could raise a tizzy.
If anyone perchance would happen by, they couldn't possibly believe
That the Peabodys would ever be guilty of a skinny dipping spree."

'Twas true, Albert had been hauling hay from the field.
He was hot and covered with dust and sweat.
Still Lizzy looked warily and cautiously around
To see if there could be some regret.

Albert's the preacher and Lizzy helps, so they could ill afford
Any breath of scandal, as they could be impeached by the church board.
Reverend Peabody himself had set the rules for the law-abiding,
And here he was in a moment of ecstasy, yielding to wicked backsliding.

At Morgan Creek the Reverend hastily removed his darling's modest attire,
Before she changed her mind and squashed his passionate, risqué desire.
After the fun Lizzy crawled out, still quite dripping wet,
Then unknowingly, in a nest of fiery red chiggers, she did carefully set.

Now this is the lesson we learn from that romantic interlude:
Be sure, your sins will find you out, as the Peabodys must conclude.
This wage of sin came from "Old Scratch" himself, laughing down below,
As Reverend and Lizzy Peabody paid dearly for their out-and-out sinful dido.

"We at the Paw Paw Times wonder if this was the work of our teenage boy wonder. He'll be a literary genius, for sure, if he continues his talent. We'll keep you informed of these turbulent times."

After reading the poem and without saying another word Otis jumped from the porch and started for home. As he came through the front door, gasping for breath, he yelled, "Maudie, Maudie, come quick. Something terrible has happened."

Maudie started reading the paper. Her face blanched white as she read the appalling news. "Otis, this has to be our Jimmy. He is the culprit of this drastic poem! Oh, my goodness, the Peabodys could be churched for this disgraceful conduct." Horror-stricken, she fell into a chair. Otis ran and got the smelling salts and had to carry her to the bed.

Jimmy was still delivering the paper and yelling the disturbing news when he got to Miss Idy's house. She rushed out into the yard, bought one, and began reading the article.

The first thing she thought of was phoning the Peabodys regarding this shocking news but caught herself just in time. If she dared to do that, half of Paw Paw would be listening in. She walked the floor, wringing her hands, trying to decide what to do. As usual, Miss Idy felt it was her duty to handle the situation since the men on the porch were lax in their own duties of the church.

It was now almost dark, so she lit her lantern and walked to the Peabody's. Thinking that maybe they hadn't received the paper, she took it with her.

When she arrived, she stepped up onto the front porch and started to knock. The lovely glass front door revealed the entire house. The Reverend and Lizzy were just getting up from the supper table when all of a sudden Albert grabbed his wife and whirled her around and around the room. Every once in a while, he would kiss her. They stopped just short of doing a hoe-down dance.

Suddenly, Albert turned Lizzy upside-down and tried to

kiss her that way, but her dress and slip were over her head. Miss Idy was aghast to see that Lizzy had pink bloomers on with lace at the legs, instead of the white or black that every other woman wore. Hysterically laughing, they both fell to the floor in each other's arms.

Disoriented and confused, Miss Idy didn't know what to do. Fearing the worst of what this could lead to before her very eyes, she loudly knocked on the door.

Both faces turned several different colors as they welcomed her in. "I can see by your actions tonight that all of these charges are probably true," she said as she waved the paper.

They both sat down and read the article. Poor Lizzy was trembling and on the verge of tears; Albert was so embarrassed and ashamed that he felt awkward before Miss Idy.

Albert was the first to speak, "Of course, we never dreamed that anyone was near us at the time, but we are guilty and you have come to us as the Bible teaches. But to spare the church in this foolish and stupid thing we did, we will resign our positions in the church right now."

Miss Idy held up her hand to them saying, "Reverend, Lizzy, I don't think you should resign; I think we should have you judged by the church. This judgment should be open to all, that way if there is any complaint about the reprimand or chastisement, it can be settled at once. This sort of thing could drag on and on, and we don't need this kind of publicity.

Reverend Peabody echoed, "Yes, we must get this settled at once."

Miss Idy grimly remarked, "Why not have it at Wednesday night's prayer meeting? And I think it should be announced in the paper. I would like for Jimmy Simpson to be there, then we can be sure that everything will be laid to bare." At this unfortunate word, Miss Idy clicked her heels and took a hasty retreat.

Early Tuesday morning, the Paw Paw Times did announce on the front page, "Reverend Peabody and Lizzy have decided to confess and come clean on Wednesday night at the weekly prayer meeting. Miss Idy told our reporter that justice would be served swiftly and surely, if these charges were true. Then she said that no further word would be forthcoming until after the meeting."

The Wednesday night prayer meeting at the Paw Paw Baptist Church was crowded. For years there had been just a handful of people who came to church, even ones who didn't declare they had done their praying on bended knee beside their beds at night. However, that night dust clouds were seen from the road caused by the cars, wagons, buggies, and hacks coming to the church's prayer meeting.

Miss Idy Crandall went to the podium and pounded her gavel. "Friends, fellow members of our church, we need to sit as close together as we can to let other people have a seat. There isn't enough room to put our children on pallets, so you will need to hold them on your laps. Since our Reverend Peabody's conduct is under a cloud of investigation, we can't ask him for his usual prayer at this time, though, for sure, we need prayer. So, we will pause for a minute of silent prayer."

The little church was very quiet for a moment while everyone prayed that this would have a good outcome.

"We know, without a shadow of a doubt, that all of you have heard of this meeting and what it is all about," she told the congregation. "Please keep in mind that the guidelines, the rules and regulations of our church, have been authored by the accused himself. One of the expressions he used was, "We must live holy lives, free from sin and transgressions."

"I will read from the Bible about our church strategy." Miss Idy opened her Bible and read Matthew 18:21-22. '"Then came Peter to Jesus and said, Lord, how often shall my brother sin against me and I forgive him? 'Til seven times? Jesus said to Peter, I say seven times, but until seventy times seven." She paused a minute to let this sink in.

"Now will the Reverend and Lizzy Peabody and Jimmy C. Simpson please come forward." Many had a smile on their face when Jimmy was called.

"Please sit down," she said politely. "I will add here that Otis and Maudie Simpson have been very cooperative in the quest for the truth and should be commended by all. Also for Jimmy C., but that took a trip or two to the woodshed, so I heard."

Bowing just a trifle, she continued, "Reverend Peabody, would you take the position of spokesman and tell us this sordid conduct in the water of Morgan Creek?"

Reverend Peabody walked to the podium with a pure, unsullied look upon his face.

There were a few titters among the ladies. "Why the Reverend looks downright handsome; Lizzy has put a little weight on him. And it didn't all go to his belly like some of the menfolks." They would discuss this phenomenon later at the Ladies' Sewing Circle.

"Good evening to the members of our Baptist Church and other friends who have come out to judge us. My beloved wife, Lizzy, and I have talked of our trial by fire, and we graciously will step down from the high position of governing this body of believers, if you see fit. I want to say further, we will never feel ill toward you no matter how it goes.

"Miss Idy has read her scripture to you, and I want to thank her for the compassionate one she picked, so I will read mine. This is a love story written by the hand of God of His love toward us and His church. It also tells of our love to the Lord. You all know I am a newly married man and not a credible witness, but I think it is also good marriage advice for a husband and wife. I will read a few verses from the Song of Solomon.

'Let him kiss me with the kisses of his mouth. As the apple tree among the trees of the woods, so is my beloved among many sons. I sat down under his shadow with great delights and his fruit was sweet to our taste. He brought me to the banqueting house and his banner over me was love.'

"When you go home tonight, read all the chapters. It is a very short book. King Solomon uses the word beloved over thirty times. Beloved means very much loved. So let us everyone love his wife as Christ loved the Church."

They all sat immovable by the gracious words he had spoken. Miss Idy's face beamed with a trace of a smile. Reverend Peabody had preached the greatest sermon that he would ever preach. She was sure that next Sunday the little Baptist Church would be packed out. However, he wasn't through. He turned to Jimmy C. "I do apologize for our wrongdoing Jimmy, but are you sure you have seen all the things that you have so cleverly put together in your poem?"

Jimmy was speechless for the first time in his life. White around the gills, he reluctantly stood up.

"Most of my poem I just made up for fun," Jimmy said meekly. "All that I really saw was that they were in deep water, baptizing one another. I quickly left before they got out of the water, as I was a trespasser on Peabody land. But, about those chiggers on Mrs. Peabody, I know I never exaggerated about that. We all know about chiggers. If anyone goes to Morgan Creek, they will be covered with them, that's a fact!"

"Reverend Peabody, I ask your forgiveness and Miss Lizzy's too."

Then he excitedly added, "I have several more poems at the house that I will gladly read, if anyone is interested."

Hastily, the Reverend said, "No, not right now Jimmy."

Then he turned to Miss Idy and said, "This is all I have to say."

Miss Idy quickly took the podium. "I think all of you know how we conduct our church elections here. If you want the Peabodys to stay, say yes on these little pieces of paper; if you think they should step down from their positions in the church, say no. Of course, you already know you can't vote unless you are a member of the church."

Jeremiah jumped up, passed his hat around, and collected

the votes. After they all were counted, all read yes, except one. Then Miss Idy announced, "The people have spoken, Reverend Peabody will take the pulpit next Sunday. I am sure our little house will be packed out. Please do not add fuel to the flame by hashing and rehashing this over and over. Let us forgive and forget with decorum and dignity this sordid happening." Then she clicked her heels, marched down the center aisle, and out the door.

Jimmy stood quite forlorn until several gave him a wink and a smile.

Albert and Lizzy continued their little pantomime of baptizing one another when they went home and laughed hilariously for the next few days.

That next Sunday, Reverend Peabody was in the pulpit with an anointed sermon, preaching up a storm. His dear Lizzy was sitting on the ladies side on the first seat. He happened to look at her and she gave him a wicked smile and moved her arms as if she was baptizing him in water. No one saw her do this, so the congregation was in utter dismay when Albert started laughing uncontrollably and had to hang on to the podium to try to stop. The people were aghast, especially Miss Idy.

Lizzy jumped to her feet, "I know I'm probably out of order, but can't you see what this laughter means? Spiritually, there is such a thing as a holy laughter. You who have read the Good Book know this. King David said, 'Let our mouth be filled with laughter and our tongues in singing.' Sarah, Abraham's wife, laughed at angels who told her she would have a baby, though she was far too old. She must have laughed for nine months, because she gave birth to Isaac, whose name means laughter. In the Book of Ecclesiastes, Solomon wrote, 'There is a time to weep and a time to laugh, time to mourn and a time to dance.'"

Then a mischievous glint sparkled from Lizzy's eyes. "So maybe there is a time to baptize and a time not to baptize."

The entire congregation was smiling and laughing when they were dismissed. Miss Idy heard many say they would be back next Sunday, as they so loved every minute of the service.

Before the Peabodys ate their Sunday dinner of chicken and homemade dumplings, they fell across their bed hysterically laughing in a very unorthodox manner.

And when Rachel saw that she bare Jacob no children,
Rachel envied her sister; and said unto Jacob,
Give me children, or else I die.

GENESIS 30:1

Chapter 25

The Tender Blue Room

When Albert and Lizzy Peabody went to bed, from habit Lizzy always slept near the window. There was some cold, lazy winter snow still on the roof of their house, and like the fringe of a crocheted doily, crystalline icicles hung from the eaves. They appeared content to just release their beauty drop by drop, but once in a while a big one gave a wild cracking sound as it took a fast journey into the dark welcoming earth. Lizzy had to turn her head a little, so both ears were uncovered to hear the tiny icicles fall.

Thin as straw from a broomstick, they barely made a whispering sound when they released their hold and shattered in sharp points like needles. She remembered the day she had dropped and broken one of her crystal iced-tea glasses. As she swept the sharp splinters into her dustpan, she cut her finger. She felt that pain again as she wept, "Oh, maybe I should go out now with my broom and sweep the broken icicles up."

Then she remembered from somewhere that there was a man who played tall crystal tea glasses with silver spoons. "Why, I can hear them now. They were all cradlesongs. 'A Baby's Lullaby,' 'A Baby's Serenade,' and there was another one. I can't remember that one." She wept again, thinking of the missing song and the cut on her finger long ago.

All night she heard the rustling sounds of spring. She could hear the crocuses making their slow ascension from their dark entombed chambers, up through the snow to promenade their feathering yellow buttercup petals. In her fancy, she heard the blossoming petals of the cherry, apple, and wild persimmon trees struggling to be free, to flaunt their brilliant display on every branch and twig.

Albert was fast asleep as Lizzy quietly arose and shut the door to their bedroom. She went to the kitchen to make their coffee. When Albert built their house, he put a big window in the kitchen. She never failed to gasp at the glorious drama and pageantry outside. The distant mountains voiced their messages of the season, and in some magic way drifted their pantomime across the shining floor of her kitchen.

From her window view, she could see the pastureland, the corrals, the well, and the outbuildings. She could also see the high hay and tobacco barn, the smokehouse where they smoked their ham and bacon, the springhouse where they kept their food cold, and the door to the cellar. All too soon, their vegetable garden, fruit orchard, and vineyard would be bursting forth their bountiful harvest that Lizzy would then preserve in jars for their winter fare.

Before they married, Albert bought her a small rocking chair so she could sit at her window. He placed his mother's exquisite marble-top table next to it for her to set her tea and coffee on. He placed his Bible on it and always left it open to one of his many favorite scriptures, verses that he would carefully underline as he considered their meaning.

Lizzy rocked for a little while that morning, holding the hot cup of coffee in her hands to feel the delicious warmth. God had turned off His night stars, was arranging the epic of his daystar that was ready to say "Good morning" to Mr. and Mrs. Peabody.

Lizzy saw her little dog emerge from his own little house. Albert had painted his name, Casey Jones, over the door. Casey was stretching out in length, as far as he could, and was starting to go through his morning yawning when he caught sight of Doomsday, the calico cat, and her three calico kittens.

Doomsday was busy teaching her babies just how to step lightly and daintily to keep their little paws from getting dirty. She kept one eye on Casey Jones and the other one on her babies. If, perchance, he made a move towards them, she would snarl and hiss as her hair stood straight up on her head. Casey Jones always backed off, as he realized he was no match for her deadly claws. One day he had come into contact with them, so he avoided suffering that mishap again.

The calico mama acquired the name Doomsday when she was in the milking barn begging Albert to pour some milk into her dish. For some unknown reason, she felt she couldn't wait any longer. She hovered over the bucket, and Albert squirted some milk into her open mouth. Apparently, old Creamer, the cow, didn't like her getting too close to one of her faucets, so she deliberately raised her foot and stepped on the mama cat. When Albert jumped up to rescue her, he spilled the bucket of milk and screamed for Lizzy to come quickly.

They both examined the cat for broken bones. They didn't find any, but she certainly had been flattened. Lizzy kept her in the kitchen. Then one day she left; she moved under the porch and had her babies. There she was this fine morning with her calico babies, showing them the delights of a kitten's heaven.

Lizzy couldn't see the pigpens from her window, but she knew the mama pig was there. Lizzy named her Misses Gobbler because she gobbled up any kind of food they gave her. Even at this early morning hour, she would be stretched out as far as she could on her side. She had nine piglet babies; and she would let them fight, shove, and squeal at their breakfast table. Except for one, the runt.

Albert had told Lizzy, "Honey, in every pig litter there is always one that's a runt. Some men do away with them, but I've always tried to save them. With extra feeding and care, they usually catch up." Excited, Lizzy had carried the baby pig to the kitchen and put it into a basket and fed it from a bottle. Very soon, it caught up with its brothers and sisters, so he was sent back to his mama.

Lizzy counted one by one the five baby lambs in the sheep-birthing pens. They were dancing and frolicking with one another. All the mothers kept a wary eye on their little white woolly babies. Every once in a while, the babies would make a mad dash to their mama for their dinner, then just as quickly, they'd go back to their games of hide-and-seek.

Two huge white-faced cows strolled into the barn. Each one had a small replica of itself. At times the babies butted their mother's udder to give them more milk. The mama cows paid them no mind. They just chewed their cuds, gazed up to the heavens with brown liquid eyes and thanked God for His precious gift of their babies.

On the far side of the pasture, the brood mare, Jenny, was grazing. Lizzy had named her baby Jenny Two. Both mama and baby had white stocking feet. Jenny One was kissing and nuzzling her baby with soft whispering neighs.

Yes, it was springtime, a time to surrender and a time to yield the sweet burden, the fruit of the results of the begetting. She had counted the months since her marriage; she too should have been suffering the sweet pain of birthing a child as God had promised in Genesis 3.

Lizzy finished her second cup of coffee and carefully set the empty cup on the little table. She picked up Albert's Bible and looked at the verses he had underlined last night before they went to bed. They were both in the Song of Solomon, 4:12 and 8:8. She read the first one aloud. "A garden enclosed is my sister, my spouse; a spring shut up, a fountain sealed."

Then she read the second. "We have a little sister and she hath no breasts. What shall we do for our sister in the day? When she shall be spoken for?"

Lizzy felt her throat tighten with a feeling of numbness. She didn't know what meaning Albert drew from the two underlined verses, but to her they both referred to one thing—a barren womb.

She carried a hot cup of coffee to the bedroom and set it down on the table beside Albert. Then she reached over and kissed him.

Suddenly he grabbed her and pulled her down into their bed. "Do you know, my little Liz, you have a bad habit of kissing men awake when they are sleeping! What kind of punishment do you want me to give you?" He looked at her face and saw a serious look.

"My dear husband, I do want something from you. This is going to be a beautiful day. Let's paint one of the bedrooms upstairs in a lovely shade of blue. We could buy a little white bed, and I will make a fluffy blue down quilt with little white lambs frolicking and dancing on it. We will need a wee chest of drawers, white, of course; a white rocking chair; and a powder blue rug. My darling, I feel that Albert Peabody Jr. will be spoiled rotten."

Albert could tell her pain and growing fear had gripped her heart and soul. He knew that she had carefully rehearsed the words that she had just said to him.

He leaped out of bed and danced her around the room. "Lizzy, sweetheart, I think that would be fun. So get your frilly bonnet on while I drink my coffee."

Laughing with rapturous joy, they went to the General Store for the blue paint. They had heard of the huge amount of paint that Jacob had bought some time ago from a little lass when she passed through Paw Paw taking orders.

They both knew the men on the porch of the store would be discussing them as they walked hand in hand. They saw Amos smile and overheard him say, "Did you ever see the likes of them two love birds having an affair right before our eyes?"

Otis replied, "Yes, it was indeed a marriage made in heaven when them two jumped the broomstick."

"Yes, indeed!" they all chorused.

Lizzy and Albert still holding hands ran up the stairs. Lizzy was the first to speak. "Now you men don't need to ask what we are going to do because it's a secret between Albert and me." Then she looked up at Albert with dancing eyes.

They went into the store, and together, they chose a soft shade of blue. Lizzy whispered to Albert, "Darling, I shall call it a tender blue color."

Clara got out her order catalog, and they chose a small white bed, a chest of drawers, a white rocking chair, and a large fluffy rug. Then Albert went out to chat with the men on the porch.

Clara helped Lizzy pick out her material for the comforter for the little bed. When the ordering was done, Clara came around the counter and hugged Lizzy. They both had tears of joy in their eyes.

Lizzy went out to the porch, grabbed Albert's hand, and they ran down the steps, eager to get to their joyous task.

When they finished painting the Tender Blue Room, Lizzy made a little sign on some pink furled paper and tacked it on the door. It read:

> This room is for Albert Peabody Jr. And this little pink sign
> is sending a message to God to order a baby girl, a Lizzy Jr.

Laughing together and covered with paint, they fell into each other's arms. Albert started kissing her.

Abruptly, with no warning, she pulled away from him and slowly knelt at his feet as if offering homage to him. In the hush of the moment, her voice was a wounded whisper. "My darling, my darling. Give me a baby."

Albert sat down on the floor and took her in his arms. There were no words to say. They had already been said.

He hath led me, and brought me into darkness,
but not into light. Surely against me is he turned;
he turneth his hand against me all the day.
Also when I cry and shout, he shutteth out my prayer.

LAMENTATIONS 3:2-3,8

Chapter 26

Lizzy's Breakdown

Out in the far distance, a stark black thing crouched, bearing a burial shroud. It was writhing along, inch-by-inch, gaining strength for a foothold in the home where Albert and Lizzy abided. Then from deathly silence, they heard a funeral hymn being sung and a wreath of fear enveloped them both. And Lizzy fell under the fury of a breakdown.

The ladies of the church came, bringing them food and helping with Lizzy. However, they were hindered, as no one knew what was wrong with her. One day she would be fine, then the next day she might stare at them with blank and questioning eyes. This sorrow and grief was felt from the men on the porch to all the inhabitants of Paw Paw. They all loved their little Lizzy Peabody.

Albert found her one day curled up in a fetal position on the carpet of the Tender Blue Room. She had cried so long that a puddle of salty tears lay on the rug. Gently, he picked up her tiny waif-like body and carried her down to bed.

She whispered to him, "I thought you wouldn't come for me."

They both were weeping now, heart-rendering sobs. He kissed her brow, her teary cheeks, and—eagerly—her salty lips. He kissed her neck. Then rocking her back and forth, "Oh, my darling, what are we going to do? What are we going to do?"

There was no answer from the shrouded room. They were like two lost children who couldn't find their way home.

That night he knelt at their bed, praying and weeping, and he fell asleep on the floor, agonizing to a God who did not hear him or the tiny form that lay so helpless and still.

Then for several days, Lizzy had been well. She cooked their meals, and, though they were meager, Albert was glad.

"Honey, I need to go and hunt for some of our cattle that are ready to deliver their babies. Do you think you will be all right while I'm gone?"

Lizzy smiled, "Oh yes, for sure. I have several little jobs in the house to keep me busy."

He was late in getting back to the house because he could not find a cow he was concerned about. He gave up the search, as it had started to rain and darkness was upon him.

When he got back to the house, he didn't see any lights. He called out, "Lizzy darling, I'm home." When he got no answer, he fearfully rushed through the house, calling her name. In panic, he ran up the stairs to check the little blue room. She wasn't there either. He ran out the front door, screaming, "Lizzy! Lizzy, where are you?"

He stopped for a moment as he heard a little moan from his gravesite. She sat huddled down inside the circle of plants and flowers.

"Oh my darling, what are you doing here?" he asked as he knelt beside her in the mud.

She whispered in his ear, "I thought I was your little girl, laughing and dancing over your grave."

He pulled her into his arms and rocked her back and forth, whispering his love for her through bitter tears of despair and grief.

When he picked her up in his arms and tenderly carried her to their bed, she murmured, "Albert, I love you so much."

She was soaked and her clothes were muddy. Thankfully,

there was plenty of hot water on the stove. He bathed and powdered her and tucked her between some warm blankets.

She seemed to come to herself and looked into his eyes with a big smile. He brushed her hair and braided it into two braids. He got a mirror so she could see herself. He saw some of her red ribbon and tied bows on each braid. He lifted each bow and shook it in her face. She started to laugh, and there was a sparkle in her eyes. Then saucily and with impudence, she pulled him down into the bed with her.

"Lizzy dear, I must take a bath. I'm all wet and muddy."

She clung to him. Albert was clothesless and supperless that night. She slept on his arm all night between her little tricks of kissing him awake now and then. He reveled in her intense, wondrous response in their love. His heart and soul sang with joyous anticipation that she was well.

They both awakened as the rising sun made a path of gold across their bed. Trembling with anxiety and fear, he looked into her eyes. She stared back at him through eyes that were empty and void of understanding.

All day he tried to arouse her and make her eat. She refused the food but did drink a lot water.

He moved his big chair from near the fireplace to beside her bed, so he could hold her hand. Every once in a while, he would turn her palm up and fill it with kisses of love, whispering a Bible verse into her ear. "Oh my beloved is mine and I am his, until the day break and the day spring on high hath visited us, and our dark shadows flee away."

As he looked at her fragile porcelain face, he detected a smile on her lips. All day he sat holding her hand, sometimes falling asleep with his head next to hers. But, alas, Lizzy's dark shadow did not flee but instead stealthy stalked into their bedroom, their living room, and their kitchen. They both heard it climb the stairs to the little Tender Blue Room. As it entered the room, it brushed against the little ruffled pink sign on the door and left it dangling askew, held up by just one small tack.

Lizzy's breakdown now had enveloped her like a gray cloak. Sometimes she would cry and beg, "Please take this cloak off of me." In her agitation and imagination, she would sometimes try to cast aside this agony in her soul. Sometimes she would nervously and feverishly try to fasten it to her.

And sometimes she would be her delightful self once again. If those days were sunny and warm, he would take her out to his work. Albert called it her sunny and cloudy days.

In many ways, she became a child in a charming world of her own. Her face took on an innocent, angelic calm; her actions were trance-like in her other world. And Albert could not enter into that unholy sanctuary.

Blessed are the peacemakers:
for they shall be called the children of God.

MATTHEW 5:9

Chapter 27

Some Days Angels Are Everywhere

To say Miss Idy was orderly would be a mild expression; systematic would be a better word to describe her. She woke early with the cocks crowing in every henhouse around Paw Paw. Then she prayed for whatever the day would bring. This was a short prayer compared to the one she would pray at night. The evening prayer generally was for the problems she had encountered that day. This prayer always ended in her confessing her sins and shortcomings, although she rarely could think of any. She heard a preacher say there were secret sins one did, so just to be sure she prayed about them also.

After the prayer, she dressed, dampened her hair, and skinned it back to a knot on top of her head. Then she fixed her breakfast, one thin slice of bacon and one coddled egg on a warm biscuit with a bit of jelly.

She had just sat down to eat her breakfast when a loud pounding began on her door. Hastily she opened it. There stood Clossy Hanford in his beggarly attire, speaking in a teary voice. "Miss Idy, could you come and lay out our baby girl, Idy May? She left us last night."

Though startled by this request, she answered, "Clossy, I have never done that before, but I will gladly come and do what I can." Her breakfast was forgotten as she grabbed a wrap and started out with him. He took such long strides she almost ran to keep up. He never spoke a word on their journey.

She remembered Bessie Hanford whispering to her one night in church. "Miss Idy, if my baby is a girl, could I name her Idy May?"

Miss Idy was so touched by this question she put her arms around the woman and brushed her a kiss on her cheek. "Oh Bessie, I would be honored if you would do that."

The Hanfords lived in one of the most squalid, poverty-stricken dwellings on the outskirts of Paw Paw. A large cedar break cut them off the main road, so they weren't in sight of the other residents of town. When the area was mentioned, the men on the porch often said, "Out of sight is out of mind."

Mr. Hanford opened the door to the little house and led Miss Idy to the bed. Bessie lay with her back to them; she was asleep. There, curled around her back, lay the tiny Idy May, so still, silent, and hushed. Miss Idy picked up the wee miniature of Bessie Hanford, and despite the soiled condition of the baby, she clasped the little body to her breast. She had always thought dead bodies would be stiff and cold, but that wasn't so. The baby was soft and cuddly as she nestled her close to her heart. Suddenly, she found herself trembling, not from fright, but from a sensation of rapture.

"What is happening to me? Does this happen to all young ladies or just to a spinster?" She was aware that everyone described her as such. Then mysteriously she felt her nipples becoming firm against her dress. Alarmed at the surging swell, she again asked herself, "What is happening to me?"

Then the answer came to her and she almost said aloud, "Oh yes, this is the divine, the sublime of God's performance, the heavenly. Why here in my arms lay the kingdom of God."

She knew with her calling that she would never have a baby of her own. She also knew that God wanted her, for just a little while, to taste and drink in the depths of His wonderment in the form of a baby. She didn't know that God was teaching her this lesson to ready her for what would be coming down the road.

Looking around the unkempt room, she saw several dirty little faces peering at her with big frightened eyes, not understanding the commotion that circled around them. Even Mr. Hanford stood by looking helpless. Miss Idy realized she must take hold the helm to get things done that were needful. Speaking firmly, she said, "Mr. Hanford, I want you to go over the hill and ask Dick Bayley to help you build a little wooden coffin for our baby."

She was startled at his reaction. He changed from the meek lowly man as his eyes turned angry. "Miss Idy, I can't do that," he blurted out. "We haven't spoke to each other for years. There has always been bad blood between us, so we avoid any chance of meeting each other. We fear it could develop into the same violent behavior as it did in the past."

Miss Idy was shocked. "How did this come about from two grown men? Tell me."

A little meek from Miss Idy's outburst, Clossy pointed, "Yonder over the hill is twenty acres of prized land. Someone long ago got the surveying mixed up. My name is on the deed and Dick's. It has laid idle all these year's, so no one benefits from it."

Immediately, Miss Idy came down to earth. The spiritual sensation she had had with her tiny Idy May vanished with irate anger, which she didn't know she had. She raised her voice. "Both of you should be ashamed of this foolish behavior. I don't give a hoot about your silly feud. You are to go immediately to Dick and ask him to help you build a little coffin for your baby.

"Mr. Hanford, it wouldn't take the wisdom of Solomon to settle this foolish quarrel between you and Dick. Just divide it up. You take half and Dick can take the other half. Or you could farm it one year and Dick the next. If you want to help settle this peaceably, that I will gladly do." She looked up at the ceiling with consternation and muttered, "Men! Men! Men!"

After the spiritual experience with Idy May and the earthly confrontation with Mr. Hanford, she laid the baby on a towel on the table. Then she realized the children were looking at her from behind chairs and doors. Still embarrassed from the rapturous moment of holding the baby to her breast, she smiled and said, "Good morning, children. I am Miss Idy. I have come to take care of your little sister, Idy May."

A teakettle of water was singing and whistling on the kitchen stove, so she filled a dishpan with warm water. She looked for some soap, but when she didn't find any, she asked the oldest boy, "Where is your soap, honey?"

"Ma'am, we don't have any."

A little startled Miss Idy asked, "Doesn't your mother make lye soap?"

"Oh yes, ma'am, but we have used it all up, and she is too sick to make anymore."

"Oh dear God, please give us help in this terrible drought and Depression, so people can have enough money to buy the things they need. When will it all end?"

Miss Idy trying to think what she should do remembered that soda was a cleansing agent. She found a big box along with a box of cornstarch to powder the baby. The baby had scurfy, a thick dandruff on its tiny head. She made a thick paste of soda and water to loosen it, then she took a fine comb and it came off easily. Then she tenderly put the baby into the warm water and bathed her. She dried her and powdered her with the cornstarch. The baby felt soft and silky as Miss Idy again held the "glory of God" to her breast.

Clossy was not a big praying man, but he prayed now with every step he took as he headed to face his enemy of long standing. He didn't see any activity around the house but was greeted by two dogs raising a fuss and wagging their tails at every bark. Gingerly Clossy knocked on the door. There was no answer, but the knob on the door was turning slowly. Then it stopped for a second and started turning again. There before him stood a little girl with huge blue eyes and blond curly hair.

She clapped her tiny hands in glee. "I did it, I did it. I opened the door all by myself. My name is Angel Bayley. What is yours? Would you like to come into my house?"

Immediately, Dick Bayley appeared behind his angel.

Faltering, with a sob in his voice, Clossy asked, "Dick, would you help me build a little coffin for my Idy May? She left us last night."

Dick Bayley reached out and placed one hand on Clossy Hanford's shoulder and with the other shook the hand of his longtime enemy. This gesture was something that took the place of words. Yes, they both realized the bondage of hate took flight, and unshackled and unfettered, they were free at last.

Early the next morning when the Hanford's were still asleep, another angel placed a big box of soap on the back step; some bars were for washing clothes, and others smelled of sweet lavender to bathe in. Oh yes, sometimes there are angels everywhere.

A little child shall lead them.

Thy wisdom and thy knowledge,
it hath perverted thee.

ISAIAH 47:10

Chapter 28

A Chicken in the Hand is Worth Two in the Henhouse

One Saturday morning, Jimmy needed to go to the newspaper office, so he was stepping around lightly, hoping his mother wouldn't notice him. No such luck, his mother yelled at him, "Jimmy, don't you leave this morning. I am going to cull out the chickens that are not laying eggs. I have them all in the henhouse, so we can catch them easier.

Jimmy knew that a hen should lay an egg every day. One sure way of knowing if she was doing that was to see her hop into the nest and lay her prize. Another way was to feel the egg itself to see if it was still warm. He had wondered many times about their clucking. The question was, were they proud of their ability to produce an egg or just happy to get rid of the big round thing that was tormenting them? He finally decided it was a little of both.

One thing his mother had to watch for was a hen that was prone to her nest outside the henhouse. Hens could be enticed to lay an egg if there was one already in the nest, so his mother had brilliantly placed a white porcelain doorknob or a white darning egg into each nest. But even with these allurements, it didn't always work. Some would venture to other places to lay their eggs, and Jimmy was the one elected to find their hiding spots.

The only way to do this was to watch the questionable chicken and see where she was heading. Sometimes, strangely, she would cast suspicious glances at him. Jimmy called this playing hide-and-seek. Sometimes he was rewarded and discovered maybe a dozen eggs in a hidden nest, but in the meantime, he lost perhaps half a day from his other various projects.

"Jimmy!" his mother yelled, "Get your head out of the clouds and get to the chicken house!"

He knew there were two ways to deal with this hateful operation. He could languish and just mosey along, which would ensure his mother's wrath upon him, or he could get to work and snatch up that first chicken.

"Now Jimmy, turn your chicken upside down, putting her head toward your back, and then put three fingers between the pelvic bones. If it's wide enough, it means she is laying. But if the bones are real narrow and close together, you can believe she is not laying, so off to the market she goes."

"Mother, does this procedure always work?"

"Not always, but this is the way all the ladies of Paw Paw do it."

Fascinated now, Jimmy was still examining his hen when suddenly one of his many lights came on in his head. He looked a little closer at the tail of the hen, and there was the hole where the egg would emerge. Turning his back to his mother, he put his finger in the hole, and lo and behold, an egg fell into his hand! His heart began to race and quiver in excitement. "I have found a gold mine under my finger! This is a breakthrough of enormous possibilities. Everyone in Paw Paw has a few chickens in the backyard."

Throwing caution to the wind, and the hen too, he raced through the gate and down the road. He was heading for the newspaper office to put an ad in the paper. He still had the egg in his hand; his mother stood with a chicken in each of her hands, screaming at the top of her lungs. "Jimmy, come back here this instant!"

The next-day's paper had an ad that read:

Esteemed Ladies and Gentlemen of Paw Paw,

Are you fed up to the gills feeding chickens that refuse to lay an egg every day? If so, you need to call a genius, who has a 100 percent, foolproof, surefire method of culling chickens. Just call the Paw Paw Times and leave your request there.

—Jimmy C. Simpson

Dead flies cause the ointment of the apothecary
to send forth a stinking savour:
so doth a little folly him
that is in reputation for wisdom and honour.

ECCLESIASTES 10:1

Chapter 29

The Miracle in a Chamber Pot

One Sunday morning Reverend Albert Peabody stood behind the podium and loudly read his Bible scripture from the book of Ecclesiastes, Chapter 10. "Dead flies cause the ointment of the apothecary to send forth a stinking savor."

Reverend Peabody had a certain pattern he would follow when he read a difficult verse that was hard for his congregation to understand. First he would raise his voice like Gabriel's trumpet, then he would suddenly settle down in a sing-song way, then he would explain what it meant in everyday living, in coping with the world in general. Next, he would move to the spiritual realm, by lowering his voice to almost a whisper. He had discovered that this was a good way to keep his congregation awake, especially the men who had taken their coon dogs out on a midnight serenade of their prey the night before.

Jimmy always stayed alert to everything he said. This was one of his special tools he used in dealing with the older men and ladies of Paw Paw. He would memorize a few words from each sermon. They were always impressed, and it had a tremendous effect on some of his shady dealings.

This morning's sermon was preached with an anointing, and every word the Reverend spoke seemed meant for him alone. He, for certain, had two dead flies in his ointment; they were his twin brothers, Paul "Pete" Lee and Saul "Repete" Lee. He constantly had to take care of them, and since he had less time to work, his supply of money in the coffee can never increased. Surely he did wail from morning to night, but it didn't do any good, as his parents paid no attention.

Jimmy hadn't realized the rich blessing he had had being the only child in his family until the twins arrived, especially since they arrived under such spectacular circumstances. Now there were two crosses to bear. The pain and suffering he had to endure was sad; and he rued and lamented because their home was never quiet or peaceful anymore.

He had hoped things would get better, but he couldn't see that they had. When he had to take them somewhere, every little old lady he met would cluck her tongue, "Oh, here are the twins. Yes, we remember the nights and days that stork got befuddled and bewildered about his depository at the Simpson's house." Then she'd go on her way, still clucking her tongue.

Jimmy was fast asleep the night little Paul Lee was born. He had heard a lot of racket going on but he just turned over and hurried back to sleep. He always tried to get enough rest, so he could be at his best in the daytime. He awakened, saw it was getting light, and heard the commotion still going on in the house. His dad called, "Jimmy, come in here quick and see what happened to us in the night. You have a new baby brother."

He looked at his mother; her eyes were sparkling and dancing, "Jimmy, here he is," she said, as she turned the blanket from the baby's face. "Isn't he beautiful?"

Miss Idy saved the day for him. He thought the baby looked wrinkled and shriveled up, when she, in her best military voice ordered, "You men will have to leave for a while, I'm going to make Maudie eat a bite." Then she coyly added, "And this baby boy has to eat some dinner himself." Jimmy was glad to escape; he needed time to try to figure out how this baby would fit into his way of life.

Two days after baby Paul Lee—Jimmy was determined to

call him Pete—was born, the house was still in an uproar. Miss Idy stayed on and spent most of her time with Maudie, while his dad looked haggard and worried indeed. For the first time in his life that he could remember, he was glad to go to school. Jimmy was late in coming home, having to stop and see the widow Anna Merry Reece about hoeing the weeds from her garden and flowers. He entered through the back door and was shocked to see so many people running to and fro. His father grabbed his hand, he was pale and almost speechless, but did blurt out, "Jimmy, our home has become a madhouse! I am so taken aback my wits are addled, I can hardly think straight. We have another baby boy that came today! None of the ladies that have been here helping us has ever seen the like."

Seeing his father shaking and so distraught, he put his arm around him, "Dad, take it easy now. It appears it is here, so we'll just have to welcome the little guy." Jimmy realized that it was up to him to stand as tall as he could during this upheaval in his family.

His father led him over to the kitchen table, and there in a dresser drawer were two baby boys covered with two little blue blankets, fast asleep. Jimmy was astonished at himself, as a lump rose in his throat and he found himself smiling and crying at God's gift to the Simpsons. Jimmy and his dad stood with their arms around each other, gazing in a hushed reverence. "Jimmy, we are going to name them Paul Lee and Saul Lee. We don't want to hear them whining in a few years that they have no middle name." They both started to laugh at the same time. "Dad, I am going to call this newest baby Repete," Jimmy said. Then, still with their arms around each other, they went to the bedroom to see and love the new mother.

Miss Idy, and Tabitha from the Paw Paw Times, were standing and talking to each other about the babies, especially the last one. They were discussing how to word this sensational news in the paper, as already this second baby was causing a big stir all over Paw Paw.

The men on the porch, with Otis' chair being taken up by

Sam Doolly, were laughing hilariously and slapping their knees as they reviewed over and over the twins at Otis and Maudie Simpson's and how they made their appearance. "They came to dwell with us mortals in a pretty spectacular way," Sam said.

Maggie Jenkins, the telephone operator, declared again and again that the telephone wire was overheated by the ladies of the town as each one tried to be the first to bear the exciting news.

The next day the Paw Paw Times carried the birth of the Simpsons' twin babies. Tabitha had to write and rewrite the article several times before she was satisfied. Generally, birth announcements were put on the page of "What Fell Out of the Wastebasket Today," but she thought this deserved the front page as so many citizens were clearly disoriented with rumors flitting hither and yon. Hoping to lay those rumors to rest, Tabitha, with pen in hand, wrote the whole story of the Simpsons' twins:

> Baby number one's arrival was just a run-of-the-mill delivery, nothing spectacular except from the family's point of view. Miss Idy was there to direct everyone that came to help. In fact, all the ladies from the Sewing Circle were there to lend a hand in the baby's birth. Miss Idy brought her smelling salts just in case Otis needed a smell, but he came through like a trooper. Otis and Maudie named him Paul Lee—they were determined on the second name. And, as usual, Jimmy put in his two cents by saying, "I am going to call him Pete." So, we will have to wait and see how this controversy is solved. It will be interesting.
>
> Now fellow citizens, after consulting with Miss Idy for several hours, we have agreed how this bizarre story could be told. I will discreetly and cautiously handle this matter.
>
> It is no secret that Maudie did not snap back after the birth of Paul Lee, as she had to linger for two days longer in

bed. Miss Idy stayed on to help take care of her. So, reluctantly, I report that dear Maudie got out of bed, aided by Miss Idy, and sat down on the chamber pot. Our dear Maudie gave a loud, piercing, ear-splitting cry and fell back onto the bed. But with that one terrific pain, little Saul Lee had just plopped out and down into the receptacle.

Again, I hope that none of our citizens will take offense at this very embarrassing situation.

Otis came running. It was a sad sight, indeed. Miss Idy almost lost control of this plight right then, but as usual, she quickly rallied round and fished baby Saul Lee out of the pot before he drowned.

Naturally, he was screaming bloody murder. Miss Idy quickly gave him a thorough examination. He seemed to be nonetheless for wear, so she hastily put him in a pan of warm water. The baby screamed at this procedure too. She dried and powdered him and wrapped him in a soft, blue fuzzy blanket. When she put him down beside his brother in the dresser drawer, he gave a sigh of contentment and proceeded to go fast asleep.

So dear readers, we hope this will still the rumors immediately and that everything will quickly blow over.

Tabitha knew for sure that the men on the porch would not relinquish this juicy story right soon, and in time would repeat it over and over until it had little resemblance of what she had printed in the Paw Paw Times.

In the beginning, Jimmy's mother, using her wily ways, attempted to make him change their diddies, but she had to give up on this task. He purposely made bad matters worse as he would take the contents and smear it around.

His mother yelled at him from morning 'til night, except when he was in school. Her yells were mostly, "Jimmy, check the twins" or "Jimmy, do you chores."

Jimmy examined this relationship between the twins and

himself. They tried his patience every day. At times he would have loved to have given them a big spanking or a good shaking but feared his mother's wrath would descend upon him. Then, on the other hand, would come this overwhelming love for them. When this happened, it seemed like they were lacing their little hands around his heart in a sweet smothering kind of way. The boys were now two months old and growing by leaps and bounds.

It was before daylight when Jimmy was awakened out of a sound sleep. Both of the twins were screeching and screaming. Suddenly, his door opened and in marched his distraught mother with a baby under each arm. She had a terrible glint in each eye as she grimly declared, "Jimmy, you are going to take your turn in helping with your brothers. Your father and I are completely exhausted!" and with a dramatic flair, she charged out the door, making the house shake as she slammed it shut.

Pete gradually calmed down but not Repete. (Jimmy could tell them apart as Repete had the beginning of a cowlick in his hair.) He blew his breath into Repete's open mouth, startling him for sure. The baby quit screaming as he tried to catch his breath. When he once again started screaming, Jimmy once again blew in his face. In amazement, he stopped crying and Jimmy thought for sure they both had tiny smiles for him.

He heard his mother starting breakfast, so he got dressed and with a quiet baby in each arm walked into the kitchen. His mother was shocked, "Jimmy, what did you do to make those babies quit crying?"

"Oh Mom, it wasn't nothing, just one look on my sweet face was all it took."

Maudie was surprised as Jimmy placed a soft kiss on her forehead.

She put her bacon on the stove to fry and rolled out her biscuit dough on the counter. When she turned to check the bacon, she had her back to the biscuit dough. The twins were barefoot and there in the soft dough were four little footprints.

She looked at this son of hers and could see he already had the footprints of the babies in his heart and soul. Smiling to herself, she recalled what Miss Idy said when she started to go home, "Remember, Maudie dear, a little child shall lead them."

And into whatsoever city ye enter
and they receive you,
eat such things as are set before you.

LUKE 10:8

Chapter 30

The Barrel of Dill Pickles

Old Plenty Bethel had been sitting on the porch of the General Store some said all his life. How old he was, no one knew for sure. He was often asked, but he'd just smile innocently and say, "I don't remember, but I'm glad you asked."

Jimmy C. said he had a built-on smile on his face. It was round and pinkish, like a cherub, and his bright blue eyes twinkled in a joyful manner.

Old Plenty wasn't very tall and his girth was a little on the ample side, but everyone in Paw Paw loved him. His greatest claim to fame was that he had furnished free water for Paw Paw, all the water the town needed.

Old Plenty had never married, although there had been numerous occasions when this could have happened.

Amos, the prize question-asker of the porch, piped up one day, "Boys, do you think the reason Old Plenty has lived so long is because he never got married and had to deal with all that goes along with it?"

The men were a mite puzzled that Otis didn't join in on this wrangling back and forth; he was always quick-witted. He just sat with a smirking grin on his face and waited until Jeremiah left for home before divulging his story, as Miss Idy would say.

"The reason I had to wait until after Jeremiah was gone was

because this story is about his kinfolk—his father, nonetheless—when he was a baby. This deplorable story was gravely handed down by my dear mother-in-law, so it is a reliable source.

"Old Plenty was called Young Plenty then. He was sitting on this very porch, calm and peaceful like, when Jeremiah's granny arrived one Saturday morning to do her weekly shopping for commodities. She was carrying a six-month-old baby—Jeremiah's father. She paced over to Young Plenty and bravely asked, 'Plenty, can you hold my baby for a while? I want to shop for several items today and could do it a mite easier if I didn't have to cart this youngun' around.'

"Would you believe she never waited for Plenty to answer but just plopped the youngun' and his diddy bag down on Plenty's lap?

"I have to stop here and ask you to take into consideration that Young Plenty was an only child, so he was not familiar with the sort of debacle that was coming to pass. I'm afraid this story gets quite rancid and gamy here. Granny never returned when she said she would, so an explosive situation was foreordained to happen."

"Young Plenty looked wildly around for help, but no one came to his rescue. So, he had to "bell the cat," so to speak, and change the baby's diddy right then and there. But not being familiar with this oft-encountered natural event, it unnerved him. He lost control and was botching the plight he was in. Oh yes, his labor was in vain.

"Now, no one could believe that any sane man would do what he did next. He jumped to his feet and tossed that baby through the air. It landed on the lap of an innocent stranger who had stopped to rest for a few minutes. Then Plenty took a flying leap off the porch and headed home to change his clothes.

"The stranger became very violent. He was like Miss Idy's expression, 'the beast in man let loose.' He yelled out, 'This

Paw Paw town will never see my face again!'

"It was a blessing that Jeremiah's granny came back just then as I believe that stranger was also fixing to toss that baby as it was still very messy.

"So, in winding this story down, Young Plenty never got over this. He was heard to have remarked, 'If this is a sample of married life, I will remain single.'

"My mother-in-law said that on account of this happenstance of fate, Plenty was never the same again. He became very insecure and odd in his ways."

"Well, so be it," Fred Pinkham defensively asserted. "I believe he has always had one foot on the ground and the other one in the heavenlies."

No one challenged him on this presumption.

Old Plenty always sat on the porch until cool weather arrived, then the men moved his big chair into the store. There he sat hugging the big, fat, potbelly stove. Beside him was a barrel of dill pickles, and every once in a while, he dipped one out and ate it. Clara and Jacob paid little attention to this, it had been going on so long it became a fixture of the store.

One day, while doing invoices, they realized they were not making any money on their pickles. Mystified, Clara said, "Jacob, maybe we should not stock them anymore. What do you think?"

Jacob, a little irritated, said, "Clara, look on the summer invoices; we always make a profit on them then."

So there was always a free pickle for Mr. Plenty. In fact, once in a while he would stop a stranger entering the store. He would give them a smile and say, "They have free pickles inside the store."

Old Plenty had the only rocking chair on the porch; it was reserved for him alone. It would shriek, creak, and squeak as he rocked to and fro. When the men didn't hear it, they knew Plenty was asleep. There was much talk about reinforcing the old rocker, so it wouldn't make so much racket, but Tom Curry adamantly declared, "I am against fixing the rocker. We all know he drops asleep at the ruckus of it. I believe it is music to his ears." They all agreed this was sound advice.

When they left the porch that day, Old Plenty was still asleep in his rocker, but the men didn't think anything of it, as he was always the last one to leave.

As they started for home, Jeremiah remarked, "I think we are having a cooling in the weather. We should move Mr. Plenty's chair into the store in the morning."

The next morning, shocked and horror-struck, the men discovered Mr. Plenty had rocked himself right on into heaven.

"Well, there is one thing we know," Ray commented, "Mr. Plenty now has a golden rocking chair to squeak, shriek, and creak, that's for sure."

They all said, "Amen."

But whosoever drinketh of the water
that I shall give him shall never thirst;
but the water that I shall give him
shall be in him a well of water
springing up into everlasting life.

JOHN 4:14

Chapter 31

The Well of Plenty

There was a huge gathering at the Baptist Church for Plenty Bethel's funeral. They moved in extra chairs and filled the aisles. They opened the windows, so the men and boys outside could see and hear.

Miss Idy was the first to get up and open the service. "Now we are all here to pay tribute to our most august and stately resident, Plenty Bethel, Old Plenty to some. I think our Reverend Peabody can explain it better."

Reverend Peabody took the podium. "Miss Idy and I went to the newspaper office to put in the announcement of our dear Mr. Plenty's passing into yonder heaven. Jimmy C. Simpson was there putting in one of his endless ads, tying to get more money in his coffer. Oh, I mean, his coffee can."

There was a ripple of smiles from the congregation.

"While we talked, Jimmy said that he would like to say a few words if he might. Maybe the eulogy. We were a little startled, but knowing how our 'boy wonder's' journalistic, reporting, and book-learning skills have made everyone sit up and take notice, we ask none other than our own Jimmy Chores Simpson to come forward.

"As he speaks, remember the scripture from Isaiah 11: 'And a little child shall lead them.'"

There was a slight murmuring and whispering from the

audience, as they'd never heard of one so young speaking at a funeral. Of course, they were very proud of Jimmy. The numerous venturesome tactics he had used over the years had caused many to smile, but all admitted he had God-given talents with no end.

Slowly and reverently, Jimmy C. Simpson walked to the podium and then looking the vast audience over carefully began. "I humbly stand in awe and wonderment of Miss Idy and our Reverend Peabody asking me to do the eulogy for our beloved friend and, yes, our Mr. Plenty Bethel. Did you all know that the word Bethel means 'the house of God and the gate to heaven'?

"I'm just going to read a portion of scripture in Proverbs, Chapter 20. 'The Spirit of a man is the candle of the Lord.' So we will take a journey today back to Bethel, perchance it can be with Mr. Plenty and we can bask in the warmth of his candle."

There was a slight rustling of the people as they listened spellbound to Jimmy's words.

"My first awakening of our Mr. Plenty came to me one night. It was dark, and I had been sent to get some wood for the stove. The reason for this late-night chore was because I had failed to do it when it was light." At this, Jimmy looked at his mother with a knowing smile. "I was standing at the gate of our fence in the backyard. I think I was doing one of my favorite things, looking at the moon and stars and all of God's Creation. Then I heard Mr. Plenty playing his new Jew's harp as he walked down the road. He quit playing and started to sing that old song 'Amazing grace, how sweet the sound that saved a wretch like me.' Then he played his harp again, then sang again, 'Once I was lost, but now I'm found, was blind but now I see.'

"His playing and singing drifted far away 'till I could hear no more. Many of you will say that Jimmy Chores Simpson is a little 'tetched in the head,' because I realized that wherever he was, the birds in the trees hushed their singing. The red and gray squirrels in the high oak tree hesitated in their little chatter and prattle, and a mama rabbit in the carrot patch bid her babies to be silent.

"It has come to my ears that the men on the porch once said that even when Mr. Plenty was miserable, he was a happy man.

"I have noticed in my young life, one question is always asked after a funeral: How did he die? I want to share a little poem that I have kept in my writings. I don't know who wrote i;, there was no title or name on it. This is for Mr. Plenty.

The silver cord has been loosed,
And the golden bowl broken at the fountain.
Not, how did he die, but how did he live?
Not, what was his station, but had he a heart?
And how did he play his God-given part?
Not, what was his church, but what was his creed?
And had he befriended those really in need?
Not, what did the sketch in the newspaper say?
But how many grieved when he passed away.

"Reverend Peabody found a small diary at Mr. Plenty's house and asked me to read it. For some unknown reason, he quit writing for several years." Jimmy abruptly stopped, as he was becoming so emotional. He collected himself and then continued.

"This is what he wrote about his well that he dug years ago in the front of the General Store.

> This is Monday. I have finished my daily reading from my Bible. Today was about Joseph, God's dreamer he was called. God sent Joseph a dream about vast starvation that would come to Israel. And Joseph would be the one to save God's chosen people. "Joseph, you are to store up food and grains for a seven-year famine." Well, dear diary, I had a

> dream last night. I dreamt everything in Paw Paw was brown and dry. So, dear diary, I am going to dig a well starting this morning. I don't know why, only God can answer that, but I am to dig a well. I shall dig it deep and I shall dig it wide.
>
> Dear diary, it is Monday night. I went to the porch and told the men my message from God. Some doubted and some laughed, but they all said they'd help.
>
> Dear diary, it is Saturday night. We discovered much water yesterday. Several said it is deep enough for anyone. I said no, we're going to dig until we hit a vast supply that cannot be diminished under constant drawing. Today, at last, it was completed. A superabundance, a gushing fountainhead, is flowing out to everyone.

"My friends, these were the last pages of Mr. Plenty's diary; he never wrote anymore. But he left a heritage with us before he passed on. We, in Paw Paw, will always remember not only his well that surges out to this day it's life-giving water in the natural, but also the spiritual water that we drank from him.

"Oh yes, Plenteous, the God of Plenteous for all. He has entered into heaven where we, the rank and file, have not yet entered."

By now, tears had dampened every eye in the church; even the men and boys standing outside at the windows were seen to wipe their eyes on their sleeves. Jimmy C. Simpson took a deep bow to the congregation while saying, "Nor shout, nor rush, but hush for God is here. The king is dead, long live the king."

The people sat spellbound, entranced, as silent as white falling snow at the gracious words Jimmy spoke. They knew he spoke under God's anointing. Maudie, Jimmy's mother, tucked all of her son's poignant words into her heart. She pondered them and wondered about this son of hers. Was it true, as Miss Idy said that a little child would lead them?

For several days the men on the porch hashed and rehashed the life and death of Old Plenty. Jeremiah spoke. "I wish there was a way to keep his memory and his gift of this life-giving well alive in the years to come."

The men didn't see Miss Idy standing in the doorway of the store. Overhearing what Jeremiah said, she stepped out. "Well gentlemen, I have heard your conversation of wanting to leave a memorial of our dear Mr. Plenty. There is something you can do. It won't cost you anything but a little work." When she mentioned work, she detected a slight tremor among the men, but she plunged ahead. "In Morgan Creek there are some huge white rocks. Some resemble headstones. You could move one here to his well and carve in the words: 'Plenty's Well, Plenty for All.' However, I and all of Paw Paw realize that you are probably too laid-back to get up and do this."

With these words, Miss Idy made a dramatic gesture, like washing her hands, and then briskly sallied down the steps toward her house. The men were stunned and dazed at this direct attack on them. It demanded that they take action to save their pride; plus it was a good idea. This would save Mr. Plenty's memory for posterity.

Jeremiah lamely said, "Well my friends, it 'peers to me that we have been caught in the trap of our own wagging tongues."

It took two days to get the huge white rock from Morgan Creek to the side of Plenty's Well. And a bit more time to get Mr. Plenty's legacy engraved in it: "Plenty's Well, Plenty for All."

And when neither sun nor stars in many days appeared,
and no small tempest lay on us,
all hope that we should be saved was then taken away.

Acts 27:20

Chapter 32

The Three Storms of Reverend Peabody

The time had come for Albert to get some help, so he went to the General Store. He had to hold on to the wobbly banister for support to get up the steps. All the men jumped up to help him; they could see he was on his last leg.

"Gentlemen, I have come to see if you know of any men I could hire to work for me. I need to have someone to do my work on the ranch while I take care of Lizzy. All the ladies from the church have been very kind in bringing food and taking care of Lizzy. However, I have had a hard time with Miss Idy. I had to speak rather firmly to make her go home before she collapsed."

They promised to help him find someone.

He barely made it into the house when Maggie Jenkins called. "Reverend Peabody, Jacob just now called me to say that he knew of two men that were desperate for work."

Overjoyed, he said, "Maggie, if you can get word to them to come to the ranch today, I would be obliged."

That afternoon, the men arrived with their meager belongings. Albert showed them to the little cabin where they could live. "Now gentlemen, I have credit at the General Store. Get what you need to eat and charge it to me, but I intend to watch that you don't waste my money—remember, just the bare essentials you need."

Albert was free now to do one more thing to help Lizzy. He had been reluctant until now to take her to a doctor. He was afraid of what the doctor might say and afraid that his faith would be shattered if she did not get well. He began preparing to leave early in the morning to take her to the town of Whippoorwill. He knew it would be an all-day ordeal for them.

He bathed her before they went to bed, as he would be rushed for time in the morning. Sleeping fitfully, he arose early for their journey. He fixed her something to eat, hoping she would eat on the way. Then he quickly dressed her, braided her long hair, and carried her to the buggy. All the while, she was crying and begging to go back to bed. He ignored her pleas; she wouldn't hear his answers anyway.

Finally arriving in Whippoorwill, he carried Lizzy's tiny fragile body into the office where a nurse in a white starched dress and cap had him lay her on a bed. Albert introduced himself to Dr. Summers and his nurse and told them all he could of her breakdown—if that was what was wrong with her.

He told them of their special storybook marriage in the past year. He answered their many questions. They both listened carefully and seemed deeply concerned for him. Then they asked him to please wait in the other office.

Finally, the doctor came out, sat down beside him. "Reverend Peabody, what do you think has happened to your wife?"

Albert looked up into kind eyes, choked back tears, which threatened to overflow, and said, "I think, Dr. Summers, the trouble is she cannot have a baby."

The doctor left him saying, "I think I'll give her another evaluation. This will take a little time."

Albert sat waiting for over an hour, going back and forth between wondrous elation and dark despair. Then the nurse opened the door and said, "Do come in, Reverend Peabody."

Lizzy was lying still on a little bed, seemingly asleep.

"Please take a seat Reverend," the doctor invited. Then he continued, "My nurse and I have given your wife a very thorough examination. In fact, there is nothing more to do than what we have done. We can't see anything that would prevent her from conceiving a baby. We wonder if you have asked yourself if it could be you. Now, we both know you will have a difficult time accepting this, but it is the conclusion we have come up with."

The doctor and his nurse were prepared to tell him more about why they had come to this conclusion, how something like this could happen and try to comfort him.

"What about adoption?" the nurse said.

"How much do I owe you?" Albert snapped.

He paid and without another word picked up Lizzy and went out the door. He put her in the buggy, wrapped a blanket around her, and started for home. He didn't remember how he got there, but his horse, Agatha, knew as he regularly laid his lash across her back.

It was dark when they reached home. He carried Lizzy to her bed, and as he started to cover her, she clasped his hands in hers. He rudely shook his hands free and went to put Agatha in the barn.

Albert could hardly walk back to the house. Desolation and hopelessness weighed down over him, and he dragged his feet all the way.

He pulled some red coals from the banked fireplace and warmed up some soup and hot chocolate for Lizzy. "Darling, I have some supper for you," he called out.

When he put a spoon of soup in her mouth, she spit it out on her nightgown. She turned her head away from him saying, "No, no, leave me alone." He carefully set the bowl down on the table beside her bed, but she reached up and knocked the dish on the floor, breaking it.

Violent anger and anguish bubbled up from somewhere deep in his soul and overflowed as he screamed at her in rage.

Trying to control himself, he walked back and forth the length of the big room. Afraid now that he might hurt her, he leaned over the back of his big chair and held it in a tight embrace, shaking and trembling, trying to calm himself.

Suddenly, there was a crash of thunder. Lightning raced across the room almost blinding him. It flashed across Lizzy's bed, but she did not stir.

Then a torrent of rain burst from the sky and pounded down, punishing the earth with its deluge. The wind whipped and howled around the corners of the house. It beat its savage message on every windowpane, demanding entrance. Then it crashed through the lovely, big, oval, stained-glass window in the front door, hurling splinters across the floor.

Albert gave a blackened scream and dashed through the shattered door. He never felt the jagged, cruel glass as it cut his arms and hands.

If one happened by in this raging, furious storm, he would certainly wonder why a wild and savage man, drenched in mud and blood, was pulling up the plants and shrubs that formed a semi-circle around a sacred burial plot. And why he was throwing them onto his front porch. And if that person had dared to fantasize, he might see a white marble monument engraved with the words, "Oh death, where is your sting? Oh grave, where is your dark victory?"

And Albert could scream back, "It is here! Look very close! it is here! I am the sting! Oh yes, grave, you have gained your dark victory. I am here."

Now they both were mad, Albert and Lizzy both utterly insane, lost in clouded chambers of sinister images.

Albert was nearing quicksand and an undertow whirled before him. Somewhere out of the blackness, a question was hurled at him. "Are you going to let your love, your desire, fail? Are you going to let that silver cord be loosed and the golden bowl be broken?"

He babbled a vicious, "No!" Frenzied, like one possessed,

he screamed, "And here is my burial shroud!" He tore off his filthy wet garments, threw them in a heap on his burial plot, and ran naked back into his house.

In a delirium of wonder and joy, he got in bed and pulled his Lizzy to him. Heartlessly and profanely, he made love to his darling. Just then, the huge towering shade tree beside the front porch gave a violent shuddering convulsion and, like a thousand cymbals, crashed across Albert Peabody's gravesite, as he sank into waters of oblivion.

Albert awakened to the light of day with no memory except his dashing through the glass door.

The storm, in all its fury, had abated. He could hear and feel the heavy silence, the calm, quiet and still. He felt like he had been beaten and bruised. He was shocked when he realized he had slept all night in their bed. Why was he covered with mud and blood? Why were the sheets and Lizzy covered with them too?

Her head lay on his arm; he felt her warm satiny belly against his own. She had entwined her tiny frail body around him. He looked at her lovely face, her long dark lashes against the pale and creamy face. Her exquisite pale pink lips were parted just a little. He felt her breath whispering on his face. He looked at the tiny throbbing pulse on her neck. However, he felt no response to her. In the past, he would have been wild with desire for her, but now he was unmoved.

Whispering to him was the word "finalized." Yes, that was the word he searched for. It echoed through their sweet house, encompassing him, hugging him tight in its cruel message.

In shock, he looked around. Through the arched doorway, he saw shattered stained-glass shards lying like broken dreams across the floor. He leaped out of bed and ran to the door to survey the damage surrounding them. He was stunned and frightened of what had happened in the storm. He remembered dashing through the glass door. What in heaven made him do that? Then he saw all of the shrubs and debris on the porch. Why, those were the plants from around his grave, why would he do that? And the huge tree. It barely missed the house but fell right across his gravesite. That was a blessing indeed, for if it had fallen a few feet closer, it would have crashed onto their bed.

Then Albert saw his clothes on his grave. Why, he was naked! He ran out and got them, wadded them up and hid them in the far closet upstairs. He would take care of them later in the day.

I must be in Purgatory and this must be my penance, he thought.

Bewildered and tremulous he, as if in a nightmare, hastily washed himself and wound some bandages around the cuts on his arms. He built fires in the big fireplace and in the cook-stove. Then he bathed Lizzy and set her in the big chair in front of the fireplace while he began changing her bed. He fixed a big bowl of oatmeal with lots of cream and sugar and a cup of coffee for her. She never said anything but eagerly ate it all. Then she withdrew back into her wretched cell, and he carried her back to bed.

He ate some oatmeal and set the coffeepot beside him at the fireplace. He relaxed a little from what had happened, gazed at the bright flickering fire before him, but felt not a flicker for his love that slept in a fetal position in their marriage bed. This "heaven of heavens" he entered into for just a little while was gone. He put his head down on his hands and wept for the new man that was no more.

"Oh my Lord, forgive me. I have knelt at your golden altar of incense. I have eaten of the shewbread of the table, which I had no right. It was reserved for your high priests. It wasn't meant for me, a common man. But Lord, I'm not even a common man. I am less than that. I am evil, warped, and shaped into a different mold from the ordinary."

"I am three storms: the storm of the house, which I can fix; the storm in my soul, that only You, Lord, can fix; and the storm that carried away my love, my life."

Had God's Holy Spirit fled from him forever, leaving him desolate and forlorn? If that was so, he was now on common ground with other sinners. Maybe he had never entered that paradise, that utopia, with Lizzy. Was it just a sweet and wild dream? He sat up straight, thinking that maybe the storms came from Satan himself.

"And if that is true, then my anguish and agony will be prolonged and will ever be with me," he moaned.

Why should he ever attain such joy? Why should he aspire to the sweet life, which he had barely tasted?

How could he ever fill the pulpit again in the little, white Baptist church? Did they not know of who he really was? Of whom he had been all his life? He was selfish. He was greedy. He wasn't just thrifty; he was stingy, irritable, and sullen. Why did people come to hear him preach? Why? Just because there wasn't any other minister in Paw Paw? He should have been barred from the podium long ago.

Oh yes, he had always acted so pious, so sanctimonious. Jesus called them, such as he, whited sepulchers full of dead men's bones. "My bruises are incurable," he shouted aloud. He found no place for repentance, no place for solace though he sought it with bitter tears.

There was a light tapping on the broken front door and Miss Idy walked into the house. "Good morning, Reverend Peabody," she said as she hung up her coat. She took a big apron out of her bag and put it on. She was so small, it almost covered her up. "You are free to do what needs to be done, or if you need to go somewhere, I'll be here for the day. I assure you I will take good care of your Lizzy." And with that, she got a broom and a dustpan and started sweeping up the glass from the floor. Miss Idy asked no questions about what had happened.

Albert hastened to the workmen's cabin. "Gentlemen, I want you to help me repair the house and to cut up the big tree that fell last night."

Several shingles had blown from the roof in the storm. They used extra ones he had stored in the shed from when he roofed the house. They boarded up the beautiful front door, and he knew it would never be replaced.

Then they started on the tree. They cut the limbs off first, sawed the tree into fireplace lengths, and stored the wood on the porch. If anyone wondered why the plants and shrubs lay on the porch, they never asked. All the debris was carted off; they even raked up the leaves.

Gone. All gone. And gone also were Albert's dreams of his little children playing and laughing on his grave.

In the twilight, in the evening, in the black and dark night:
And, behold, there met him a woman
with the attire of an harlot, and subtle of heart.
So she caught him, and kissed him.

PROVERBS 7:9-10,13

Chapter 33

Enter Gertrude Miller

Gertrude Miller was born in Alabama into dire poverty. She was the last of eight children. Uncle Reuben Donahue, of Paw Paw, was her father's brother, but her father rarely spoke of him. By the time she started school, she had vowed to herself that someday she would escape the madness of her family. Maybe she would move to Paw Paw.

Her brothers that had left the house had come back home because of failed marriages or from just being too lazy to work. Their small house was slowly turning into total disaster. There wasn't enough food, enough beds, or enough clothes for them all. Her father did work hard, but he liked to relax at night by drinking; her brothers did too. Her mother was a timid, shy woman who rarely spoke to her husband or sons about their drinking. Gertrude often tried to talk to her about the problem, but she would just become distant or agitated. So, she vowed to escape this never-ending nightmare. She quit her angry tirades against her family, as it always ended in some violent uproar with no solution.

When she was sixteen, she eloped with an older man who had led her to believe that he was very well off and would give her all her heart's desires. All his promises came to naught, so she left him. When she had to move back home, her family never stopped ranting and ridiculing her, saying that she was one of them now.

She later got involved with a handsome man, no money for sure, but she did love the man—and so did several other women. The competition left her in pain and completely exhausted. She was ready for a change of scenery, so she caught the train and headed for Paw Paw.

Gertrude almost went into shock when she arrived. "Why, this is in the middle of nowhere," she gasped. If she had had the money to leave, she would have done so right then. But she had just barely been able to scrape together enough money to get there. Trying to make the best of a bad situation, she took a deep breath, stood up straight with shoulders back, and headed to the General Store.

The five men on the porch had been kinda sleepy, but when they saw her coming their way, they came to full attention. They watched her closely. They noticed that when she came up the steps, she did not need to take hold of the wobbly banister.

"Gentlemen, I am Gertrude Miller. I am looking for the Donahue's house. Mr. Reuben Donahue is my uncle; his wife's name is Sarah." They all visited for a while before directing her to the Donahues' house.

As she started to leave, Miss Idy came up the stairs. Otis introduced them. "Oh, Miss Idy, you must meet Miss Gertrude Miller, a newcomer to Paw Paw. She has come to see the Donahues. Reuben is her uncle. Miss Miller, this is Miss Idy Crandall, one of our genteel and important residents of our community."

Pleased by this welcoming, Gertrude hastened down the road to her destination. But Miss Idy's traveling eyes focused on her until she was out of sight.

If Albert had listened in on Maggie Jenkins' party line or spoken with the men on the porch, he would have known of Gertrude Miller's visit to her aunt and uncle. He would have known she was attractive, blond, and what some called a "mite ample"—not skinny, that's for sure. All of the men on the porch tried to guess how old she was, but they evidently did not agree on that subject.

A couple of days later, Tom Curry excitedly called him. "Reverend, there's a new lady that's come to Paw Paw, and she's looking for work. Would you want her to help take care of Lizzy? She looks mighty strong and healthy, not puny. She is staying at the Donahues' for a visit.

"Thanks, Tom. I'll go see her in the morning."

When Reverend Peabody went to the Donahue house, the guest herself greeted him.

A little hesitantly he said, "Good morning, I am Reverend Albert Peabody, a man of the cloth. Is Sarah or Reuben here?"

"No, Reverend, they aren't here. They won't be back until evening. My name is Gertrude Miller. Sarah and Reuben are my aunt and uncle. If you wish to leave a message, I will give it to them as soon as they return."

"Miss Miller, I will tell you of my mission here. My wife, Lizzy, is very ill, and I need some help until she gets better. I'm sure she will be all right, but, for now, I need someone desperately. Would you consider coming to work for me for a while? The work will be mainly in taking care of her and cooking the meals for us. I am a rotten cook, barely able to eat my own cooking, and Lizzy absolutely refuses to eat what I fix for her."

Albert waited for her to say something, but she just looked at him.

"If it's a matter of money," he continued, "I will gladly pay you whatever you charge for this kind of work. If you want time to think about it or ask your aunt and uncle for advice, I will wait until they return."

Stunned and dazed, Gertrude looked at him. So this is the richest man in town, in the whole county, in fact. Her aunt and uncle were always talking about his wealth. And his wife is sick? What a gold mine to find here in this woebegone place.

Albert was quite taken back by her eagerness, as she warmly and fervently replied, "Oh, yes, Reverend Peabody, I will gladly come as I do need a job. And you will find I'm quite able to do any kind of work that you want done."

Heaving a sigh of relief, Reverend Peabody said, "Miss Miller, we must agree about your wages. How much does one make in this kind of work? I do not know."

"Very well Reverend, I will charge you what I received from my former employer. I have some recommendations if you would like to see them."

"There's no need of that," he said.

They finally agreed on her salary, and Albert left for home, mopping his sweaty brow and muttering to himself all the way, "Why, this is the highway robbery, having to pay such wages." But he had to have someone to take care of Lizzy. He was sure that there had been lots of gossip on the porch of the General Store about why he hadn't used any of his ill-gotten gains to nurse her back to health.

As soon as Reverend Albert Peabody left, Gertrude leaned back against the door, shaking, trembling in excitement. At last her time had come and without any effort on her part. What a day! What a gold mine right under her nose! She always believed that once in a lifetime there would be one opportunity to make good, and this was it.

She poured herself a cup of coffee and sat down at the kitchen table and began her strategy. "Oh, I must be aware of everything around me, and I must always be in good humor no matter what happens. I must be cunning and subtle. Oh yes, even the Good Book said to 'Be sly as a serpent and harmless as a dove.'" She had never read the Good Book herself, but had heard this from someone.

"Maybe I should try to read it," she thought out loud. "There could be other jewels lurking in it."

Calmed down a little, she took a bath and washed her hair. She wound it with strips of rags so it would be curly. She was so excited thinking of her good fortune that she could hardly sleep.

She finally dozed off but suddenly sat bolt upright. There it was again, another story from the Good Book guiding her way. From the Garden of Eden, Eve insisted that Adam eat a bite of her delicious fruit. So, the old adage was true: The way to a man's heart begins in his stomach. Gleeful now, she knew where to start because she knew she was an outstanding cook. Asleep again, golden coins of "filthy lucre" danced in her head.

Early the next morning, the Reverend had barely put his clothes on before there was a knock on the door. He hurried to open it.

He was astonished, at first, as he didn't recognize Gertrude as the same lady he had talked to the day before. All he could remember was that she was a tall, big woman.

Before him now was a buxom, full-blossoming woman in her thirties. She looked at him with a wispy hint of a smile in her big blue eyes. Gold-covered clasps held her golden curls away from her face, and the rest fell in golden tendrils down her back. And he was sure she had powder on her face and paint on her lips, which was a big no-no in the church.

Embarrassed for looking at her so long, he blurted out, "Come in, come in. You can see that everything is a mess. Lizzy is in bed refusing to eat my cooking—I can't eat it either." He smiled at this remark.

Gertrude stepped into the room and as she passed him, he could smell her sweet perfume. She took off her coat and from her bag, got out her apron.

"Reverend Peabody, I would like to be introduced to your Lizzy," she said, tying her apron tightly around her small waist.

"Of course, Miss Miller." Albert led her into the bedroom.

She was shocked at Lizzy's condition but more shocked at her youth. This was not what she expected at all! She had expected an older woman, more the Reverend's age. Still, she was nothing but skin and bones. Gertrude leaned over and said, "Mrs. Peabody, I have come to help take care of you. Do you think you could eat a few bites of food?" Lizzy looked at her but never answered.

Gertrude and the Reverend went back to the kitchen where she searched the cupboards and pantry for something to eat. She set some milk on the stove to heat then sliced a big piece of bread and put it on the stove to warm. When the bread was nice and toasty, she buttered it and put brown sugar on top of the butter, then she poured the hot milk over it.

Gertrude pulled a chair up beside the bed and, talking soothingly, put a spoonful of the toast into Lizzy's mouth. Lizzy was startled but began eating the delicious bread. She looked at Gertrude with questioning eyes but never said anything. She ate the whole dish of toast. Gertrude held a glass of water to her lips and she drank half of it. Triumphantly, Gertrude returned to the kitchen.

"Reverend Peabody, she ate the whole piece of toast. Isn't that wonderful?"

He was elated. "Miss Miller, you have given me a little hope. What can I do to help?"

"Well, you will need to go to the store and get supplies," she answered. "I'll give you a list, but first I'll fix you something to eat."

Gertrude hurried out to the smokehouse and got a slab of cured bacon. She sliced it and made some biscuits while it was frying. Then she made some gravy from the bacon drippings. Albert prayed over the food for quite some time then commenced to eat the delicious meal.

Gertrude sat down at the table and made her list. "Now Reverend Peabody, I'm sure you might think some of the things on the list are not necessary, but I will need all of them if we are to get Lizzy well. While you are gone, I'm going to plan my schedule and some meals for you and me, which I'm sure I can get her to eat as well."

Albert reluctantly took the long list from her and left for

the General Store.

Gertrude checked Lizzy again. She was fast asleep. "Does she look a little better?" she murmured to herself. She went out to the chicken house, checking each hen to find the fattest one. None of them were really fat, but she took the best one, wrung its neck, scalded it with hot water, and picked its feathers. She cleaned it and cut it and put it on the stove to simmer.

Then she got a huge pan of warm water and carried it to Lizzy's room, talking all the while. "Miss Lizzy, how about a nice warm bath? I found some clean sheets and blankets. How about if I change your bed?"

Lizzy never answered.

Gertrude took a hot wet cloth and washed her face and eyes. All the time she was washing her, she spoke words of encouragement. She turned her on her side and washed and rinsed her back. She got some more fresh warm water and this time set the pan in the bed. Then, by raising her knees, she put both of Lizzy's feet into the warm water.

Lizzy whispered, "Oh, that feels so good!"

Gertrude gently spread each toe apart and washed them as Lizzy smiled.

After she bathed her, Gertrude went to her bag, got out her powder, and powdered Lizzy. She deftly changed the dirty bed linens and put fresh ones on. She dressed Lizzy in a clean gown then began to brush her hair, being careful not to hurt her.

"Tomorrow, Reverend Peabody is going back to the store," she told Lizzy, "for some powder, lotion, two new gowns, and some soft house slippers."

After straightening the room, Gertrude returned to the kitchen where she made some egg noodles to cook with the chicken. She found some cocoa and a lot of rich milk, which she used to make a pan of chocolate pudding.

Reverend Peabody arrived home with all the purchases she

had requested. He immediately went to see Lizzy. When he returned to the kitchen, he said, "Mrs. Peabody appears much better and certainly smells better." Gertrude smiled and served their supper. She told him of the places she had worked and the funny and tragic things she had seen in caring for people.

After their supper she fixed Lizzy's plate and took it to her room and fed her. An idea came to her that she knew she must act upon immediately. While doing the supper dishes, she nonchalantly said, "Reverend, what do you think of moving a cot into Lizzy's room for me? I can sleep there and take care of her, so you can get a good night's rest."

Hastily he said, "If that's what you want. I'm just grateful for whatever you can do."

After moving a cot into Lizzy's room, Albert climbed the stairs and, exhausted, went to bed. But Gertrude was too excited by her good fortune. Yes, it was obvious Albert cared little for his wife. When he was home, she would manage to take care of Lizzy well. She had to make it appear that she could do wonders. She had a smile of triumph on her lips as she finally went to sleep.

Albert awakened the next morning to the smell of cooking bacon, floating up the stairway. How could he have slept the night without stirring? It had to be that he didn't have the burden of caring for Lizzy. Then, startled and shocked indeed, he saw that Gertrude had carried a big china pitcher of water and a basin into his room. Ill at ease he washed, combed his hair, and rushed down the stairs.

She was at the stove, but she turned to him and smiled. "Good morning, Reverend Peabody. Just sit down and make yourself at home." Then coyly she added, "As if you weren't already."

"Miss Miller, I want to apologize for sleeping so late; I will see it won't happen again," Albert said nervously.

While Gertrude set the food on the table, he went to see Lizzy. She never aroused when he called her name.

Going back to the kitchen, he ate heartily of the biscuits and gravy and bacon. "Thank you for the wonderful breakfast," he said as he turned and quickly went out the door to his work.

Albert had attended to some business transactions in Paw Paw, so it was late in the afternoon when he returned. He could scarcely believe his eyes. Gertrude had carried all the rugs from the house and hung them on the clothesline. That task in itself would need two men to perform it. She had found the dust beater and the broom, and dust was flying in all directions. She gave the rugs a few last strokes before following him into the house.

The floors had all been scrubbed and polished in some remarkable way, the furniture shined and rubbed until it gleamed. The kitchen range had been newly blackened, and the silver nickel had been rubbed to a brilliance. Hot yeast bread sat on a reservoir of warm water, and on the dish cabinet rested two apple pies, wafting their cinnamon smell into the air. A white, linen tablecloth covered the table that was set for two, and in the center was a big vase of wildflowers.

For the lips of a strange woman drop as an honeycomb,
and her mouth is smoother than oil:
But her end is bitter as wormwood,
sharp as a two-edged sword.

PROVERBS 5:3-4

Chapter 34

In the Family Way

The church members were a thorn in Gertrude's flesh that she had to cope with when they dropped by unannounced. She told them very sweetly that they were welcome but that she would like them to phone her when they were coming. Only Miss Idy blithely ignored her wishes. Therefore, Gertrude still had to be on her guard for a visit from her.

Gertrude would fill the visitors' ears with tales of what she had been doing and how difficult it was to care for Lizzy. About the fever that had raged through the night, and how she kept cool cloths on her brow. How she was sure to keep a pitcher of lemonade by the bed. How Lizzy had vomited all night. The mishaps were endless, and they made her have to do the wash every day. On and on, she would complain to the visitors.

One day Miss Idy came by later than usual. Albert had not come home yet from his work, but she decided to wait for him a little while. When it began getting dark, Miss Idy finally decided to go home but told Gertrude she needed a glass of water first. This provided her an excuse to look at the kitchen. While drinking, she made a remark that frightened Gertrude. "My, my, here we have a tablecloth on the table and a bouquet of wild roses in the center. I can see you have time to go pick flowers, even with all your pressing workload."

One morning, Gertrude started to give Lizzy her bath and

change the bed linens. She knew Miss Idy could pay them a visit at any time, so it wouldn't do to neglect Lizzy in any way. She had heard one of her sharp-tongue tirades, and she sure didn't want to go through that again. Every time Miss Idy came, Gertrude didn't have a minute's peace until she left. In some uncanny way, Miss Idy seemed to read her mind. It was absurd, of course, but she seemed to know the secret plot she was brewing.

Most mornings, Gertrude would put Lizzy in Albert's big chair while she changed her bed and did other chores in the bedroom. This was not going to work out today because Lizzy violently refused to get up. Gertrude was quite vexed and muttering when she turned Lizzy on her side.

Then something exploded inside Gertrude's brain, a realization so strong it was like a physical blow to her head. Lizzy was going to have a baby! Horrified and outraged, Gertrude turned into a babbling idiot. She fell down on Lizzy's bed; her legs wouldn't hold her up. Quivering and shaking in disbelief, she knew she must regain control of herself.

How had this happened?

She had deliberately held back food from her, except when Albert was near, of course. And she had noticed a strange weight gain, but she never put two and two together.

She had slept in Lizzy's room every night, so she knew there was no intimate contact between husband and wife.

How had this happened?

She had to sort this out. She had been here six months, so Lizzy was six months along, or more. She leaned over, put her hand on her belly, and carefully felt the baby. She kept her hand there for some time and never felt any movement. In Lizzy's weakened condition, this pregnancy and the trauma of birth might kill both mother and child.

Panic-stricken, Gertrude covered Lizzy up and began walking the floor, wringing her hands and wondering what she should do.

She remembered hearing about a violent storm in this area just before she moved in. She and Albert had talked with each other about it and the damage it did. Albert had said it was indeed a wild night. Then there was the mystery of the bloody, muddy clothes and sheets she had found in an upstairs closet. Yes, for sure, Albert had been out in that storm.

But why? Why would he go out in the storm and leave Lizzy alone? Could the baby have been conceived in the violent fury of that night? Were those sheets from Lizzy's bed?

Questions. Questions. There were no answers.

One thing she knew for sure, she had to make her evil moves in a quicker fashion than she had planned. After waiting all her life in dire poverty, she must get Albert to fall in love with her, so she could get part of the Peabodys' wealth.

Gertrude suddenly realized that in the last few days, Lizzy's health had gotten better, not worse. What was the reason for that? She had thought Lizzy was near death when she moved in. Could she know she was going to have a baby? No, she had to erase that thought!

She must get Albert to have an affair with her, then she could blackmail him, if need be. She knew she was far prettier than Lizzy, but if Lizzy didn't die, would he divorce her? That was too far-fetched, as he was a minister and a divorce would mean he'd have to give up his calling. However, he wasn't making any effort to go back to church even though several of the church members came to inquire why. They all knew she would take care of Lizzy, if he wanted to go. But he clung to the excuse of not wanting to leave his wife.

She made herself a strong pot of coffee and sat down in the little rocker in front of the big window where one could see forever, as Albert would say. Everyone in Paw Paw had talked and laughed at Albert and Lizzy's continuing love affair with each other. Everyone who came to the house never failed to tell her of their devotion to each other. However, that was not true now. Gertrude had never seen him kiss her when he would feed her or tell her goodnight. Was it because of her having a baby? No, of course not. He didn't know about that. She consoled herself that it was because it was evident he did not love Lizzy anymore. Fortified by the two cups of strong coffee, she realized she had less than three months to play out her deadly game.

Gertrude knew Albert had been desolate and feeling helpless since his darling had gotten sick. His body and soul were easy prey as she began, step by step, to work her evil wiles. A little here and a little there, and he would be all hers.

Some time ago, she had splurged by buying herself some fragrant perfume. She called it her "Come Hither" perfume. She was careful to bathe every day and use just a little dab. She had never used much of it because the time had not arrived, but now the time had come to make her move.

Every night at supper, Gertrude would ask Albert questions regarding his ranch and his various duties; about the cattle, farming, and sharecropping. She never had to act at this because she knew nothing about this farming occupation and was interested. He was pleased to answer her questions.

Albert found himself laughing when he told her about their wedding night when the young men put his hack on the barn roof. Then he suddenly stopped laughing and, looking crest-fallen, climbed the stairs to his room.

Whenever she got close enough to him, she managed to touch him—just his hands at first. She was delighted. She felt she was making clever advances.

The next morning, while Albert was eating his breakfast, she slipped up behind him and covered his eyes with her hands. "Can you guess who this is so early in the morning?" she sang out, as she pressed her ample bosom against his shoulders.

Startled, he never answered but got up and went out the door. Gertrude watched him. With a puzzled look on his face, he scratched his head for a minute and looked at the house.

One morning as he was going to work, she helped him put on his coat. Then shyly said, "Reverend Peabody, I would rather have you call me Gertrude instead of Miss Miller, and I would like to call you Albert. I wouldn't call you that in the presence of other people, of course, but here we live under the same roof and we should be less formal." Seeing a puzzled look in his eye, she added, "Now, don't you do this until you think it over."

As he went out the door he said, "Good-bye, Gertrude." That was the first time he had said it. Stone upon stone, her plot was taking shape.

Gertrude loved to wash and iron his clothes. She loved to give his shirts a spray of her perfume. "Gertrude," he asked one day, "how do you manage to make my shirts smell like the roses in the yard?"

"Well, Albert, my dear, I put a little of my "Come Hither" perfume on them," she coyly whispered to him.

"Gertrude, if I wasn't already married, I could believe you are trying to get me to fall in love with you." Aghast at his own words, he hurried out the door.

Gleefully she smiled and whispered to herself that she was making wonderful progress.

He didn't try anymore to get Lizzy to respond to him. Often he blamed himself for her condition, and he would go day after day, trying to drown himself in hard work. He drove himself harder and longer, so he could sleep at night from pure exhaustion. Sometimes when he came home, he would skip his supper and go immediately upstairs to his bed. He finally quit kneeling by his bed, begging his God to restore life to his darling and bring her back into his arms.

One night when he came home late, he saw the supper on the table, but he passed up the lovely meal to go to bed. Thinking Gertrude was with Lizzy, he went upstairs and opened the door to his room. Gertrude was lying on his bed. Stunned, he looked wildly about. Gertrude started laughing,

"Oh Albert, I wish you could see the look upon your face. I have a tub of hot water, and I'm going to stay and wash your back tonight."

Albert, clearly shaken, went around on the other side of the bed, knelt down, and started to weep as he began praying. Gertrude was so stunned and horrified at this that she hurriedly went down the stairs to attend to Lizzy.

Albert had been gone now for two days on business, which was unusual for him. But he would be home tonight. This had given Gertrude time to think and to review her plan of action. It had to be tonight or never.

She carefully felt for the baby again. She thought it had moved a little lower than the day before. She didn't know if this meant anything, but it reinforced her plan of action.

She knew if Lizzy died, she would be the next occupant of the Peabodys' grand home. If the baby lived, it would be wonderful, as it would make Albert happy and she would be pleased. She shivered with joy and glee at what awaited her.

Gertrude would be rich at last.

Though ye have lien among the pots,
yet shall ye be as the wings of a dove covered with silver,
and her feathers with yellow gold.

Psalms 68:13

Chapter 35

Gertrude's Scheme

Gertrude baked a chicken and made cornbread dressing, then she made a lemon pie for their supper. She bathed Lizzy and changed her bed so that if Albert did come in to see his wife, he would know that she wasn't being neglected.

After Gertrude bathed, she put on a beautiful, icy blue, satin robe. She brushed out her blond, curly hair and let if fall down her back. She put on quite a few dabs of her "Come Hither" perfume and preened in front of the mirror. Yes indeed, she was lovely. No one would deny that.

Then, with a clap of thunder, it started pouring down rain. Albert would be soaked, even if he were near to home. She went in to check Lizzy, as she could have heard the storm and been roused. But, as usual, she just lay there with that transparent look on her face.

Then Gertrude heard Albert at the door. When she went to greet him, she saw that rain was running down from his hat and coat. She helped him take off his jacket and hung it up. She was talking to him, but he failed to answer her. So, daringly, she put her arms around him and kissed him.

"Oh, honey, I have missed you so bad and was worried about you in this storm." He seemed unaware of her kiss. She put her arm around him again and guided him to the table. "How was your trip, honey? What did you accomplish? You look so tired and exhausted. I hate to see you drive and push yourself like this."

She took his plate and filled it with the chicken and dressing. He idly pushed it around, untouched. She knew he was somewhere else in his thoughts and that they didn't include her.

"Oh Gertrude, what am I going to do? I bought twenty head of purebred, whiteface cattle today for just a song. By this time next year, I will double, maybe triple, my money on them easily, but I just don't seem to care anymore."

Albert exhausted from his trip and the anguish of pain in his soul for his beloved Lizzy, he laid his head on his outstretched arms and began to weep. Then to Gertrude's appall and horror, Albert fell asleep and began to snore like a whistling trumpet. Anyone, except Gertrude, would have been daunted and stymied by this unexpected turn of events. Her enthusiasm was damped a little, but all was not lost. She knew this was the final curtain for her, so she played it to the hilt. She moved to the back of his chair, putting her arms around him and began kissing his neck, his hair and whispering in his ear, "Oh Albert let me comfort and love you. After a good night's rest you will feel better in the morning. Come my love, my dear sweetheart."

As she tried to awaken Albert, a loud, terrifying, piercing scream came from Lizzy's bedroom. At the same time there was a loud knocking at the door and someone yelled, "Let me in! Let me in!" They rushed to Lizzy's room. She was sitting straight up in bed, beckoning them, and she was laughing and crying. At the same time she was looking at a tiny baby boy that was also screaming bloody murder.

Albert couldn't move or speak because, in that instant, he was secured forever by a miracle of joy and wonder. Oh yes, God in His heaven reached way down low for Reverend Albert Peabody and Gertrude Miller.

Lucky for them, Gertrude knew what to do. She moved quickly to Lizzy's aid. She tied and cut the cord of the squirming baby boy. The baby was breathing well, so for one glorious moment, she held him tight against her and felt his tiny breath in her ear. She felt her throat tighten; no, it was her heart that was tightening in tumultuous joy that overwhelmed her.

Albert stood petrified, dumbfounded by this "crowning act of God." Gertrude tenderly placed the tiny, wet, and slick Albert Peabody Jr. into his daddy's arms. She snuggled the baby's tiny heart against Albert's heart, so they could beat as one.

She had heard that a baby's breath is just one breath away from God. Now, she too was breathless in wonder as she experienced a transformation in her spirit, soul, and body. She soared into God's highest heights and plunged into the deepest realms of Spirit alone.

The pounding and yelling on the door had been forgotten in this medley of confusion that reigned supreme. Then it began again with someone shouting, "Why don't you let me in? I'm drowning out here!"

Albert couldn't be depended upon there to do anything, so Gertrude ran to the door. It was Miss Idy. She had a lantern in one hand that was sputtering and hissing from a crack in its globe. In the other, she had a big suitcase. When she stepped inside, rivulets of rainwater poured from her hat and coat.

Gertrude was bewildered and shaking from this carnival of events, but trying to control her voice, she said, "Miss Idy, why are you here? And in this terrible storm?"

"Well, Gertrude, I have come here to take care of Albert Peabody Jr."

Gertrude, already unnerved mentally, saw Albert in the next room with his baby. He had him cradled in his arms, as he commenced to dance back and forth, the length of the room. She could hear him singing "Amazing Grace."

She was by this time a basket case, as she grabbed hold of Miss Idy's arm and pleaded, "What is going on here? Don't the church forbid dancing, especially the clergy?"

"Well, Gertrude, King Solomon wrote in the Ecclesiastes, 'There is a time to weep and a time to laugh, a time to mourn and a time to dance.' Now, my dear Gertrude, it is time to dance, and I might be able to dance a few steps myself." Then laughing, she hugged the stunned and astonished Gertrude.

Gertrude stood in the doorway. She was dazed as she watched the enchanting drama unfolding before her eyes. Albert was still singing his "Song of Songs." She caught a few more words: "Once I was blind, but now I see...." Oh, yes indeed as Gertrude Miller began singing along with him.

Tears of joy like jewels ran down her cheeks. What bliss she felt, all of her sins (which had been many) had been erased and were now cast into God's Sea of Forgetfulness. Oh yes, she had touched the hem of God's garment, and He had opened His box of alabaster and anointed her with His precious perfumed ointment. God whispered, "Gertrude, from the womb you belonged to Me. All souls do."

She would go. She knew they didn't need her anymore, and she realized that she didn't need them. She did not know where, but He would lead the way. Her bad years were gone and new ones lay in store for her. Old things had passed away, and all things were now new. Out there somewhere she would find her lover. He was there, and so was her own little boy or girl. She was smiling inwardly for she now understood why.

Miss Idy came in the storm. It was a spiritual journey to save her and Reverend Albert Peabody from falling into the habitation of fallen angels.

It was written in the Good Book that a little child would lead them.

Delight thyself also in the LORD;
and he shall give thee the desires of thine heart.

PSALM 37:4

Chapter 36

A Small Diary Book

Little eight-year-old Priscilla Brooks pressed her face against the glass counter and gleefully observed how it made her nose flat. What she was looking at was a small diary book. It was pale pink, and all around the book were dancing bright purple pansies. It had a golden keyhole and a tiny golden key, which was attached with a pink grosgrain ribbon. Every time she came to the store, she would run and see if her little book was there.

Jessie Chadwick stood by and watched her, knowing that her old skinflint father, Rufus, would never buy if for her. Priscilla had asked her mother for it, and her answer was always the same, "Absolutely not, your father would never give me permission to buy what he would call 'utter nonsense.'"

Priscilla went to the store with her mother, and, as usual, she ran to the glass-covered counter to look at her lovely treasure, which she always claimed as her own. She stared in dazed astonishment; her book was not there! Her face became pale and ashen. She didn't dare cry, but tears lay somewhere smothered away. Her pain was a dry anguished hurt that came up to her throat with a choking sensation. She didn't say anything about it being gone to her mother.

When they arrived home, she said, "Mother, I don't feel well. I'm going to my room and lie down."

She lay on her bed, hoping the tears would come and

relieve her distress and grief. They did not. Finally, she fell asleep and didn't wake up until morning.

She hurried down to the kitchen. Her father and mother had just sat down at the table. Her mother asked, "Are you feeling better?"

Priscilla was glad to do all the chores that awaited her. She even did a few extra ones voluntarily just to keep her mind from her lost treasure. She helped her mother fix dinner and supper, then washed and dried the dishes. She went back to her room as soon as her work was finished.

Again, she lay on her bed, and this time the hot tears ran slowly down on her pillow.

Quietly, her mother came into the room, whispering, "Priscilla, here is a present for you from Jessie Chadwick. She knew I could not buy it for you because of your father's wrath. She insisted I bring it to you and said it belonged to you from the very first. In fact, she said we had already paid for it with all the years we had traded at her store and that she owed us something in return. Just keep it hidden away somewhere, so no one can find it, because we could get into trouble if your father sees it." She sat on the bed and took her daughter in her arms. "I love you so much, my darling."

She watched as her little girl carefully took the paper and ribbon from the gift. They both sat entranced with delight at its beauty. Priscilla was overwhelmed and shaking.

"Mother, this border of pansies is just like the beds of wild pansies down by the creek." She didn't know that the pansies on the book and the wild pansies down beside the creek would become the sweet, tangible, wonder in her life—and the most painful. Her mother kissed her goodnight. "Now Priscilla, don't stay awake all night; we have a lot of work to do tomorrow.

As her mother left the room, Priscilla put the little book at her heart and tried to get to sleep, but any chance of sleep had now fled. She put it under her pillow then back to her heart again. Still no sleep. Finally, she sat up in bed and started writing on the first page of her lovely diary.

She decided to write of the events in her life up to the present time. Most of what she wrote was about her three years in school, starting at age five. She wrote of her lovely teacher who had given her so much attention and had been the person who tried to instill confidence in her. She wrote about her first doll and the dollhouse that stood in the corner of her room. She wrote about how she had made all the tiny furniture for it herself. She wrote about playing "house" and how, in her mind, Jeremiah was always there beside her. About how she would pour him tea and slip a cookie from the kitchen for their tiny plates. Mostly, she wrote of her goings on at school and Sunday church—about how her father and mother always sat in the same seat with her beside them.

"Oh, I must get to sleep," she whispered to herself. She quickly read the first two pages in her little pansy treasure. Horror-stricken, she realized most of her writing was about Jeremiah and the pranks he tormented her with. Then she fell asleep, smiling to herself, hugging her book to her heart.

Thy lips, O my spouse, drop as the honeycomb:
honey and milk are under thy tongue;
and the smell of thy garments is like the smell of Lebanon.

SONG OF SOLOMON 4:11

Chapter 37

The Wild Purple Pansy Day

Jeremiah Jones didn't know when it started. It was as though their love had no beginning or ending; it had always been there between them. "Jeremiah and Priscilla are in love" was like a song that he would sing to himself.

They saw each other at church on Sundays. Jeremiah would rush to get the seat behind her and her parents. The first things he noticed were her thick, honey-colored, flaxen braids. Each had a ribbon bow the color of her dress. There were little thatches of hair hanging loose below the ribbons.

One morning at church, surprised at his own courage, he touched the end of her hair. Did anyone see him? He furtively looked around. No one seemed to have noticed. Then he became excited as the preacher had the congregation stand while he read his text.

At this time, Jeremiah realized he was so close to her braids of hair that he could hold them against his body. This caused him to tremble like a leaf in the wind.

At school, he always rushed to claim the desk behind her, so he could feel her presence near him. Sometimes he would play a little game with himself; he would close his eyes for a few moments and picture her gone. When he opened them and found her still sitting before him, he would be flooded with a delirium of joy. She was his sunshine, day after day, year after year. He watched her; he knew she belonged to him and that someday he would hold her in his arms forever.

One day at school, he skillfully maneuvered one of her braids with a blue ribbon bow on it across his desk. Then he dropped the end of the braid into his inkwell. Terrified at what he had done, he grabbed his handkerchief and tried to blot the ink out. This fruitless task only spread the ink and made the problem worse. When the bell rang for dismissal, he jumped up and ran as fast as he could for home.

Jeremiah knew that Priscilla's father hated him, so he was in deep trouble. As soon as he got home, he forgot his usual snack and began his many chores. Before he realized it, he had completed not only his chores but also many jobs he didn't have to do.

His father arrived home and was mystified at the amount of work his son had completed.

Every time the phone rang, Jeremiah would feel weak and his face would turn pale, as he knew this call would be from Priscilla's father.

It was suppertime, and so far that dreaded call had not come. Suddenly Jeremiah looked at his father and innocently asked, "Dad, how did things go today on your job? Just how hard did you have to work? I don't think you have shared this information with me and Mother."

Astonished, his father looked at him. "Jeremiah, what is the matter with you son? Are you sick?"

"No, Dad, I'm not sick. I guess I worked too hard since coming home from school. May I be excused? I'm going to bed early."

"Of course, of course, my son. Maybe you are working too hard around the house." His father gave him a pat on his shoulder and wondered if this son of his was growing up too fast.

Jeremiah was breathing a little better as he felt that Priscilla's father would have called before now if he knew what he had done. Yes, the crisis was over, he thought as he crawled into bed. He promptly went to sleep. In a dream, a nightmare, there was a huge braid of honey-colored hair wrapped around his neck, slowly choking him to death.

Priscilla knew that Jeremiah was doing something to her braids. She tried to sit still, but in this delicious wonder, she started trembling in spite of herself. When school was dismissed, all the children started to leave for home. She waited for him to tug on her braids as he had always done. This time, however, he just jumped up and rushed out the door.

She waited until all the other children had left, and then Priscilla walked up to her teacher and shyly asked, "Miss Anderson, what is the matter with Jeremiah? He teases me so much. I really like him, but he keeps doing terrible things to me. He jumps out from behind a tree and tries to scare me. And when we're in line, he pinches me. Now just look what he has done." She showed her ink-stained braid.

"Priscilla, I am not laughing at you, but this little prank convinces me that God is still on His throne and all is right with the world. You see, Jeremiah likes you very much, and this is his way to get your attention. Would you like me to put you in a different seat?"

Priscilla's eyes glowed with merriment. "No, Miss Anderson, I think I shall continue to sit in front of this terrible person."

Miss Anderson hugged her. As she started to go home, she said, "Priscilla, when you get home, soak that lovely braid in a cup of milk before you wash it. It will remove the ink stains." She stood in the doorway and watched Priscilla skip happily down the road, braids flying behind her. One honey-colored, the other black with ink.

Jeremiah remembered the first kiss he gave her. There were times when he would manage to steal a little peck on her cheek, but this was his first real kiss. It happened the day their teacher, Miss Rose Anderson, dismissed the school early. She had been handed a note saying that her mother was gravely ill.

"Now children, I will have to leave, so get your studies and take them home and do them. I will let you know when I return."

The children grabbed their coats and lunch pails from the cloakroom and ran for home; Miss Anderson gathered her things and hurried off to see about her mother.

Priscilla and Jeremiah lingered. Jeremiah cleaned the blackboard, while Priscilla slowly went to the cloakroom for her coat. When she turned around, there he stood looking at her. He reached out and touched her satiny face then boldly took hold of her braids and gently pulled her to himself. His heart was pounding so loudly he knew she must have heard it; she didn't because her heart was racing also. He looked into her lovely gray-blue eyes. She closed them as he tenderly kissed her.

At first, she resisted a little, and then he felt her barriers go down one by one as she responded. Quivering in awe and wonderment, he started kissing her again. Frightened by the surging love that swelled between them, they quickly drew apart.

Priscilla grabbed her coat and lunch pail and ran toward home. In her hasty retreat, one of her red ribbons was lost. Jeremiah was standing at the door of the schoolroom watching her, and he saw the red treasure float down to the path. Smiling, he ran and picked it up. He kissed it and smelled her essence then tucked it into his pocket. "I am one lucky young man, oh yes, indeed."

Their love grew as the days, weeks, months, and now years slipped away. They lingered behind the other children, so they could be alone. Jeremiah's house was closer to the school, but he always walked her as far as he could without her father seeing him. Just holding her hand made him tremble and his heart race. They whispered their love for each other, sometimes just silently drinking in the sweetness of it.

With each passing day, Priscilla grew lovelier. She budded

and blossomed from a little girl to a bewitching and glowing young lady. Jeremiah shook with fear of her beauty. He was always fearful that he might lose her. His life was an up-and-down seesaw, as there were other young men who also worshiped her, but only from afar. Not even the young men from Whippoorwill High School dared challenge Jeremiah for her affections.

One afternoon, he was at the General Store, buying some supplies for his mother, when he caught a glimpse of Priscilla coming down the road. He grabbed his purchases and ran around the side of the store, so she could see him before she arrived at the porch. When she saw him, she ran into his arms. He pulled her to himself and hungrily kissed her over and over again. Suddenly, his tender and soft devotion changed, as he roughly pulled her tighter to him. He whispered hoarsely, "Oh, my sweetheart, what are we going to do?"

"Priscilla gave a gasp, "Well, if you continue your courtship very long this way, you will surely have squeezed me to death."

"Priscilla, how can you laugh at our love? I am always consumed by pain, knowing that I'm not allowed to be with you."

She pulled away from him, taunting and teasing him. "What has changed you from your tender, soft, lovemaking to this brash, insolent young man?" Although she said this in a mocking way, his actions seemed harder and more urgent. They frightened her.

They both were out of school now for the summer, and Jeremiah was working every day, and sometimes overtime, at the mill. He was frustrated by not seeing Priscilla as often as he wished. This frustration drove him to work harder than the other men. The only thing that consoled him was he knew she belonged to him.

One afternoon, as he stood looking out his bedroom window, he became filled with rage. He flew out the door and ran madly to the back fence that separated their land and began screaming, "Old man, she is mine. She belongs to me. If you don't let her come to me, I shall take her by force and then she will lie in my arms forever." Luckily for Jeremiah, the Brooks weren't home to hear his tirade.

One evening after supper, Jeremiah's father spread some legal papers out on the table. "My son, your mother and I have decided to deed our acreage, all 150 acres of it, and our house over to you. And we have a little nest egg, which will be yours. We know at our age things could happen to us.

"We thought out near the old fence stile would be a wonderful place for you to build a new house. It has a vast supply of water from Big Morgan Creek. That site has a view of the entire valley and of Paw Paw. And, my son, with a wink and a smile, this might encourage Priscilla's father to let you have his daughter. Anyway, whatever you decide, your mother and I will be there for you."

They were left speechless when Jeremiah emotionally hugged and kissed them both then rushed out of the house.

The moon was bright as day as his long legs brought him to the corner of his new property. He could see Priscilla's house; there was a light at an upstairs window. Could this be her bedroom? Was this where she slept? He had to find out. Coming down to earth, he could see what his father meant when he said this would be a glorious building site. "Oh, I shall build the most beautiful house in Paw Paw for my precious darling."

He ran back home. His mother was washing the dishes, but he grabbed her anyway and danced around the room with her. They all laughed and cried with so much happiness.

Jeremiah got very little sleep that night, thinking of his house. Someway and somehow he must get Priscilla to come and see where their new house would be. Could a miracle happen that she might come? Although Jeremiah scarcely prayed at all, he whispered a prayer to God as he fell asleep.

The next morning, he dressed up in his suit, necktie and all, because he was sure she would be at church. He rushed to the same seat he always sat in, and there she was coming in the door with her parents.

"Oh, what a ravishing beauty she is, and she's mine," he silently sighed. She smiled at him, but he didn't dare smile back as her wicked father would see him.

Jeremiah hardly dared to breathe when he saw her reach into her pocket and carefully drop a note on the floor under her seat. Shaking and all aquiver, he used the toe of his shoe to pull it, inch by inch, to himself. He gave a couple of coughs, pretending that was the reason for the various movements he was making. He didn't know that God had answered his prayers, that the answer was contained in the little note that was burning a hole in his pocket, the note he didn't dare read until the service was dismissed.

While he waited for the preacher to finish his sermon, he looked at his love's pretty little ears. "When I marry her, I'm going to buy her diamond earrings, a diamond necklace, and diamond combs to pin up her lovely curls."

Once outside, he read her note.

My darling,

My parents will be gone next Sunday, and if all goes well, I will meet you at the old stile in the morning.

Your love,

Priscilla

All week long, he worked like a man afire at the mill. His fellow laborers thought he had lost his mind, and, of a truth, this was so. He went to order the material to start his house. He bought his lumber at the mill where he worked with a huge discount. The other materials were ordered from Whippoorwill's wholesale house.

Every evening after he came home from work, he grabbed

a few bites of food and went to his property. All the while as he worked and planned, he sang his little song, "Jeremiah and Priscilla are in love."

Jeremiah arose at the breaking of the day Sunday morning. He wasn't going to church, he was going to the old stile to meet Priscilla. His mother scolded him. "Jeremiah, that child is not going to meet you this early." Her words never had any effect on him. He knew that if her folks were gone, Priscilla would be there early. He ate his breakfast, grabbed the plans for his house, and rushed out the door.

He sat down on the lower step of the old stile and began looking at his house plans again. He was so exhausted from the frenzied week, he rested his head on the upper step of the stile and fell asleep. He dreamed an angel was kissing him on his lips. Oh yes, this dream was true as he pulled his love down on himself. Jeremiah was barely able to control his love for her. He showed Priscilla his plans, and together they picked out the house site. Like little children, they gathered rocks and placed them where the rooms would be. Stopping to kiss as every room was finished, it was a slow project.

They ventured down the hill at the back of the house-to-be to a little wet-weather spring. Jeremiah said they should go across the stream to see their house from the other side. To get across, they had to step very carefully from stone to stone. Jeremiah had hold of Priscilla's hand to help her over. Once they made it to the other side, they began laughing joyfully as they fell down together in a bed of wild purple pansies that was like a soft velvet quilt.

They lay motionless, crushing the fragrant blooms. The perfumed essence enveloped them with fiery petals of love. They whispered their love to one another, as lovers have been wont to do from the beginning.

Jeremiah carefully picked up three velvet pansy stems, and slowly braided them together into a tiny ring, which he slipped on her wedding finger. "My darling, this is a token and keepsake of our love."

Priscilla closed her eyes and started to weep.

"What is the matter, honey?"

"Oh, my love, I am so happy."

He kissed her ring over and over, as Priscilla murmured, "I shall keep this forever."

They planned how to write notes to one another. "Jeremiah I will tie a note on a string and hang it out my bedroom window every Saturday night. Then you can tie your note on, and I will pull it in before Sunday morning."

All too soon, the day ended. Jeremiah was full of frustration, kissing her one minute, pacing back and forth where their house would be and threatening her father in another minute.

Taking her in his arms, he said, "My darling, unless a miracle happens for us, we will have to wait two years to marry. You will be eighteen then, and your father can't stop us. I have already concluded that it will take two years to build our house, which is going to be the finest in Paw Paw.

Then once again, Jeremiah shook a clenched fist toward her house, swearing out vengeance to her father. Priscilla began to shake and cry, trembling at his outburst. He pulled her close and said, "Oh, my darling, forgive me. Forgive me for the things I say. You are my love, my life giver for living, my flesh and my bones. When I think I can't have you for two years, I am beside myself with grief."

"Oh, Jeremiah, I must go now," Priscilla said, weeping openly.

"My beloved, write it on your calendar," Jeremiah said. "I shall do the same. June 9th, two years from today, shall be our wedding day. Run now, my love."

He watched her go. When almost out of sight, she turned and they waved to each other.

Behold, I will lay thy stones with fair colours,
and lay thy foundations with sapphires.
And I will make thy windows of agates,
and thy gates of carbuncles,
and all thy borders of pleasant stones.

ISAIAH 54:11-12

Chapter 38

Love and Hate Build a House

Jeremiah hurried back to his home, happy and elated, filled with excitement. He rushed into the house, grabbed his mother, and whirled her around in circles. "Oh Mother, Mother, she is going to marry me. What do you think of that?"

"Well Jeremiah, I knew she would, but don't you think she is a mite too young? Her father will never allow it, you know?"

Jeremiah called for his father to come and hear his plans. "Dad, Priscilla's overcome with happiness about the house site, but we certainly will have to wait until I get it built before we marry. We both decided to wait two years. I can build the house in that time, I think. She will be eighteen then, and her father can't stop us. We pledged our love for each other but feel it would be best to wait. I know I can't go and see her, but I'll see her at church and maybe at social doings."

He told them about the note exchanges once a week.

Impetuously, he grabbed the calendar off the wall and made a cross over the date. "Every day, Priscilla and I are going to mark off the days until we shall be together forever. In two years, I will be at her door, to take her by force if necessary. I am so happy. I have the best parents in all the world. Mom, can you get us supper? I found out that I can't live on love alone; I do need some nourishment to go along with it."

Jeremiah and his father sat down at the table and began

pouring over his house plans. The kitchen could hardly contain the excitement of the Jones family.

Jeremiah arose before daylight the next morning, still basking in the flow of the wild purple pansy day. He rushed straight to his house site and began taking measurements. The forms had to be built before the foundation could be poured. Jeremiah knew his father would help him, as he was almost as excited as Jeremiah was. He hurried back home and was barely able to snatch a few bites of his breakfast before he had to rush to his job at the mill. Later, he and his father worked at the site until dark drove them home. He ate a quick supper and immediately went to bed. Jeremiah didn't dream of castles in Spain, but he did dream of the castle he was going to build for his ladylove.

In his fervor and zeal, he worked like a madman both at the mill and on his house. His coworkers were not very happy, as his leadership required them to work harder. They complained to him to slow down a little, but he pushed their complaints aside and went on in his hectic, frantic pace.

His father and mother were not the only ones worried and anxious about him. His actions caused a little stir and enlivened the conversation of the men on the porch of the General Store.

Jeremiah had rushed by them one day and just gave them a nod. Then after getting his supplies, he rushed out the same way, without so much as a word. They all shook their heads in disbelief.

Fred Pinkham commented, "Jeremiah, he is going to work himself to death if he keeps up that pace. He won't be here to live in his house or with Priscilla either. If you ask me, he looks like death warmed over. And I heard Granny Octavia say that his eyes look like two burnt holes in a blanket."

They all agreed that this description fit Jeremiah Jones.

On the hill overlooking the purple pansy bed were large, glistening alabaster stones. They were breathtakingly beautiful.

Jeremiah began to probe and delve into the ground and was elated when they proved to be easy to unearth. He hauled them down to his house for the magnificent fireplace he was building in his living room. He dared not haul them over the purple pansy bed, so he had to take a much longer path around them. At every load, he would stop and remember their love tryst.

On one trip, he was tired and exhausted, so he lay down on the velvety quilt that he and his Priscilla had lain on together. He rested and remembered the wedding ring he made for her and the purple corsage he had tucked between her breasts. He even remembered that the moist petals had been crushed in their embrace and left a trace of purple on one breast. He lost the joy of this yesterday yearning when he thought of Rufus Brooks, Priscilla's father. From somewhere deep inside him arose an uncontrollable hatred that overshadowed his love for Priscilla. When those hateful thoughts clouded his mind, all he knew to do was to work and labor harder on his house.

Rufus was the one who stood between the lovers. He was a wicked tyrant who controlled everyone and everything in that house. For sure, he wasn't going to let any young man court his daughter.

The weeks, months, and a year had passed. The neighbors, townspeople, and the men on the porch were stunned at the progress of Jeremiah's house, especially since they knew that all the work had been done while he was still working at the mill. However, a few whispers could be heard here and there that perhaps, just maybe, Jeremiah's mind was slipping away.

Jeremiah's mother and father were frantic yet felt helpless as they watched their beloved son destroying himself. They scolded and threatened, but he pushed aside their words as he rushed back and forth to his house.

The house was finished on the outside, and he began in earnest to finish the inside and also to build his furniture. He ordered a huge kitchen stove and the latest style of icebox. He put running water and a pitcher-pump by the sink. He had abundant water supplied by Big Morgan Creek.

His father quit helping him as his health was failing. And he could no longer face his son day after day and witness the mysterious changes in him.

Half the time Jeremiah never came home to eat, so his mother brought his meals out to him. She also brought him clean changes of clothes, although there was little reason for that as he seldom changed his clothes anymore. She brought wool blankets for him, and he used them when he slept in front of the fireplace. He quit shaving and failed to get his hair cut. He became a fearful-looking character and the little children looked warily at him. Some of the townspeople looked in pity at this disheveled young man who had been so handsome in days gone by.

In the beginning, it was subtle. It wasn't anything that a person could really lay a finger on. It first started when Jeremiah quit writing his notes to Priscilla on Saturday nights. His mother called this to his attention, and he was surprised by the fact. Then she began helping him write them and he took them to the window where the white string was waiting.

One night, as he was leaving his love note, he was so overcome with fatigue that he lay down under Priscilla's window and fell asleep. When he awakened, his clothes were wet with dew and the shape of his body was outlined on the crushed grass.

Jeremiah built a wide circular staircase in his living room leading to the upstairs bedrooms. He never tired of going up and down the elegant stairs, caressing the rail, sliding his hands on the polished wood that gleamed like glass. As he stroked the banister, he whispered in his madness, "Oh, my darling, how lovely you are. How soft your face. You feel like the velvet petals in our bed of wild purple pansies."

At times, there was a voice that he heard when his love for Priscilla overcame him. "You are not going to have her, you know," it taunted.

Then immediately came a spirit of bitterness and hatred for her father. Jeremiah realized that in some terrible way, he was being controlled by an evil spirit, a spirit that was pressing him down, pushing him back and forth. He loved his house the way he loved Priscilla. Why, he was in love with them both. How could this be? What was happening to him? It was insane to think a man would love a house the same way as a girl he would marry. Yet his house became a shrine, and his massive fireplace became his altar as he knelt and slept before it night after night.

Somewhere, somehow, Jeremiah had turned his mind and soul from his living God to worship a dead, lifeless god of wood and stone. And a deep dark anger, filled with the spirit of hatred for Rufus Brooks, had gained a foothold in his heart and his being.

Jeremiah sat in front of his altar of worship and fell asleep.

The little calendar on the wall beside the magnificent fireplace had been sadly neglected. No X's had been made on it in a long time. And he didn't realize that the two long years had come to an end.

And in the latter time of their kingdom,
when the transgressors are come to the full,
a king of fierce countenance, and understanding
dark sentences, shall stand up . . . and he shall destroy
wonderfully, and . . . he shall magnify himself in his heart,
and by peace shall destroy many:
he shall also stand up against the Prince of princes;
but he shall be broken without hand.

DANIEL 8:23-25

Chapter 39

The Beating

Priscilla ran upstairs to her room and looked in the mirror over her dresser to see if her lips were bruised, the color of the pansies from the passionate kiss Jeremiah gave her when he said good-bye. Gleefully, she took her flower-stem wedding ring off and tucked it between the pages of her diary book. Then she began writing page after page about this most beautiful day of her life, the day she would always remember as the wild purple pansy day. The fragrance of the pansies created an aura around her and her little diary that was now embellished with purple petals.

She made the first cross on her calendar; she would make one every day for the next two years until Jeremiah came to take her away and they could be married.

Endless days, weeks, months, and now a year passed by, yet still the only time they saw each other was at church. She looked forward to the love notes they exchanged. On Saturday nights she hung a little string from her window, and they would tie their notes to it.

Then excited one day, she wrote a long letter to him.

Oh, my darling,

Mother has bought several skeins of crochet thread. And she is teaching me how to crochet beautiful scarves and doilies, how to put edges on pillowslips and how to make a tablecloth for our table. And I am going to crochet a bedspread for our bed. Oh, my darling, can you feel me blushing? The way I have it figured, these tasks will keep me busy until you come for me. I can only work on my crochet work when father is gone.

I love you so much. I think of the wild purple pansy day constantly!

Your love, Priscilla

Then a series of events happened that Priscilla didn't understand. One Saturday night, Jeremiah didn't tie his note on the little string. In some questioning and wondering way, it frightened her. When she wrote him, asking him why, he answered her and asked her forgiveness for not remembering.

His notes began to take on new meanings that she didn't fully grasp and left her with a feeling of apprehension and uneasiness. She tried to read between the lines of his words. What was he alluding to? She was anxious to go to church because she was sure that if she saw him, she would get an answer to her bewilderment somehow. She needed to quiet her fears.

When they arrived at church the next day, her father did an unexplainable thing. He guided them to the opposite side of the church. Why, they had never sat on that side. What had happened? She felt it was because Jeremiah always sat behind them. She gave a glance at Jeremiah sitting in the same place he had for years. Her heart and soul ached. The pain reached up and filled her eyes with hard dry tears. She knew that Jeremiah couldn't move behind them, her father would immediately know why. Jeremiah would know that she would be punished by her father. To add to Priscilla's distress, Jeremiah quit going to church after that.

Jeremiah's mother kept a close eye on Priscilla at church on Sundays. She watched this precious girl wane and grow pale, the laughter and sparkle in her eyes fade away. Priscilla had always given her a certain shy tender smile because she was Jeremiah's mother, but that seldom happened anymore. She knew that Priscilla was living in the depths of despair over the changes in her son. "I am with you, my dear Priscilla. I do not know the reason for these changes, and I see him every day, my precious little friend," she whispered to herself.

Through the second year of waiting, it was a year of winter sorrows for them both. Finally it was finished, just as Jeremiah predicted. Both of his parents came over one day and walked through his magnificent house. Jeremiah was delighted they had come but was a little disappointed in their lack of enthusiasm.

Jeremiah knew there had been drastic changes going on inside him these past few months. He didn't understand what it was but knew he was being continually torn apart in this strange relationship between his love for his house and his love for Priscilla.

Then his father ventured, "Jeremiah, I hope you know that you promised to marry Priscilla in a few days. I don't want you hurting that lovely girl. It's high time you get your priorities straight in this baffling world you have moved into." With those words they walked out the door.

All week long, Priscilla read and reread Jeremiah's last note. In it, he said that he would come for her at the stroke of midnight Saturday night. She lay awake all night with the note between her breasts, just as the bouquet of purple pansies had lain, knowing that tomorrow would be her freedom day.

She heard her mother starting breakfast, heard her father's heavy footsteps. Did he hesitate a moment by her door? This was the day that Jeremiah would come and take her away, yet she was filled with panic. She was tormented by a fear that almost overshadowed love. She was afraid of her father, of course, but also of Jeremiah. Why? She knew that every minute of this day she must act normal, calm and composed. She surprised herself as she nonchalantly sat down at the table.

As usual, there was no greeting to each other. Her father just handed her a hot biscuit and then the bowl of gravy. She managed to eat a few bites and swallowed them too. Then her father broke the deadly silence. Turning to her mother, he said, "Finny Lou, I think we might have a prowler around. It could be a big dog. I found the grass matted down below Priscilla's window. So we need to be on close watch, and I'm going to carry my gun with me."

He never looked toward Priscilla, which was fortunate, as she could feel the blood drain from her face and icy fear clutch her throat. Did he know? If he were looking for some reaction from her, he would surely have looked at her, wouldn't he? Was this a warning or tantalizing torment, which he was so skillful at? He enjoyed playing with his victims. Yes, he knew about Jeremiah coming for her. No, maybe he didn't know. Either way, she had to continue in this deadly game. She had no way to let Jeremiah know that her father was carrying a gun. Again, that icy fear grabbed her throat, and she gave a little sigh as she fell faint onto the kitchen floor.

She awakened to find her mother kneeling beside her and washing her face with cold water. She was crying, "Priscilla, Priscilla, my baby. What is the matter with you, my darling?" She opened her eyes just as her father went out the door without once glancing in her direction. Her mother helped her up the stairs to her room.

Her mother was still crying and weeping. "Mother, I'm all right. Can't you see? I'm all right now. I was just dizzy, that's all. I'm going to lie down a little while."

Priscilla didn't leave her room all day. Her mother brought her soup and some buttered toast, which she forced herself to eat. She became more in control of herself. She knew this day would take clear thinking. It was important not only for Jeremiah, but also for herself. Their happiness was dependent on her getting away. Her biggest fear now was her father and the gun he had beside him.

Priscilla lay motionless on her bed. She held her little

alarm clock close. The bright moonbeams slipped through her window, giving her enough light to watch the time. She knew she must do something to make the time pass more quickly, so she got her diary out and with trembling hands wrote her last entry in it.

> My Dear Diary, my close friend for many years,
>
> He will be here tonight, you know. My sweet love will take me with him.
>
> We will be married and I shall lay in his arms forever.

She breathed deeply of the wild purple pansy ring that she had pressed between the pages of her book. There was no fragrance anymore, and as she held them in her hands, they crumbled to the floor and lay in ruins, looking like colorless ashes at her feet. Hot burning tears gathered in strength, fell, and mingled with the symbol of their love. Why was she crying? Was this an omen, the forewarning of a storm cloud on the horizon? How foolish these thoughts were. Why, in just a few minutes, she would be in his arms and there she would stay forever!

She hastily dressed but carried her shoes in her hand. She knew where each squeak in the floor was and the squeaks in the doors. The grandfather clock nearby pealed out its message that midnight had come to Rufus Brooks, Finny Lou, and Priscilla's house.

As Priscilla slipped out the back door, the man in the moon was shining forth in all of his glory. She didn't see the black, ominous specter beside the big oak tree. It melted and huddled into the tree's dark trunk. No one just walking by could see it. Priscilla didn't see the brightness of the moon reflecting off the cold blue steel of the deadly weapon in the hand of her father.

What was keeping him? She was so weak she had to sit down where her lover had slept long ago. What had happened to him? A hoarse whisper gathered in her throat as she started to pray to her Lord. However, He too seemed not to hear. What must she do? Where could she go? He said he would be there to get her.

Priscilla became horror-stricken, paralyzed with fear, when her father stepped out of the shadows, holding the blue cruel gun in his hand. He began screaming at her. "Oh, now I see! You have been meeting him here, night after night. I should have known you weren't any good, with that beautiful face of yours. I should have known that men would be hanging around you. Now I know what kind of daughter I have. A good-for-nothing tramp of the streets."

He continued to scream at her. "So, this is why he built that fancy new house. The men told over and over about the furniture that he built for some ladylove. Well, here is something you need to hear. You will never live in that new house and neither will he!"

Priscilla struggled to tell him she hadn't been meeting him, but only gurgling sounds came from her throat.

"Shut up and get to your room!" he roared.

When Priscilla struggled to her feet, he kicked her so hard she fell down again in the matted grass where her lover had slept. She crawled through the kitchen door and up the stairs to her room. She quickly locked her door and lay down on her bed.

Then she heard two shots ring out.

"Oh, he has shot Jeremiah." She started screaming in terror, but no sound did she make. Rigid with fear, she heard the kitchen door slam. She heard her father slowly come up the stairs. There were eleven steps; she counted them one by one.

He tried to turn the doorknob, but she had locked it. So he took his booted foot and crashed open the door, leaving it in splinters. He stood in the doorway with a huge leather strap in his hand, fire raging from his eyes. First, he looked at the doll-house she used to play with when she was a little girl. He demolished it. Then he saw her diary book lying beside her. Laughing like a madman, he read it through then dropped it to the floor and ground it in circles under his heavy boot.

Priscilla sat up in bed to talk to him, but he made a big lunge at her and slapped her on both sides of her face. She fell back, trying to turn her face from him. Then he took the leather strap and, possessed by a legion of demons, began to beat her until blood seeped through her blouse. Just as she fell into the waters of oblivion, she heard her mother screaming. "What are you doing? Are you going to kill her? If you are, you will have to kill me first."

He turned and looked at his wife and slammed her down on the floor. Then, with a dazed cruel look on his face, he stumbled out the door, down the stairs, and out the kitchen door into the darkness.

Then the earth shook and trembled; the foundations
also of the hills moved and were shaken,
because he was wroth. . . .
He made darkness his secret place;
his pavilion round about him were dark waters
and thick clouds of the skies. At the brightness
that was before him his thick clouds passed,
hail stones and coals of fire.

PSALM 18:7,11-12

Chapter 40

The Fiery Furnace

Jeremiah's mother was restless. With eyes wide open, she began thinking again of her beloved son and the changes in him. What could she have done to help him? Had she missed something that only a mother would know? She heard their clock in the living room, chiming forth the midnight hour. Wide-awake now she thought, Isn't this the night Jeremiah is to go get Pricilla? She had been crossing the days off on the calendar; Jeremiah had stopped doing it. She knew that Jeremiah's salvation would depend upon Priscilla. She jumped up, put on a robe, and raced to Jeremiah's new house.

She burst through the door, screaming. "Jeremiah! Jeremiah! This is the night for you to go get Priscilla. Did you forget? You do still love her, don't you? Are you going to get her?"

Jeremiah leaped to his feet. "Mother, I forgot. Yes, I love her. You know I have always loved her. How could I have fallen asleep on this night, the night I have waited for for so long? Yes, for two years."

He grabbed a jacket and rushed out the door. He jumped into his car and raced like mad down the road. "Oh yes, she will be mine tonight. I shall carry her over our threshold in just a little while." He was laughing and crying for joy. "I intended to bathe, put on clean clothes, and I intended to get my hair cut and to shave off my beard, as I do intend to kiss her all night long. We will go and be married early in the morning." He was overwhelmed in his joy.

Jeremiah parked his car behind some trees across the road from her house and ran to the window beneath her bedroom. Priscilla was not there. What had happened? Rufus! Oh yes, Rufus had found her. Everything was silent, too silent. Rufus had found her, of course.

"He is waiting for me," Jeremiah said through clenched teeth. "Well, I shall be glad to meet him. I shall be glad if I can kill him."

Crazed with hate, he pounded on the back door with his fists and began screaming, "Old man, don't you know she is mine. She has always been mine. If you don't believe me, ask her. Don't you know she has been with me every day as I built a house for her? We planned it together. The floors, the doors, they were all designed with her in mind. She is mine forever."

The reason Jeremiah received no answer was that Priscilla's mother, Finny Lou, was holding her silent, beaten daughter in her arms, and in their misery, they never heard any sound.

The door he was pounding on was locked, and he was just about to kick it in when he saw a bright orange flame, like a meteor or a mass of falling stars, bursting across the sky. He forgot the door and raced toward his house. Above the flames, ominous clouds soared with black plumage above the carnage below.

As Jeremiah ran, he heard the loud popping sound of glass windows exploding, and then he heard a larger burst and knew it was the big oval stained glass in his front door. Just as he arrived, the timbers were crashing down one by one. Then he saw his big curved stairway ablaze. Raging fire whirled and swirled in a big fiery circle, likened to a funeral wreath as it engulfed the last remnants of his dream house.

Then came a silence, a sweet sickening silence that Jeremiah felt and tasted on his tongue. He sank to the ground as a piercing knife plunged through his heart and soul.

If perchance someone happened by, they would have been repelled by the sight of a wild grotesque figure on the ground curling into the shape of a fetus in the womb.

His parents came. His father stood on one side of him and his mother on the other. They put their arms around him as they knelt and wept for their beloved son.

They found his body in the smoldering blackened ashes stretched across the threshold. He had tried to crawl away from his fiendish crime. His body was burnt to a crisp, yet still clutched in Rufus Brook's claw-like hand was the gasoline can, which had held satanic witches brew.

As the daystar brought forth its first glow of morning, the three figures were still kneeling before Jeremiah's house, his shrine, and his altar. The massive fireplace was still standing, but the black smoke had covered over the sparkling and glistening lights of the alabaster stones, the stones from the wild pansy bed.

After eons, Jeremiah arose in total madness. "Mother, I'm going to get Priscilla and bring her home."

Will a man rob God?
Yet ye have robbed me.
But ye say, Wherein have we robbed thee?
In tithes and offerings.

MALACHI 3:8

Chapter 41

Will a Man Rob God?

The little town of Paw Paw absolutely reeled and rocked on its heels, no ifs and no buts about it. But it took three days before the truth really sank in. As soon as he learned the facts, Otis Simpson, Jimmy C.'s dad, wanted to run out right away and tell his friends, the men who sat on the porch of the General Store, this unbelievable story.

"Now Dad, I want you to act nonchalant when you tell them of this," Jimmy had told him. Then Jimmy had to coach his dad for a while on the meaning and pronunciation of the word nonchalant.

Although Otis was quivering with excitement and his skin blossomed with goose bumps, he casually meandered up the steps of the General Store. He was disappointed that his friends had not yet arrived, but that gave him time to think of just how to announce his son's fantastic good fortune.

Finally, the others arrived and got themselves settled in. Otis passed around the "baccy" before he said anything. He was silent until they had all taken a big chew. They were almost ready to spit when he began his tale.

"You know my friends, something unusual has happened to my Jimmy C." He knew he was acting nonchalant now, as no one had asked what it was. Therefore, he tried again. "My friends, do you remember the day that Tibet Grey gave him that little runt of a dog? I'm sure you never forgot how his new wife, Ella May, drowned most of that litter in the rain barrel, did you?"

"Otis, if you have something to say, just go ahead and say it," grumbled Fred Pinkham.

Oh, how I'm relishing this, Otis thought to himself. "Okay Fred, I'm talking about that little runt dog, the one he named Goliath. Well, my Jimmy sold that dog last night for, are you ready for this, five hundred dollars!"

The men on the porch were too stunned to speak. Miss Idy often commented that they acted like they were dead from the neck up, and this was a perfect example. Instead of spitting, Amos was so dazed he swallowed his brown tobacco juice.

Still acting nonchalant, Otis continued. "Well, my friends, it all came about on this wise. Without telling his mother or me, Jimmy began to hunt with Goliath. We should have noticed something was up as Jimmy's grades in school took a dip and sometimes he was late in delivering the newspaper. He didn't stop and chat with his customers as much, and he had nothing to report to the newspaper. Plus, we never heard any money dropping into that coffee can under his bed. Now that in itself should have told us something strange was going on.

"Well, the reason for all these changes in him was that some nights he'd crawl out his window and go hunting with Goliath. He was worn out from lack of sleep. Course we didn't know that. I even warned him one day that if he didn't straighten up and stop his dilly-dallying around, he wasn't too old to take to the woodshed."

Oh, how I'm enjoying this nonchalant way of telling this story, Otis again thought to himself.

The men were staring at him, dazed, with their mouths hanging limp and loose. And they were failing to eject the brown juice!

"Now, you all know about those big black fancy pickups we have seen going by. Well, the men in those cars would drive them into the woods and meet my Jimmy there. They brought their own dogs and Jimmy brought Goliath, and together they would hunt 'coon all night.

"Then last night it all came to a head when one of the men said he wanted to buy Goliath. At first, Jimmy said no, but when the man offered five hundred dollars cash for him, Jimmy reluctantly turned the dog over.

"Me and Maudie grieved for him, of course, as this was a decision that fairly broke his heart. Then he said something that made Maudie and me very proud. He said that he wanted the money so that he and his two brothers, Pete and Repete, could go to college. Now, I hadn't said anything about college to the kids because I realized it was just a dream. I knew we wouldn't ever have the finances for it."

"Yes, my friends, I'm kinda proud of my son," Otis proclaimed nonchalantly.

Miss Idy didn't hear about Jimmy C.'s good fortune with Goliath until the next day when she opened her paper. There, spread across the front page, was the story and the amount he received, five hundred dollars.

Where money was concerned, Miss Idy's eyes and ears became like radar—not for herself, but for the church. She grabbed her Bible, quickly underlined the scriptures on tithes and offerings, and raced to Jimmy C.'s residence. She knocked loudly and he opened the door. "Well, dear Jimmy C., I just wanted to stop by and congratulate you on your good fortune. All of Paw Paw is abuzz with it. Truthfully, I am here for a reason, so I will make my spiritual speech. Jimmy, as chairman of the church deacons, I wonder if you have given any thought to tithing any of it. Offering 10 percent of your good fortune to the church would amount to fifty dollars.

"All the church would thank you for your generous contribution, and I, myself, would see to it that it does not get squandered. I realize that you might think this is truly filthy lucre and that it could be called tainted money as it has come to you through the questionable manner of selling Goliath.

But Jimmy, I am sure that I have the answer for that. We all know that when we give, we're not to let the left hand knoweth what the right hand doeth. But if you bring the fifty dollars to church on Sunday and calmly without any fanfare lay it on the men's altar and let it lay there throughout the Reverend's sermon, I think that would cleanse it and sanctify it. As a matter of fact, I am sure of it." She opened her Bible and read it to Jimmy. "'Honor the Lord with thy substance and with the first fruits of all thine increase. So shall thy barns be filled with plenty and thy presses shall burst with new wine.' I am certain you don't believe in drinking wine, this is just a proverb, you know."

"Well, my dear Jimmy, it has been delightful talking to you. And just as an afterthought, I'm sure you will continue to be successful in the hound-dog business." Then Miss Idy turned and fairly skipped down the road. She never even came into the house.

Jimmy C. Simpson, dazed and befuddled, closed the door and braced his back against it.

But his word was in mine heart
as a burning fire shut up in my bones.

JEREMIAH 20:9

Chapter 42

The Calling of Miss Idy Crandall

It had been too hot for man or beast for several days. All the horses, cows, and dogs lay lifeless. It was the same for the men on the porch. Jacob had given away the last hand-fan that advertised the General Store to a cute little housewife with her first baby. Clara had watched the harmless little gesture and pouted and sulked all morning in jealousy. Of course, Jacob, man-like, had no idea of Clara's surly and crabby attitude so was unprepared for her announcement.

"Now Jacob, I'm going in the back to get into a cool bath to get some relief from this terrible heat, so you mind the store." She was still irritated when she got down the number three washtub and filled it with cool water. One always had a difficult time sitting down in it, but she finally accomplished the feat. She basked in its comfort and consoled herself in the cool water.

Jacob stood at the screen door, looking over the lifeless bits of flotsam and jetsam of humanity that graced his porch. A stab of pity for his friends came over him. He made a big bucket of cool lemonade and took it out to the men. "Now my brothers, if you have the strength to hold these glasses, I have a little treat for you."

"Oh Jacob, 'pears to me we can rally around for such an 'endowment' as my son, Jimmy C., would say," remarked Otis.

All of a sudden, there was a loud uproar as a car came

speeding down the road, a whirlwind of dust encircling the driver and car.

"Well, who in tarnation could be recklessly gallivanting around in this heat?" exclaimed Amos.

Before they could guess, the car came to a screeching halt in front of the porch and a rather hefty man crawled out waving his hands.

"Well, I'll be switched. It's Henry Thompson from Junction City." Fred Pinkham yelled out to him, "You old scalawag, get up here and I'll give you the best and most comfortable chair on the porch. It has a woven inner tube seat that expands to everyone's curves. It appears to me you will need this expanding piece of furniture."

As Henry had to use the wobbly banister to come up the steps, the men later on would have a rousing conversation about whether his health had diminished or whether he had eaten too many biscuits and gravy.

Henry Thompson had moved away from Paw Paw over three years ago. He had fallen in love with a pretty little girl named Cary McPherson. He wanted to live in Paw Paw, but Cary had lived in Junction City all her life and she was not going to live anywhere else. So like Adam in the Garden of Eden, Henry had succumbed to his pretty little Cary's wiles and cunning and had moved from Paw Paw.

Cary's father had spent his entire life in one political scheme or another. Using the conniving methods thought up in back rooms filled with cigar smoke, he managed to stay just shy of breaking the law. When his lovely child married Henry, he immediately convinced Henry that one could have a very cushy living in politics and not by working one's hands to the bone.

"Howdy, boys, howdy. I can plainly see you are still sitting in those same chairs you were when I left here three years ago." Henry remarked.

They greeted each other with slaps on the back, laughing

and taunting. Jeremiah said, "Now Henry, we can see that you have prospered quite well since you left us. Instead of eating pickled pigs feet, looks like you have crawled a little higher on the animal and are now feasting on hickory smoked ham."

They joked, kidded, and pestered each other as they remembered the fun and the escapades of past years.

"Well, my old friends, I have to tell you I am on a mission coming here today. I am running for mayor of Junction City and tax collector thereabouts. I know you can't vote for me, but I thought maybe someone might drop by the store here that would likely be voting material for me. I know all about your pleasing personalities and winning ways, and your handsome faces do indeed carry a lot of weight hereabouts."

"But Henry, asserted Tom Curry, "in my opinion you are defeating your purpose, aren't you? If you take that hated position of tax collector, they won't vote for you to have the mayor's duties. And, look at this big new car you drive, we know you have to be either doing something right or doing something underhanded in that political field you're in."

They laughed and spun a few more yarns about Paw Paw and its citizens.

"Well, my dear brothers, I must be on my way. Jacob could I have another swig of the lemonade?" Henry asked.

Jacob filled his glass. He drank it and started to step off the porch when he looked down the road and caught a glimpse of Miss Idy going into her house. "Well, I'll be a monkey's uncle, if that isn't Miss Idy Crandall."

The men exclaimed as one, "Do you know her, Henry? We have asked far and near for someone to tell us about her, but nary a word has come to our ears!"

"Boys, I hope I can do justice to who and what Miss Idy was when I knew her. She wasn't what a man would call a drop-dead beauty; she was more like an angel, within and without. She gave the appearance and made one think she was on talking terms with someone a little higher than us mortals.

My friends, she was as cute as a speckled pup, oh yes, she was."

"She was the only child of Pansy Crandall's. We didn't know who her father was and for sure, Pansy Crandall never revealed this secret to us. There was another secret Pansy; she fell heir to a little sum of money, (of course we believed from her father) and she used that money to send Miss Idy up north to go to college. But mind you, even with all that education, she still had the ability to make herself one of us when she moved back. She was always involved in everything and would help anyone who needed her. Oh yes indeedy, she was the cream to skim off the top of the crock of milk. She was the sweetheart of Junction City. If we had ever had a contest for the most beautiful woman in town, Miss Idy would have worn the crown."

"Everyone thought she would marry up north, but no, she came back. There she was an 'old maid,' everyone whispered. But to be truthful, there wasn't much in Junction City to pick from." Then Henry gave a smirky grin, "You must understand I was already married."

This brought on loud laughter from the men.

"Then on account of her high education, she went to work for old Judge Marshy in his law office. We all know Miss Idy went through much tribulation in working for the judge. He was always in a foul mood and mean too. The talk was bandied about that he took money on the sly to keep some young men out of jail, for certain, if the boy's parents had a little money, he drained it from them."

"Then the unheard of happened. Miss Idy announced she was going to marry him. It sure shook us up. Everyone felt sorry for her, but they all said she knew how he was since she'd worked for him so long. Everyone also knew Miss Idy was real smart, what with her college education and living in the city and all. Some thought the reason she was going to marry him was because he was a high-up judge; we just didn't know. We all thought he was a dyed-in-the-wool bachelor. He had a high seat over at the county court. We knew his caseload had been over burdened with all the shenanigans going on in the community; moonshine stills, cockfights, dog fights, and a big gambling ring.

"Everyone loved Miss Idy so much, including my wife, Cary. The women went hog-wild in the preparation of this wedding. They were in the height of their glory. Pansy, her mother, passed away and left Miss Idy a tidy little sum, so she tried to spend it all on this wedding. For sure, we had never seen the like. They painted the church house, washed scrubbed, and varnished every little spot. While this was going on, Sadie Meade, our seamstress, just plain moved into Miss Idy's house. She made Miss Idy's silk and satin white wedding dress, fancy lace nightgowns, and other things you will have to guess. They ordered a new white hat and white slippers from the city."

"Now my friends, here is something that you never heard of. It is called a wedding shower. Not the kind that God sends just in time to save our crops and gardens. This is a shower of presents, gifts for the judge and Miss Idy. Well, this was one time I opened my mouth. I innocently stated this could be construed as begging. Well, all those Baptist ladies jumped all over me, and my Cary was the biggest spoke in the wheel. I still wanted to find out where this shower thing came from, so Cary wrote her shirttail cousin, a high-falutin, hoity-toity gal who lives in the big city. She wrote back that it was the latest fashion thing they were doing. So, it was announced far and wide that everyone would bring the presents to the church on the wedding day. While all the ladies were setting the food for dinner, Miss Idy and the judge would open their gifts."

"Then came the dawn of the wedding day."

"Under some dire threats to my very life, we had rushed to the church. I was burdened down with an armful of Cary's fresh flowers. Never mind that I was in another attack of my asthma. Well, it turned out we weren't the first to arrive. One of Miss Idy's cousins was there. And, my friends, there tied to a tree was the prettiest Jersey milk cow you ever saw. This fella had put a huge white bow on top of her head. He told us that she gave four gallons of milk a day that was like sweet cream. When Cary was out of hearing, he informed me that she was bred to the finest bull in the country."

"Now this is not all. In a chicken crate was a huge rooster, a mother hen, and twelve baby chicks just chirping away. They were all Dominekers, which I am most partial to. And, tacked to one newly painted wall of the church was a beautiful flower-garden quilt made by the Sewing Circle of the church. Alongside, they had tacked a huge goose-down feather bed. Under that sat a big chicken crate of the six geese that had given their part and portion in the making of this outstanding gift. Well, I shall not bore you with all the other gifts to our sweet little Miss Idy, but it all resembled the opening day at the county fair."

"I almost forgot, Miss Idy was going to sing the judge a love song when they stepped up to the altar. My Cary said this would be an unexpected gift to the judge. Oh, say, you guys, I guess you really enjoy Miss Idy's singing. That was one of the best blessings we had from her."

No one answered, and Henry seemed to be looking toward heaven as if searching for an angel.

Barely missing a beat, he continued. "Yes indeed, she could sing the birds out of the trees, soothe little old ladies out of their ailments, stop the babies and children of their fussing and whimpering, and remind us old men of our youth when we were caught up in the sweetness of our first love affair." Suddenly Henry, a little embarrassed from his reminiscing of her, wiped his eyes, cleared his throat, and returned to his story.

"All the ladies brought their potted blooming plants to church. They set them across the front and tied big white satin bows on them. They hung bows on the end of the benches. The wedding was scheduled to start at ten in the morning.

"Well, like I said, the big day arrived and what did all the ladies do but gather at Miss Idy's home to dress her. Mind now here, my Cary used these very words 'to dress her.' This made me a mite flustered, and I said that was nonsense as Miss Idy had been dressing herself for years. I was clean taken aback again by the words my Cary used on me. I don't want to quote them as some of our children might hear about them. My sweet patient Cary had become a snarling critter overnight.

"This is not all tomfoolery. Mercy, sakes no.

"I and Matt Horner, the judge's best man—and between you and me and the fence post, I would hate to see a worst man appearing for a wedding—we had to go the judge's chambers and escort him to the ceremony. Now the judge hadn't been escorted since he was five years old. Dear friends, I think you know what happened during the night. The judge had fled, neither hide nor hair could be found of him. Someone said later that he had run away and joined the army. I don't think so; he was too old for that. And it wouldn't be too good for his health if he came back to Junction City, I'll tell you.

"Boys, this story about Miss Idy gets worse. However, you must take into account and remember that old saying, 'God works in mysterious ways,' just to keep us mortals on the alert. I'm sure you can imagine what our Miss Idy was going through. With the embarrassment and all, she sank into a kinda depression. She locked herself in her house for weeks. Once in a while, she would let a lady or two come in and they would prepare her something to eat. My Cary said that if something didn't happen, she would starve herself to death.

"Well, that something did happen, and it goes like this. One of those circuit-riding preachers came by to start a protracted, long, drawn-out revival. Of course, several attended. The windows were all open, and he had a thundering voice that easily carried outside of the church. There was the usual group of men sitting under the windows and against the trees outside. They were whittling, spitting, bragging on which one's hunting dog was best. Of course, their women folks were inside the church.

"Every night the preacher plainly and grimly took for his text 'the flames below' but seldom preached on that realm above. Therefore, his audience grew smaller every night with no results. He thought he might have a breakthrough of new converts, but it just didn't happen. One night, the Laurence kid, who was about eight or nine years old, got tired with the long sermon and lay down on one of the benches next to a window and went to sleep. One of our teenage young men got a long switch, reached in the window, and gave him a hard blow across his body. Well, Laurence gave out a loud scream that fairly stopped the preacher's sermon. He thought he had a new convert, but when he discovered what had really happened, he announced he would close the revival the next night.

"Now here it gets very interesting. My Cary went over to Miss Idy's house and begged her to come to the last night of the revival. I was right proud of my Cary, as Miss Idy came with her. When Miss Idy walked in, everyone was happy to see her. She looked like warmed-over death for sure, but we thought she would be better as she had taken her first step to pulling herself together and to being around those who loved her.

"My friends, from here on out, the story will be hard for you to believe but this is true, let me assure you. The preacher read his text as usual about fire and brimstone, and then a sudden stillness came over him as if he was lost somewhere. Everyone looked at one another. Then he kinda shook his head and announced, 'I have changed my mind, let us turn to the first book of Corinthians, Chapter 7, verse 34.' He read, 'There is a difference also between a wife and a virgin. The unmarried careth for the things of the Lord, that she may be holy both in body and in the spirit. She that is married careth for the things of the world, how she might please her husband.' To cap it all off, the preacher reached into his case, got a small bottle of oil, and dipped his finger in it. Then he walked back to Miss Idy, laid the spot of oil on Miss Idy's head, and said, 'You have been chosen and anointed by God to do marvelous things.' Everyone within hearing distance, and that included the men outside the windows, shook in their boots.

"Miss Idy rushed to the 'altar of repentance' as he called it. That wasn't all. Several dyed-in-the-wood sinners rushed in from outside, and they too went to the altar of repentance and took their stand for the Lord.

"Boys, I am proud to say I was one of them. But in this political field I am in, it does require a bit of restraint in my speeches.

"I know I have taken up a lot of your time, but there is much more to relate.

"Well, everyone called it prophecy and the preacher a prophet, indeed. This revival spread out in the country and to all the towns nearby. So many people came that they couldn't all get in the church house. Since it was hot weather, the men all got together, built a brush arbor, and hauled in a truckload of clean sawdust and chips to cover up the ground. We carried the Bible stand out of the church and all the seats. We made many plain benches for the crowd to sit down. Some, of course, sat in their cars and wagons. Many of the little kids sat on the wood chips and had a heyday time. Well, this revival caused such uproar in the community, for the better surely, that some of the men quit the dogfights, cockfights, horse racing, and the bootlegging. Yes, they closed down their stills and quit the gambling all through the holler. I will have to confess that one man with a still had backslid and started it up again with vim and vigor. He had to work day and night to keep up with the demands from the public.

"Oh yes, boys, we kept that preacher in our church for our pastor. He is a good one too. Our church is bursting at the seams with new converts.

"I must tell you about this perpetual gambler that got converted at the revival. He gambled away everything from his house that wasn't nailed down. Why, he even gambled some of the leghorn chickens out of the henhouse. His wife told me he took the only ones that were laying eggs. His little woman had pieced together a lovely quilt. She had stored it away in a trunk, but he found it and gambled that away too. It was nearing Christmas, and he told his wife he would like one of those big red handkerchiefs. It was the style to let one corner hang out of the back pocket of the bib overalls. Well, his wife took two of the non-laying chickens to the store, sold them, and got this gambler-husband three handkerchiefs, two red ones and a blue one. Well, he lost them in one night of gambling. His wife told me that he never won anything and wondered why he kept it up; it didn't make sense.

"Well, this fella went to one of those revival meetings and he got converted and delivered from his gambling habit, drinking whiskey, and chewing tobacco that very night. He testifies about this to everyone he meets, if they will listen.

"Now to continue about Miss Idy. Well, she fell in love with the Bible. She buried herself in it, nearly learning it by heart. She began to approach everyone she met, telling them that they needed to be converted. She started to dress all in black; the only color she wore was a red or pink rose on her hats. I need to tell you that Miss Idy read in the Bible where the Lord said to 'Go out in the byways and hedges to bid all to come into the kingdom.' So sure enough, Miss Idy left us, but I am glad she is living here in your fair town of Paw Paw. She is a might fine sweet gal and will do you good.

"Well boys, I must be on my way, campaigning for the offices I'm running for." Henry said good-bye to his old friends and hurried off in another cloud of dust.

When Henry bid farewell to the men on the porch, he knocked the props out from under them and put them out of commission for some time.

Here they sat with the answer to a huge secret in the palms of their hands. The big mystery regarding Miss Idy solved. They now knew what had brought her to their fair town. They also knew that everyone in Paw Paw had been consumed with curiosity about her. Who was she? Where had she come from?

What was her background? She always quite cleverly turned the conversation to something else if she was asked, so finally through the years, they had quit asking.

Amos was the first one to gather enough strength to speak. "Well, my good friends, what a kick in the teeth we just got. All our surmises and guesses have just taken flight. Who would have thought that our Miss Idy had been left standing at the altar alone? Why, that old judge should have been tarred and feathered for doing such a thing."

Tom Curry, his voice like a whisper, said, "That would be the height of shame and embarrassment any lady could endure."

Jeremiah responded, "Tom, I agree wholeheartedly with you. It would be the worst humiliation that a woman could suffer. But now, men, we have a problem of our own. What course of action shall we take regarding this news? Are we going to be the ones who tell and make this public? We have the power to tell or to keep it secret. So far us keeping a secret . . . well, we don't have a very good track record in that. Remember Granny Octavia calls us blatherskites."

The men all laughed at that.

Otis Simpson said, "I don't think we have really been cruel in our judging of Miss Idy. But, I for one think we should keep this to ourselves. If it gets spread around, it will only do harm to her. And, of course, it will eventually get back to her ears. No woman should have to carry that burden twice."

They all agreed.

Jeremiah spoke up, "Men, I feel good about our decision. 'Course the sad thing about keeping this secret is that no one will ever know we kept it."

"Sad, sad," they murmured as they got up and, after hand-shaking and pats on the back, headed for home.

He that ruleth over men must be just,
ruling in the fear of God.
And he shall be as the light of the morning,
when the sun riseth, even a morning without clouds;
as the tender grass springing out of the earth
by clear shining after rain.

2 Samuel 23:3-4

Chapter 43

The Unheard of Goings-On in Paw Paw

All the inhabitants were up in arms in a hysterical uproar. The men who sat on the porch of the General Store immediately lost self-control, for which they always prided themselves. Even the relaxed Jeremiah Jones gasped, "I am flabbergasted and at a complete loss of words."

This startling news had not come down via the grapevine that flourished on the porch but was heard right from the horse's mouth herself. Miss Idy Crandall was going to run for deaconess of the Baptist Church!

It had all happened yesterday morning, and they had no inkling. Fred Pinkham suddenly said, "Boys, look who's coming down the road. There has to be something wrong with Miss Idy today. You can fairly see she is very flustered, and I'm afraid it concerns us men sitting here on the porch."

Before they had time to analyze her and farther, she hit the porch, announcing, "Gentlemen, I already know that I am a lone voice of one crying in the wilderness. Therefore, I will quickly state my mission here today. First, this is not just something out of the blue and certainly not a flighty, fanciful, hair-brained idea of a lady. I have chosen this course of action after much consideration and prayer. I am going to run for deaconess of the Baptist Church. I want a woman's voice to have a vote in the church. With this honored position, I shall be the main spokesman at board meetings. I insist this privilege must go hand in hand if I am elected. Without the principle voice, I will not accept the position. There are many things that need to be changed in our church and many projects that need to be started. Some of these will enrich all our community even outside our church.

"For instance, our bell in the belfry. Its clapper hasn't clapped for a long time. What a waste! It used to peal and ring out every Sunday morning and every Wednesday night for the prayer meeting. Old Granny Smith asked the church board to ring it three times at her funeral and sing 'When they ring those golden bells for you and me.' It wasn't done, as its clapper couldn't clap. I wonder sometimes just how many people would have come to church if our beautiful bell had rung a few times as a reminder.

"If I get on the board, this will be fixed and I have a method to get it done. I will see that the bell will ring at everyone's wedding and at the birth of our babies. I shall see to it that the deaths in our community will receive three soft muffled tones at their funeral. In fact, I will gladly take this task myself. In addition, to show all our citizens that we will do the right thing, we shall ring it at the times of our town functions.

"You remember a year back when that windbag, full-of-hot-air politician came to Paw Paw? Only you men on the porch heard him. No one else even saw him. If the bell had worked, everyone would have known something important was going on and could have come. Just by hearing of some of his promises, he most assuredly did not get my vote, but we must make that decision ourselves. Every citizen can and should vote in our democracy, the land of the free and the home of the brave.

"Speaking about that, we must have the flag of our country displayed. We must raise it high. We must salute it ourselves and most certainly have one in our schools and one in the church.

"I can hear your outcry, 'We don't have the money for a flag.' Well, I will take care of that in our church sewing circle.

"The first flag which was raised up high to wave over our democracy was made by one woman. In 1777, she took the white shirt of a soldier; the red color, I hesitate to say this, but the red came from the donated petticoat of a fallen woman; and the blue came from a captain's blue coat. We can do better with our modern techniques. I thought you men could come up with a flagpole, so you can feel you have done your part.

"And it wouldn't hurt you men to brush up on your Bible reading. I know most of you will not do it, so I will tell you that I have just read about Deborah, a prophetess who judged Israel for forty years. The Israelites had been under bondage and severely oppressed for twenty years, so she decided to do something about it. They called her a mother in Israel, and indeed she was. So, if one lone woman can judge and control millions of those contrary, sinning, unbelieving Jews for forty years, I think I can handle my part here in Paw Paw, or I would like to try!

"Before I leave you gentlemen, I would like to sing part of the song Deborah sang after her victory." The men were astonished as her melodious voice rang out. "Oh yes, I will praise Him, He that made the earth to tremble and heaven itself dropped down clouds of water."

The men were hushed and stupefied. Not so much by the song itself, but by Miss Idy's clear enchanting voice that rang out so loud and clear. It had gone unnoticed since she arrived in Paw Paw because she had taken great pains to hide this talent for some unknown reason.

Miss Idy quickly composed herself by straightening her black hat and nervously patting and smoothing her black dress. She caught her breath then plunged ahead. "And another thing I shall do if elected to this high and lofty position on the church board is to see that the hole in the roof of our church is repaired. As it stands now, when it rains we have to listen to that loud ping, ping, ping as the rain drips into the large bucket behind the podium. And we have to endure the snickers of our youth. I noticed a few Sundays ago when we sang, 'There shall be showers of blessings' there emerged quite a loud cackle from our youthful audience. I made an effort to find the guilty culprit, but they all denied it, so I had to let the matter drop. But here and now, I will confess before this holy body of believers that even I could hardly refrain from smiling. This sort of nonsense will be stopped.

"And another thing that must be done is to get our lovely organ player a bench to sit on. Now, as you know, she has to precariously balance on what some have declared was a tall fortified milk stool which came from somebody's barn.

"We also need new altar benches, one for the ladies' side and one for the men's side. I noticed some lovely cedar at the sawmill, which I am sure they would donate to such a worthy cause, and you men can build them. Now if there are no volunteers for all this work, I have an alternate plan, which will emerge when needed."

Then she bowed slightly to the men, turned and marched down the road to the Paw Paw Times newspaper.

Amos Hammon murmured, "What is this alternate plan of hers?"

Down through the years, the same men were always voted back into their same positions as deacons of the Baptist Church, so there was very little excitement about that election. The men were glad to have Miss Idy do all the many tasks at church. She taught, chaperoned the young ladies, and kept a close eye on the young men. She cleaned up the church, took the ashes from the stove in winter, and even carried in the wood and stacked it in back of the church. She dusted the old organ and got water for the speaker and anyone who needed it. Just before Easter and Christmas, she was a flurry of activity as she moved the seats outside and scrubbed the old floors until they were spotless. She made sure all the windows were washed squeaky clean, except for the broken one that had a piece of roofing over it. Miss Idy knew that on Easter and Christmas, people came to church who never attended the rest of the year. She thought this was a sad state of affairs, but there wasn't anything she could do about it unless she could get on the church board.

The men on the porch were stunned at this proclamation. There was a hushed silence akin to fear of what could happen if she were elected to this high position. An aftermath of chaos would be certain. Still reeling and floundering in bewilderment, they were finally calm enough to talk.

Jeremiah was the first to speak. "Hold your horses now, let us be poised, as Miss Idy would say. Let's not get all 'het up' and go into a tirade or let our anxiety make us do something foolish. I know you will agree that Miss Idy is no social climber. No, this will go far beyond that. Her underlying motives will be to make drastic changes in our church and who knows where else, if she gets her powerful little foot in the door. I think we talked one time about a camel getting his head under a tent and the consequences of that. And we have to admit that she did put forth a convincing loud harangue using the Good Book. Many of her passages I often do confess I did not know. Maybe all of the confusion will make us read the Scriptures a little more."

Tom Curry echoes a loud "Amen" to that. The other men gave pitiful, long, drawn-out sighs.

It was just a month before the annual Baptist Church board election. The rules and regulations of the church said the seats were open to all members. The women had a vote on who would serve on the board, but all the rest of the year the meetings would be private.

Jeremiah said, "As I am the chairman of the church board, I will attempt to speak and then you will have your turn. We have to do something drastic about this uprising. In doing this, we must use our three "Cs;" we must be collected, cool-headed, and confident. The first thing that comes to me is that we have to start this in our homes. We must try to convince our wives to stay at home the night of the election, so they won't vote for her. So I ask you, how do we accomplish that?"

None of the men spoke up.

"Well men, I think we must use our most engaging manner."

Suddenly Amos spoke, "Jeremiah, I already tried that on my Minnie. And she insisted that we wait a full year for her to say 'I do.'"

"My friends pay close attention to what I am saying. You must use the same procedure that you used when you were courting your beloved. Just do the same thing, the natural thing. However, this love action must be in a prolonged and prolific way; this is what our women want. Be loving. Help with the chores. Wash dishes together. Slip a little unexpected kiss or hug on her neck. We must be as sly as serpents and harmless as doves with sweet-talking action. If you have any trouble in your lovemaking, get the Good Book down and read the Song of Solomon. He had seven hundred wives, so he was an authority on the subject. But be careful and don't make your wife suspicious of anything.

"Now comes the last, the final action. This is a mite dangerous and only to be used in the most hazardous cases. Get down your Bible and read to your wife the verse that says, 'If you want to know anything, ask your husband at home.' Again, I must warn you about this, as you will be treading on thin ice. I have to confess that I read this to Priscilla once, and instead of accepting it graciously, she got downright mean over me reading it to her. But I have no qualms about my Prissy; I can handle her all right. Just wait and see." He pompously hooked his thumbs in the bib of his overalls and leaned back in his chair.

"Men, this is a maneuver process—I hope I pronounced that word right. When Elmo Bright got back from the army, he taught me what it meant. It's a subtle, sneaky attack to come out a winner. Men, we have nothing to fear but fear itself."

Tom Curry added, "So that we don't have to do any leg running hither and yon on this subject, we can just stay on the porch and meet every man in Paw Paw in a week's time. We have to be sure that one of us is always here to carry out our plan." He went into the store and got broom straws, and by straw vote, they decided who would get there early and who would stay late.

After finishing their plan of attack, they all got up and shook hands with one another.

Then next day the men on the porch were greeted by the front page of the Paw Paw Times. In big bold letters it said:

> DO YOU WANT A CHANGE? DO YOU WANT A NEW FACE TO LOOK AT? DO YOU WANT A NEW RENOVATION OF THE BAPTIST CHURCH, SOMETHING YOU CAN POINT TO THAT WOULD MAKE YOU PROUD? THESE ARE NOT IDLE WORDS THAT ONE HEARS FROM EVERY POMPOUS POLITICIAN, BUT I PROMISE TO MAKE A DIFFERENCE IF I AM ELECTED AS DEACONESS AND HOUSE SPEAKER.

It was signed, "Miss Idy Crandall."

Tom Curry drawled, "Miss Hoity-Toity sure do write a might fine speech."

Unless the Lord had been my help,
my soul had almost dwelt in silence.

Psalm 94:17

Chapter 44

The Intercessory Prayer of Priscilla Jones

This was the day the church's Sewing Circle would meet at Miss Idy's house. They were sewing on a quilt that was to be entered and sold at the county fair. The money was to be used for the church house and other benevolent charities. Since it needed to be of the finest quality work they could do, Miss Idy had taken it upon herself to put it in her living room, so she could work on it in her leisure time. The other ladies wondered how in the world she could find any leisure time.

The ladies always arrived promptly, and soon glittering twirling points of silver flashed as they worked. They sipped tea and ate the delicious cookies Miss Idy served them.

Miss Idy rose to her feet; since she was a tiny woman, she always felt she could speak better while standing. In her best church-house voice she said, "Dear ladies, I am happy you could come today to my humble home. I want you to know that at this very moment I am proclaiming, or as a man would say, I'm throwing my hat in the ring, for the coveted position as deaconess of the Baptist Church."

The ladies were so startled that several pricked their fingers with their needles and caused their fingers to bleed. Later on, because of this, the men that sat on the porch of the General Store would call this campaign a blood bath.

"I know I'm pursuing new and unknown territory. I know also that I am at a dire disadvantage because I'm a lady. I will tell you why I'm running for this office in a few short words, which I think, will convince you. For I know that if I am elected, it will be because of your vote. I want to make some changes in our church and in our little town. So here goes.

"I think we need our church painted white. We have stared at the ugly thing long enough. Clara Johnson of the General Store couldn't come today, but she said they have a huge supply of white paint in the back room, so just maybe we could get her and Jacob to donate the paint to the church. If there is any hesitation on their part, maybe we could, in some subtle way, convince them this gift would make us so grateful we would always shop at their store instead of going over to Whippoorwill. I know you might be thinking this is a bit uncouth, but all's fair in love and war and in getting the church painted."

The ladies chuckled at that turn of phrase.

"Another thing. In our church, all the ladies sit on one side and the men sit on the other. Where this custom came from, I don't know, but I don't support it.

"If you have noticed, our organ sits on a platform in front of the men. If and when I am elected to our governing body, the first thing I shall do is move that organ to the ladies' side of the platform. Now, I do not want what I'm about to say get out of these four walls. We have a new organ player, and by the way, I think she is very good. Anyway, I can see from where I sit that when she sits down at the organ in her delightful and charming way, her dress has a habit of showing quite a bit of her well-shaped legs. I have noticed a few sheep eyes toward her from the men. These shenanigans must be nipped in the bud.

"Now my friends, I am not accusing anyone in our church of improper conduct. I'm sure there isn't any, as I have not caught a whiff of anything. However, we must be careful and prepared. Remember Adam and Eve in the Garden, and we should brush up on our reading of King David and Bathsheba. Remember, all David did was take an evening walk on top of his mansion, and presto, he was long gone in his shameful conduct with another man's wife.

"Enough of that subject.

"There are also many things which need a man's input, like putting on a new roof or cutting weeds around the church. Sometimes I feel like a forest is taking over our church. We desperately need new benches with backs on them. Just thinking of our crude benches makes my back hurt. The men who sit on the porch of the General Store are more comfortable than we are in church! Now I realize that we have very little funds to work with, but the men of the church could easily build them. They could use some of the trees that surround us. I'm positive that the sawmill would donate their time and effort.

"Think of this: we ladies can help get many things done in our own way. We know that we were endowed with an aura of beauty, charm, and grace from our Maker, but what good is it if we don't use it to our benefit?"

Miss Idy could plainly see that the ladies were taken aback by this suggestion. She would now have to take the low road to wheedle them over to her way of thinking.

"Dear ladies and friends of mine, I was hoping that I would not have to tell you of the underhanded conspiracy by our own governing body of our church board. They have stooped to a new low in this diabolical plot. It was brought to my attention by a phone message very early this morning. In fact, I was sleeping soundly when the phone rang. I always sleep soundly unless involved in a ruckus such as this. Yesterday, I met with the men on the porch face to face and publicly stated that I was campaigning for the position of deaconess. I knew for sure that I would be a target for every man in Paw Paw. I knew that I would be accused of untold atrocities, but I said to myself, 'So be it.' I was ready to meet their challenge head on. So my friends, I will reveal to you what the strategy is they intend to use against me.

"The first plan is to start in the home with their wives. They are to start subtly romancing you with love words and love actions like those that they did on your honeymoon. They plan to do this using some kind of love tool. I think you know the method of your man. They hope with this kind of feverish excitement you will slowly be brainwashed to agree with them that I should not be on the church board.

"Lastly, they will try to read scripture to you that goes, 'If you want to know anything, ask one's husband at home.'

"One of the men on the porch gloated, 'Boys, I think you will agree that I have a voice of wisdom and knowledge.' These were the words he spoke as he put his thumbs in the bib of his overalls and smiled very smugly. Then he said, 'I know I will not have trouble or problems with my little sweetie!' Maybe you ladies know who he is.

"All our buildings and our houses need painting, and our yards need cleaning up. We need to get those men off the porch and to take more interest in their homes.

"The children should be taught to work. I have heard there is a rustling in the mulberry trees that our government is about to say that children cannot be made to work until they are almost grown. This is serious. We need to teach our children to work. If that law passes, they won't work when they are adults. This is nonsense!

"So dear friends, it is up to all of you to change things. Change your men to be better fathers, models for their children, so they will look up to them.

"I know you are going to ask how I could be an authority on what I'm saying as I'm not married. I have been close, but it's all in the Bible for everyone to read. The Song of Solomon is most captivating. Another thing, and this should have been said at the beginning of my speech, is to pray for your husbands. Pray for them to be ideal husbands. Prayer can move mountains, you know.

"You can make me deaconess with a voice in the church, or I will just help as I can as I have done in the past. I want to say here and now that I will graciously accept and be content with whichever way it goes. So it is your decision now."

Miss Idy sat down and started sewing on the quilt.

A deathly silence followed. All the women kept sewing, but they were beginning to see that their stitches were getting crooked and ugly. Almost as one, they stood up and voted to go home. In some strange way, their footsteps were a mite longer and unduly heavy, planting and penetrating the ground with righteous indignation.

Could it be that they were wishing their husbands' heads were under their heels? Oh no! Not the ladies of the Baptist Sewing Circle!

There was one lady who wasn't angry with her husband. That was Priscilla Jones. It just wasn't her nature, but as she walked, bitter tears burned her eyes, fell down her face, and dropped unheeded on the little sweater she wore. How long had it been since the atrocity, the cruel Armageddon, had seized Jeremiah's heart, his very soul and spirit? Why, startled by this memory, it had been twelve long years since that nightmare. In their first two years, she didn't remember anything except him leaning over her, shaking her, and trying to get her to speak.

"Priscilla, Priscilla, my darling, my sweetheart, just say 'I do, I do take this man.'"

Years later, when she was well, Jeremiah told her of their wedding day. He would tease her. "Miss Hoity-Toity, you never got married, but I did, as you refused to answer 'I do' to the preacher." He repeated the story to the men on the porch to get a big laugh. Priscilla wanted to tell him she had answered, "I do," from both her heart and spirit but couldn't say the words because she couldn't get her lips to move. She never told him, as she knew he would share that too with the men on the porch.

Priscilla was exhausted when she got home because she had taken baby Blossom with her. The baby was just walking, so most of the time she had to carry her. Baby Blossom fell asleep as soon as she was put down for her nap.

Priscilla was still bowed down with the pain and grief that Miss Idy in her quest for church deaconess had resurrected today. Repeatedly, through the long and lonely twelve years, she thought of that "wild purple pansy day." Of how the strong, handsome, exuberant young Jeremiah ran in circles, around and around. Of how they had laid the stones for their house. How he had suddenly grabbed her and whirled her in circles with him. How her pink gingham-ruffled skirt had billowed out as their turbulent love got out of control and they fell down in the lush bed of wild purple pansies. She could feel the soft velvety purple pansies now and smell their fragrance all around her.

Then Priscilla thought of what Miss Idy said about praying for the mountain to move. She went into their bedroom and knelt down at the side of their bed. The Bible said that the marriage bed was undefiled and holy. Did that mean their bed was less than that? Was it an unholy bed? It had failed to give them the joy, the fulfillment that God had ordained. Yes, certainly they had their children, which was expected of them, but the tenderness, the passionate love they had experienced on the purple pansy day was gone forever. For sure, it wasn't all Jeremiah's fault. The perpetual, eternal horror of the day her father had poured gasoline on Jeremiah's house and burnt it to the ground still haunted her, as well as the two years before their marriage when Jeremiah had driven himself almost to the breaking point in building the house just for her. There was also an evil thing, something shrouded in mystery, that seemed to possess Jeremiah and hold him captive. It seemed as if he grieved for the house much more than for her two year's near-death darkness.

She was thankful that he ceased to talk to her about her father. Ceased stirring up the cold gray ashes of burning pain and agony of that night twelve years ago. She also knew he hadn't forgotten. How could one? It was always between them.

Oft times the dark thing would rear its ugly head. Even now she felt the haunting ghostly phantom of her father hovering over her in all its fury and felt again the beating of the strap cutting her body over and over.

She prayed, "Oh Lord, explore down to the deepest springs of my spirit, where the spirit makes intercession for us, and read the prayers I cannot utter." At first her eyes were dry and hard, then she remembered the Bible said that one could weep tears into the ears of God.

In her travailing, wounded spirit of intercessory prayer for herself and for Jeremiah, she lay down on the rug beside their bed. She was exhausted and drained from this encounter with her God and her memories, and she fell asleep. The boys awakened her when they arrived home from school. Baby Blossom began to fuss. It was time for her to start supper for her little family.

Priscilla didn't know that God, from His high and lofty throne, leaned way down and heard her whispers as she kneeled by her bed.

Know ye not that they which run in a race run all, but one receiveth the prize? So run, that ye may obtain.

1 Corinthians 9:24

Chapter 45

"Political Unrest in Paw Paw"
(an article printed in the Paw Paw Times)

Jimmy C. Simpson has been covering the turmoil that has erupted in our town over Miss Idy running for church deaconess, so we owe this outstanding piece of reporting to our "boy wonder." He not only is a paper delivery person (always on time we might add), but he gathers much material for this paper. He rushed to get this to the press on time.

The Baptist Church prayer meeting will be canceled because of the election Wednesday night but hereafter will be resumed as usual. With his "tongue in cheek" humor, Jimmy said, "I think they should have the prayer meeting right after the election is over."

Jimmy returned from his deliveries and taking a poll from his customers, and he says most of them are split right down the middle. Those astraddle of the fence are going to attend this hotly contested election and decide in the ninth hour.

The Paw Paw Times reluctantly took this next news item to be put on the page of "What Fell Out of the Wastebasket Today." Some of our most charming housewives demanded we print it. We quote: "To the men and gentry of Paw Paw who are going to the church election, if you don't vote for Miss Idy, be sure and wear your neckties. We need them around your neck because every day, little by little, we shall tighten them until you choke."

They didn't give their names, so this threat remains anonymous.

Therefore, we beg you to go out and vote. It is your duty. Blood has been spilled all over the world for the freedom we enjoy. Psalm 11:3 says, "If the foundation be destroyed, what can the righteous do?" Our elections are part of the foundation.

GET OUT AND VOTE.

It has come to our attention that this campaign is causing a deep division among our citizens and has become most disruptive in our households. Our innocent children are seeing for the first time an unholy rancor between their parents. One uneasy child was asking what the word divorce means! Shame! Shame! Shame!

One of our concerned citizens has insisted that the rules and regulations of the Baptist Church be announced and printed before the election. They were afraid there might be serious trouble, so we gladly print this.

Only the members of the Baptist Church can vote.

They must have attended with some regularity for six months.

They must have contributed financially during the year.

All ladies can vote in all elections.

The board meetings will be held once a month, with only the church board members attending.

Off the record regarding this last rule, many wives complain that what they learned from their husbands about the meetings they could hang on a single thread.

But dear reader, could there be a deaconess on that board meeting next Wednesday? We don't know but will wait with bated breath.

The afternoon of the election found everyone, and their kith and kin, descending upon the little town of Paw Paw. The crowd of men on the porch was overwhelming. The regulars on the porch gave their seats to the elderly. The long benches that had been placed against the wall of the General Store were full too. That left the regulars seated on the steps of the porch, aiming at a different location on the grass, which was becoming soaked in amber juice.

A peculiar stillness had settled down on these men. Could they lose this election? And if perchance they did win, why weren't they feeling good about it?

Soon everyone from the porch got up, walked over to the little church, and filed in. It was the church custom for the men to sit on one side and the women to sit on the other. The place was packed out. The ladies didn't have room for a pallet on the floor for their babies, so they had to hold them on their laps. Many had two or three little ones, and they demanded to be held by their mothers. So with all this frenzy, the ladies weren't happy. The men sat in silence, waiting for Jeremiah to come and take charge of the meeting.

Minute by minute the house grew more silent, except for a few whispers on the men's side of the church. Where could he be? He was the ringleader of this brigade. Frantically, they looked at one another, trying to decide what to do. None of them was versed enough to take charge. Then all of a sudden Miss Idy got up and took the podium.

"Well gentlemen, it looks to me that Jeremiah is not coming tonight. We should not make any judgment against him because we don't know what has delayed him. But do you have another spokesperson that would take his place?"

They all said no and admitted that they didn't know what to do next.

"Well dear friends and neighbors, do you want me to take charge? I know this is an unexpected turn of events for us, but if I am elected tonight, I will be permanently taking this position. This will just be a week ahead of time. All who want me to take charge of this meeting please show by raising your hands."

Any casual observer would have said 100 percent of the men held up their hands. One reason being that many of them were too frightened of their wives to do anything different.

"Now my fellow Americans, I see that we have more than a quorum tonight to hold this election. I have the minutes of your last meeting, which someone tucked under my door. I do not know who it was, but I'm grateful for this historical document. If I am elected tonight, I shall be the one who will record our movements—until my term has expired, that is.

"It is recorded here in the minutes of the last board meeting that a vote was taken and the board decided unanimously to continue things just as they are. I see no adjournment of this meeting, so I presume that they started talking about their hunting dogs."

Then Miss Idy began carefully reading the rules and regulations that had been published in the Paw Paw Times. "Does anyone here in this august body have any questions?"

All was still until Sam Dooley spoke up. "Miss Idy, you know I come to church just twice a year. On Easter, to show off my wife in her new dress, and on Christmas, the Lord's birthday, for the kids. Can I vote?"

"No you can't vote Sam Dooley. Sit down."

"Now if there are no objections, we will hand you a little slip of paper. If you want me as your servant, vote yes. If there is something you object to about me, just write no. I shall consider that from the Lord, and I will continue doing as much as I can for this lovely church and the town of Paw Paw."

There was quite a scramble hunting up paper and pencils and passing them out. After a few minute's pause, Miss Idy said, "Amos please gather up the votes." Amos quickly took his hat and gathered them up. Then she said, "Fred please help Amos count the votes." All the church members felt a trifle uneasy, as the men did the counting out loud.

When they had finished, Miss Idy was voted into the high position of deaconess. There was only one no vote.

Miss Idy stood very calmly. "I want to thank you all for this vote of confidence in me. I will call this a landslide victory. I will also do my best as I take up this 'sweet burden' so that all can be proud of our church and our town. When we all catch our breath, I will call a board meeting to discuss the many projects that we shall soon undertake. We can't live in shadows but must all put our shoulders to the wheel and pull together to better our lot. There have been frightening whispers and murmurs of a Depression in our country, which we might encounter in the next few years. So we must prepare ourselves, keep our ears to the ground and our spirits toward heaven. And here is another little tidbit to consider: as our town grows we must be thinking about choosing a mayor for Paw Paw.

"But tonight let us all join hands and hearts for the new day that starts tomorrow. Let us bow our heads and pray for God's blessings on our new ventures that will commence in the immediate future, if not sooner."

Right after the prayer, Miss Idy bade them all "good night," clicked her heels, and marched out the door, leaving most of the membership with mouths agape.

For many days after the election, all the talk by the men on the porch centered on who might have cast that no vote against her. They were very careful to refrain from talking about their own votes.

In the same hour came forth fingers of a man's hand,
and wrote over against the candlestick
upon the plaster of the wall of the king's palace:
and the king saw the part of the hand that wrote.
Then the king's countenance was changed,
and his thoughts troubled him, so that the joints
of his loins were loosed, and his knees smote one against another.

DANIEL 5:5-6

Chapter 46

Priscilla's Intercessory Prayer Is Answered When Jeremiah and Priscilla Meet "the Thing," "Our Conscience, Our Souls' Companion

Jeremiah awakened early and stretched his long legs the length of the bed and cuddled in its warmth. He could hear Priscilla in the kitchen getting breakfast, and he could hear the boys' squabbling and bickering as they came down the stairs for school. Suddenly he gave a gasp, why this was the day of the election. He jumped out of bed and looked out the window. "Oh, tarnation!"

It was foggy and murky, a dark mist hung suspended in the air. All is not lost here, he thought. This disagreeable weather will keep several wives home with the children, so they won't be able to vote. He smiled at this shrewd idea and the insight he possessed.

Jeremiah didn't have to work at the mill today, so the men had decided to come early to the porch of the General Store. As Amos Hammon had commented, maybe they could snag a few more votes from the ones who were straddling the fence. They had decided early in this campaign that there would be no smearing or mud-slinging against Miss Idy. However, this would be a good time to hint at a few things, very subtly of course, and she wouldn't have time to answer or deal with them.

Jeremiah peered in the mirror at himself; he looked a mite bedraggled. Priscilla said he looked like a dragon that had pulled himself backward from the end of a rain barrel. He hurried through the kitchen to the washroom. Priscilla was at the stove making a skillet of gravy. As cheerfully as possible he chimed, "Good morning, my dear". She grimly ignored him.

All the Jones men sat down to a lovely breakfast, while Priscilla went upstairs to get baby Blossom.

In a slightly cautious manner, Jeremiah remarked, "Priscilla, are you going to the election tonight? I need to be there on time, you know, as I am the spokesman."

"No Jeremiah. My one little vote would not make any difference, as our male population does not want a woman's voice trying to better our community. And there will be all those boresome speeches before and afterward. Plus, the children have to go to school in the morning. No Jeremiah, I will not be going, but you'd better hurry off to the campaign you're waging from the porch of the General Store."

In a promising, hesitant voice, "Well, my sweet family, I am off, but I will be back here for supper and then go to the election tonight." He gave them all a hollow, lame good-bye and rushed out the door.

Jeremiah was elated as he rushed to the porch to tell the men his good news. "Friends, I told you Priscilla wouldn't come. Now you can see who wears the pants in the Jones family. And this is a sign to me that our Miss Idy will suffer defeat tonight."

The other men didn't seem as confident as Jeremiah. Tom Curry in a whining, doubtful voice said, "Well, I wheedled my Alice until she became quite violent and emphatically declared that she was one of those that was astraddle of the fence and would wait until the last dog is hung before she would decide."

The day passed swiftly. Jeremiah gloated all day about his victory over Priscilla to the many men that promenaded to the porch that day.

There was a lull in the politics on the porch, so Amos Hammon hesitantly remarked, "You know, my wife Ada has drastically changed the last few days. She refuses to bake hot biscuits and corn bread, making us eat store-bought white bread. The house is going to need a complete renovating unless it is cleaned up right away. And I hate to confess to you men that she took the feather bed off of our bed and is sleeping on the floor, which we all know is breaking one of the commandments of the Good Book."

"Oh, now Amos," Fred Pinkham argued, "that isn't in the Good Book. And if it is, it's the first time I ever heard of it."

"Well, it is there in plain sight." With these words, Amos went into the store and came back with Jacob's Bible. Jeremiah is a better reader than any of us. Jeremiah, turn to I Corinthians 7."

He read, "Husbands and wives should not defraud each other in their lovemaking, unless they are fasting and praying. And that shouldn't last very long."

At this quotation, the men were in an uproar. Ray vehemently said, "This is not what it means!"

Jeremiah butted in, "Now boys, let's don't argue about this."

Each one of them had a different explanation and interpretation. Seeing this was one of the verses of the Bible that would not be settled in a few minutes, Jeremiah asserted, "Now boys, we must bring this conversation to a halt. We have more important things to discuss this day, like how to keep Miss Idy off the church board. He continued by asking who they could and couldn't count on not to vote for her.

"We cannot count on Jacob's vote, because he will have to vote the way Clara tells him to," Ray said.

Amos interrupted, "Is there a possibility he could write a small no without Clara knowing?"

"Rest assured," Jeremiah added, "Clara will not let up until she finds how he voted. We all know Jacob would not tell a lie, but I will put a question mark on his name.

"And there is no way that Reverend Peabody and Lizzy will vote no, as Miss Idy was the one who brought them together. They are so much in love, like a sick calf calling to its mother. They are certain to vote for her."

Since seemingly the beginning of time, real politics and elections have flourished in some cigar-smoke-filled back rooms, so it was with the men on the porch. They chewed their tobacco and spit and carried on their pitiful campaign to keep Miss Idy from being elected deaconess of the Baptist Church.

Yet, there were some mysterious shenanigans at play from these men. Each man was going through his own "dark passage" with his wife. Some wives had refused to cook, some had refused to clean the house, and some had even moved to the living-room couch to sleep. So each man concocted a plan of secretly voting yes for Miss Idy. By this confession to their wives, they could live again in their good graces. They reasoned to themselves that one little vote wouldn't make a difference in an election anyway. They would have happy homes again, and no one would be the wiser. Of course, they couldn't admit to each other what they were about to do.

Jeremiah lived farther away from the store than the other men. He was startled to realize it was almost dark. Never intending to stay this long, he didn't bring a lantern. The moon wasn't shining, so he had to guess where the old familiar path was. Tripping over tree limbs, stumbling over rocks, ranting and railing, cursing his stupidity at staying so long on the porch, he was a stone's throw from his house and lost. Lunging forward, he hit a big tree limb across his throat and fell backward onto the ground. It was such a stunning blow that everything turned black before him. He thought for sure he was going to die as he lay gasping for breath. Then suddenly he heard a voice that paralyzed him with fear and brought on an instant cold sweat.

"Jeremiah, what are you doing groping in the darkness? You should be home with your family."

"Who are you? What in the world is happening to me?" he

said in a strangled gulping voice to no one.

"Was that my own voice?" he cried fearfully.

He didn't know how long he lay there. Calmer now he carefully examined his throat where the limb had struck him. He realized gratefully that no lasting harm had come to him. Then in terror, panic-stricken with the memory of the voice, he scrambled for the limb he had struck and pulled himself to his feet with it. Groping along in the darkness, he finally found the door to his house. However, before the light of another day, Jeremiah would feel the terrifying darkness, the rancid, foul taste in his mouth and smell the burning flesh of Priscilla's father as it lay on the threshold of his house he loved so much. Oh yes. He was going to sink again into his own pavilion of hate that he had grimly constructed so many years before.

Exhausted, Jeremiah turned his back to the door, pressing his body against it, trying to calm and compose his panic before he entered the kitchen. He heard the children playing and laughing. Why are they still up? Why had they not been put to bed? It must have been only a short time that he lay on the ground. But what was happening to him?

It was back. The "Thing" was back. It was feeling his neck where he had met the limb and trying to whisper in his ear. Why now? Why after all these years was it here again?

He remembered then that he called it the "Thing" when he first met it. Why that was twelve years ago, wasn't it. Oh yes, the "Thing" had come back into his life.

In desperation, he opened the door.

Priscilla was putting their supper on the table. The three little stair steps were seated on their chairs, waiting to eat. As if in a trance, Jeremiah tried to brightly remark, "How is my little family tonight? Would you think your daddy could get lost coming from the store to the house? Well, he did. But it won't happen again, as I will be sure to carry a lantern with me next time."

Cautiously he sat down at the table, trying to compose himself. Why did everyone seem the same? Did he think that something or someone was after him? What foolish thoughts he was having tonight.

Getting no response except the children's chatter, Jeremiah watched Priscilla as she put the food on the table. He gazed at her as she moved. He became a little stunned at himself for not noticing until now that Priscilla wasn't just pretty, she was beautiful. Her golden hair had escaped the bun on her head, and the curls were in disarray as she worked. Why she was the most lovely woman in Paw Paw and maybe the world. Her figure was still tiny after giving birth to three babies. How long had it been since he had told her how lovely she was? Had it been twelve years since he had told her that? He wasn't aware of when he stopped really looking at his lovely creation from God. Strange indeed, he couldn't remember when he stopped talking to her and the children.

"Children should be seen but not heard" had been handed down to him. It seemed the only reason he talked to them was when they had been unruly and needed some punishing or chastisement. There was no way to pinpoint the exact time that he started neglecting her. Had it always been?

Clearly, he saw again on his desk at school her big fat sunny braids with the big bows on the ends, the bows that always matched her dresses.

Suddenly a sharp pain from his innermost being arose, moved like a closed fan opening, and spread to his bruised throat. It left him breathless and overcome with anguish and despair.

Jeremiah pushed his half-eaten plate of food aside. Priscilla did the same. In the tense atmosphere, the children looked with questioning eyes at their father and mother. The only one that was acting normal was baby Blossom, and she was beating her spoon on her plate.

Priscilla picked up the baby and went into the other room,

changed her, and got her ready for bed.

Suddenly Jeremiah gave a big clap with his hands. "Hey you guys, let's jump up and do the dishes for our mommy."

Startled at this rare happening, they quickly cleared the table. Then Jeremiah washed and the boys dried the dishes. They seemed to enjoy this little task.

Priscilla finished with the baby and broke the heavy silence. "Thank you all for doing the dishes. I was a little tired tonight. Jeremiah, would you tuck the children into bed for me? You have time before you go the election tonight."

Jeremiah's ears weren't tuned to the pain and distress in Priscilla's voice. Then he noticed that the sofa had been made up. Before their shocked and horrified eyes, Priscilla put on her nightgown and lay down on her new bed. This was new for her also, as she had always slept with her husband for twelve long years.

Jeremiah, bewildered and addled, was adrift in a sinking ship. He was seeing Priscilla leave him, finally cutting asunder her love for him. In looking back, he knew she had done it along time ago in her spirit; this was just the physical part that as emerging now.

The children ran and kissed their mother then bounded up the stairs with squeals of laughter because their daddy was going to tuck them in. Jeremiah bent over to pick up his tiny baby girl, his Blossom. "Me walk, Daddy," she babbled. He stepped behind her as she crawled up the stairs. The little boys put on their pajamas. They slept in one bed, Blossom in another smaller bed.

"Now my little stair steps, jump in your beds."

Shyly, David whispered, "Mommy always lets us pray before we go to bed."

"Oh my goodness, Daddy forgot." Jeremiah knelt down between their beds. They laced their fingers together. They did not know that as they did this, they were also lacing their fingers around their daddy's heart, something that he had unknowingly severed a long time ago.

They prayed. "Dear Jesus, we love You, and we know You love us too. Bless our mommy and our daddy. See, our daddy is tucking us in tonight." After a loud "Amen," they jumped into bed. They closed their eyes, while visions of lollipops danced across their beds. Their daddy had tucked them in.

Jeremiah was still on his knees between the children's beds. His mouth was dry, as he trembled with fear for himself, for Priscilla, and for his children. For somewhere outside of his house was his larger fear, fear of the unknown. He kissed his little boys who were brown from the sun. Across each nose was a scattering of brown freckles. Why had he never noticed that before?

Although baby Blossom was asleep, he lifted her into his arms and held her to his heart. Her blond curly hair lay in ringlets on her damp forehead. She had long blond eyelashes that graced the pink porcelain face. Her tiny rosebud mouth was wet. She had started a little habit of sticking out her tongue and blowing a little spit bubble when she slept. Oh yes, she was a tiny wee elf Priscilla. In a magical and holy gesture, Jeremiah kissed the lips of his little baby girl and she sleepily kissed him back.

From somewhere (was it heaven?) came a song, "Let the little children come to Me. They are the ones who make up the kingdom of God."

Jeremiah whispered, "Why, such as these sit on the lap of God."

Then he heard Priscilla's voice echoing in his memory, telling him again what she had said so many times before. "You must hold all sweet reminiscing of your babies tight in your heart. Those memories must be handled softly and tenderly because they are delicate, fragile, yet they have the power to break your heart."

He realized now what he had done, within and without, he had severed the bonds with his family.

The small lamp between the beds tried desperately to shed its golden glow over the wounded man that knelt between his children's beds. But his eyes were closed and his hands were clenched in fear. The "Thing," once again, was trying to clutch his throat and drain his strength from him. His mind seemed to draw a dark gray curtain between him and his children as the "Thing" whispered, "You have to go out the door."

Why, oh why did the "Thing" want him to go out tonight? He had to go, there was no escape, nowhere to flee, the "Thing" had dominion over him. He rushed down the stairs, out the back door of his house and began to run. Stranger still, he never ran to the Baptist Church to stop the election of Miss Idy as deaconess and chairman of the church board.

Priscilla hadn't gone to sleep; she was wondering why Jeremiah stayed so long after putting the children to bed. What was the matter? Had he fallen asleep? Yes, that must be the reason. She certainly wasn't going to awaken him. In fact, she was pleased that he had snuggled his children in his arms. She must get some sleep herself. The boys had to go to school, and she had a large washing to do in the morning. But the couch was too narrow and very lumpy. She turned over several times, but that didn't help, so she jumped up and changed ends. What is the matter with me, she wondered? She was still determined to go to sleep when she heard it.

"A keeper of the home, not a keeper of the house. I hope you know Priscilla, there is a big difference in these two words."

Priscilla sat bolt upright. Why, that's a scripture from the Bible that Reverend Peabody preached about one Sunday morning. Trembling, she arose and got the Good Book, as Jeremiah called it.

"Here it is in Titus, Chapter 2: 'The wife to be discreet, chaste, keeper of the home.'"

"Why that is who I try to be," she said aloud. "I must find out for myself what is happening to me." She got the Bible dictionary and read what a "keeper of the home" meant: a protector, a guardian of the harmony in the home.

Then the mysterious voice spoke again. "Priscilla, you have been keeping care of a house, not a home. There is a big difference. A house is a tangible thing of wood, bricks, and stone, a dead thing. The man builds a house, but a woman builds a home. What a difference. A home is where the heart dwells, it is alive with love and laughter and even tears. A home is where a sick child can become well. We never say that a person is house-sick, they are homesick.

"I know you had a bad time the first two years you were married; it certainly wasn't the kind of honeymoon a girl dreams about. I'm sure you will agree that it wasn't what that passionate, full of vinegar, Jeremiah wanted either. But all is not lost, you have your children, and you have fully recovered from that frightful time in your life.

"While you have the Bible in your hands, I want you to read Proverbs, the last chapter, and then I want you to read the Song of Solomon. Study it carefully. Oh yes, you could easily become flushed, scarlet at this book, but this is where you leave that house you have been living in and move into a home. Remember that 'wild purple pansy day'?

"Oh, I almost forgot, Jeremiah is going to take a visit there tonight."

Sitting stunned and dazed, she heard the "Thing" laugh at every step he took as he climbed to where Jeremiah knelt beside his children. Priscilla wasn't unduly alarmed when Jeremiah and the "Thing" rushed down the stairs and disappeared into the night.

"This surely is an unusual night in the Jones house," Priscilla said. Then she quickly changed the word house to home as she took the blanket off the couch and returned to their bed.

He brought me to the banqueting house,
and his banner over me was love.

SONG OF SOLOMON 2:4

Chapter 47

Jeremiah's Salvation and Homecoming

The moon was now shining in all of its bright glory. Had God with His infinite wisdom and power illuminated the way for Jeremiah and the "Thing" to run? In stark terror, Jeremiah thought he had forgotten to put Baby Blossom back into her bed and that he had her now in his arms as he ran. He tried to squeeze her close. He didn't feel her little body, but in some shocking spiritual way he felt her presence with him. In his madness, he cried out. "Oh, my baby, my baby, my darling Blossom. Your daddy loves you so." Though she never answered him, he felt a waft of warm wind touch his cheek as he ran on.

Exhausted and weary, he finally stopped running and looked around. Why, this was the foundation of his house he had built for his Priscilla twelve years ago. High weeds, thistles, thorn bushes, blackberry vines, and wild pink roses grew in abundance. They seemed to be wreathing the debris and ruins like a funeral shroud. He felt a deep smothering sensation down in his chest and throat; no, this pain was coming from his heart. He remembered the pact he had made with Satan himself that long-ago day when he said he would never return to this corner of his property.

The "Thing" beside him interrupted his thoughts. "Well, take a long look Jeremiah. This is where it started twelve years ago. I warned you then that the spirit of man is the candle of the Lord, but you begged me to extinguish that candle. And since I do this quite often, I consented gladly. So do not blame me for your tawdry behavior, your mean habits and actions through these many years."

Defensive and angry, Jeremiah yelled, "Shut up for a few minutes. I'm trying to remember that night."

In looking back, he knew the "Thing" was correct. He remembered screaming and clenching his fists at his God, profanely and brazenly as imps of darkness danced around him in glee. "Come on hate," he remembered screaming. "I give you permission to possess me if you can. Here is my heart and soul. Take your abode within me and all my shattered dreams." Hate entered and he nursed that hate as a babe would nurse at its mother's breast. In words liken to blasphemy, he proclaimed, "I shall never step my feet in this black corner of land again."

This "Thing" that he had adopted hugged closely to him. It made him happy, so he had taken it with him everywhere he went. The men that sat on the porch and all the other residents of Paw Paw agreed that they too would be bitter and full of hate. This black beast was due him after all that had happened. As time went on, the men on the porch ceased talking about it and the "Thing" itself became muffled and vague. But tonight the "Thing" moved back in full force.

In several places, the stones of the foundation could be seen. Jeremiah pushed aside some thorns and briars, sat down, and rested his face in his hands. He struggled to control himself, but his heart was beating fiercely. The "Thing" sat down beside him right on the thorns and thistles, which startled Jeremiah. Why, the "Thing" has no feelings, he thought. Then, when he crossed his legs, the "Thing" crossed his also. This terrified Jeremiah so much that he began trembling and shaking.

The "Thing" picked up a handful of ashes, "Jeremiah, I want you to smell this."

Jeremiah leaned over and took a deep breath. In the darkened crumbling ashes was the smell of putrid flesh, the death of Priscilla's father but also the death of his and Priscilla's love.

Suddenly, the "Thing" said, "Jeremiah, look a little to your left. What do you see?"

He hesitated for a minute. "I see a basket."

"Jeremiah, this basket is filled with your hate, bitterness, and numerous other sins, which I don't have time tonight to rehash, but you can plainly see it is running over."

Fearful, Jeremiah screamed, "Are you crazy?"

The "Thing" calmly replied, "Well, that is one of my names."

"Jeremiah do you know that your hatred is self-punishment? The one you hate is gone. This is a coward's revenge. It is time for you to let go. It is a puzzle to me that I am saying all these things to you, as it appears to me that I am trying to help you. This puts me in unfamiliar territory and is against my religion. Don't you think that's funny?"

The "Thing" was grinning ear to ear as Jeremiah cautiously asked, "Who are you? Do you have a name?"

The "Thing" finally answered. "That question is a mite hard to answer, my friend."

Jeremiah spit out words of anger, "I am not your friend, and you will never be my friend after this night is over."

The "Thing" continued his conversation, ignoring Jeremiah's appeal. "I am more than shirttail kin to the angels God so rudely cast out of heaven. However, since you no longer read your Good Book and don't go to church anymore, you don't know about such things. I have many names, but to you my name is Bitterness and Hate and Neglect.

"The way you neglect your family, especially Priscilla, is my doing. Oh, how that girl loved you. I'm sure you know you have lost her love and respect.

"Some folks like me to hang around them all the time. Let me see, I have been with you now for twelve years. You see I am able to lay dormant for a time. Some think they are rid of me, and then lo and behold, here I am again, my old delightful self." At this, the "Thing" let out a peal of horrid laughter.

"But sad to say, there seems to be something mysterious going on here tonight, and I have a feeling I may not be hanging around very much longer. Of course, that don't bother me very much, as there are plenty out there begging me to chain them as my prisoner.

"Jeremiah, since I have ventured this far, I will offer you this advice: Abstain from being involved in anything that wars against the soul. Oh, this good advice, I didn't know how clever I was."

Jeremiah got up when he saw something sparkling in the grass. It was the bits and pieces of the stained glass from his front door shining in the moonlight. He was standing in what was his parlor. With poetic insight, he saw his wide-sweeping stairway that led to the bedrooms upstairs. He saw the curved wooden banister that he had polished 'till it glowed a satin amber and reflected the fire from the fireplace. He had stood night after night, amorously stroking it, as a man would do when caressing his lover.

He brushed aside the brambles and stinging nettles, and he stood where Priscilla and his bedroom would have been. He had put two big windows in that room, and now in a flight of fancy, he envisioned himself holding her in his arms as they looked out at the moon and stars and watched the sun come peeking over the hills. He saw himself drawing her closer and heard her murmur in her teasing way, "Oh, my love."

Jeremiah turned his gaze to his ornate fireplace that was still standing like a black sentinel guarding precious jewels, remembering a lost love that was so sweet but couldn't endure the fire of destruction.

He remembered asking, "Prissy, where do you want your stove to sit? And would you like your kitchen sink in front of this big window, where you can see me and I can throw you a kiss as I pass by? Then when it's bitter cold and the window gets frosty, I will write 'I love you' on the pane. Then I'll rush in, lift you up in my arms, and we will dance around the room."

Even now, Jeremiah could hear her voice sigh.

The "Thing" arose and led Jeremiah through the kitchen to where his back door had been, then out into his backyard. There was the wet weather spring that he had helped his sweet love across just before they both fell down together on the wild purple pansy bed. Jeremiah remembered, how could he forget, how they both lay there so still, so trembling.

Now he saw that through the years, the wild purple pansies had reached out their fragile tendrils and made a long velvet path all the way to the back door of the foundation. His feet crushed the purple glory, and they sent up their fragrant perfume. Jeremiah breathed deeply of the sweet nectar. The "Thing" breathed also.

What was this "Thing"?

Then he wept and ached with pain as he thought about the wedding ring that he had so painstakingly braided for Priscilla from the tender green stems of the pansies. He remembered her excited words, "Oh darling, I shall keep it forever." Then he remembered one of the notes that he hung from the string out her window.

Oh my precious love,

The pansies are dancing the Polka right before my eyes. My darling, my darling, my darling. May I have this dance with you? Maybe that will erase the pain from my heart.

Your Lover

"Jeremiah, don't be getting too sentimental on me. You haven't heard it all, and the worst is yet to come. I'm sure you will try to deny it, but it is so. Instead of loving your Priscilla, as you should have, your house became your mistress. You loved it with the same intensity as you loved your Priscilla. You became unfaithful by choosing a house to be your lover. I have never seen anything to equal that; and I have seen everything diabolic, evil, and wicked."

Then Jeremiah screamed at the "Thing," "You are insane to think I would do something like that!"

"Now, my friend, calm down. Although, I shall admit that several have called me insane down through the years, 'Let the devil have his due' is my favorite quotation, you know.

"You were wildly in love with Priscilla until you started your house. But we can't blame the house, you know; it was entirely your fault for allowing me to move in. I was always nearby. I might even say I have dogged your steps, excuse my uncouth remark. I have watched your progress for nigh unto twelve years, and I was satisfied with your downfall, your anger, and your hate. Oh yes, I relished that hate. Oh yes, indeedy!"

Jeremiah sat down again on the foundation and bowed with his face in his hands. For the first time in twelve years, a torrent of hot tears flowed down on his tormented, unforgiving soul and filled his cupped hands to overflowing. He thought of the wasted years he had been consumed with hate against a man who had fathered his beautiful Priscilla.

He remembered his wedding day. Priscilla's broken and bruised body lying so still in her bed. His marriage was a mockery. 'Do you take this woman on her sickbed; or do you take this lovely house that you built? Do you take our holy abode in heaven or your holy bond on the earth? Is there anyone who objects to this union?' For sure, there should have been many voices crying out yes in protest. Yes, there is a reason. He loves them both with the same depth of feeling, the same passion, and the same fervor.

Spent and afflicted, Jeremiah whispered to the "Thing," "I'm insane, aren't I?"

"Jeremiah, your so-called Good Book says man can't serve two masters. God or mammon. He will love the one and hate the other or hold to one and despise the other.

"Do you realize that there was the possibility that you could have killed Priscilla's father with your own hands? Neither one of you could ever have erased that memory and that kind of pain. So it 'pears to me that though you have left your first love, there is still time to return to that magic you once had. The way I interpret your Good Book—and by the way, I'm an authority on it—there is no sin, however grievous, that your God will not forgive. Is that right, Jeremiah?"

"Yes, that 's the truth. It also says to work out your own salvation with fear and trembling. For sure, I've done a lot of that tonight," Jeremiah whispered.

Jeremiah forgot about the "Thing" sitting beside him and started to pray. "Oh my heavenly Father, if it is possible take this bitter cup from me. Or have I crossed the line of no return? Am I like Esau who sold his birthright for a morsel of meat and pottage of lentils? He who never found a place of forgiveness though he sought it carefully with tears. Lord, would You give me back my treasures, my lovely Priscilla, my Baby Blossom, my sons. Is there no deliverance for me? Is there no balm in Gilead? Is there no physician for me?"

Jeremiah rose to his feet and in some way looked refreshed and renewed from the ordeal he had been through. "Mr. 'Thing,' I perceive that you have been offering me deals that I think have been inspired from heaven, certainly not from your abode. So how about another deal with you?"

"What is it?"

"Well, I feel that I have just been forgiven for my past deeds, which you have been in control of, especially my hatred for Rufus Brooks, Priscilla's, father." At these words, Jeremiah lifted his hands to heaven. "I am going to build again a house on this same foundation. It is going to be built again in love, not hate. In fact, Priscilla and I will build it together. Of course, we will have to watch our step, so we don't trod on the wild purple pansies around the back door."

Then laughing at every step, Jeremiah jumped over the foundation and ran to his toolshed behind his house. Amazingly, the "Thing" ran beside him. Jeremiah grabbed a hoe, rake, and shovel, then raced back to the foundation. The "Thing" watched and smiled as he began cutting and slashing the briars, thistles, thorns, and bushes from in and around the foundation.

The "Thing" cautiously spoke, "Jeremiah, why don't you pile all of your rubbish in the center of your foundation."

"Okay." It took a few hours to get this done to Jeremiah's satisfaction.

The "Thing" spoke in an offhanded and nonchalant manner, "I think you should burn the debris, so you can start your house."

"I think that would be fine," Jeremiah said, "but I have no matches."

"Don't worry Jeremiah, I always carry some with me. This is one of the fun things I do." When the "Thing" struck a match, fire lit up the sky as the one that had burned twelve years ago. However, this time Jeremiah had a big grin on his face, thinking of Priscilla's new home.

He heard the "Thing" as it cried "Good-bye," saw it leap over the wild pansy bed, laughing hilariously, and heard its last words: "Jeremiah, Priscilla has dabbed some perfume behind her ears and also on her pillow."

Priscilla got up from the couch, pulled the blankets off, folded them and put them away. Then she hurried to their bed. As she lay down, she pressed his pillow into her arms and smelled his essence. She wept for the young Priscilla who never remembered her marriage vows.

"Do you take this man for your husband to cherish, to love, and to obey until death do you part?" Did he kiss her then? She never asked him. It was two years before she was well enough to take over the care of herself and her house. Her mother had stayed for the entire time, taking care of her, and then she left.

Then she heard a whisper in her ear. "Weeping can endure for a night, you know, but joy comes in the morning."

Suddenly Priscilla sat up with a loud gasp, remembering the "Thing," remembering the passionate prayer she had prayed beside their bed. "Oh, there is something very different about tonight. What is it, dear Lord?" She never heard an answer, but she knew that out there somewhere a miracle was waiting to happen. She shivered with excitement.

She yanked the sheets and pillowslips off the bed and stuffed them into the hamper. A long time ago, she had bought new flowery sheets and pillowslips and had never used them. Now it was time. When she got their new bed complete, she got her bottle of perfume and sprayed it on the linens. She stood in awe as she realized the flowers were wild purple pansies. "Why, I do believe they are dancing the Polka!" she said aloud.

Suddenly the phone rang. Who would be calling so late? It was Maudie Simpson. "Sorry Priscilla, for calling so late, but I just had to tell you that Miss Idy is our next deaconess. She won a landslide victory with only one vote against her. Oh yes, what happened to Jeremiah? He never got here." Maudie was laughing so hard that Priscilla didn't have time to answer before Maudie hung up the phone.

The fire hadn't gone out in the kitchen stove, so she added more wood and set two big buckets of water on to heat and took her bath in the warm kitchen.

"Oh, how I wish I had a pretty gown to wear," she said. Then a light went on in her head. She remembered one day when she was ill her mother had slipped one of Jeremiah's undershirts on her while she washed her nightgown. Priscilla went to Jeremiah's drawer and slipped one on now.

Meanwhile, the big golden moon was straining itself to

show Jeremiah Jones the way home. He was running faster now than he had ever run when the "Thing" was with him. He was laughing and crying and singing at the same time. "I'm forgiven, I'm forgiven. I'm redeemed. I'm free, free, free! Oh yes, my Lord, my Priscilla, your prodigal has returned."

Then he heard a voice saying, "Bring out the best robe and put it on him. Put a ring on his hand and shoes on his feet."

Jeremiah slowly opened the kitchen door. In the little washroom, there was a big tub of hot water. On the shelf was his razor. He picked up the bottle of aftershave. Where in the world had this been lost? Where were his clean clothes? Then with a tender smile on his face, he murmured, "Oh, I don't need them until morning anyway."

In the distance, coming from the foundation of his new house, he heard sweet voices singing a song of restoration. Every one of the singers had a harp and a golden vial full of sweet odors. They sprinkled their essence of healing all over Jeremiah and Priscilla. The number of them was ten thousand times ten thousand. And they all guided Jeremiah through his bedroom door.

It was after midnight. Where had the night gone? Quivering in anticipation, she sat down on her little bench in front of her mirror. She took down her hair and began brushing it, the light of the lamp reflecting it's glowing sheen. Then she saw him in the mirror standing in the door.

Jeremiah looked at her exquisite, flawless beauty. Not unlike a holy hush enveloped them as they stood in wonderment of each other. "Is there any reason of why this man and this woman be not joined together?" Adam's voice echoed from Eden's Garden. "This is why You created us, my Lord. In my sleep, You hovered over me, took out a bone over my heart, and made me this woman. This is now bone of my bone and flesh of my flesh."

Jeremiah, with quiet muted steps was behind her. Still without speaking, he took the brush from her hand and began stroking the voluptuous mass, liken to ripening golden wheat, until it fell down like a mantle around her. In reverence, as at a majestic shrine or an altar of royalty, he knelt before her. He held her tiny feet in his hands and buried his lips on them as the liquid beauty of her hair closed around him. Surely, this was a place where heaven and earth did meet. There was no sound unless it was the fast beating of their hearts.

Priscilla whispered to her heart, "If this is all I ever receive from him, it will be sufficient." Yes, this kind of love would be enough to last a lifetime.

In delicious fear and trembling, Jeremiah picked up her tiny body and soundlessly carried her to their bed, whispering, "My darling, I've just come from our wild purple pansy bed, and they are still dancing the Polka, you know."

Oh yes, Ecclesiastes, the Divine Cleric poured out His blessings upon them. With poignant intensity, Jeremiah bruised her lips with his. The swelling came like the ebb of flood time; the receding like a spent melodious symphony. Innumerable heavenly beings stood by with folded wings watching this joyous pantomime of love unfold before them.

Oh, sweet restoration, sweet redemption. God stood up from His throne, reached down from heaven, touched the heart of Jeremiah and sent him home—a home he had been gone from for twelve long years.

As arrows are in the hand of a mighty man;
so are children of the youth.

Psalm 127:4

Chapter 48

A Quiver Full of Arrows

For quite some time, tranquility reigned supreme in Paw Paw. Clamoring had ceased and law and order prevailed. Fred Pinkham commented, "My friends, there have been less feathers to be ruffled in Paw Paw lately than I have ever seen. Yes sir, no one's stroked the cat backwards to make it squall in a long time.

"Well, my neighbors," he continued, "I hope you have gotten a glimpse of Lizzy Peabody lately. That little gal do look pretty these days. She has that sparkle in her eyes again and them cheeks are a rosy red. I don't see how she manages to smile all the time. Peers to me her face would get tired. And our Reverend Peabody do look plum pretty at times too, if you can get him in a certain light.

"And here is something else that was discussed quiet freely at the ladies' Sewing Circle last week before Lizzy got there—Albert Jr. had slowed her down some and made her late. That little Jr. is saying dada now but refuses to say mama, and that has Lizzy a trifle piqued."

The men were all surprised by Fred's new word but let it pass by.

Then Otis butted in, "My Maudie indeed did verify what Fred has related. She also added that Albert Jr. has several teeth for his age, and if he don't stop clamping them down, Lizzy is going to cut off his milk supply."

They all smiled at the thought of the happy dwelling place, where the Peabodys lived, laughed, and loved.

The next Monday morning, the men gathered on the porch of the General Store as usual. Otis Simpson was the first to speak, and strangely, he had his Bible under his arm. "Now gentlemen, you were not in church yesterday, but I was, so it will be my job to tell you of some circumstances that might add up to a rift and a skirmish in the Baptist Church.

"It happened this wise. Lizzy Peabody phoned Jimmy early Wednesday morning. She wanted to know if Jimmy could do a little work for her, and she added she would be the one to pay him—indicating that he would be blessed with more money than if paid by our Reverend Peabody. Of course, you all know my Jimmy. He never turns his back if there is a nickel in his sight. When he hung up the phone, Jimmy declared that Lizzy was bubbling over with joy and happiness. Then he went over to the Peabodys' and that was the beginning of the little mystery here.

"Lizzy had marked off a little plot of ground shaped kinda like a semi-circle or a horseshoe right near the front porch. She told Jimmy to go down near the springhouse and dig up several plants and shrubs and to make sure a couple of wild roses were thrown in. He was to carefully leave some soil around the roots when he dug them up, so they wouldn't die in the transplanting.

"Well, this next thing, it do beat all! Jimmy said the reverend came home unexpectedly and saw what Miss Lizzy was doing. Jimmy said it made his heart race around a bit when he saw Albert grab Lizzy, kiss her, and whirl her around in a circle. Then her dress tail flew up and he saw she was wearing pink bloomers. The reverend and Lizzy were both laughing like crazy right in front of my innocent child! Now, who would do something so crazy, can you tell me that?

"Lizzy paid Jimmy very generously, and—now you won't believe this—the reverend reached into his own pocket and gave him a few more coins! I'm inclined to say this is just a 'little more wood in the fireplace' as you try to unravel this mystery.

"Jimmy hurried home and told us this news. The next day, Jimmy headed for the newspaper and put in a new ad. It read:

> To all the ladies in Paw Paw,
>
> Do you want the latest look in your front yard? It is a semi-circle of flowers by your front door. If desired, call the newspaper office. I will be waiting for your calls twenty-four hours a day.
>
> Jimmy Chores Simpson

"I think you can surmise that there hasn't been one call.

"Now we go to the next episode, to see if there is a connection.

"Now remember, we left the scene of the Peabodys singing, dancing, and laughing hilariously. Well, they came to prayer meeting that night the same way! And in the church house! They finally quit laughing but were still smiling. Now mind you my friends, I was there with my Maudie. It sure 'peared to me that the reverend cut a little two-step when he went to the podium. He had Miss Rose Turner to sing two of her special songs and Old Matt Collins to lead in prayer. He didn't make any leading speech. He just told those who had their Bibles to turn to Psalm 127 in the Old Testament."

The men on the porch now understood why Otis brought his Bible that morning as he opened it and began to read the reverend's passage: "Children are a heritage of the Lord and the fruit of the womb is His reward. As arrows are in the hand of the mighty man; so are the children of the youth. Happy is the man that hath his quiver full of them."

"Well neighbors, when Reverend Peabody finished reading that passage, there were more than a few whispers. Then a hushed silence penetrated the room. Even the kids on their pallets, the ones that hadn't gone to sleep, looked warily around. Lizzy was sitting on a bench at the side of the wall where everyone could see her face, and she never blushed a mite as everyone looked at her. It was truly amazing how she kept that big grin on her face. Then, on account of the silence that one could cut with a knife, Albert said the Twenty-third Psalm and dismissed the congregation.

"We were all stunned at this, so we hurried out the door.

"You might ask if this the end of my story. Indeed not! Yesterday morning, Sunday, Maudie and I went to church. There was an unusually large crowd, I do say. Miss Rose Turner sang her special song, and Old Matt Collins said the morning prayer again.

"Then, soberly and a little gravely, the reverend took the podium and said, 'I will try with my usual dignity to say things that might sound harsh. I will confess I am a mite testy and my feathers have been slightly ruffled in the wrong direction. A rumor has been spread up and down, near and far, about the scripture I read in your hearing Wednesday night. And this rumor has not come via the grapevine of the porch at the General Store, which indeed is a surprise. The scripture was taken out of context by some church members and turned into a sordid implication. This passage was an innocent form of speech in Old Testament times. Yet, the shock waves have spread like a prairie fire to every nook and cranny in Paw Paw. The very words that are being so flippantly used are: "The reverend's quiver is acting up again."

"'Enough of that. I will proceed to make you understand that the word of God is always spiritual. Let us turn our Book to the New Testament, the book of Galatians. The apostle Paul said, "Taking the shield of faith, wherewith ye shall be able to quench all fiery darts of the wicked."

"'Now, does this mean to run out and buy a shield? Of course not! I will not answer another question about this sordid tale that has been bandied about in Paw Paw. I beg you to do the same.'

"Well, the reverend shut the Good Book a little peevishly, and he stalked out the door. He never stood beneath the belfry to shake hands with his flock as he departed. Poor Lizzy had to carry that unruly Albert Jr. in her arms along with her Bible and the pallet, which Junior had refused to lay on. She was the one who shook hands with everyone and invited them back to church.

"Now mind you, my friends, she was still smiling ear to ear. Me and Maudie have come to the conclusion that Lizzy is in the family way again and that despite the Reverend's churlishness, he is a happy man. That's why he read that quiver verse from the Good Book."

Fred Pinkham spoke, "We should be on our guard of what we say. We might do untold harm to our unsullied children, and I will add here there are several verses in that Book that we should read at home."

The men on the porch had talked for two days, trying to figure out the great mystery of why Lizzy had hired Jimmy C. to plant all those bushes beside their front porch. Oh, how they did love a mystery.

The next morning the ladies of the Baptist Church had their Sewing Circle. Clara loudly announced, "Jacob, I don't often get to go as we are generally too busy, but this day I'm going, so you stay on your toes and take care of our customers, so they won't grumble or complain. Do you hear me, Jacob?"

"Clara, how could I help from hearing you. The men on the porch can plainly hear you."

With that warning, Clara rushed out the door to the church.

Jacob was pleasantly surprised that their customers must have stayed home. This gave him a chance to sit on the porch with the men. They were all delighted that he could join them. They related to him the mystery that had occurred at the Peabody home.

Tom Curry adamantly declared, "This baffling tale has

some connection with the reverend's text he read out of the Good Book."

"Oh dear," Jacob said. "I happen to know all about this. Lizzy told Clara about it. The night of the big storm, a big tree fell on the gravesite where the Reverend wanted to be buried. He requested this, so he could hear his children playing and singing over his grave. Well, we all know that so far Albert Jr. is the only one to play all by his lonesome there. That spot is so important to Albert, it must mean that Lizzy is in the family way again. Therefore, that is why this whole tawdry mess has happened. Men, I think that clears up your latest puzzle."

Jacob looked at them for some thanks, but none was forthcoming. It looked like he had spoiled their day by solving their mystery.

Judge not, that ye be not judged.
For with what judgment ye judge, ye shall be judged:
and with what measure ye mete,
it shall be measured to you again.

MATTHEW 7:1-2

Chapter 49

A Plug of Chewing Tobacco in a Rolled-Down Stocking

Once again there was squabbling and bickering in the Baptist Church. This time it was about Reverend Peabody's barn and what was stored in it. He had the biggest barn in Paw Paw and in fact, the whole county. It was used to store the hay and feed for his livestock and to house vast crops of tobacco, which his sharecroppers grew. The tobacco put a lot of money in the reverend's coffer. The complainers did admit that both the barn and the crops were there before his conversion and before his becoming their preacher.

The problem was tobacco itself. Some of the members of the church thought it a sin to chew or smoke tobacco. Some thought it wasn't right if one grew it but didn't use it. Some thought it all right if they used it and grew it. Of course, some diehards thought it a sin to do either one.

Now this complaint had reared its ugly head among the ladies at the Baptist Sewing Circle. The day started out to be another joyous day of fellowship. Then, out of the wild blue yonder, Anna Bell Sawyer, with her needle pointing upward, cautiously remarked, "What are we going to do about the tobacco questions that keep popping up in church? The complaints are flying hither and yon. There are whispering accusations of our high elite and even from people that don't fellowship with us.

"And it has come to my ears that little Kathy Hawthorn was

caught chewing tobacco at school recess and on the sly during the class. Where she spittles, only the Lord knows. If you are wondering why I'm using a Bible term, it is because I can't say S.P.I.T.! It sounds too vulgar to me.

"We mothers know that as soon as our daughters get to school, they roll down their dark long stockings. Sometimes in the winter, they roll up their long underwear and then the stockings go down. I'm sure our excellent schoolteacher knows nothing of the cud of tobacco that Kathy rolled up inside her stocking. Two of our children reported this to me. So what do we do now, Miss Idy?"

Miss Idy was stunned at this revelation of little girls chewing tobacco. Aghast, nearly speechless, she said, "I will see that this outrage is dealt with immediately. I'm sure Kathy's parent know nothing about this. We know that Mr. Hawthorn uses chewing tobacco, so she probably slips some from his big cud. What an example we are setting before our innocent children."

Moaning and lamenting, she wrung her hands. "I think we should dismiss our gathering today as I am forced to do something about this revelation."

The ladies looked askance at one another as they gathered up their belongings and left. Then Miss Idy jumped up and clicked her heels together with more deliberation than usual and raced to the porch of the General Store.

It was extremely lucky that three of the board members were there. With no outsider being around, she thought it was safe to repeat the talk about tobacco as it had been discussed at the Sewing Circle.

"Gentlemen, we are aware of you partaking of this 'devil's brew,' so you must consider long and hard about the predicament we are in. This problem must be nipped in the bud now. This is so serious it could cause a church split. Look at what happened in Whippoorwill. Half of the congregation went down the road and built another church. There they stand, in sight of each other. I have heard that it was the puritanical members who pulled away, calling the ones that were left 'another tawdry group.' You all might not have noticed, but there has been a subtle indication of that already in our flock.

"Since I am chairman of the church board, I am calling for a meeting at Wednesday night's prayer meeting. You men scatter this news abroad; only church members can come."

Wednesday evening, all the members of the church were present. They all were quite nervous, and a light commotion of unrest and whispering went on. Miss Idy used her gavel unusually lightly. "Now, my brothers and sisters of this church, we will discuss this quietly and try to come to a pleasing ending."

She calmly reported her findings of this turmoil they were in, cautioning that they must settle this tonight, then forgive and forget this conflict.

Miss Idy made a slight bow to a new convert, Jerome Daniels—everyone called him "Sad Face" when he wasn't nearby. "People, I call Brother Jerome to the podium. He is a babe in Christ and will be a new voice in our church, and just maybe we could learn a lot from him."

Shaking violently with stage fright, Jerome walked to the podium. The elders, and indeed the whole assembly, were pleased as he carried his Bible with him. "Dear Friends, you all can see that I am almost scared to death, but I will do my best to answer some of your questions. Just last night I was reading some passages in my Bible, and maybe this might help us. Please turn to First Corinthians. These are the words of our great apostle Paul: 'I was with you in weakness and fear and much trembling.'

"Boy, this sure describes me right now." He gave a big laugh and the members' laughter rippled across the room.

"Our beloved apostle Paul wrote this also, 'I am determined not to know anything among you save Jesus Christ and Him crucified.' I can see that inside the church and outside of the church, we are all divided. We know for sure that our Lord can solve this problem, even tonight. But can we be divided again next week by something else? Maybe by someone saying we can't grow corn because it could be used to make bootleg whiskey.

"I can truthfully say I was miraculously delivered from tobacco the next morning after my conversion. And I must confess that Miss Idy had a hand in this. One day, on the porch of the General Store, I heard her quote, 'Taste not, touch not, handle not, but be ye separate from the world.'"

Jerome stopped his shaking and controlled his nervousness. "My questions is this, who has made us a judge over one another? I thought God was our judge. Who among us wants to throw the first stone? Men judge on the outward appearance of a man, but God looks at the heart and how much we love Him and our fellow man. How does one love God, who he hasn't seen, and not love our fellowman?"

Jerome gave a slight bow and took his seat. The members all sat stunned and hushed from these gracious words that came from a "babe in Christ." Unashamed, all did weep as Reverend Peabody slowly rose from his seat.

"We will never forget this message tonight. You know, I think this would be a good time for us to hug one another before we dismiss."

All the laity said, "Amen."

Reverend Peabody turned to Jerome, smiling broadly, "Welcome to the ministry Reverend Jerome."

As usual, nothing was settled and they continued to love each other in spite of their complaints.

A little child shall lead them.

These six things doth the LORD hate:
yea, seven are an abomination unto him:
a proud look, a lying tongue,
and hands that shed innocent blood,
an heart that deviseth wicked imaginations,
feet that be swift in running to mischief,
a false witness that speaketh lies,
and he that soweth discord among brethren.

PROVERBS 6:16-19

Chapter 50

The New Mayor of Paw Paw

Miss Idy often appeared defiant of all the conventional methods and accepted ways of doing things in Paw Paw. At times, the men on the porch were quite nettled, irritated, and angry with her.

One day, Fred was brave enough to whine and wail, "Why do we, mature men, allow Miss Idy to ride roughshod over everyone that disagrees with her? Tell me that if you can."

"Well now Fred," Jeremiah lamely replied, "the reason is because she is a woman and we have all been raised to show love, honor, and courtesy to this weaker sex."

Ray Linden, a mite testily added, "I have heard several people describe a person as one who lights up a room when they walk in the door, but 'pears to me that Miss Idy lights up a room when she leaves it. Explain that to me."

Otis added, "Life is too short and sweet to become embroiled in such an altercation. It would require too much effort, and I, for one, won't use or exert the sweat of my brow to try to change things."

Fred still whining said, "Otis, I wish you wouldn't use those new-fangled words; they could trip us up someday!"

Otis drawled, "I just can't help it. My Jimmy insists on me trying to increase my vocabulary."

With these solemn and somber words, there wasn't any

more to say. Therefore, with a look of penance and suffering, Fred passed around to his friends a plug of chewin' tabaccy. Jimmy declared it was just "a short pause between the wars of Miss Idy and the men that sat on the porch of the General Store." Peace dominated on the porch until the paper came.

From the beginning, it had caught the men on the porch completely off guard. Some said they were dozing and nodding, so they were not aware of what was going on right under their noses.

Jimmy C. had stopped by this morning to chat for a few minutes, while on his way to school, and mentioned vaguely that they were studying democracy in school. "We are learning how the electoral system works in our United States. The people have the right to vote for whom they want to govern over them. However, I am going to question Miss Anderson this morning about the word acclamation. I think a person could be put into office without a ballot just by speaking yea or nay, by applause, or by just raising of one's hand."

Otis, growing testy at his son said, "Now Jimmy, you go on to school, as we can do without all this rigmarole that you're talking about. We have more serious things to discuss than the word acclamation."

With a leap off the porch, Jimmy ran on to school lickety-split.

Later that week, school let out a little early, so Jimmy decided to deliver his papers before going home. He raced by the men on the porch and threw the paper to them with a bit more vigor than usual and without his customary banter with his dad and his dad's cronies.

Otis remarked, "I hope he displays the same vim and vinegar when he faces the wood pile when he gets home."

Ray Linden picked up the paper. "Well, I'll be horns waggled, how in the world did this happen? Why, that Miss Idy do look good in this picture."

"Come on Ray," Otis remarked, "what does it say, and

what cockamamie scheme is she involved in now?"

They all gathered around Ray, and there on the front page was a very flattering picture of Miss Idy smiling one of her rare smiles. Under the picture was the explanation.

> For the first time in its history, Paw Paw has a mayor. It is Miss Idy Crandall. This paper congratulates our boy wonder, Jimmy C. Simpson, on how this came about.
>
> It was a calm and serene election, and the people of our town should be proud of its orderly fashion. It bore none of the chaotic turmoil of our last election of Miss Idy to the position of Deaconess of the Baptist Church.
>
> We understand that our own Jimmy C. had a head-to-head encounter with Miss Idy before embarking on this questionable journey. He bluntly asked her one question. "Explain to me, Miss Idy, what are your qualifications for the lofty task of mayor?"
>
> Scheming and conniving as always, Miss Idy obliged, "Jimmy, if I am mayor, I will be a tireless worker for every citizen in Paw Paw, the dignitaries and the distinguished but also the meek and lowly with the same devotion. I am qualified for this position as I have the 'pot of oil' to lubricate social contacts that will stimulate growth in our economy. I know I have the dignity and polished manner and can be a gracious host representing Paw Paw. I am willing to burn the midnight oil, which I often do now, as all can attest. If I do hold this position as mayor, I shall be a hard taskmaster."
>
> To our reporter she said, "If anyone wants to call this election null and void or challenge me, I will be glad to turn this important and vital task over to him or her."
>
> The Paw Paw Times discovered that as mayor, she receives no money, and, in fact, she will use her own money on her travels and innumerable duties.

For the second time in Paw Paw history, (and that went back several years) the men on the porch were tongue-tied, lacking the power of speech completely. If perchance a stranger should have happened by just then, they would have wondered about the stark white, immobile faces of the men.

When they finally regained the ability to speak, someone whispered, "How did this happen?"

Fred Pinkham whined, "I thought that everything in a newspaper was the truth, the whole truth, and nothing but the truth, so help me God. This can't be the truth. We didn't have any election."

Ray Linden lamented, "This word taskmaster Miss Idy uses, that comes from the days of slavery. It means 'tyrant.' Only the Lord knows what lies in store for us in the days to come."

Otis stood up. "I think we should all go home and cool down a little. I will talk to Jimmy tonight and find out how this happened. I'll also try to figure out if we can stymie 'Miss Steamroller' from her latest campaign." They all managed a laugh at that.

Around every supper table that evening, the hue and cry went on. "Dad, explain this please, so we can challenge Miss Anderson on what she is teaching us about the electoral system of our nation. Miss Anderson calls it acclamation yet you tell us that Miss Idy got the position of mayor in a sly, cunning, underhanded way. This sure puts a little excitement into a boring subject."

The master of the house, sighing with the patience of Job, raised his voice a trifle and said, "Children are to be seen but not heard. All of you get to bed, and I will help Mother do the dishes tonight."

Whenever there was utter confusion in town, the men gathered a few minutes early. The shenanigans that Miss Idy pulled off involved every working male in Paw Paw. It rendered the brave men that sat on the porch at the General Store powerless in her little hands.

The men brightened a little as Otis and Jimmy C. came down the road. Their hopes turned to misgivings when they saw defeat on Otis' face. Even his steps betrayed defeat.

"Well, my friends, here's my son. I'll gladly let him speak." The men saw Jimmy C. was uneasy and a little scared about his part in helping Miss Idy into the position of mayor. "Go ahead Jimmy, tell them what you told me. Maybe this will be a learning lesson to you that you have overstepped yourself this time."

"Well gentlemen," said Jimmy, (Did the men detect a tear in Jimmy's eyes?), "we all heard Miss Idy say at her election as deaconess that we needed a mayor here in Paw Paw. That no town can succeed, operate smoothly, or gain wealth or fame without one. I thought all of you would like that, as for sure we are a long way from being wealthy." Jimmy was beginning to feel better now, as he was at his best when speaking. "Well, one day Miss Idy and I were talking this over, and in school we were studying this very same thing. She told me that one way to be elected was by acclamation. This could be done by applause or by raising one's hand or by saying aye. I checked with Miss Anderson, and she said it was true.

"So when I delivered the paper, I just asked everyone if they would like to have a mayor in Paw Paw. I couldn't believe the response. There were a few that refused to answer yes, so I asked them to clap their hands, which they did. And you know, I left them laughing. I remembered the verse in the Bible that said that laughter is as good as a dose of medicine, and I know you all believe the Good Book.

"There is something you can do if you don't want Miss Idy to be mayor. We can declare this to be a breach of law and custom and call for a bona fide election."

Jimmy C. looked helpless and contrite. His dad still had that testy look on his face, but he was sure there was a twinkle in his eyes.

"Dad, can I go to school now? I think Miss Anderson will

finish the subject of the electoral process in the United States of America today." Then, without waiting for his dad to respond, Jimmy leaped off the porch and ran to school. Just before he was out of sight, he yelled back to them, "Miss Idy said that this overwhelming vote for mayor, it automatically put her superintendent of our school system."

Did someone say a little child would lead them?

Although the fig tree shall not blossom,
neither shall fruit be in the vines;
the labour of the olive shall fail,
and the fields shall yield no meat;
the flock shall be cut off from the fold,
and there shall be no herd in the stalls:
yet I will rejoice in the LORD,
I will joy in the GOD of my salvation.

HABAKKUK 3:17-18

Chapter 51

The Depression/Drought Decision

The drought and Depression was no respecter of persons living in Paw Paw. It had rapidly and pitilessly moved into the home of Reverend Albert Peabody and his beloved wife, Lizzy.

It was before daylight, and they were sitting in the kitchen drinking their first cup of coffee. Their two little boys were sound asleep, but there had been no sleep for them. They were facing a frightening disaster and were in a dire dilemma about what was to be done with their one hundred head of white-faced cattle.

"Dear Lizzy, in a week or maybe ten days, we will have no more water for the cattle. No water means no pasture. The two boxcars of hay and corn we had shipped in from Nebraska will soon be gone too. There will be no more of it as Nebraska has begun to feel the Depression and drought. Therefore, my dear, we must make up our minds today. We soon will be land poor, you know, as no one can buy acreage at this time. So we are facing something threatening out there that is rather chilling."

Lizzy pushed her chair closer to her husband's. She pulled him into her arms to her soft breasts and stroked his head. "Now you listen to me, my love, you must do what you feel is the best. I don't know what the best decision is, that's for sure. Remember Albert, no matter what happens, we have each other and our babies. You are always preaching about how our

Lord will take care of us in trying times. You read from your pulpit that our Lord will never leave or forsake His children. So, my love, you be on your way, and I must get busy making our little baby girl some nightgowns." With her eyes sparkling, she reached over and put Albert's hand over her swollen belly. In her happy and joyous mood, she began kissing him.

"Oh, my darling, my love, why have I been given so much?" Albert murmured in her ear. "I don't deserve the happiness you have given me." With these words, Albert stood up a little taller with his back a mite straighter as he went out the door. For sure, Lizzy was the pattern and helpmate that God had provided Adam in Eden's Garden long ago. "I am blessed over all men." Albert said humbly.

Now if perchance a stranger should have happened by the Peabody home as Albert was leaving his house, they would not have guessed that this was a rich man on his way to sell his livelihood. And maybe that stranger would think that this Baptist preacher had experienced life to its fullest when he saw him dance a little two-step out in his yard.

The Reverend Peabody went to the telephone office. He was in search of a buyer for his livestock, and he knew he would get the best price in St. Louis or Kansas City. He also knew that if he found a buyer in either of those cities, he would have to send the cattle by railcar. With Maggie Jenkins' help, he made good contacts with the buyers, but there was no market for the cattle, and no one offered him any hope. His last and final hope was his lifelong friend, Andy Fremont, who lived in Whippoorwill. He owned a big ranch on the White River, which still had plenty of water in it.

Reverend Peabody went to Whippoorwill. Luckily, he spotted Andy coming out of the feed store just as he was fixing to head back to his ranch. After greeting and embracing each other with jokes and banter, Albert said, "Andy, let me tell you, I'm in big, big trouble. You know, of course, that I have the best herd of whiteface in the county. Some of them are registered animals. However, I am out of water, or will be in a few days.

Big Morgan Creek is fast drying up, and you are the only one I know who could take my cattle. What do you say, my friend?"

Trying to steady his nerves, Albert picked up a small piece of wood and started to whittle while Andy walked in small circles, kicking up the dust with this boot. Those familiar with business transactions, trading, and bartering in this part of the country knew this was the quirky mannerism that all the men in the vicinity indulged themselves in when thinking about a deal. The one who was pressed to sell, maybe with his back against the wall like Albert, was the one who picked up a stick and began whittling. The value and worth of the transaction would determine the size of the stick. Both men would warily eye each other while trying to appear not to. If the one whittling happened to unintentionally cut his thumb, the dust-kicker knew he had won the upper hand. The men on the porch called it a "bloody enterprise" when this happened. Fortunately for Albert, there was no reason for playing this little game anymore, not in this hour of want and disaster. This was a plea between friends.

Andy was the first to speak. "My friend Albert, I can tell you, as you already know, we are living in perilous times. We don't understand what is happening now, and we don't know if it will be worse tomorrow. I don't want your cattle. I do have water as you say, but if this drought doesn't break, my pastures will dry up too. The only thing I can do is give you thirty-five dollars a head."

"But Andy, I paid over $250 a head for my registered stock."

"Yes Albert, I know that, but this is all I can give. Take it or not. It is my only offer."

"Andy, I have to accept it. I have no choice."

They shook hands and began planning how to move the cattle. Andy insisted that the move take place at night, as it would be cooler and easier on the cattle than facing the blazing afternoon sun.

"I will have to beg, borrow, or steal enough trucks to move them in one night. We will be dealing with old ramshackle, dilapidated trucks," warned Andy.

Andy saw the worry and distress on Albert's face. He put his arm across his friend's shoulder. "Old buddy, I want you to know I am sorry for you, I would do better if I could."

Then all of a sudden the worried, anxious look left Albert's face. "Andy, I must tell you what has happened in my life. I have married the most beautiful girl in the world. I have two little boys and another child on the way. I know you have heard that I am a pastor of the precious Baptist Church in Paw Paw. Andy, who could ask for more, except for maybe a little rain." Albert laughed. "None of us knows what tomorrow holds, but we do know God holds tomorrow in His loving hands, so we can rest in His promise."

As Albert left, Andy watched him go. "Why, he is a new man. Maybe the Spirit dwells within him. I am going to go to church Sunday and see what this is all about, that's for sure," he murmured.

All day long, the huge, magnificent whiteface cattle of the Peabody Ranch displayed a spectacularly gruesome sight as they clawed and pawed in the mud for the last of the moisture of Big Morgan Creek. Huge clods of clay clung to their hoofs like grotesque deformities, as they struck wildly in their frenzied efforts to find water.

Just as dusk was falling, five trucks arrived at the corrals to load the cattle. It was almost an impossible task as many of the animals could barely stand.

All Saturday night, the residents of Paw Paw heard the faint lowing and moaning of the cattle as they were being loaded into the trucks. The men, the breadwinners of the family not involved in the move, were chilled and apprehensive. They lay in bed with their eyes wide open, wondering about the ominous veil of gloom that, in the darkness, was lowering itself over the town. If a rich and powerful man like Reverend

Peabody was being brought to his knees, where did they fit in this vast Depression-and-drought drama? Although it was a hot night, each worried man pulled his sheet closer as cold fingers from icy hands rippled up and down their backs.

All through that day, Lizzy and Reverend Peabody's two little boys had cried, fussed, and whined. Since they were always happy little boys, she knew that in some uncanny way, they were feeling the strange silent upheaval in the Peabody household. She decided that they were so upset she would take them into her bed. One lay on each side of her. They had promptly gone to sleep, which she was grateful for.

Then it began. A muffled lowing sound of bereavement coming from the cattle. Then, as if in sympathy for the precious cargo, the trucks began making a sad grinding noise, as if they were fighting against a grindstone as they slowly crawled and wormed their way up the slight hill just a few steps from Lizzy and Albert's bedroom.

In fear, Lizzy hugged her little boys tight against her body. Then she thought the unthinkable; she thought of the text that Albert had preached a few weeks ago. It was Revelations 6: "Come and see, and I looked and behold a pale horse and his name that sat on him was Death." Ere this drought and Depression would end, the pale horse and its rider would have traveled and crept into every nook and cranny in every house in the little town of Paw Paw. Lizzy put aside the terrible verse and remembered what she had told Albert before he went out the door, about God's watching over them in this hour of travail. She believed it then and she believed it now. No sooner had she settled that in her mind than suddenly, unexpectedly, the baby girl they hoped for took a jump and a leap in her belly. It made her laugh in spite of this heart-crushing, terrible ordeal.

The boys were still asleep as Lizzy crept out of bed after a sleepless night. She went to the kitchen and made some coffee, then sat down in the small rocking chair. She looked at the tiny antique table that held Albert's Bible, which he always left open to his last reading. Outside the big window, she watched the sun's burning eye peek over the small hill by the house. It seemed to pause a few minutes and look at the deep ruts in the road left by the big trucks as they toiled through the night with their prized cargo. She watched as tiny particles of soil loosened their hold and fell down into the ruts in the road. She scolded herself for this frivolous, piddling, pointless observation. Then the diligent sun resumed its task of searching unrelentingly for any tender green foliage that might be lurking anywhere around the Peabody ranch.

Then her vigilance and watchful longing was rewarded when she saw Albert coming through the yard gate. Her husband, her lover, yes, her friend, was home. So many of the wives complained that their husbands never sat and talked with them, but she never had this problem. Maybe the reason was that their conversations as close friends inevitably led into friendships of fire. Again, she smiled to herself as she opened the door for her beloved.

Lizzy tried to keep Albert from going to church after the heartrending ordeal he had just been through, but he refused. While he was bathing and dressing, she dressed the boys and herself for church. She noticed a piece of paper he slipped into his Bible as they went out the door. When they got to church, their friends looked concerned for their misfortune and the financial loss they had experienced.

The service proceeded as usual. Miss Idy began with a silent prayer, asked the congregation to sing a song from the hymnbook, then bowed and gracefully turned the pulpit over to Reverend Peabody. He in turn bowed to her. Lizzy was a little surprised that his countenance fairly glowed with radiance as he bowed before his congregation.

"I greet you all this morning in thanksgiving, giving thanks especially for my beloved wife, Lizzy. She has opened doors to a bright new world that I never knew was out there for one such as I. She led me through heaven's gate. The family, yes, this is the most precious gift God has bestowed on us mortals."

Then, instead of opening his Bible, the reverend took out a sheet of paper and began to read.

Riches in Christ

One by one, He took them from me, all the things I valued most
'Til I was left empty-handed, every glittering toy was lost
And I walked earth's highway grieving in my rags and poverty
Until I heard His voice inviting, 'Lift those empty hands to Me.'
Then I turned my hands toward heaven, and He filled them with a store
Of His own transcendent riches 'til they could contain no more.
And at last I comprehended, with my stupid mind and dull
That God cannot pour His riches into hands already full.

Author Anonymous

Reverend Albert Peabody turned and murmured to Miss Idy, "I don't think I could say anything that would lift us up more than that." Then turning back to the body of the church, he said, "I thank you, dear congregation, for the love you have bestowed on my family."

Then he reverently picked up his Bible and walked back to his beloved Lizzy. He picked up one of his sons, Lizzy took the other, and they walked through the door where "servants ride horses and kings walked by their sides."

The LORD is my shepherd; I shall not want.
He maketh me to lie down in green pastures:
he leadeth me beside the still waters.

PSALM 23:1-2

Chapter 52

The Dark Woods

Miss Idy had been to Reverend Albert Peabody's house, and she decided to take a shortcut through his vast acreage to her house. She had never been this far from the reverend's big, white house, but with her usual uncanny sense of direction, she felt very sure of herself. After walking for over an hour, she began feeling a little concerned about where she was.

The fields that lay before her gave no indication of ever having been cultivated for growing corn, wheat, or any other grain. It didn't look as if cattle had ever grazed here either. Maybe the reverend was so wealthy he never bothered with this out-of-the-way place.

Again, she was puzzled and bewildered as she came upon a field of high grass. A brisk wind was blowing the grass, which was swaying back and forth, looking like the sea.

Suddenly, as if hearing a bell ringing, she gasped in wonder. Why, these fields were growing broomcorn. When the short leaves and bright flowers had been harvested for the cattle to eat, the dry stalks were used then for making brooms.

Miss Idy shivered with this discovery. Right now, this was a godsend. This was a means to help those that were hungry and could be facing starvation if something wasn't done. Emotionally, she raised hands to heaven, thanking her Lord. Abruptly she thought of someone else she needed to thank, that old scalawag, Lommis Carouthers, her professor in college who had insisted she take a course in agriculture and animal husbandry.

Coming down to earth, she found she was laughing. She couldn't remember how she got through the sea of broom-corn. Had she walked on the waves as the Lord had done? Of course not, veering on blasphemy she quickly brushed that thought aside, still laughing.

She grew somber when she thought of how to approach Reverend Peabody about the treasure he had growing on the far edge of his ranch. She knew about his stinginess in certain areas of life. She also knew he didn't know about broomcorn or he would have already had it harvested. Yes, she knew it would take careful scheming on her part to persuade the reverend to give it to Paw Paw's citizens in these trying times. Therefore, she must be "sly as a serpent and harmless as a dove." She must also keep this quiet until she could finagle around and get him to do this generous deed.

Looking around, she thought she should be near the store by now, but nothing looked familiar for as far as she could see. What had she done with her head in the clouds? It was a cloudy day, so she couldn't see the sun for telling the time of day. She knew she had walked over two miles from the reverend's big white house.

Being exhausted, she sat down under a tree to rest a few minutes and give herself time to get her sense of direction under control. Should she backtrack to the reverend's house and get him to take her home? No, she was too exhausted to walk that far. Yes, she was lost. The little know-it-all spinster was lost probably just a few steps from the General Store. Bolstered by this thought, she got her "second wind," as the men on the porch would say, and increased her steps in the direction of town.

The faster she walked the farther away from Paw Paw she journeyed. In doubt and apprehension, she trembled. No one would know where she was or even realize she wasn't home. She had to slow down now as it was getting dark, and she had to be careful not to fall down over a branch or a stone.

Night closed around her, so she prayed very seriously, trying to stir up all the faith she had. She knew she needed to stay near a tree for support. So when she felt a large tree trunk with her hand, she sat down. Then she felt water with the other hand. Her throat was parched after the turbulent, chaotic day, so she cupped her hand in the water and drank her fill. Then she put her wrap around her back and hugged the trunk of the tree tightly for a little protection from the cold night air.

Then sitting up startled, she thought, What is happening here? Why, Big Morgan Creek went dry several months ago! Although exhausted, she barely slept as she excitedly wondered about where the water came from.

She was awakened in the morning by the dappling, mottled spots of sunshine in her eyes as they filtered through the leaves on the tree. She uncoiled herself from the tree, which she had hugged all night, and then grimacing in stiffness and pain, she got to her feet.

Then she saw the water. She was dumbstruck. Water? Stupefied, Miss Idy stared at this phenomenon before her. Finally, she walked the length of this pool of water. At its end was a short strip of dry ground and then another pool of water. Then she noticed another miracle. These ponds were teeming with silvery catfish. Oh, what a treasure she had found. She raised her arms to her Lord, as she knew He was looking down on her, in spite of her doubts.

She knew there would be a few non-believers in town when she delivered this news, so she had to come up with a logical, sensible explanation for the water. On the other side of the ponds was a steep mountain, which had clefts, ravines, and chasms. Since there had been no rain in over two years, she reasoned that these ponds were being fed by an underground spring. All the trees and underbrush must have hidden them, plus the fact that they are on Reverend Peabody's ranch, must be the reason why no one had seen these ponds before.

Why was she trying to seek some answer when she should accept God's miracle?

After she had solved the mystery of the two pools, she walked briskly toward Paw Paw. All the way, she was thanking the Lord for His provisions. She finally came to the old sawmill that had been silent for nigh on to two years. Resting for a few moments on a stack of wood, she said, "What a waste of this fine lumber!" Then a light came on in her head, flickered and started to flame. She spoke her new idea aloud, "Why not make cedar pencils? Kids had to have them for school, and the adults too. No matter what happens, there will always be a need and a big market for pencils. All we would need is graphite. The men could get that from Alabama. They could make them without pay until they established a growing market. Maybe even a company."

Miss Idy's heart was beating overtime. She didn't need to rest anymore, she had a mission, and under God's direction, she would accomplish it. Tiptoe she must, because all the males in Paw Paw, especially the men that sat on the porch of the General Store, practically breathed their lackadaisical, lazy way of life.

Miss Idy never ventured into anything unless she covered all the areas in her mind of what could happen if, by chance, the project backfired on her. She almost literally wet her finger in the wind to test for any skirmishes she might encounter. Finally, after getting home she ate a bit and took a little nap.

The next day, as she returned to the Peabody home, she went over and over how to approach him, and if need be, finagle him into giving that big acreage of broomcorn to the church and the needy people of Paw Paw. Fearing she might come to the house and startle them in one of their passionate moments, which had happened before, she started singing "Amazing Grace" as loud as she could. She had always thought that kind of behavior only happened in the night, but she had to admit she wasn't an authority on the subject. Just singing that song increased her faith that the reverend would be in a generous mood. Her faith once again was rewarded as she found Albert with one step on the earth and the other in the glories of heaven. His darling Lizzy was in the "family way" again.

When she stepped through the door, Lizzy grabbed her in a big hug, knocking her black hat off her head. "Oh, Miss Idy, we are so happy that the Lord would bless us again. I'm afraid that Albert's grave will be a mite crowded for all our children to dance and play on."

Miss Idy agreed quite dryly, "You are right about that, Lizzy."

Later on, she would tell that God had gotten to the Peabody home before she did, softening Albert's heart into giving the most generous gift.

"Brother Peabody, I will quickly state my position of why I'm here. We have people, whole families on the verge of starving in and around our town. We must do something immediately. Now, you have several acres of valuable broomcorn that I stumbled onto, and if you're not going to harvest it, why not give it to the church to help those who are so desperately needing help?"

The Reverend and Lizzy sat with a still concerned look on their faces. "Miss Idy, I do thank you for doing a job that I should have been doing. I'm sure you have heard the gossip of the vast holdings I have accumulated over the years. Maybe some would say it was true; anyway, I will gladly give this corn to the church. What do you say Lizzy?"

"Oh, honey, I agree with you."

Albert looked at his darling with worshiping eyes. "Miss Idy, this wife of mine has so changed my life, I will count this gift as tithing to our church. Please feel free to do what you want with it."

Miss Idy got up and started home happy in the knowledge she had been God's instrument. After getting out of sight of the house, she held up her long black dress and started skipping down the road, singing at the top of her lungs. "I have crossed over Jordan to Canaan's fair land, and that is like heaven for me."

They helped every one his neighbour;
and every one said to his brother, Be of good courage.

ISAIAH 41:6

Chapter 53

Depression Co-op

It took two weeks for Miss Idy to plan, explore and canvas Paw Paw and the surrounding areas. Clara was amazed at how many legal letters and documents Miss Idy sent and received back. One day there were three big letters and she entertained the thought of holding one in the vapors of the teakettle, but she quickly changed her mind. If Jacob found out about it, there would be havoc in and around the General Store.

There were many mysterious long-distance phone calls too. Maggie Jenkins from the telephone exchange didn't offer much help, as she said Miss Idy used too many words that were in college-graduate lingo.

Rumors swirled around town and on the grapevine on the porch. When these drifted to Miss Idy's ears, they only spurred her on. She still needed a little more time to get everything into a nutshell. When the evening paper arrived at her doorstep and the whole front page carried the announcement that President Franklin Roosevelt and the government were setting up a vast welfare program nationwide, Miss Idy knew she must act immediately.

She grabbed her pages of paperwork and headed toward the Paw Paw Times newspaper. As she walked into the office, she slammed the door so hard the old Hines building fairly shook.

"Now listen carefully Tabitha and Timothy, and you too, Jimmy C. (Why was Jimmy C. always around during any important issue in Paw Paw?) If I have my way, our residents will not accept the handouts and welfare program from the government. This is degrading, humiliating, and disgraceful to the fair name of Paw Paw. I think I have a solution. I want the whole front page of the next paper to blare out these words in big letters."

> ARE YOU SICK AND TIRED OF BEING SICK AND TIRED AND LIVING IN WANT AND DISASTER IN THIS DEPRESSION AND DROUGHT? ARE YOU SICK OF WATCHING YOUR CHILDREN GO HUNGRY AND IN NEED OF SHOES?
>
> I HAVE A SYSTEM WORKED OUT WHERE WE WON'T NEED TO ACCEPT THESE GOVERNMENT HANDOUTS, BUT THESE PLANS WILL NOT WORK UNLESS I HAVE THE COOPERATION OF EVERY ABLE-BODIED CITIZEN IN PAW PAW. THAT MEANS THE FATHERS, MOTHERS, GRANDPAS, GRANDMAS, AND THE CHILDREN. IF YOU ARE INTERESTED IN SAVING YOUR FAMILY, BE AT THE WEDNESDAY-NIGHT PRAYER MEETING AT THE CHURCH!

"Timothy, I will pay out of my little nest egg to get this on the front page."

"No, Miss Idy, we will gladly print this free, as we are all in this disaster of want and poverty."

Suddenly, Jimmy had an idea—something that happened to him quite often. "I don't know if there is any way to do this, but how about me getting some red pencils and underlining those words in red? This is a red-letter day."

"But Jimmy, that's a big a project; it might take all night."

"That's okay, Timothy. I'll call my folks and tell them what I'm doing."

Miss Idy, Timothy, and Tabitha looked this lad over and pondered in their hearts who Jimmy C. was. Was he the one the Scriptures wrote about when it said 'a little child shall lead them'?"

All four of them worked through the night on the red-letter edition of the Paw Paw Times. On Wednesday night at seven o'clock, Miss Idy started ringing the church bell, giving it a few extra tugs to announce this important meeting. Later she became alarmed but pleased at the crowd who packed out the room. She made all the children join her on the platform in order to give their seats to grown-ups. For sure, the children weren't happy with this arrangement because they knew their parents would watch their every movement and whisper.

Reverend Peabody opened with a prayer, and then he said, "Now Miss Idy will take over in this very important meeting. I have already gone over the many ideas she will share with you, and I have wholeheartedly agreed with her. Jimmy C., you can take the minutes of this meeting."

Then Reverend Peabody bowed to Miss Idy, as she grimly took the podium.

She began by shaking the newspaper back and forth. "I am ashamed of this article in the paper about our government taking over our lives with this aid and welfare program. I think it is demeaning and degrading to have to accept these government handouts. This is nonsense! This is what churches are supposed to do when there are people in need. There is great news right now. If you have read the Bible, as you should have, that is where your help should come from.

"I have worked on a plan that I think can succeed in getting us through this hard time without the government's help, but only if—and that's a big if—we all put our shoulders to the wheel and pull up our boots by the straps. I know I don't have all the answers, so our Paw Paw Times will accept any suggestions. They will all be examined to see if we can use them.

"Now for my ideas. I have divided them into plans, and

each plan has many parts.

"Plan Number One starts in the home. Now for many of you, this may be only a rehash of what you do every day, for others it is new, but we all need to be on the same page so to speak.

"Many households do not live near Plenty's Well but must haul the water they use from it. All of us ladies, after we finish washing our dishes and scalding them, should keep that rinse water and use it to wash the next meal's dishes. Every drop of water has to be put to use—dishwater and wash water. Mix it in the pig feed, water the fruit trees or a few garden vegetables."

"Also, save every drop of grease from your kitchen to make your soap. If you are a new bride and don't know how to make it, you can ask Grandma Octavia. She will be happy to show you how. She said she would share her secret of scented soap for your bathing.

"Many of you don't know that I went to college near New York. Well, I have a dear friend there, and I contacted her. She said she would buy all of our quilts, handiwork, and crocheting. She said there are still people who didn't lose all their money in the crash of the stock market.

"Now ladies, it is important that you cull your chickens, every little whipstitch, to see if they are laying eggs. Jimmy C. has a surefire method for doing this. If they aren't, you should eat them right away or they can be canned using a pressure cooker.

"Now Plan Number Two I call the Co-op. This actually has five parts.

"Part One concerns fish." Then she told them about finding the two ponds of fish. "We shall immediately start canning them, and we shall make fish cakes which are wonderful eating. I have a pressure cooker, I phoned to Whippoorwill, and they have four in their general store. Jimmy, I want you to get them in the morning. I will put up the money for them, but I expect the Co-op to pay me back when we get up to full speed.

"Part Two of the Co-op Plan is broomcorn. Our esteemed Reverend Peabody has given us a very generous gift of twenty acres of broomcorn. We shall make brooms, and I have already taken orders for them. Every woman in the world needs a broom to clean up after her kids and her husband too." Miss Idy tried to smile but failed in the effort.

"We shall feed the fish in the ponds with the tops of the canes, as they are good feed. This would be a good job for our children.

"Now for Part Three of the Co-op Plan. We shall start making pencils from the piles of cedar lumber at the abandoned mill. I have plans for how this is done, and I have already ordered the graphite from Alabama. It will be here in a few days. We know Depression or no Depression, every child needs a pencil—and adults too.

"Part Four of the Co-op Plan. We shall start making railroad ties from our big trees. I know this is going to take our most able-bodied men; several men who sit on the porch of the General Store fit that category.

"Now I will tell you of the largest project to be implemented. I call this Part Five of the Co-op Plan. This will take several meetings of the Co-op committee to bring this to pass, and all the distinguished leaders of Paw Paw will be able to vote whether we do it or not.

"This plan involves the ten-acre field of wildflowers. We all know that those flowers have died in this drought. And we know that land is the best acreage anywhere. Even though we have been careful in plowing our fields, we still lose topsoil to the fearsome hot winds.

"Now you men will need to study this closely. Why don't we go in and use a light, double shovel on that field and scratch the surface, maybe even do it by hand. This will take the efforts of the entire population of Paw Paw if we do this."

Miss Idy heard whispers and shuffling of shoes where the men were seated, so she knew she was treading on thin ice.

"We are the envy of every little town around us, as we have an abundance of water from Plenty's Well. We know Mr. Plenty's inspiration to dig it came straight from God, and it has never failed us. However, gentlemen, why can't we install a pump on it? We could pipe the water across to the field. We can even get the water there by a bucket brigade if need be. I think if we plant that field, we could have all the vegetables we would ever need in Paw Paw. Whatever we have in abundance we can put up for winter. This big project must include the children. They can hand-water the plants if need be.

"Now gentlemen, I have laid out a plan which I believe will work for us in this hour need, but for everything to get done, we must work shoulder to shoulder, hand to hand, heart to heart. We know that many will cry that they've done their share. There will be complaints of every description, so many of us will need to go the second mile without any thanks. The rewards are endless here on this earth and in heaven. There will be a band of angels waiting to put a golden star on your crown, which will adorn your head when you arrive there. Heaven forbid the thought of you going anyplace else! Then here on earth in Paw Paw, all of us will stand taller than we ever have. The men especially can hook their thumbs in the bib of their blue overalls and say, 'Look at us.' And indeed your wives, your children, your neighbors will burst with pride, even awe at these giants of men."

Bowing deeply before the men, Miss Idy ended her presentation by asking Reverend Peabody to offer a prayer for the success of the plan. Once again the residents of Paw Paw sat in astonishment, bewildered by the manipulative finagling of Miss Idy to get her way once again.

For the bed is shorter than that a man can stretch himself on it:
and the covering narrower than that he can wrap himself in it.

ISAIAH 28:20

Chapter 54

Elastic

Elastic is capable of standing stress without injury (which could be stretching the truth a mite). The General Store had a big box of it amidst the sewing needs on the dry goods counter, but Clara had noticed for some time that none of this was selling. One day she remarked to Jacob, "There is something going on in Paw Paw that I can't figure out. Every lady and girl needs to have elastic for garters and other unmentionable garments. Why Jacob, she would be foolhardy and reckless just stepping out the door without them. But we haven't sold any in a year."

"Clara, maybe they don't have the money to buy elastic in this awful Depression we're in."

Clara frowned. She wasn't one to let sleeping dogs lie, especially if it curtailed the cash flow into the coffer of the General Store. Just then, little Reba Bower walked through the door. Clara murmured to herself, "Why, this is an answer to a prayer I haven't had time to pray yet!" Cautiously she asked, "Reba, my dear, how do you little girls hold up your stockings and bloomers?"

"Oh Miss Clara, mother makes them out of strips of old inner tubes. They don't work very well, but we can't afford store-bought elastic right now." Little Reba skipped out the door before any more questions were asked, leaving Clara with her mouth agape and asking herself, "What am I going to do with all this elastic?"

Now Clara had the positive and tactful ability to say and do the right thing at the right time. She first called Granny Octavia (sure enough a homerun). Pearly answered the phone, "Yes, Granny is here but she has taken to her bed for two days, fasting and praying for all the sinners in Paw Paw."

Elated by this gossip, Clara almost forgot what she had called about. Then, in her angelic and innocent voice (Jacob called it her hypocritical voice), "Is it any person that I would know, Pearly?"

"No, Miss Clara, just the good old everyday sinners in Paw Paw."

She knew she must ask this question with diplomacy, lest it look like she was pressing them to buy her elastic. "Pearly, can you tell me how to use inner tubes for elastic?"

"Oh yes I can, Miss Clara, as we have been hassled from every side of how this is done. It appears to me that Granny warns of what not to do instead of how to do it. The first thing you measure is the inner-tubing strips, not too wide and not too narrow, not too loose and not too tight. These inner-tube strips will never be ideal or picture-perfect. They tend to be buoyant and hazardous when you tie the ends together, and one must tie three times, as this knot is prone to have a mind of it's own. It can unloosen for no reason at all. You will notice there is quite a handful of knots where this is tied, so one must do a fair amount of maneuvering to get this bulge in back of the knee.

"I know you have observed that dresses are getting shorter. By the way, that is one of the burdens that Granny is fasting and praying about right now. She saw quite a bit of pink flesh above Polly Owen's knees when she sat down in church. Granny has forewarned that it is possible a tragic thing can happen if you are involved in any strenuous activity, fast walking, or running. The inner-tube elastic can spring undone.

"There is whispered talk that Silas Meade took his ladylove

over to Whippoorwill to a dance. He was going to propose to her while they were dancing. When he put his arms around her back (she had put the knot there), thinking this was a tumor he skidaddled out the door with a fast dip, leaving her standing in the middle of the room. It's been told that he gave up dancing altogether, as this experience left him with a strange phobia against dancing forever. I never did hear if he ever got married."

Without even saying good-bye, Pearly slammed down the phone. Once again, Clara was left with her mouth wide open and murmured, "What am I going to do with all this elastic?"

(Dear Reader, I must put your mind at ease. As soon as the Great Depression had waned and diminished a little, the genteel and refined females in Paw Paw began buying Clara's elastic. Granny Octavia declared far and wide, up and down, it had lain so long that it had lost most of its stretchery.)

By faith Abraham, when he was called to go out
into a place which he should after receive for an inheritance,
obeyed; and he went out, not knowing whither he went.
By faith he sojourned in the land of promise,
as in a strange country.

HEBREWS 11:8-9

Chapter 55

Doctor Allen

Doctor Graham Jonathan Allen was the youngest doctor on the staff at General Hospital in St. Louis. He had just finished shaving and was combing his hair, when he discovered a small patch of gray near his temple. Surprised, he got his magnifying mirror to study it closer. Sure enough, there they were. He started to smile, "And men call women the vain ones." There in the mirror staring back at him was a fairly good-looking man that any mother might love. The nose would look a little better if it wasn't so large, but he did agree with what he'd heard many times, that he had dark gray eyes that seemed to sparkle and laugh a lot. He chuckled at the thought.

The eyes are the windows of the soul. As physicians judge the heart by the pulse, so we by the eyes. Where did that expression come from?

Maybe I should have majored in Philosophy. Have I missed my calling? He burst out laughing at all the nonsense he was thinking. Then he grabbed his coat and hat, jumped into his car, and drove to the hospital. It was his day to pull a double shift.

Doctor Allen, after weighing the pros and cons, decided that he was going to sell his house and move into an apartment. He generally called it his monstrosity or his mausoleum anyway. He often wondered what his grandfather had had in mind when he designed and built the huge thing. Did he think he was going to have many children? If that was the reason, he failed miserably as his mother was their only child and they were getting up in years when she was born.

Maybe there was another reason for this house to be the biggest and most prominent in all of St. Louis. Maybe his grandfather's ego wanted power to reign arrogantly over his fellow man. He felt this last reason was the truth. No matter, he was getting rid of it.

His colleagues warned him that he would have a hard time letting go of his grandparent's and his mother's home where he had lived all his life. Yet, he didn't feel any qualms or remorse when he boldly made this major decision. Why? he wondered. Was it because he had never had any happy memories?

He was amazed that the house sold so quickly, as the long ghostly specter of the Depression had reached its bony finger into everyone's life here in St. Louis. He had only thirty days to pack up and move out before the new owners moved in. He took a few days off from the hospital to tie all the ends together. He engaged a man to auction off his priceless antiques. The Depression took its toll, and he only received a small pittance of the furniture's worth.

It was evening by the time all the furniture was gone, so he sat down on the floor in his grandfather's office and spread his grandfather's yellowed and faded worn documents beside him. They all told a story of shame, graft, and corrupt means his grandfather had employed in his business dealings. In one paper, his grandfather recounted the time he had been arrested for one of his unscrupulous deeds and bragged about how he bought off both the lawyer and the judge. Money he loaned with high interest and usury he would quickly gain back by foreclosure. He took advantage of a widow-woman when her husband had died and foreclosed on her immediately, even though she had five children. There were letters from people begging him for a little extra time to pay for their houses, but he obviously thought nothing of forcing people out on the street. He bragged that he owned the public officials. He had letters that told of his cheating people in horse and cattle dealings and even some false claims used to collect money from insurance companies.

Why had he kept all of this information? It should have been destroyed over the years, or better yet, never kept at all. Did his grandfather relish reading them over again? Yes, that was probably the reason. Thinking back through the years, he remembered him chuckling and laughing at some of his schemes.

Doctor Allen found out that the big house he grew up in was built with "slave labor." What in the world did this mean? There were no slaves. Did his grandfather think the workers who built the house were his slaves? Yes, that was clearly written within the yellow pages! Then Doctor Allen noticed that his mother's signature was on many of these documents. Did she know of these wicked deeds? Questions, questions, tormenting questions. Would he be able to find the answers? Then, stunned indeed, he realized he had received his education because of someone else's pain and suffering.

By this time, he was visibly shaken and unnerved, but he thought he might find the answers in the metal box he found under his mother's bed. It was locked and no key had been found. He got a knife and broke the lock.

There on top of the contents was a picture of him; on the bottom of the photograph were his name and his age—ten years old. Was this the only picture that was ever taken of him? Why hadn't he been photographed more often? He had often wondered why there was no ornate silver framed photograph of him on a table or hanging on the wall. After all, he was from a wealthy family. He studied the skinny pale-faced boy in the photo, whose eyes were too large for his face. There was something he could see in those big saucer-like eyes, a questioning look or fear. Which was it?

Doctor Allen was abruptly taken back to the years of his childhood, and he remembered clearly what it was. It was fear!

The fear the little boy felt every time he heard the chime ring for supper. He remembered telling his mother he was too ill to eat anything and clinging to her. However, she would firmly say, "Now, Graham, we have to eat. Just be brave and take your seat at the table." Then she'd lead him by the hand to the dining table and sit him down next to his grandfather.

His grandfather sat at the head of the long table and never spoke. Oh yes, it all became clear to him now. In his pain, he had tried to make himself even smaller than he was, to shrink within himself and become invisible. The little boy understood that even though his grandfather didn't look directly at him he could still see his plate and his food.

His grandfather would begin supper the same way every night. Year after year, it was the same. He would say, "Go ahead Graham, read it."

Then in fear, he would begin to read the blue velvet motto that hung on the wall across the table from him. "Christ is the head of this house, the silent listener to every conversation, the unseen guest at every meal." As he took the first bite with heart-pounding terror, an icy chill began to sneak up and down his back; it circled his neck then lodged in his throat. It filled his ears with pain then reached down to his trembling knees.

As Doctor Allen looked back to that every-night ritual, he knew that his grandfather relished the pain and anguish he and his mother suffered. This was, indeed, a mystery, to a little boy until an older boy was teasing and taunting him about his name being the same as his grandfather's. So year after year, he wondered who his father was and what his name was.

Now he would find who his father was and what his name was. Did he want to know? He had started his search, and he must finish this journey. His hopes were dashed; the only things that he heard were the dark shadows that crept around him in the old mansion, and shadows don't talk. In the metal box, Graham found a sealed envelope with his name written across the front. A feeling of apprehension engulfed him, and his breath quickened as he slowly opened it. It was a letter written to him by his mother. Strange, even after all the years, he could still smell her essence, that same wonderful perfume he remembered smelling every night when she tucked him in. After Grandfather was in bed, his mother would bring him something to eat; then she would hold him in her arms and tell him of his father until he went to sleep. "Oh my darling," she would say, "he came from a place where you can sit on a big porch and see across acres of flowers. If a soft wind blows, the perfume from those flowers will waft to the porch. I remember he said one could become drunk easily from their essence. We both laughed at that. He said in that place, love welds all the families together and the families weld the town together."

My Beloved Son,

I don't know what age you will be when you read this letter; my only hope is that you can forgive me and remember how much I loved you. This letter is a confession of possibly the greatest sin a mother can put on her child.

I met your father one day when your grandmother and I had to go to the office to sign some papers for your grandfather. I didn't know the particulars of them, I was never told. Your father was there, and I was introduced to him.

Oh, my darling, in that moment I loved him and he said it was love at first sight for him too. Grandfather was sending him to Africa on a mining operation for diamonds. In some wonderful way, your father managed to take me to a restaurant for a bite to eat. This was the first time in my life I had ever been alone with any man other than your grandfather. I was eighteen years old. I fell madly in love with him. Your grandfather was so caught up in preparing for this expedition (there were two other men going) that little attention was given to me. The men stayed three days and three nights at our house. My beloved son, it was the most glorious three days and nights I had ever spent. I had always been kept like a prisoner in that big house.

Your father was so handsome. You get your beautiful eyes from him. You would have loved him. He said that as soon as he returned, we would get married. He promised to bring me the biggest diamond in the world, but I didn't want the diamond, I only wanted him.

Those three men, including your father, never came home from Africa. Grandfather left no stone unturned trying to locate them, not because he cared for them, but because he knew they had found some precious stones. But all was in vain. The only thing they came up with was that they were probably killed by the natives.

I do know that your father loved me, and, if alive, he would have come back for me. I suppose you already know what is coming next. I soon realized I was going to have a baby. I kept my secret from your grandfather for a few months. I quit going down for supper, pleading that I was ill, which I was. Then one night, Father screamed up the stairs for me to get myself down to supper no matter what was wrong with me. I knew my mother hadn't told him anything, in fact, I don't think she even knew about it herself. Mother was a weak, forlorn woman, and my father had destroyed her reason for living years ago.

When I came down to supper, there wasn't any way to hide my shame as I walked to the table. Father started to rise from his chair then gave a choking sound and grabbed his throat. I thought for sure he was going to die. I ran to him to help him. Then he came out of this attack, whatever it was, and threw me across the room. I almost lost you that night, and maybe that would have been the best thing for your grandfather. But, my beloved son, I wanted you so badly I prayed that God would give you to me. My life was so empty and barren, and I so desperately wanted someone to love me and I knew I would love you.

The day you were born, my life and my prayers were fulfilled. You have always been my beloved one. Please forgive me and remember me with kindness. I was in the hospital several weeks, near death I was told. They gave my maiden name to you since I wasn't married.

Love forever,

Mother

Doctor Allen was shocked, bordering on angry. Why didn't she tell me my father's name? Why? Why Mother? Didn't you think someday I would want to know? He cried out in his grief.

Then he got up and walked around his house. The letter shook him to the core, but at the same time, it answered many questions he had had when growing up. He went into the kitchen and made himself a cup of coffee. He drank it slowly, as echoes resounded from his past.

When he returned to the metal box, he found a little blue napkin. It had "Graham Jonathan Allen, 10 years old" printed on it. Oh, yes, it was his birthday napkin. Why had he blocked the memory of it out of his mind?

He remembered the morning his mother came into his room, dancing and singing. She sat down on his bed. "Graham, get out of that bed, we are going to have a birthday party for you. Your grandfather is going to Europe for a month on business, and we are going to have a wonderful time. This will be the 'party of parties' because you are going to give each child a gift. On each invitation card, we will ask that child what gift they would like to receive if this was their birthday. We will include a stamped return envelope, so they can mail it back immediately when they have written their answers. That will give us time to shop for their presents.

"You know, son, the Bible says it is better to give than receive. But, wait a minute here; this is not the end of the presents. When we buy the gifts, we will buy two of each, one for you to give to your guests and one for you to keep. We will hide them in the attic, and every day as soon as your grandfather leaves for work, we will run up to the attic and play with them together. Oh my darling, how I love you."

Then she pulled him out of bed and they danced around the room as his mother sang the "Happy Birthday" song over and over. He remembered his grandmother scolded and begged his mother not to have the party, but she ignored her. As they planned the party, she said, "I know Father will have a fit, but I don't care. The party will be over by then, and I'll face the consequences."

Oh yes, the birthday party. He could still feel the excitement, the tingling, and the goose bumps of that little ten-year-old boy. He didn't know many of the children that came, but that was okay with him. Behind each chair, the present for each child was placed on the floor. The children were excited as his mother brought in the cake and set it in the middle of the table. It had ten candles on it, and his mother lit each one.

"Now Graham, make a wish and then you can blow them out."

But, he never got that chance. They were snuffed out by a fierce, brutal wind that swept in through the front door as his grandfather entered the house. In black rage, his grandfather screamed profanities and stomped on the presents. All the children began crying hysterically and running for home. Doctor Allen could see it now, the cake in ruins on the floor with the candles and little frosting flowers in broken disarray. At the same moment the cake hit the floor, his grandfather died of a violent heart attack. It was all too much for the little boy, who fell in a faint beside him.

His grandmother followed her husband in death a few months later. She always walked in his shadow, and this was no different.

Graham's mother went on a long journey too, but it was to her bedroom. She never laughed or played any games with him after that day. Through the years, the little boy searched for her but all he ever found was a wan wraithlike figure that always dressed in black. Now he realized that she carried an aura of sin every day of her life after that.

Doctor Allen couldn't remember much about his mother's funeral, but he did remember that no one came.

There in the middle of his room, Graham lay down and wept in anguish and pain for that little ten-year-old boy, his mother, and his grandparents.

When he awakened, the sun was shining brightly through the window. He called the hospital and notified them that he didn't know when, or if ever, he would be back. He was startled that he would have such a good feeling about not going back.

He had his work cut out for him. He gathered up all of his grandfather's papers and took them downtown to his lawyer's office. He instructed his lawyer to find the people his grandfather had robbed and to give them interest on the money they had lost from their transactions with him. Then he had his address changed to the lawyer's office.

"I don't know where I will be or where I am going, but I will get in touch with you often." With those words, Doctor Allen walked out the door. He didn't know that he would never be back.

When he returned to his house, he noticed a magazine that had dropped from his mother's box, which he hadn't noticed the night before. There on its front cover was a picture of a huge field of wildflowers. What was mystifying to him was the thought that he had seen this place before. He even knew the names of all the flowers. The magazine was fragile from being handled so often over the years, and there seemed to be dried teardrops on the cover. Then like a bolt from the blue, he remembered. His mother had told him repeatedly about this place on the nights she lay with him until he went to sleep. Why, this was the place where his father had lived.

"A Poem From God Without Words" was the caption under the picture. He could barely read the name of the town where it had been taken, Paw Paw.

Early the next morning, Doctor Allen packed his belongings and, shaking and trembling with excitement, began his odyssey to that little town.

He didn't know that the drought and Depression had destroyed the beautiful field. He could never dream what God had in store for him there.

Who shall roll us away the stone from the door of the sepulchre?
And when they looked, they saw that the stone was rolled away.

And, behold, there was a great earthquake:
for the angel of the Lord descended from heaven,
and came and rolled back the stone from the door,
and sat upon it. . . . His countenance was like lightning,
and his raiment white as snow: and the angel answered
and said unto the women, Fear not ye:
for I know that ye seek Jesus, which was crucified.

MARK 16:3-4; MATTHEW 28:2-3,5

Chapter 56

The First Doctor in Paw Paw

It was early in the morning when a stranger drove into Paw Paw in a sleek black automobile. Instead of parking at the General Store, he parked in front of the telephone office.

Maggie Jenkins had barely gotten out of bed when she heard him drive up. She still had her flannel nightgown on and her hair in rag curlers. She stuck her head out of her bedroom window, which was next to the telephone office—actually a part of it. The man was as startled as she was.

"Oh, I'm sorry to intrude on you so early. I'll sit out here and wait for you to get dressed."

Maggie, like a scared deer, pulled off her nightie and almost yanked out the hair on her head in her rush to get the rag curlers off. She brushed her hair with a "lick and a promise," dressed quickly, and scurried into her office. She opened the door and let him in. He offered his hand to her along with an engaging smile.

"Miss Jenkins, I presume. I saw your name on the door. I'm Doctor Graham Allen. Would you be kind enough to put through a long-distance call for me to St. Louis?"

Maggie went to the switchboard and quickly put the call through, but she was so excited and nervous she failed to hear what was being said.

After his call, Doctor Allen asked, "Miss Jenkins, could you tell me if there is somewhere I can stay for a few days? Who knows, it may be even longer."

"Oh yes," she said. "Just go over to the General Store. The Johnsons have a fabulous guest room to take care of our visitors." Maggie, still shaking like a leaf in the wind, went back to her tiny kitchen and made a pot of strong tea, sat down and drank several cups, and began taking some deep breaths.

She quickly recovered enough to begin calling various ladies in Paw Paw and one man. She knew just the right ones to tell who would spread the news all over town. "My dear, I am just recovering from the excitement of the morning. A Doctor Graham Allen has come to town. I think he means to take up practice here; at least those were the unspoken words from him. You know I am qualified in the reading-between-the-lines department. He is young, tall, dark, and handsome."

All that day the phone lines fairly sizzled with the news. By evening, the gossip had escalated and intensified so much that they now had Doctor Allen with patients standing in line on the porch of the General Store.

Doctor Allen had settled in the lovely guest room at the store and was very comfortable. He arranged to dine with the Johnson's until he decided what he was going to do.

Doctor Allen was awakened every morning by a highbrow, sold-out concert performance. The performers—offensive culprits he thought—were the roosters that dwelt in Paw Paw, who would have this predawn sing-along in a variety of musical tones. Laughing to himself, he was trying to figure out which "cock-a-doodle-do" came from whose henhouse. One thing he did know for sure, there was no "sleeping in" in this sleepy little town.

Doctor Allen joined the men on the porch several mornings. Their main topic of conversation was Miss Idy. "Doctor Allen," Jeremiah declared quite boldly, "Miss Idy runs this town. She just walked in one morning, quiet-like, and before we realized it, she became the head deaconess of the Baptist

Church and the mayor of our fair city. She is responsible for the newspaper and our library. She is the superintendent of our school, although of course we found out later. We all have different opinions of her, but even our opinions of her can change before the day passes. She is constantly poking her little nose into everybody's business, and she works endlessly for the better of Paw Paw."

Otis defensively spoke up, "Some claim she has a private line right up to heaven and a special angel at her beck and call. What do you think of that Doctor Allen?"

Ed ventured his opinion, "The Good Book says be careful because we could have angels in our midst."

Doctor Allen was absorbed and enthralled by this description, as he was puzzled about her. There was quite a distance between being an angel and a busybody. He was excited to meet her; they pointed to her little house up the road.

One morning he awakened early. Clara and Jacob were still in bed, so he decided to take his morning constitutional, as the men on the porch called it. He deliberately chose the road that would pass by Miss Idy's little cottage. To his delight she stepped out of her house just then. "Lucky for me," he murmured to himself. He adjusted his pace, so he would meet her at the gate. He gave her a slight bow, "Good morning, Miss Idy. I am Doctor Allen, and you must be the mayor of Paw Paw. The men on the porch told me where you lived."

"I can imagine, Doctor Allen, that wasn't all they told you about me!" She gave him one of her rare smiles. "Our little town is abuzz about you coming here, and I admit I am one of the buzzers." Again, her smile, but this one was a little more pronounced. "Have you decided to stay with us?"

"Miss Idy, I keep looking at the small place across the road from the store. Fred calls it a moth-eaten building, not fit for man or beast." At this remark, both of them laughed.

"Now, Doctor Allen, I must be on my way to a small problem to take care of before it escalates and intensifies into a hornet's nest."

Doctor Allen watched her until she got out of sight. "Well what do you know. She is a lot of woman!"

Doctor Allen had been in Paw Paw for quite some time just lolly-gagging around, as the men called it. 'Twas true that he hadn't decided one way or another of where he would put his office, and he couldn't understand why he was not in a big fizz to start his practice. Otis loudly commented, "Doctor Allen, I have never seen so much sickness in Paw Paw since you came. I hope we are not having one of those epidemics in our midst." So, the sweet banter and teasing continued with Doctor Allen and the men on the porch.

Doctor Allen and his morning reverie and wool gathering always ended in thinking of Miss Idy. She was the most controversial figure he had ever met. He had to smile at how she cunningly and cleverly took control of everyone's life in Paw Paw. At times, she betrayed a combative and belligerent attitude in her finagling to get her way. But, he had to admit, she never demanded or asked anything from anyone, if she hadn't already tasted the dregs of the residue herself. He knew she saw her most difficult and Herculean task was reforming the men who sat on the porch of the General Store.

Doctor Allen heard Clara bustling about in the kitchen, fixing breakfast. When he walked in, they were in their "Sunday go to meeting clothes," as the men on the porch would say. "Oh good morning, Doctor Allen. Come and eat your breakfast. We are going to church. Why don't you come with us? I'm sure you will enjoy it."

Startled at himself, he replied, "Clara, I think I will, but I might be late."

Jacob said, "Doctor Allen that will be all right."

Doctor Allen walked to the church instead of driving his car. What has come over me? Why am I walking? Why, I have never walked anywhere except from my car to a building or through the halls of the hospital. Before he could come up with an answer, he was at the church.

He was astonished; the whole town was there. Why are the women on one side and the men on the other? he asked himself. The men on the back bench quickly squeezed together to make room for him to sit down. He was a little surprised to see Miss Idy, still dressed in black, in charge of the meeting.

The singing had ceased, and she called several members of the congregation to stand and give testimonies of how God had blessed their lives, how they walked where the Holy Spirit led them. One could indeed believe this, as there was such a sweet and moving radiance on their faces. The whole audience seemed lifted up into a holy atmosphere.

Reverend Peabody stepped up to the podium with calm assurance and began his sermon. He read his scriptures and turned back to them several times in his message.

Why did Doctor Allen feel that he had always dwelt in this tiny town? Why did he feel like he had always come to this church on Sunday mornings? Oh, questions, questions.

He drank in the words of the sermon, yet he didn't hear them. When the sermon ended, he knew they were going to sing their last song. Why, he knew the words, even though he had never heard them before. As their voices rang out, "I've anchored my soul in a haven of rest, I'll sail the wild seas more," all the tense, rigid feelings he had acquainted with his patients and the grueling hours at the hospital were gone. Oh yes, God had leaned way down and had lit his candle, his Deity that dwelt in every man. Sweet tears coursed down Doctor Allen's face as he walked back to the General Store. There was no doubt that he had come home to stay.

Now was the time to find his grandparents, whom he knew lived in the blessed little town called Paw Paw.

This morning he gathered with the men on the porch and chatted with them. He told them about the hustle and bustle and frantic ways of life in the big city. Then they in turn told him what the sages had handed down to them, the colorful legends, romances, the myths, even a tale of a murder on the porch of the General Store. This morning they went into great lengths, telling him about those that had gone to sleep in the tiny graveyard beside the Baptist Church.

Otis asserted loudly, "Doctor Allen, would you believe there is an empty grave yonder inside the gate of the graveyard?" he pointed to the graveyard, "It even has a tombstone and the name is Graham Jonathon St. Claire. Uncle John and Aunt Sissy insisted that they feel closer to their son that disappeared years ago. Yes indeed, it is a mystery. I conclude that everyone has different ways to handle their grief and sorrow."

Doctor Allen sat frozen and rigid, from somewhere it came. "A man dies, but his words live on." Was this from his heart or soul? He would not be quieted until he found out. He went to his room and got the pictures of the field of flowers, yellowed and tear-stained, that his mother had left him, and took them to the porch.

He spread the pictures before the men. Jacob gave a gasp. "Why, these are the same pictures we have in the store!" He ran into the store and brought the old, framed pictures out, sheepishly wiping the dust off them. He laid them down next to the magazine. They all agreed they were the same.

Fred Pinkham said, "Doctor Allen, the drought killed all those pretty flowers. They used to grow on that hill yonder."

Doctor Allen opened his heart to the men. "I first heard of these flowers in this 'Poem from God Without Words' from my mother. When I was a little boy, she would tuck me in at night, and then she would tell me about the field of flowers and name every one. I knew in some way my father was involved. I knew she had never been here, so it had to be his description of this little town that she was telling me about."

Before anything else was said, Uncle Frank and Aunt Sissy arrived, walking hand in hand as usual. After the introductions and greetings ended, Uncle Frank began his morning report of all the news. Doctor Allen didn't hear any of it because he was watching and studying the old man, his features, his bearing. He could feel goose bumps rise on his arms; his heart was racing. He even had difficulty breathing. Could this be his grandfather? Or did he just want to believe it so strongly that his imagination was overwhelming him? He realized he must go slowly with this thought, as he could plainly see both Uncle Frank and Aunt Sissy were quite fragile. Too much excitement might push them over the edge.

When the "news" was over, Uncle Frank and Aunt Sissy came over to Doctor Allen. Sweetly, Aunt Sissy asked, "Doctor Allen, would you like to come and visit with us for a little while? I have a warm sorghum molasses cake, and I can make a mean cup of tea."

He wasn't surprised. This was the next step he would take. "Oh yes," Doctor Allen remarked with a smile, "how kind of you to ask me." He slipped her arm in his and touched Uncle Frank at times as they all three walked to the couple's modest home.

The lovely old woman didn't need to help her husband through the door, because Doctor Allen was there and he helped them both in. Was this the last step he needed to take to erase the pain in his heart?

Aunt Sissy started bustling around. "Now Doctor Allen, I want you to sit in the most comfortable chair in the house."

"Oh no, Aunt Sissy, I want Uncle Frank to sit there."

She went into the kitchen to make their tea. Doctor Allen didn't sit down but walked to a little table in the corner of the room. There was one picture in a silver frame. It dominated the corner. Doctor Allen picked it up and looked at it. He was looking at himself. Was he surprised? Not really. This was meant to be. He turned to help Aunt Sissy, his grandmother, set the pot of tea in front of his grandfather.

He placed the photo on the table facing them. Gently, carefully, he guided them step by step down his long journey home to them. He heard their intake of breath. Grandfather and grandmother sat in wonder and fascination as their tears were being kissed away by their grandson. There was no need for words to explain. This was just a grandson who happened to stop by for a cup of tea and piece of cake with his grandparents.

After the tea had been drunk and a big piece of the cake had been eaten, they all three walked to the cemetery to view an empty grave. They felt the warm summer's sun upon their faces and a waft of wind kissed their cheeks. Doctor Allen knew his sojourning was over and that he had come home. What manner of God had he found who was willing to come down and visit with a man of clay?

They opened the gate of the cemetery and walked to the grave, the empty grave of their son. A man had carved the marble headstone. No, the finger of God carved it. "He is not here, he has risen."

He hath hedged me about, that I cannot get out:
he hath made my chain heavy.

LAMENTATIONS 3:7

Chapter 57

Chessy Lou Darnell

Jimmy C. Simpson commented to the men on the porch that the Darnells lived on one of the routes leading from "nowhere to nothing."

In their tiny house, Chessy Lou Darnell sat on a pillow on the floor with her head on her grandmother's lap. The small rocking chair complained and threatened with endless squeals. Her Grammy, as she called her, was brushing her curly hair until it shone.

"Grammy, tell me again about my mother and father," she said.

"Oh, my child, you know every word about them. I think you know them better than I do," she said as she gave a loving tug on one of her curls.

There was a large mirror on the wall across the room, and it reflected the beauty of her grandchild. Her young eyes were a brilliant blue, varying at times to a sparkling sea green, and her lashes were dark and long. Her nose was a trifle upturned with a spattering of freckles across it. She had lost her winter pearly porcelain look, and her face now was very brown from the hot summer sun. Chessy was totally unaware of her stunning beauty. In fact, she portrayed a look of shyness with an inner quality of innocence. A calm, ethereal glow surrounded her. It was as if all the cherubs from heaven had descended, taken up their abode in her, and sprinkled her with their bewitching charms. She saw everyone through the eyes of love. In her delightful innocence, she thought the world was all her own.

Her grandmother, however, was filled with fear and anxiety because of her granddaughter's beauty and her childlike, pure heart. Because Chessy was guiltless herself, she thought others were also. In a way, Grammy thought Chessy would understand, she warned her of what could happen to her with men. However, after hearing the facts of life, Chessy just seemingly smiled them off. Therefore, Grammy pondered and wondered every day about what lay in store for her beloved granddaughter.

From the very beginning, the ladies of the community were in awe and a little guarded when they met Chessy Lou. They knew it was their Christian duty to be pleasant to her, but their greetings were always "safe" talk about the weather, about the church's activities, about their gardens.

Chessy felt more comfortable talking to the men on the porch. They were always amazed at her wisdom when talking about God's love. One day she was excited, "My Gram gave me a little sparkling motto and I put it up in my room. It says, 'Be kind to everyone you meet, they might be having a hard time.' Love is a fruit of God's Holy Spirit, you know. My Grammy taught me that a dog would wag its tail just for a pat on its head. She also said that is a gesture that a deaf person could hear and a blind person can see. Don't you think that is wonderful?"

She would say things like that, then smile her captivating smile, jump off the porch, and go skipping and running to her tiny home.

Amos remarked, "It's as though she came from another world to grace our lowly everyday lives."

"Yes, for sure! I can see her maybe living half here in our little surroundings and the other half in heaven," Tom Curry cautiously murmured.

Ray Linden asked, "Can one be possessed and inhabited by an angel, like sometimes we say that a person is possessed by a demon?"

They agreed that if this was so, God lost His pattern, as no one else could measure up to Chessy.

Chessy's grandmother saw her smiling face in the mirror as she started the old story again. "Your mother was the most beautiful lady in the world. She looked like you, my love." She gave Chessy a love pat on her head as she smiled in the mirror at her. "Chessy, my dear, there are two kinds of beauty, one on the outside and one within. The one within is the most important.

"Your mother and father met in church. Your father had been away attending a seminary for young ministers. However, when he walked into our little church and saw your mother, it was love at first sight. Oh, my darling, how they loved one another.

"They lived with me in Wichita, Kansas, for a while. Then the governing body of the church wanted your father and his lifelong friend, David Hoffman, to move here and establish churches in the nearby small towns that didn't have an assembly. Of course, they both came. The organization gave them money for their livelihood, for horses and for a house, while establishing those churches.

"The only sweet problem was that you were on the way. Your mother insisted that your father and David answer the call of the church, so we all moved here to Paw Paw—I insisted on coming to help your mother with your arrival.

"We had hardly settled in when the governing body of the church in Wichita wrote. They asked your father and David to go to a meeting in Butler County as soon as possible. The meeting was with businessmen and mayors and influential men who wanted to start two churches there at once. They would be gone for two weeks.

"There had been torrential rains for a couple of days, and

Big Morgan Creek was near to flood stage. They were going to have to cross it to get to where they were going. David came over, and they talked and discussed whether they could ford the creek safely. Your father vehemently declared that he did not think it was safe, and he was fearful about your arrival. Your mother wasn't due for two months, but he knew that new mothers had a habit of delivering early. Your mother knew of your father's spiritual calling, so she encouraged him. David said he knew they could make it. As they packed their bags, I remember your father holding up his Bible and saying with a laugh, 'We mustn't forget this; it is our weapon wherever we go.'

David kidded him back and said, 'Yes, my friend, we'll need that to hold us up when we cross Big Morgan.'

"Your mother took your father into the bedroom to tell him good-bye. She tried to calm his fears and told him that she would be all right. She must have accomplished this, as he looked serene when they left. We both stood in the door waving at them. Then we went into the kitchen and made us a pot of tea.

"Your poor mother's feet were swollen, so she took off her shoes. We talked for a while about babies and especially about what to name this baby. I remember her saying, 'Mother, I don't know whether it will be a boy or a girl, but I do know that I will love it. Oh, I can hardly wait!'

"I laughed and said, 'Well, my darling, you soon will know.'

"Then suddenly, my precious, as if in concert with what was about to happen, an angry wrathful wind started shrieking in all its fury around the house." Chessy's grandmother stopped talking and took on a look of wounded pain. She hugged Chessy tight against her and whispered, "It was the kind of wind that blows out the lamp of the mind.

"Then we heard a chilling sound. We thought it might be an animal screaming and crying for help. Fear gripped our hearts as we ran to the door. A cry of agony ripped the air with these words: 'My God, my God, why hast Thou forsaken me?' It was David. He was crawling on his hands and knees in the mud through the front gate to the house, and he was screaming. I still remember his every word. 'Oh Kathy, Kathy. Danny has drowned. I tried to save him, but I wasn't able to. Oh Kathy, why wasn't it me? He loved you so much, and you need him so. Dear Kathy, please don't ever forgive me. I need to carry this evil thing the rest of my life.'

"Your mother, still barefoot, ran to meet him. She was trying to help him up, but she couldn't, as he was kissing her feet. She sat down in the mud beside him and held him in her arms. In that unreal moment, they rocked back and forth in their grief and sorrow. Then, in their heartwrenching despair, your mother began her labor pains.

"David carried her into the house and laid her on her bed. Ere that night was over, you were born. So tiny, so still, so quiet. And your mother also lay so still, so quiet, as angels wafted her to heaven. She was swept away on angel's wings to join her beloved Daniel, who was waiting for her.

"David stayed with me for two weeks as we battled to keep you alive. I don't know if you would have made it without him. Later on he told me the strange thing that had happened the night your father was swept away by Big Morgan. As he was being carried downstream, he managed to throw his Bible up on the shore where it caught in the crook of a tree. The horse got out of the river downstream, but your father didn't."

Grammy lowered her voice to a soft whisper and said, "They told me your daddy's Bible was seen high in an old oak tree with its pages fluttering and turning in the wind, page after page. Maybe it is still there, my darling. I have never gone to see."

Curse not the king, no not in thy thought;
and curse not the rich in thy bedchamber:
for a bird of the air shall carry the voice,
and that which hath wings shall tell the matter.

ECCLESIASTES 10:20

Chapter 58

Chessy's Hair

Chessy's hair was a mass of curls the color of chestnuts and had a radiant glow. Those curls were always escaping the bondage of her hairpins. Once in a while, tiring of this task, she would let it fall loose around her shoulders and tumble down her back.

When she got to the General Store, Chessy knew she was in trouble with her hair being down, because Miss Idy was there; she had faced her wrath before when her hair was down.

Miss Idy, though reluctant to do her Christian duty, knew what must be done. Squaring back her shoulders, she bravely met Chessy face to face. "Chessy, I hope you don't think I am too bold to mention this, but you should fasten your hair a little more securely, and it should always be on top of your head. When it is down, it looks very untidy and messy and certainly not ladylike. You know the Good Book says, though a little subtle and vague I admit, that a woman's hair is her glory. Yes, her crowning glory. A crown has to sit on top of one's head, doesn't it? I certainly hope you agree."

Not giving time for surprised Chessy to answer, Miss Idy hurried on her way, pleased that she had the strength to chide the child and show her shortcomings. She thought it her duty to carefully check out all the young girls regularly. Generally, that task took place in her Sunday school class.

She had spoken to Chessy in her sweet and silky-sounding

voice in a most holy manner. She called this her church-house voice (only to herself of course). One never bragged on one's self. A person's good deeds spoke for themselves.

Now she was so excited she could hardly wait until morning for the ladies' Sewing Circle at the church. She would calmly wait for the hot tea to be poured, then she would take center stage with the ladies evenly divided on both sides of her and loudly announce, again in her sweet church-house voice, the news she had.

She practiced what she would say. "I know we have discussed this problem before. Well, I have finally had the courage to do something about it. I met Chessy yesterday at the General Store, and she had that gorgeous head of hair tumbling down her back again. I used the Good Book scripture as I always do. So now, we can rest easy regarding this problem, hoping of course that she will not let this happen again.

"The way I look at the situation, mark my words, only despair and grief can come to this beautiful and seemingly serene girl. There is no escaping it. Since we are women, we all know how that girl could take our male population off guard. They see her at our various functions, church, and the General Store, of course. With her hair down, they can see her coming a mile up the road. It is not only the single young men in our community who are affected, but we should not be shaken by the fact that husbands could also be sidetracked. It has happened before and not very far from here, so we must closely watch and be on the alert. That is the end of my story except to say, remember Bathsheba and King David!"

After she had delivered this speech at the Sewing Circle the next morning, she smugly sat down. She was disappointed that not one person congratulated her on her holy boldness. She recovered swiftly from this as she considered it one of the crosses a person has to bear in Christian warfare.

"We can't win them all, but I can surely try," she told herself.

And, behold, a woman in the city, which was a sinner,
when she knew that Jesus sat at meat in the Pharisee's house,
brought an alabaster box of ointment,
and stood at his feet behind him weeping,
and began to wash his feet with tears,
and did wipe them with the hairs of her head,
and kissed his feet, and anointed them with the ointment.

LUKE 7:37-38

Chapter 59

Chessy's Birthday— A Cake and A Token of Love From Clint

"Chessy, get out of bed you lazy bones! The sun is doing his best to shine just for your birthday. Your sweet-sixteen-and-never-been-kissed birthday. My darling, postpone that as long as you can," Grammy teased.

As Chessy walked into the kitchen, Grammy brought out the lovely birthday cake she had made for her granddaughter. She had decorated it with pink and blue rosettes of sugar icing. Chessy was delighted. Then she spotted the gift on the table. Her eyes beamed with joy as she looked at her grandmother and gingerly asked, "Is that for me?"

"Yes, my darling girl, it is. Open it."

Chessy was excited, and her hands shook as she carefully untied the ribbon.

"Oh, Grammy it's beautiful," she exclaimed, as she held up the snow-white, linen petticoat. It had two ruffled edges near the bottom, one with pink tatted lace and the other with blue tatted lace. Excitedly, Chessy put it on and danced around the room, the blue and pink rosettes dancing with her.

"Grammy, when did you make this? I didn't see you working on it. I remember you told me that tatting takes a long time. How did you do it?"

"Well, my dear granddaughter, here is a little hint. I'm not the one who did the tatting. Every day an angel descended from heaven, snatched it out of my hands, sat down on my little rocking chair, and went to work. Now, my love, what do you think of that?"

Chessy squealed with delight, "Oh, Grammy, I don't believe that."

Grammy's old treadle sewing machine stood in the center of the room. Chessy gingerly took the petticoat off and spread it over the ancient machine, so she could look at it.

"Chessy the pink and blue tatting is called 'love tatting.' You must pack it away carefully in lavender; I'll show you how. It must be saved to wear under your white wedding gown." Then with a mischievous smile she added, "My love, the blue rosettes will bring you a baby boy, and the pink ones will bring a baby girl when you are married, but don't get in a rush about that my darling."

They had just heaped their little plates with huge slices of this delectable cake when a car came roaring down the road and stopped at their gate. They ran to the door and opened it just as a young man started to knock. Too flustered to even give his name, he said, "I'm from Whippoorwill. Are you Eva Wright?"

"Yes, I am her," Grammy answered perplexed. "What is the matter?"

"Your daughter in Wichita is near death and wants you to come at once. I have been told to wait until you pack, and I will take you to the train station."

"Oh, Chessy, my dear child, what must I do?"

"Grammy, I think you should go. I'm not afraid to be alone for a short while, I'm a big girl now." They both hurriedly packed the lone suitcase.

"Chessy, I will get someone here in Paw Paw or someone in Whippoorwill, some young girl or lady that needs a few coins, to come stay with you while I'm gone. Here, my darling is three dollars now. I will send you three dollars a week in a letter. That will safely tide you over until I return." As she pressed the money into Chessy's hand, she hugged and kissed her. Then she climbed into the car, tears running down her face, and waved until she was out of sight.

Chessy's birthday cake with its pretty pink and blue flowers still sat on the kitchen table. From the heat of the day, the pretty pink and blue flowers had slowly melted and formed a pink and blue wreath around the little birthday cake.

The leaving of her Grammy had been so hectic and frenzied, she immediately plunged into dark despair, as this was the only time she had ever been left alone.

She needed to walk, that always made her feel better. Why not go to the store and talk to the men or Clara? She knew when she got to the old stile over the fence that she was halfway to the General Store. Her huge Paw Paw tree, she couldn't remember when she first started calling it "her tree," always sent out its inviting branches, beckoning her. It was usually all dressed up with deep, dark, emerald green leaves, but now, because of no rain, the leaves were faded dark brown. A soft wind rustled them, and they whispered to her. It seemed to Chessy that her tree talked to her, asked her how she was, and wanted to know what was on her mind. It was a very good listener.

Through the years, her tree had tried to swallow up the old stile, which she also called hers. Her stile was her private hideaway. Someday she would have to get someone to trim back the branches, but that would be taken care of some other time. Today, she just sat on the top step of the stile, hugged her knees to her chest, surveyed her little kingdom, and wondered about the world. Then she remembered.

It was her birthday and an enchanting feeling washed away her loneliness. Her Grammy had been right; she never had been kissed.

"I wonder what it will be like," she asked herself. She would soon know.

What she didn't know was her Grammy would die and she

wouldn't ever see her again.

Hurriedly, she climbed the steps, seeking shelter from the heat in the General Store. Surprise! The men weren't on the porch. She had just started to pull open the old screen door when she was suddenly startled by a head of black hair elaborately bowing before her. He was acting as if he were greeting royalty, as he stretched out his hand in a ridiculous courtly fashion.

"Oh, do come into my humble abode," he said. "I have been watching you coming down that hot and dusty road. You looked thirsty, so I poured you a glass of cool lemonade. My name is Clint Martin. I know your name is Chessy Lou Darnell; Auntie Clara has filled my ears about you."

Chessy was left speechless by this strange and exaggerated welcome.

Then as Clint looked deep into her sparkling blue-green eyes, he very gently took hold of both hands, turned them over, and kissed both palms. Chessy's face turned scarlet, and she started to tremble as he released her.

Clara Johnson, owner of the store, came through the door and rescued her just in time.

"Chessy, this is our nephew, Clint Martin. He has come to gladden the hearts of his Auntie Clara and Uncle Jacob for a little while. Oh, my goodness, I am making jelly this morning, so I will have to run. Now Clint, you take care of Chessy's needs." With those words Clara hurriedly left to go to her kitchen behind the store.

In dismay, Chessy looked around for someone that might help her escape this man, as she felt her strength draining from her, leaving her weak and helpless in his clutches.

"Well, my dear Chessy, Auntie Clara gave me orders to help you in any need of yours. So what do you need? All my needs have been take care of just by meeting you. I have been gone so long at sea, I was fearful that I might never see a lovely lady again."

Chessy was shocked as he once again commenced kissing the palms of her hands.

Clint had come from the sea with the taste of it still in his mouth and the essence of it on his garments. Clearly, he walked with bold and arrogant, swaggering sea legs. His handsome and rugged face was browned from the sun and the spraying seawater. He had a deep cleft in his chin and laugh lines around his mouth that was always wreathed in smiles.

His eyes were unbelievably astonishing; one was velvet brown with flecks of gold, the other was liquid jet black. He was always delightfully amused by people's reaction when they first met him. He always took advantage of their surprise and wonder to weave the enchanting dark magic of his eyes as he glowed with the strength and the vigorous radiance of youth.

Chessy was unable to move away from him; she stood frozen in her steps. He was still holding her hands, and all of her body was melting before him. Oh the wonder of his eyes. She could feel his eyes slowly devouring her, and she felt she was drowning in them. He hastily brushed another kiss on her hands as he heard Clara returning. He whispered, "Chessy, I know where your stile is; please, please meet me there tonight."

She didn't have time to tell him that she most certainly would not be there, when and if he came to her stile.

Clara came back into the room, "Well, Clint, I see you have gone on with your prattle and never tended to her needs. Chessy, what can I do for you?"

Without answering her, Chessy just grabbed a box of salt and hurried out the door.

"Well, Clint, do you know any reason Chessy would be in such a hurry? I will have to ask her why she didn't stay and visit a while. Oh well, us old folks sure aren't the likes of the young ones nowadays."

Frantically, Chessy slammed the screen door behind her.

The men, who now had gathered on the porch, were startled a bit. They had never known Chessy to slam the door, and most of the time, she would stop and chat a bit with them. She tried to calm herself down and still the racing of her heart, which had moved from where it was supposed to be up to the vicinity of her throat. Her face was still hot, and she knew it must be the color of scarlet. As she raced down the steps, she heard Amos Hammon say, "Well, this is not like our Miss Chessy to not take time to chat a minute. I do wonder what could be the matter with her."

Chessy knew she would be the source of their conversation until someone else happened by. She slowed her walk down a little, which was certainly a good idea in the intense heat. Her breathing was almost back to normal, but now icy fingers were running up and down her spine. As soon as she was out of the sight of the men at the store, she started to run, not caring where, just running, her mass of curly hair flying behind her like a wild tempest. The palms of her hands were still burning from his kisses. She spread them open to the wind, which did not help. Just ahead was her stile. Totally spent, completely confused, and wet with sweat, she sank down on the lowest step and rested her head on the one above.

Now was the time to figure out Clint's outlandish behavior. She wished she had someone to talk to; maybe they would have some advice to give her. Since there was no one, she would have to think this one out by herself. Oh, how she missed her Grammy.

The turmoil she was in began when she opened the screen door at the store and Clint bowed outrageously before her. Yes, this was the beginning of this trouble.

The man was ruthless. He began by having the upper hand when he said Clara had told him all about her. She felt powerless and weak. When she had looked into his eyes, it was no wonder that she fell into some kind of spell. If only Clara had remained in the store, none of these shenanigans would have happened. However, thinking calmly about it, she was sure he had already hypnotized Clara with his cunning ways.

Chessy made herself stop thinking about this nonsense and started for home. When she got there, she discovered that she had leaves, grass and all kinds of debris on her clothes from when she began that wild conniption fit of running.

She hurried into her little house and attended to the chores that had to be done each evening. Then she made a pot of hot tea, got out two of her biscuits from breakfast, and spread them with butter and her homemade jam. While she sat and ate, she tried to think of some way to find out when Clint would be leaving. She would have to make do with what she had on hand in the way of supplies, so she wouldn't have to go back to the store to meet him again. She was firm on that! After eating her little supper, she got out some mending to keep herself busy tonight. She found a dress that had to be mended, but as she sewed, she carelessly jabbed her finger with the needle and now it was bleeding. More torture. She threw the old dress on the floor and was getting increasingly angry by the minute.

What kind of girl did he think she was, telling her to meet him at her stile? He did say please, but still, it sounded like a command to her. She could see him now in his room, getting all slicked up, anxious to meet this girl of the kissed hands. He knew they had never been kissed before, not like that. For sure, he was priming himself up for a little more than the kissing of hands. He had probably been hailed with cheers by every girl whose hands he had kissed, she thought. She decided she would call him the hand-kissing man. She could see him now, stepping out his door, doing a nimble, fast-footed fox-trot step. If he hadn't been whistling and singing in his room, for sure, he would start now in his eager walk to her stile. He would have no trouble finding it, for Chessy was sure that even the man in the moon was conspiring with him. Maybe the man in the moon is a hand-kissing man himself, she thought. Well, since she wouldn't be there, the moon could watch the poor rejected man mourning, perhaps with his head resting on the step above him. Let the moon send its radiant rays upon her stile and try to comfort him.

What if he was the kind of man who relished a long wait because of its aftermath? What if that wait built up his feverish passion to an even greater excitement?

Chessy got up and put on her nightgown. She knew she would be able to get a good night's sleep after this topsy-turvy day. In the morning, in the light of day, she would see this in a rational, reasonable way. She stretched out her tired body luxuriously for a well-deserved rest.

Her pillow lacked its usual puffiness, so she sat up, beat it, and turned it over. Then she felt some wrinkles on her sheet so she got out of bed, pulled it tight, and tucked it in. Once again, she gave her pillow another beating a trifle harder this time.

Thoroughly upset with herself, she got up, went to the kitchen, and made some tea. Sitting at her table, she turned up both of her hands. Her kissed hands seemed to be her biggest problem. She slowly rubbed her fingers repeatedly on her palms. She commenced kissing them herself just where he had pressed them with his lips. She laid her head down on them and hot burning tears seeped out between each finger, washing the kisses away.

Chessy knew she had lost the battle. She knew now that she really like him, maybe even loved him. Oh yes, this had to be love, as she had never felt this way before. Then she began planning her strategy for handling this unbelievable event that had come into her dull and boring life. From here on, she must be in control at all times or it could lead to dire consequences, as this sea-fairing, hand-kissing man's love might be unrestrainable.

First, she would tell him that she wanted to show him some of the southern hospitality that he had heard of in his many travels. Then let him know, very subtly, that she was interested in knowing more about him. This must begin in a public place; maybe Sunday church would be an ideal environment. That way, they could both get the clouds out of their heads and get back down to earth.

But no more kissing the palms of her hands. And no more breathtaking fever like she had experienced at the General Store. And no more being flustered like a stormy tempest. They needed to just stand back and watch this friendship unfold. Who knows? It might lead to marriage.

Having made up her mind as to what to do, she now had to decide when to do it and where. It couldn't be at the store, especially with the men sitting on the porch. Why not tonight? This might be the best place, if they both kept their emotions intact and restrained. She hastily changed to a clean dress, brushed her hair and let it fall down like a mantle of glory. She quickly ran out the door, then suddenly stopped, turned, and ran back to the house. She got her petticoat out of its lavender perfumed hiding place and put it on. The little pink and blue rosettes smiled in glee as Chessy ran out the door to her stile under her tree, and the man in the moon sprinkled stardust that made a golden path for her feet.

They saw each other at the same time. Not knowing why, tears began running down her cheeks. Clint pulled her to himself after kissing the palms of her hands. Her body was trembling as he began to kiss her tears away. He, ever so gently, picked her up and carried her to her stile. Slowly, step-by-step, like the steps of her stile itself, he took her on a downward spiral of burning desire. There was no turning back. They needed no words in this place where heaven and earth did meet. Their intense passion was like a wall of seawater that carried them with love.

Chessy was baptized with fire; Clint was drenched with salty seawater. The silver cord was loosed, and the golden bowl had broken, never to be mended again.

There is no healing of thy bruise; thy wound is grievous:
all that hear the bruit of thee shall clap the hands over thee:
for upon whom hath not thy wickedness passed continually?

NAHUM 3:19

Chapter 60

Suspicions

It was another hot and sweltering day in Paw Paw. Yet, in every household that morning, there was a frantic rush to leave for Miss Idy's house. The ladies of the church's Sewing Circle had big news to discuss according to her. There was shocking, shameless behavior in their midst.

Miss Idy shook with excitement as she opened the door, got them seated, and served them cold tea. Then she took center stage, wishing she had a gavel.

"Now ladies, the first hint of what has happened in our midst came from Clara Johnson. She hadn't seen Chessy for weeks, and then into the store she walked. Now, as we all know, Clara usually never sees beyond her nose; but she told me that Chessy looked terribly peaked, her hair was in a mess, and she looked sick. Clara said she talked for a few minutes; Chessy never said a word. Then all of a sudden, as soon as she mentioned that Clint had returned to his ship, the child left the store in a rush and without buying anything.

"I met Chessy on the steps of the store as she ran out, so I will quickly give you my reason for thinking Chessy might be in the family way. I thought I noticed a tightening of her dress across her bosom, but the gathered skirt she had on was able to conceal anything. Why would she be in such a rush? We will just have to wait and see if our suspicions are true.

"So ladies, let us be on the alert; I fear Satan has reared up his ugly head in our midst. If Chessy is in the family way, this kind of news cannot be hid under a bushel basket or under the bed. This phrase is from the Bible, you know.

"Maybe I should feel a little guilty about what has happened. I should have kept a closer eye on her. Her beauty has been her downfall that's for sure.

"Just don't forget that Chessy has broken one of the Ten Commandments of God's Holy Word," Miss Idy continued in her harsh and judgmental way. "So if we are around her, we must act accordingly, that there is a consequence to this kind of sin.

"For now, let us watch our young men, hopefully not your husbands, although remember David and Bathsheba's adulteress affair. This will give you all something to do this week.

"I don't think any of us are in the mood for sewing today, so I suggest we all go home and keep our eyes open."

The ladies nodded in agreement, then shook their heads in astonishment as they started for home.

Maggie Jenkins' telephone switchboard was getting its biggest workout since it was first installed. She complained long and loud that she needed a raise in salary, but as usual, the magistrates of Paw Paw paid her no mind.

Who was the father? Every man, married or not, literally shook in their shoes. Who was this man who was putting them all in peril? Every young man and old was stepping lightly. They knew they were all under suspicion.

Miss Idy was sure it was Clara's nephew. He was a handsome scalawag, and she could tell he was a scoundrel just by looking at him; but since she had no proof, she dare not call him guilty.

There was many a quarrel and much wrangling—the men on the porch called it being at loggerheads—in every household. This turmoil continued on, and every male in Paw Paw became subject to every whim and fancy of their wives and mothers.

Not willing to hear the scathing accusations of the female gender, the yards around their houses became free of weeds and broken windows were replaced. They hung the clothes on the line after the ladies had scrubbed them clean on a washboard. Otis and Jimmy C. even painted the house, the woodshed, and his doghouse.

Draw me, we will run after thee:
the king hath brought me into his chambers:
we will be glad and rejoice in thee,
we will remember thy love more than wine:
the upright love thee.

SONG OF SOLOMON 1:4

Chapter 61

The Stile of Love

Chessy never tired of listening, and Clint never tired of telling her about his ship and his sea. They would lie under her tree next to her stile, and he would tell her about the stars and the big universe beyond.

"Chessy, can you see it? The sky, ominous and menacing in its darkness, and the stars looming over us, the only light their silvery glow. At night when the sea is calm and quiet, you can reach up in the heavens and take hold of a star in your hand. Did you ever hold a star in your hand? Or, have the privilege of conversing with the man in the moon? It can be done, you know, when your heart, soul, and spirit is controlled by the sea; it can be done.

"Darling, why don't you come away with me and we could always be together. You and me, my ship and my sea, all my loves together.

"Chessy, I think we will take a magical journey to heaven tonight. Angels are going to sweep us past the sun, the moon, the stars, and the planets rare. Who knows, they might just bow their heads to see us there.

"There are millions of stars. Just a few can be seen. Even with a telescope, we couldn't see them all. I think God's little angels light the tiny stars, and His big angels light the big ones. There are blue stars and red ones, and I think God Himself tends to them. There seem to be more tiny ones, and they are the ones that twinkle. The angels call them 'forget-me-nots.' God puts them in clusters, so they can give as much light as the big ones. They are always asking Him to make them bigger, but God has a reason for all His creations, big and small. There are star clouds, which are always moving, sometimes even running away. There are giant stars and little tiny dwarf stars. There is a lot of jealousy and fussing among the stars. Sometimes, right out of the blue—oops, I mean black—they try to show off. We call them shooting stars, and one must get out of the way when they begin to shoot."

When Clint told some outlandish tale, Chessy would scold him. Then she would kiss his mouth until they both became breathless, hungry with desire. After which, she would drop off to sleep in his arms.

For over a month, Clint had tried desperately to wean himself from his sea and take his place among the other quiet contented men that sat on the porch at the General Store. If he could do this, then he could stay with his lovely Chessy. However, he felt this life would be a waveless, windless existence. A life of such peaceful unhurried composure it would be likened to a ship on its last journey to a port to be dismantled. Every morning when he left Chessy, he could feel the raging of his sea within him. He could smell and taste the salty seawater. Then this untamed spirit would start burning in his innermost being. Day after day he was tormented by the sea, as it called him back to his wandering, vagabond life.

Once he told Chessy that her stile was arid, stale, and barren, and that everything around her had been tamed, brought under control. On the sea, he lived a life that was forever moving, filled with the unexpected, a life that was startling and electrifying. There was always a new challenge to confront to keep his ship from being demolished by the uncontrollable defiant sea.

In her childish innocence, Chessy never tired of hearing the story of the mermaids. She would beg him to tell it over and over.

"The old men of the sea say that to see the mermaids, you have to stand staunch on firm sea legs on a rolling deck in the middle of a wild storm. You have to be drenched and baptized by the foaming spray and have tasted and savored the frothy salt water on your tongue.

"The mermaids only come out at midnight, and only during the most violent of storms. They seem to sense and hear the groans and shudders of a mighty ship. They thrill as the cruel winds whip the ship like a cat-o'-nine-tails. The mermaids come riding on the huge swells, surround the ship as the sailors curse, and pray in the same breath for God to quiet the storm. Many a rowdy seaman believes and repeats over and over again the superstition that the mermaids themselves bring on the storm. They do this, it is said, so they can capture the sailors to be their lovers. The mermaids are so beautiful they cause some sailors to jump overboard and join them. Half the mermaid's body is covered with scales that glisten like rainbows in the night; the other half is a beautiful, soft woman. They swim and circle the ship. They promise to take the sailors to the bottom of the sea and show them wrecked ships full of gold and silver, ships filled with riches just there for the taking. Then when the winds abate and the sea becomes calm again, the mermaids vanish. They return to their watery home to swim around their enormous treasure and wait until another ship is in distress."

Chessy knew that even in the heady wine of lovemaking, Clint's beloved ship was between them. She noticed that when he talked of his ship or his sea, he crushed her tighter in his arms. When he cradled her in his arms on the earth, he also cradled his ship on the sea. She knew he wanted them both with equal intensity, but she knew that was impossible. Her lover had to make a decision.

Clint knew it too, but when he weighed them in the balance, Chessy was the one who came up wanting.

"Oh Chessy, the sea is so vast and enormous, it lies out here just for the taking and can be claimed by anyone. Many don't know this and don't understand, but when they do, the sea becomes their own. The boundless, limitless spirit of the sea beckons one to come and drink of its fullness. It is a spirit that can never be quieted. This spirit so possesses you that you must sail to every island large or small, far or near, to see what secrets they hold. My darling, there are the seaports to search out for their treasure and beauty. Some men would like to live on the sea, but they are frightened. There is nothing to be afraid of. The lighthouses on the cliffs are bright jewels to a sailor, and the somber sound of the foghorn warns of the dangers that lurk beneath the surface. The sea becomes a mother and father. It's also like an unrestrained, wanton lover, a mistress, always seeking searching hungrily for a lost paradise.

"Darling Chessy, the thing I love most is the calm before the storm—the storm out there, gathering a foothold before it unleashes its fury. Your ship will rise up, be driven by its force, mighty waves cresting, then it plunges downward, almost capsizing your ship. I have stood on the deck and let the black waves wash over me, and in some uncanny and mysterious way, I felt cleansed of all the sins in my life. Then, in the light of dawn, there would be a calming down of the treacherous sea and peace would still the waves. I would feel this same peace in my body, soul, and spirit."

After this story, Chessy and her lover had fallen asleep.

Their serenade of passion and splendor had reached its peak, its pinnacle for Clint. There was now a growing restless numbness in his heart. He no longer wanted to go to Chessy's stile, her "stile of love" as she called it. In his way of thinking, he had climbed the highest mountain, trekked across the heated desert, and all that was left for him was to go back to the beckoning arms of his beloved sea.

Last night, he had made his last and final trip to the stile. Now a heavy velvet curtain was slowly lowering itself between his lovely Chessy and his ship, which was calling him back to the sea.

Suddenly, he was awakened out of his reverie by his Uncle

Jacob knocking on his door.

"Clint, come quick. There is a man here with an important message for you. He has come for you. You have to leave immediately for your ship."

Clint hurried out to meet him. He was thankful that there was not time to tell Chessy anything. Then shrugging his shoulders, as if to say everything was all taken care of, he walked out and slammed the door behind him.

When Clint left Chessy, he didn't leave her arms empty; he left her his legends of his sea. He left her his legacy, a token of the wonderment of their love.

There was no hint, no forewarning, of this shameful wounding day, but ere it would end a darkness, bereft of even starlight, would crush Chessy and her stile. Yet, even if she and Clint had known ahead of time, it would not have stopped their sojourns into paradise, even though for her it was a fool's paradise.

Chessy had thought for several days that maybe she was wrong in her findings, but now there was no doubt. She was going to have a baby. "I didn't think this would happen to me," she said worriedly to herself. "But Clint should have known. He's the one who sails around the world on his wonderful, blue-green sea. For sure, he has been involved with many other ladies." Chessy knew he loved her best because he had told her so. She knew her rival was his ship and his sea, but now the baby would make him stay with her. "So tomorrow, we will go to Whippoorwill and get married. That will solve our problem," Chessy thought aloud. "Then all my worries will have been in vain. That's what we shall do."

It was too early for Clint to come to her stile under her tree, but she decided to go anyway and sit on the top step and dream of her baby. "I wonder if it will be a boy. Most men want a boy first and then a baby girl. That's what I am going to do; I'm going to have a boy first. I shall tell him as soon as he arrives; this baby will hold us together forever." She shivered with delight. She smiled and swung her feet back and forth in her happiness.

Chessy waited all night, but Clint didn't come. She waited for him at the stile again the next night too, but he still did not come. She knew she had to go the store to see for herself what had happened to him. Maybe there would be a reason for him not coming; maybe he would come rushing back to her today. But, deep down in her heart, Chessy already knew the answer. On her way to the General Store, she rehearsed what she would say to Clara to find out about him. Maybe he would be there and look at her again as he did when she first met him. Maybe he would kiss the palms of her hands again.

As she was climbing the steps to the porch, she was glad to see that the men hadn't arrived yet. She opened the screen door. Clara was the only one there.

"Well, my, my, my, if it isn't our sweet Chessy. Where have you been? We have sorely missed your presence around here. Have you been sick? You certainly look a little peaked, that's for sure. We will be lonelier than ever now that Clint is gone. He got some urgent news from his ship, and he had to hurry back to it. I never did understand about all that urgency, but he sure left in a rush. You know Chessy, I was hoping you would come back to see him again. He sure took a shine to you that first morning here. Oh well, it probably is for the best. My gramma always said when a girl married a wandering kind of man, she was 'driving her ducks to a dry pond.' Clint is one of those wandering men, that's for sure.

"Oh, but wasn't he the handsomest man these parts have ever seen? And his eyes, Chessy, did you notice his eyes? Let me see, he was only here for about two months. I remember I put it on my calendar the day he arrived. I don't know why I did that, but sometimes it's a good thing to do. Well, here I am forgetting what I was talking about. Oh yes, his eyes. One brown and one black. With just one look from his eyes, he had every girl—and I will say all—bowing and scraping before him. Mary Thompson, down the road, was so gone on him it was just disgraceful how she carried on. But he never bothered to give her the time of day.

"Well, dear Chessy, we didn't need to worry where you were concerned. He didn't have you twisted around his finger. Every girl around should take you as an example. You know, Chessy, Clint wasn't high on working. He had to take a nap every afternoon. Can you beat that? But maybe that is not so unusual. Maybe sleeping on that big ship prevented him from sleeping sound."

Clara was busy sacking beans and didn't see the pain in Chessy's face.

"And you know, he never left me his address. What if I might want to write him a letter? All I can say is, he was a mite strange. I did my best to get him to go somewhere, but no, as soon as it was dark, he would go to his room and go to bed. Well, it seems to me that young people today aren't like they were in my youth."

Without a word, Chessy hurried out the door, leaving Clara with her mouth open.

Just then, Clara saw Jacob come in the back door.

"Jacob, what do you think? Chessy came into the store and didn't say a word. And, to cap that off, she never bought anything either. Can you come up with an answer for that? I do believe she might be sick, but she never offered to say she was. We'll have to check on her. Oh, these young folks."

Clara kept on talking, although Jacob had already gone out the back door again.

"Jacob? Are you listening to me?"

Chessy didn't remember going by the stile on the way home or going in the door of her house. Her lips moved but her voice was not heard, as she knelt beside her narrow white virgin bed that was never to be again. A whispered, wounded prayer of pain and despair failed to penetrate the darkness that had seized her. She felt smothered, barely able to breathe as dark hands clenched tightly around her throat. She felt all the punishment of sin in Eden's Garden in her Gethsemane. Drained and desolate, she crumpled in a heap on the floor. A piercing, wounded cry came from her soul and filled the room with her grief and despair, but no one was there to hear. Intense pain seemed to reach out with huge blackened claws and take possession of her. The day ended with darkness, like the blackness of a sackcloth of hair, covering her world.

But one of the soldiers with a spear pierced his side,
and forthwith came there out blood and water.

JOHN 19:34

Chapter 62

The Petticoat With Tiny Pink and Blue Rosettes

Chessy awakened after a sleepless night. This was the day she had to go to the General Store, and she was dreading it. For over two months, she barely had enough food to keep up her strength. She slowly dragged her swollen body from the bed in a numbed stupor, went to the milk shed, and milked her cow. The milk and butter were her main source of food. Trembling with fatigue, she finished milking her cow. Then she went to the kitchen, poured milk over one biscuit, buttered another one, and added some jelly, forcing herself to eat it all.

As she started out, the blazing sun beat unmercifully down on her. As far as she could see, furious heat waves were shimmering and dancing from the hot dusty road. Dazed and bewildered from this extra exertion, she wondered if her baby had moved lower in her belly, it was getting more painful to walk, she voicelessly lamented.

Chessy walked barefoot and carried her tattered shoes in one hand. Then she hesitated for a moment and put one shoe in each hand, as if this might provide some balance to her ungainly walk. With each step she took, she very carefully and purposely pushed each foot into the white powdery dust. She welcomed the exquisite hot pain she felt as it squeezed up between each toe.

Could this be her atonement to make amends for what had happened? She felt no answer to her question.

She plodded along toward her destination, the General Store. She wore a faded, flimsy, blue cotton dress that at one time had had purple violets and sprigs of yellow daises dancing on it. All that remained now were ashes of lavender and pale yellow shadows. Her dress buttoned down the front, and between each straining button, her pink belly could be seen. A trembling wash of sweat blurred her eyes, trickled down her brow and face, and dropped to her chest. Her dress was wet and clung to every distended curve of her body. She had no petticoat on.

Chessy Lou Darnell had used her beautiful petticoat to make her baby two little gowns. One was trimmed with blue rosettes, and the other had tiny pink ones. The petticoat had lost its sweet perfuming lavender. It now mingled with the harsh poignant smell of discord.

In planning this trip to the General Store, she knew she must avoid sitting down at her stile, as it would surely stir up again her passionate love for Clint. But she was exhausted, and her fragile body demanded a few minutes rest. She sat down on the first step and rested her head on the step above. For months, she had tried to shrink back within herself when she thought someone was near. Now there wasn't any reason, there was no use trying to hide her sins. Everyone knew and had known for a long time. She had been the brunt of their conversation for months.

In vain, she wiped the sweat from her face. There was a hard, dry pain in her tearless eyes. If only she could vent and somehow release the pain that was slowly consuming her mind, soul, and body with its bright intense burning glare. However, there was no solace, no ease. Her lips were parched like the world around her that was so barren and naked for the want of water. The heat had caused her hair to fall down around her face, and she tried for a few moments to pin it up higher. Her lovely chestnut-colored hair had lost its bright and bouncy luster. It hung limp and untidy with an unwashed look. In just the few months, her brow had darkened with deep wrinkles between her eyes. They too had lost their clear blue radiant glow. Her lovely face was marred with puffy, swollen reddish blotches.

She could see the General Store now. She was afraid she might fall in putting her shoes on, so she had to leave the road and go to the nearest tree. Balancing herself against it, she managed to put them on. Then she plodded down the road. Her sweat had found a new place to rest; it squashed inside her shoes although she never heard it and she never felt it.

As usual, there on the porch of the General Store sat the men. Strangely, when they saw her coming, they ceased their talking and forgot their chewing, spitting, and whittling. They sat motionless in a death-like silence; a sweetish mist akin to fear or revulsion gripped each one. She reached the steps to the porch and took hold of the shaky, wobbly banister. Slowly she pulled herself up the steps, faltering and stumbling in the effort. She never really saw the men, she had mentally detached herself from everyone and moved into her own world of anguish and desolation.

None of the men wanted to be the first to help her, so none of them moved. It was as though they were compassed about by a contagious fear or fascination. They all sat frozen to their chairs. She passed by them and disappeared into the store.

Woman, where are thine accusers?

Then one by one the men apprehensively and cowardly murmured a reason for having to go home to their sacred and virtuous little houses that were free from sin and transgression.

When at long last Chessy arrived back at her house, not one bit of energy remained. Life was closing in on her. She slumped down on the little rug beside her bed as water and blood pooled around her. The only sound that could be heard was her faint, whispered plea, "Miss Idy. Miss Idy. Help me, Miss Idy."

This image's head was of fine gold, . . .
his feet part of iron and part of clay.

DANIEL 2:32-33

Chapter 63

Peaches and Cream

It was 2:00 A.M. when the phone started ringing. A sleepy Doctor Allen answered. "Doctor Allen, this is Maggie Jenkins at the telephone office. I hate to call you at this hour, but I got a call from Ed Reed and he was hysterical. I only caught the words 'dying' and 'dead' and 'come at once.'"

"Okay, Maggie, I will hurry out there." As Doctor Allen put on his clothes, he thought he might need someone to help him. Why not Miss Idy? She was always on the go to help someone far or near. He called Maggie back. "Maggie, please call Miss Idy and tell her I need her in this emergency. I will pick her up in ten minutes." He never gave her time to answer, but he heard her give a loud gasp. Then he hung up the phone and hurried out the door.

When he got to Miss Idy's house, he found her standing at her gate. He leaned over and opened the door for her, and she got in beside him.

"Good morning, Miss Idy."

Her "good morning" was a trifle weak. Where was that assertive voice she always had? That in-control, bold, very bold, if the situation called for it, voice? What had he done in getting this prim, pious, devout lady in his car at this time of the morning? He realized that his actions had been rash and even a little crazy. The atmosphere in the car was indeed a trifle strained.

Trying to make amends, Doctor Allen said, "Please forgive me, Miss Idy. I am an impetuous fool and I used bad judgment. I should have called someone else to go with me. The only excuse I have is that you were the first person I thought of. Please believe me."

"What's done is done," she replied stonily.

The car became silent again.

Then Doctor Allen in a soft, yet bold, tone said, "Miss Idy, I'm not so sure that I really am sorry. I have for some time wanted to meet with you someplace where we could talk and get better acquainted."

Doctor Allen looked at her. She seemed someplace else other than in the car with him. He said, "Miss Idy, I can see that I certainly overplayed my hand this time, didn't I?"

Stunned, she started laughing.

What in the world is happening to her? Doctor Allen thought. He had heard the men say repeatedly that she never laughed and that even a trace of a smile was rare indeed. He became worried. "What have I done, Miss Idy? Please tell me."

"Oh, Doctor Allen, it's not you I'm laughing about, it's me. If you knew Paw Paw as I do, you would know that tomorrow would be a day that will go down in infamy. It will go something like this. The excitement will begin at the break of day because that's when Maggie will start her grapevine telephone calls. She will call three women and one man—I happen to know who they are. A short time later, the men on the porch will hear of it, then the members of the Baptist Church. They might be so shocked they might ring the bell in the belfry. Then last, our Jimmy C. will make a wild dash to the newspaper office and have it put in the 'What Fell Out of the Wastebasket Today' column."

Doctor Allen was startled at these revelations but more so by the fact that she was laughing so hard she had tears pouring down her face. Then he started to laugh with her.

Miss Idy said, "Better laugh while we can, as we might

never laugh again."

They drove into Ed's yard. The house and barn were all lit up. "Miss Idy, I must prepare you, it must be that someone's hurt seriously in the barn." As they jumped from the car, he grabbed her hand and ran toward the barn.

The big doors were open and a terrible ruckus was sounding in the back of the big barn. They rushed in and a huge mare was lying stretched out before them, making great heaving sounds and looking wildly around as if begging for help. Doctor Allen saw that she was hemorrhaging badly. Ed had her head on his lap and was trying to comfort her.

Doctor Allen shouted, "Ed, are you crazy? I'm not a veterinarian!"

"But Doc, my vet is gone and won't be home for another two weeks. You got to do something or my Betsy's going to die! What's the difference between her and a woman having a baby? Oh, please don't let her die, Doctor Allen."

Doctor Allen saw the panic in his eyes, so he threw off his coat and rolled up his sleeves. He muttered aloud, "This might get bad before it's over." Then taking charge of the situation and determined to do his level best, he began barking orders. "Miss Idy, you get over here with me. Ed, you kneel on the other side. We are going to have to pull this mother's little baby out of her."

As the old mare heaved and struggled, the colt would come into sight then it would disappear again when the heaving stopped.

"Ed, get me a clean rope if you have one. When the colt appears again, we will quickly slip it over its head and feet. It will take our combined efforts to pull the baby, and we must be gentle to not harm either Betsy or the colt."

Miss Idy was overcome by this dramatic scene before her, but she did like the fact that she was part of a team. They were working for a hard taskmaster who was bold and unafraid to do what must be done, yet she saw a soft and gentle man too.

He was working feverishly, and at Betsy's next heave, he slipped the rope around the colt's head and front feet. When old Betsy gave another heave, they all pulled and out in the soft hay a baby colt lay. Ed was crying and laughing at the same time, but Doctor Allen continued examining old Betsy.

"There is something wrong here, but I don't know what it is. We need to say a little prayer, I think."

Suddenly, Old Betsy gave another big and mighty heave and another baby colt lay beside his twin on the soft hay.

Ed Reed started blubbering and running in circles, he was so beside himself with joy. Impulsively, Doctor Allen grabbed Miss Idy in his arms and swung her around in joy, and they began babbling along with Ed. Her hair fell down in total disarray, and she failed miserably in her attempt to fix it. In her rush to meet Doctor Allen, she failed to use enough hairpins, and in this rash madcap experience, she lost the few she had in the hay.

Doctor Allen started to laugh. "Miss Idy, if a person can't find a needle in a haystack, we also can't find your hairpins in the hay."

Then he helped up one of the colts, and Ed helped up the other. They stood them up on their wobbly legs and guided them to old Betsy's life-giving milk. They could see the mare was in a quandary and a bit puzzled about having two babies, but she used her velvety nose and softly nuzzled and nickered her happiness first to one colt and then the other.

Miss Idy was bursting with joy. "Oh Ed, Doctor Allen, look. Old Betsy is smiling. Look at her!"

"Miss Idy, you are getting beside yourself if you are imagining that a horse can smile," chided Doctor Allen.

Ed finally stopped blubbering and said, "Miss Idy, I want you to name my babies."

"Oh, Ed, I can't. You must name them yourself. I would probably name them Peaches and Cream or some other ridiculous names."

"Thank you, Miss Idy, that shall be their names. Peaches and Cream. I like that."

"Ed, I was just teasing, you know."

But, Ed was adamant. He bowed to each of his babies and said, "You shall be called Mr. Peaches, and you shall be called Miss Cream."

Ed brought a big bucket of water for Betsy to drink and a basin of water for the three of them to wash up in. Then they all sat down and rested from the violent, yet emotional event of this awe-inspiring wonder from God.

Doctor Allen spoke sternly. "Ed, you are going into the house and get some sleep. You have been up all day and all night. Miss Idy and I shall stay for a few hours, watch over your babies, and make sure they are okay."

They heard him praising God for his Old Betsy and her two babies, for Miss Idy, and for Doctor Allen all the way into the house. Ed Reed was a happy man.

While Doctor Allen was giving his new patients another checkup, Miss Idy walked to the big open door behind the barn. A pinkish golden sun was barely peeking over the horizon. She knew she had witnessed again the hand of the God of the universe. He had reached down from heaven to a humble birthing room in an old barn and touched Ed, sweet old Betsy, and her two babies. Once again, she asked the question, "God, what is a man that You are so mindful of him?" Then, trembling, she turned her thoughts to Doctor Allen.

She had never seen anyone like him before, so strong and brave, so gifted and sure of himself, so ablaze with life and beauty. How she loved him! She wanted to shout it from the tops of the mountains and sing it in the valleys. She wanted to shout for all to hear: I love you Doctor Allen! I love you Doctor Allen! She raised her arms in this silent brazen shameless proclamation.

She never heard Doctor Allen step up behind her, but she felt his gentle touch as he gently clasped his arms around her and pulled her to him. She felt his face pressing and kissing her fallen hair. She never moved. This is the way it should be. God Himself had taught His creations from Eden's Garden this gift of love that He would bestow between man and woman. The design, the pattern, the hunger, the thirst, the tantalizing conception were all His. But Satan dangled this image before her eyes.

She turned to him in glorious wonder. He cupped his hands around her face and began kissing her face, her eyes, and finally her lips. Then in reckless heated passion, he wildly pulled her closer. She trembled with emotion as she began kissing him back. She felt her body yield to him; she had no strength left to push him away. In this awakening, she felt the release of old pain leaving her and tears ran down her face. Doctor Allen kissed them away. This pure, holy virgin had no defiance, no resistance. She knew she was entering forbidden territory that she knew very little about. There would be no chance of reversing, no restoration, no retracing of one's steps back to the virginal bed. Oh, yes, the mighty Miss Idy, the lady of iron with feet of clay had been brought to her knees by a man.

Suddenly, a strange specter appeared to Miss Idy. Was this her guardian angel? No! This was Chessy Lou Darnell. What was she doing here? Then realizing this was a message from God, she knew He was making her aware of her terrible sin against the child. Miss Idy began to shake violently and cried out loud, "Chessy, forgive me my beautiful child. Oh, sweet innocent Chessy, I was the one who cast the first stone. I am stained forever with this sin."

Then almost in answer to her plea, she heard Chessy calling her. "Help me, Miss Idy. Please help me. Miss Idy, please come quick."

She pushed herself out of Doctor Allen's embrace, jumped up, and ran for his car as she cried out for him to hurry.

Not one word was spoken on that frantic drive home.

Judge not, that ye be not judged.
For with what judgment ye judge, ye shall be judged:
and with what measure ye mete,
it shall be measured to you again.

MATTHEW 7:1-2

Chapter 64

Where Are Chessy's Accusers?

Doctor Allen was shook up and perplexed all day about Miss Idy's behavior in the barn and her crying out to Chessy. What had this meant? He was deeply ashamed of his reckless and sinful departure from God Himself. Why, oh why, had he done such a thing? Why was she so different from all the other women he had met? He closed his office early and went over to the store to see Clara; maybe she could answer his many questions.

She was in the backyard tending to a huge purple lilac bush. It had grown so large that it drenched the old swing with its sweet essence. She sat down on the swing and motioned him to come over and sit down beside her.

"Clara, I want to ask you something. Who is Chessy? Have I met her yet?"

"Well, Doctor Allen, that is a sad story. Chessy is a young girl who is going to have a baby, and she isn't married. Who the father is we don't have any idea. No one has seen a man around her. She is the most stunning and beautiful girl anyone has seen. If it were possible for one to be bewitched or charmed by the angels, it would be Chessy. Now that I think about it, seems like her baby ought to be due any day."

"Clara," Doctor Allen exclaimed angrily, "how can the people of Paw Paw claim to be so religious then leave this poor girl all by herself? Do you mean to say that Miss Idy hasn't even seen about her? Tell me!"

"Now Doctor Allen, do not prejudge Miss Idy harshly. That would be wrong. She is the most intelligent and efficient person I have ever known. You wouldn't believe the careless slipshod ways we had of doing things until she got here. Her favorite expression was 'cleanliness is next to godliness.' She said this applied not only to one's person but also to their house and yard, as well as to every public building, like our school, church, and library.

"You know Doctor Allen, she was the one who brought our newspaper and our library here. She demanded we paint our small courthouse and little jail. The jail has never been used and the men on the porch said that was just a waste of time, but it got painted. Miss Idy saw to that.

"Did you know we were chosen as an example and have been honored as being the most successful little town in the way we have coped with this severe drought and Depression? One tiny little lady, Miss Idy, brought all that about. She oversees our ponds of fish, the making of pencils and brooms, and the huge hand-worked vegetable garden where the field of wildflowers used to grow. She was clever, inventive, and ingenious as she fought for what she believed in.

"I, for one, believe she has sacrificed her life and her happiness as she fought a battle royal to save the town, especially the families in town. She worries a lot about the family. She confided in me one day," Clara smiled. "I called it the day she laid down her coat of arms.

"She said, 'Clara, I'm afraid there will come a day when the foundation will crumble and the family as we see it now will disappear. Home will no longer feel secure for children to run to. A day will come when many children will not know whom their father is. As these men disappear, it will mean more babies that are illegitimate. The Bible warns that without the "natural affection" of both mother and father, one never learns self-control. I see all this leading to disrupted schools, lack of discipline in both school and at home, and, who knows, maybe even people forgetting to pray. Clara, the life of God is in the soul of every man. I have tried and tried to bring this to the surface, but evidently I don't know how.'

"Doctor Allen, I believe Miss Idy was ordained, written into the Book of Life which rests on the lap of God. Everything that is good in Paw Paw was the result of her."

They both sat quiet for a moment, overcome by her description.

"Miss Idy has inspired the whole town, even the men on the porch. I remember one day, I came out to the porch and I didn't see one man sitting there, only a few of their hunting dogs who thought this was their other home." They both laughed at this.

Then, without even a good-bye, Doctor Allen, still a little angry, strode through the store, slammed the screen door, got into his car, and left in a big cloud of dust. He was headed to Chessy's house to find his own answers.

And it shall come to pass, that before they call,
I will answer; and while they are yet speaking,
I will hear.

ISAIAH 65:24

Chapter 65

A Plaintive Call to Miss Idy

All Miss Idy did when Doctor Allen dropped her off at her house was to run in the front door and out the back. The thought of Chessy, the poor young pregnant girl she had judged so harshly, preyed on her mind. She had to redeem the wrong she had done her. She knew there was a shortcut to the fence stile and a path that continued on to Chessy's house. She found herself weeping and crying out to God, "Please, dear Lord, let her be alright until I get there."

The dry leaves and grasses crushed and crackled as she ran. By the time she reached the stile, she was breathless, so she sat down for a moment.

The stile was a landmark, a resting place for the tired and weary, but Miss Idy knew that Chessy saw it in another light. She remembered what she told her one day. "Miss Idy, the old stile is my favorite spot in all the world. It is a soft place. A place to dream and make wishes." Then Chessy had pealed forth her exquisite, joyful laughter.

What had she said to the young woman after hearing this? She couldn't remember. Whatever it was, it would have been said in a curt, sharp way, probably with a scathing verse from the Bible. Oh, yes, she knew the Bible backward and forward, and she often used its verses to bow people down and humble them.

The big shade tree next to the stile might have hidden it

from view if the leaves had been green and new, but now it was bare and naked except for a few brown leaves that rattled in the breeze with a haunting sound.

Had Chessy met her lover here? Did he come night after night to meet the sweet little girl? Or had this pregnancy happened after just one tumultuous tryst, when she knew that could happen? Oh yes, indeed she knew that could happen. Had the man promised to marry her? Had he vowed to never leave her? Had he told her in sweet poetic phrases that their love might result in "red roses in the winter?"

The possibility of all this being true tormented Miss Idy now that she had experienced the power of passion between man and woman. She, who was a lot older and wiser than Chessy, had almost succumbed to it.

Things were still as death when she arrived at the little cottage. She knocked on the front door. There was no answer and it was locked, so she ran around to the back door. There was a rooster sitting on the arm of a bench and a little pink pig grunting and squealing at the door.

She stepped into the kitchen and heard sobbing and moaning. She found Chessy lying on her side on a little rug beside her bed in a pool of blood and water. How long had she been here? Her body looked wasted and ravaged, overcome by the burden of a large baby.

Miss Idy was terrorized with fear, why she should have known that Chessy was due to have a baby, but no, the righteous and holy Miss Idy had stood afar off all these months lest she would be tainted. She should have brought Doctor Allen with her; why didn't she think of that! Chessy had no phone, and she realized there wasn't time to run back to Paw Paw. If she died before the day was over, it would be her fault. Loudly, she called on God. "Please, dear Lord, forgive me of my harsh and bitter condemning words and my unholy judgments. Reprieve me of my sins and shame. I have heaped abuse on everyone when I should have been compassionate and loving."

Then the formidable Miss Idy began to take charge in this life-and-death struggle to save her sweet Chessy. She felt her pulse and her labor of breathing. All seemed normal as could be expected in the turmoil of a baby's birth. The bleeding had stopped and that was good. She knelt at Chessy's back and felt the position of the baby. She was shocked by how big it was. Was the tiny form of Chessy able to deliver this large of a baby?

In desperation, she heard a voice from heaven, "Shall I bring to the birth, and shut up the womb? No, no saith God." Why, this was a cry from the prophet Isaiah in the Old Testament.

Thanking and praising God in His heaven one minute and begging God for forgiveness and strength the next, Miss Idy began to race and scurry about. She got a large pan full of water from a ten-gallon milk can on the porch. Who had brought the water to her, she wondered for a moment?

Chessy's dress was torn apart to make room for her baby. Miss Idy got a pair of scissors and cut it off her. Then she began to give her a sponge bath, all the while speaking comforting, loving words to her about the little baby she would soon have in her arms. She gently pulled the wet soiled rug from under Chessy and pushed a clean soft blanket she found under her and gently rolled her on her back.

The activity brought Chessy around. She looked up, saw Miss Idy, and began to cry with relief. "Oh Miss Idy, I knew you would come. I really tried to wait. Please help me. It hurts so bad."

Miss Idy was stunned. How could she know I was coming? I've never come before. Then, overwhelmed, she realized that she had heard her voice while she was in Doctor Allen's arms. She was saved from immoral conduct by Chessy's cry. Chessy was the way of escape for her. And once again that night she said, "What is man, O God, that You are so mindful of him? I thank You. Please forgive me!Please forgive me, Lord!"

Then Chessy gave a loud scream, grabbed her hands,

squeezing hard, and began gasping for breath and throwing her body back and forth. Miss Idy washed her face with cool water as soon as the pain subsided.

By this time Miss Idy was so hot and sweaty from all the running she'd been doing that she took off her dress and shoes and continued to help Chessy with only her petticoat on. She hunted up a sheet, tied knots in the opposite ends, and wrapped it around the leg of the bed.

"Now Chessy, listen to me. Your pains are going to come again. When they do, I want you to pull on the ends of this sheet with your hands and push down hard to get your baby out. Can you understand what I'm saying?"

"Yes, yes, Miss Idy."

Then once again Chessy was gripped by the throes of pain. Miss Idy clasped her hands to the ends of the sheet, "Chessy, Chessy, you must pull and push my love!"

All day the pains continued, at one time, then they eased up and Chessy dropped off to sleep. Then suddenly the pains started fiercely again. With Chessy screaming and her body wrenching in spasms of pain, Miss Idy began to pray. "Oh, yes, in Eden's Garden came the cry. I will greatly multiply thy sorrow, and thy conception, in sorrow you will bring forth children.

"Please, please, dear Lord, deliver our baby!"

In Miss Idy's hands lay a baby boy. She breathed, "Thank you, Lord" and lifted the baby so Chessy could see him.

Chessy started to laugh and cry hysterically. "Thank you, Miss Idy," she blubbered as she reached for her baby.

There was a big ruckus outside as Doctor Allen drove up and slammed on his brakes. He bolted in through the back door and into the birthing room just in time to bring a tiny twin baby girl into the world. The baby boy had eyes as black as magic; the baby girl's eyes were like brown velvet with flecks of gold.

I know thy works, and thy labour, and thy patience,
and how thou canst not bear them which are evil: . . .
And hast borne, and hast patience,
and for my name's sake hast laboured, and hast not fainted.
Nevertheless I have somewhat against thee,
because thou hast left thy first love.

REVELATION 2:2-4

Chapter 66

Miss Idy Repents

For the first two weeks, Doctor Allen and Miss Idy hovered over Chessy and struggled to keep her babies alive. Doctor Allen purchased two camp cots, one for himself in the living room and the other for Miss Idy next to Chessy. He sent to Whippoorwill for two bassinets and sat them beside her bed also. She had to feed them cow's milk during the night, but Doctor Allen insisted they be put to nurse at Chessy's breast several times a day to keep her flow of milk and to strengthen the tiny babies. He purchased a fan and hung wet sheets around Chessy's bed to keep her cool.

Through Miss Idy's nourishing meals, Chessy lost the little-girl look and gradually she returned to a stunningly exquisite woman. Day by day, she began to take over more of the care of her babies. She was joyful and jubilant over her little ones. Miss Idy looked on with love and shared her happiness. She smiled when Chessy's bubbly cheerful voice penetrated every room in the tiny house.

There had been a few lacey dark clouds all day. They hovered over the hot burning sun, bringing a relief to the little town of Paw Paw. They also sent a tantalizing taste of rain that cooled the dusky twilight. Doctor Allen checked his three little patients then went out and sat down on the little porch swing. Miss Idy joined him.

When he touched the floor with his shoe and gently

pushed it back and forth, it made a creaky melody all its own. Doctor Allen murmured to Miss Idy, "This kind of noise one doesn't mind."

The kerosene lamp in the window was the only light, and it shed a soft glow on Miss Idy's face. Doctor Allen lovingly studied it for a few moments. Why, she is beautiful. She is bewitching. So desirable, why has she not married?

Then he realized she was indeed a different person in the light of her constant bustling hither and yon on her many projects. She wore a rigid, harsh masked costume as from a masquerade party—the strict Miss Idy, controlling everything and everyone with an iron fist. "Oh yes, Paw Paw residents, I am going out of my house today, so I must put on my masquerade garments."

Why, Miss Idy, Why? he wondered.

Not looking at him, she began to speak in a soft gentle voice. "My dear love, in the cold winter of my life, you have come to me. You brought me deep crimson roses, and they perfumed and pointed to a glorious spring of love and life for me. My dear Doctor Allen, it was so vivid, so clear and brilliant it will last me forever, you must know. In Ed Wiley's barn that night, I found a man who thought me desirable and more than that, wanted to kiss me, to hold me."

She imagined the taunts she would hear if anyone in town heard her say what she had just told him. "Oh, not you Miss Idy! What are you saying? That's impossible. We refuse to believe that Doctor Allen would want to marry you!"

He saw the wounded hurt, the pain in her face.

In a low whispering voice, she told him about her near wedding to the judge she had worked for. How he left her. How, filled with shame and humiliation, she stood at the marriage altar alone.

Doctor Allen reached and held her hand, but in a poignant tender move, she pulled her hand away.

"Now that I look back, it was all a childish dream of an

elaborate church wedding by a silly young girl. For sure, I never loved him. I think I was in love with love itself. My darling, a healing has begun that I searched for so long. You have given to me everything my heart has desired. In just a brief fleeting moment, you gave me the feel of love, its pleasure and its tenderness the rush of the torrent of violent passion, and yes, the desire that burns between a man and a woman.

"Yes, my darling, I wanted it all. I wanted you so bad. As I sit beside you now, it makes me tremble and shiver, this greatest gift that God has given to His creation. But I can't have you." Doctor Allen started to say something, but she reached over and put her finger on his lips. With a smile she continued. "Now you have to listen to me. Everything good, lovely, and beautiful is going to happen in the days that are ahead for us. My darling, I shall stand back and smile at your happiness that is to come.

"I know God has called me to do a mission. I was in such a hurry I didn't give God enough time to tutor and instruct me. I thought that I was the second Moses descending from Mount Sinai with the tablets of stone that He had written with His finger. I thought I was the judge and the jury. I will approach my new mission with a heart and spirit of love, compassion, and forgiveness. The apostle Paul wrote in Galatians 6: 'If one is overtaken in a fault, ye which are spiritual, restore this one in a spirit of meekness, considering thyself lest thou also be tempted.'" She smiled at Doctor Allen and said, "I was tempted, as you know, but our gracious Lord gave me an escape.

"In light of this scripture alone, and there are many others, I was tempted by the same temptation which I condemned. Like Chessy's temptation for one. She was innocent, free from guilt, pure, and without sin. She was also very lonely, desolate, afraid . . . the list can go on and on. However, with that temptation, which I only now understand, I stand guilty before her and before God. She has forgiven me and so has my God. You see Doctor Allen, He loves us, so that I think He stands with beckoning hands to forgive us.

"Doctor Allen, you and this child have led me to the place where God wants me to be: to minister, to show others the way to His kingdom. Through this valley, I have walked all these years; I have been doing things my own way, not God's way of love and compassion. I have been severely chastened, humbled, and brought to my knees by you and our sweet Chessy. I have touched the hem of His garment, and I will never be the same. By God's love and by His grace, I have been forgiven. One can have a glow within that casts a most becoming light on others. That is what I will be seeking. From the altar of repentance to a crown of victory is a long journey, but it's worth the effort. There shall be no doubt in that day that it was the superior power of divine grace that made the blessed change which turned this lion into a lamb, this earthworm into a bird of paradise.

"Doctor Allen, I'm sure you know that Chessy loves you. All through the day, she wants me to talk about you. She has this glowing radiance in her lovely face, and her sparkling eyes fairly dance when she knows you are coming. This glorious girl—no, she is a young woman now—has taught me how to love, how to forgive, and how to be soft. Yes, how to be soft. Isn't that a lovely word? I don't think I ever used that word in my life. So many things seem clear to me now."

"Yes, Miss Idy, I agree that all people should be soft."

"Yesterday, while we were bathing the babies, Chessy, so innocent, chaste, and still unsullied, I think, whispered something so sweet to me. She said she never was able to give anyone a gift; she barely could buy food for herself, you know. But here she said she found that she could give a little of herself. She always imagined she carried a big bouquet of flowers, and as she traveled, she would give the flowers away one by one. Yet, at the end of her journey, in some magical way, her bouquet was as large as when she started. Then she hugged and kissed me, and we both laughed at her wonderful story.

"She was well educated by her grandmother, who I learned had been a teacher. Her father drowned and her mother died when she was born. Her grandmother died in Wichita, where she had gone because her other daughter had died. Oh Doctor Allen, that left precious Chessy all alone in this lonely place." At this telling, Miss Idy broke down in bitter tears. Doctor Allen also wept in sympathy.

"I have prayed over and over for forgiveness for neglecting her. We, the church, should have moved her into town to take better care of her. What a lonely place this is.

"She asked me yesterday if she should tell everyone who the father of the babies is. I told her no, not unless she really wanted to, because she wasn't the guilty one. All of Paw Paw is guilty, especially me. Who knows, maybe the time will come when she wants to share this. At that time, she will know when or where because God will let her know. The town, the people, the church will love her unconditionally, I hope. I am going to ask for forgiveness from the pulpit of the Baptist Church."

In the dusky listening night, Doctor Allen, in a whispering voice, said, "Miss Idy, I too am the result, or creation, of two people who loved unwisely." He told her of his own life, his mother's cross she bore daily, and the pain he shared with her. Again, the night listened, but all it heard was the old swing, still creaking out her soft melody.

"Miss Idy, can I sit in my little rocker and hold my baby girl?" Chessy called out. The baby boy was a little slower in gaining strength.

Miss Idy helped her out of bed and put the girl baby on her lap. Miss Idy murmured to herself, "Oftentimes the face reveals the condition of one's heart." If that were true, then she was looking at the most radiant glow of happiness she had ever seen in her life. They heard Doctor Allen's car drive up, and Miss Idy sensed the quivering excitement that trembled from Chessy's little body.

Doctor Allen burst in with a freezer of ice cream and a cake decorated with the words, For the New Mommy. He kissed the babies' and Chessy's and Miss Idy's cheeks. "We are going to have a party tonight. We have fussed and fumed about our babies' names long enough, so tonight, Miss Chessy, there will be no more dilly-dallying around. I am sick and tired of calling our babies '1' and '2', or 'A' and 'B', or baby girl and baby boy.

"Miss Idy, dip us up a huge bowl of ice cream and slice us a piece of that cake while Chessy tells us her names for these two angels."

Chessy innocently whispered, "Can I name my baby girl Idy Chessy Lou and use the initials, I. D. for my baby boy?"

It was quiet in the little room. Miss Idy sat rapt, spellbound. "My darling, I would be honored if you named your babies after me." Then out of the blue, teasing and laughing, Doctor Allen, in a loud voice, said, "The only way you can name these babies after her is if you give them the last name of Allen." They all sat stunned and wordless!

The only sound they heard in the room was the rustling of angel wings.

Turn, O backsliding children, saith the LORD;
for I am married unto you.

JEREMIAH 3:14

Chapter 67

The Backsliding of Miss Idy (as viewed from the porch of the General Store)

Jimmy C., loudly declared that this alarming episode had traveled around and around the Circle Square before the men on the porch heard of it—which was a miracle in itself.

The "B" word had only been whispered, as no one had the audacity or courage to utter it aloud. Most of the Paw Pawites quoted: "Leave the straight and narrow path of righteousness and you travel down the wide road that leads to destruction."

The gist of it started with Granny Octavia, who had always claimed she had the gift of discernment. This was doubted by the men on the porch, because they knew that her granddaughter, Pearly, had caught her dipping snuff on the sly. That wasn't such a great sin, but she hid this from the Baptist Church members, and that was the sin of hypocrisy.

All the men proclaimed there was no doubt that Miss Idy did indeed have the gift of discernment. "Why, Miss Idy can sniff out trouble like Jimmy C.'s dog, Goliath, can sniff out a coon in a high oak tree," one of them remarked.

All shook up, Ray Linden said adamantly, "Now, my friends, do you know that it's been one month today that Miss Idy has stayed out at Chessy's house? I know because my dear wife puts all the major events on the calendar. It appears to me that Miss Idy has done a complete turnaround in what she believes. I can accept the fact of Doctor Allen and Miss Idy staying out there for two days and two nights. We all know that

Chessy and the baby boy barely pulled through, but I am aghast at this continuing devotion."

"Well," Amos said dryly, "it does look quite dubious and suspicious." He lowered his voice and continued. "You all know that Clara and Jacob are not above eavesdropping, and Clara told my wife that as soon as Doctor Allen closes his office, he heads right out in the direction of Chessy's house. Of course, Miss Idy is out there. All of us remember Miss Idy saying that there was a question of ringing the church bell if the girl isn't married when she births a baby."

Otis butted in, "Jimmy was out hunting the night the babies were born, and he saw Doctor Allen drive up into the churchyard. Jimmy said he was afraid that clapper would break the bell again by the force Doctor Allen used when he rang it."

Ray shook his head in wonder. "Again I do say, what is this world coming to when we celebrate a baby's birth when there is no man within yelling distance? Tsk, tsk!"

Early the next morning, as soon as breakfast was over, Jimmy C. saw his dad tucking the family Bible under his arm and starting to head out for the porch of the General Store. "Now Dad, I wish you wouldn't be talking religion or politics with the men, as you know it sometimes makes you testy and upset when you get home."

"Well now, my little smart boy, what would you have us do? Shall we sit there like dummies, deaf and dumb? With all this upheaval we are in, I think we should try to find out what the scriptures say about certain things!" With this scolding to his son, he slammed the door and left for the porch.

So far, the word backsliding hadn't been voiced. But, there it was, a burning issue hovering over them like a morose and sully cloud. Otis felt this would be the day to discuss this word. The men all greeted one another as they had always done. Faltering and stumbling over his words, Tim Curry, sad of countenance, almost whispered, "This is about the worst thing that could happen in Paw Paw. I, for one, firmly believed that we had one person we could call our solid rock."

Ray Linden gamely remarked, "Tom, get your head out of the clouds. This is not the worst thing that has happened here. How about the time Rudy Cropper was beaten so bad that he died right there where you sit? As of now, we have never discovered his killer."

With those startling words, Tom looked a little wild as he looked under his chair.

Otis, testy as usual, slapped his knee with his hand. "Oh, Land of Goshen. We need some help! Boys, listen to what we are discussing. This is about Miss Idy. So, please, stay on the right track.

"We are all thinking the same thing. Why can't we cease this little game and just say the word backsliding? We are not a bunch of scared little wimps but grown men. Therefore, as of now, we think Miss Idy has backslid and this is why I fetched the Good Book. I will read St. Luke, Chapter 9, the 62nd verse. 'No man having put his hand to the plow and looking back, is fit for the kingdom of God.' Gentlemen, that is pretty plain to me. Do you all agree?"

The argument had now escalated with all the men talking at once. Half agreed with Otis; the other half vehemently disagreed. It was like a changing of the guards, as they frequently changed their minds about what the Good Book meant.

Jeremiah spoke up and said, "God said He was married to the backslider. What do you make of that?"

Fred Pinkham, trying to get a word in edgewise, said, "How about the fact that there is no forgiveness if one has blasphemed? David committed adultery, then later David was a man after God's own heart. How about Judas? He hung himself and he was a disciple, no argument there. Apostle Peter denied the Lord three times, yet the Lord called him a 'spiritual rock.' And how about Lot's wife? She just looked back and the Lord turned her into a pillar of salt."

The harangue and tirade went on and on until darkness

drove them home.

Miss Idy had been home for six months and still the ripples of discord about Miss Idy's behavior continued. At times it escalated beyond the pale; this was one of those times. There it was on the front page of the paper, a picture of Doctor Allen and Chessy announcing their marriage in the little Baptist Church. Miss Idy was the head deaconess, so she had to give the blessing on this union. Jeremiah complained loudly, "It is not that we are against the marriage but to have it in a public place! Why in the past, couples would have slipped away to the justice of the peace and in the nighttime!"

Fred Pinkham said, "They ought to wait a year (this is the standard policy) instead of eight months. What is this world coming to!"

Everyone in Paw Paw either saw or heard of this drastic change in Miss Idy. One of the ladies in the Sewing Circle had whispered, "Could it be that she added a little pink rouge on her cheeks?" That surmise was quickly squashed, but all agreed her face had lost its wrinkled, tight lines; her look of anxiety and nervous energy had quieted; and her passionate, zealous behavior for every cause had mellowed.

This morning was no different, as Fred Pinkham voiced belligerently, "Tell me, if you can, what has happened to the high and mighty Miss Idy? Her conduct now bears no resemblance to the way she has always performed in the past? Why she has quieted her military, combative way of walking. At one time we could have predicted the pattern of behavior. Now it's 'turn about face,' no more hot or cold but this lukewarm way has confused everyone in Paw Paw."

Tom Curry butted in, complaining, "We all know she has ruled Paw Paw with an iron fist, and she had the right to do this, being head deaconess of our Baptist Church, the mayor, and superintendent of our school system. How all that happened and came about is still a mystery. Be that as it may, I think her actions are a little syrupy now. I think I prefer the former Miss Idy!"

Jeremiah said, "I want to take us to the Good Book now, in Judges, Chapter 14. The mighty Samson was on his way to see his ladylove when he met a big lion and killed him with his bare hands. Later on one day, he stumbled on the carcass of the lion, and bees had filled the carcass with honey. I am persuaded to believe that this scripture explains Miss Idy to a T." The men all marveled at Jeremiah's wisdom.

What they didn't know was the Father, the Son, and the Holy Spirit were busily involved in the sweet activity of conforming and harmonizing Miss Idy from glory to glory into the likeness and image of Christ, the Lord.

The Spirit of the Lord is upon me,
because he hath anointed me to preach the gospel to the poor;
he hath sent me to heal the brokenhearted,
to preach deliverance to the captives,
and recovering of sight to the blind,
to set at liberty them that are bruised,
to preach the acceptable year of the LORD.

LUKE 4:18-19

Chapter 68

The Calling of Jimmy C.

Miss Idy was talking to herself again; she called it talking to her heart. "Wasn't it just yesterday that Jimmy was giving the Valedictorian speech as he graduated from the eighth grade? Here we sit, waiting for him to begin his high-school graduation Valedictorian address. Oh my, how time does fly."

All of Paw Paw, as well as the residents of Whippoorwill, were here to listen to this outstanding young man. The students of Paw Paw had to come to high school here in Whippoorwill, as Paw Paw did not have one of its own.

"This is going to come to a screeching halt," Miss Idy murmured to herself. "We are going to have our own high school, and soon." She had had this on her mind for some time and she felt that God had it on His mind also. She smiled and wondered if God was smiling too.

The president of the school board announced, "I have the pleasure of giving to you the most important graduate that Paw Paw and Whippoorwill has ever had, someone who has endeared himself to every heart. I present Jimmy C. Simpson."

The hand-clapping applause started with his classmates, then everyone joined in and they all stood up. Then suddenly the large audience grew still as Jimmy C. Simpson, not hesitating or wavering, walked to the podium. Bowing low to the listeners, he began speaking in a clear, firm voice. "I am most privileged and grateful to have the honor of speaking before you, my teachers, fellow students, people of Paw Paw and Whippoorwill.

"I am going to take you to an orchard of fruit trees. Apple trees. We are going to be fruit inspectors. We are going to examine the trees' branches. We will see some branches that are laden with plump, bright apples, these branches bending down low with their sweet burden. Then we will see bare branches here and there; branches with few apples and even those stunted. Then, alas, we will see a few branches are completely dead; those must be burned.

"You can produce luscious fruit or be barren and unfruitful. I am taking to you God's holy Word for the answer of how one can bear this fruit. I will take excerpts from 2 Peter, Chapter 1."

Miss Idy's heart beat a little faster as she looked at the teachers, the principal, the parents, and the dignitaries from Paw Paw and Whippoorwill to see how they were accepting this plain biblical message coming from such a young man. She closed her eyes and, by faith and prayer, took Jimmy C. before the throne of God. Jimmy was safe now. Yes, Jimmy was safe. She smiled as she listened to the rest of his speech.

"'Grace and peace be multiplied unto you through the knowledge of God and Jesus, our Lord. By His divine power, hath given to us all things that pertain unto life and godliness. Whereby given to us exceeding great and precious promises.'"

"I will tell you there are over three thousand promises in the Bible. I tell you this so that in that knowing you may be partakers of the divine nature of God. So that by giving this message all diligence, you can add to your faith, virtue, knowledge, patience, godliness, brotherly kindness, and love. If these things be in you, and they abound, they make you neither be barren nor unfruitful in the knowledge of Jesus, our Lord. But he that lacketh these things is blind and cannot see afar for he has forgotten that he was once a fruitful branch, but now is a branch for the burning. So we must be diligent to make our calling and election sure, for if you do these things, you will never fail and shall have an abundant entrance into God's everlasting kingdom."

The audience was hushed and enthralled by the gracious yet passionate words Jimmy spoke.

The hand clapping started again from his fellow students, and they all stood up. Then everyone in the room joined them.

In spite of all the congratulations and excitement, Jimmy managed to whisper in Miss Idy's ear. "Miss Idy, I want to come to your house tonight. Is it all right?"

She nodded yes, then spoke to her heart, "For this child I have prayed."

While waiting for Jimmy to come, Miss Idy brewed a pot of tea and placed a plate of persimmon cookies on the kitchen table. When he knocked on her door, she opened it and for a minute, they stood looking at each other. Then Jimmy took her in his arms and hugged her. There wasn't any reason to say the tiresome, everyday, "I'm glad you are here" words that everyone uses. He knew she loved him as if he were her son. That knowing warmed his heart and hers too. Towering over her like a giant, he followed her into the kitchen and sat down. She poured him a cup of tea, placed a cookie on his plate, then she sat down across from him and said, "Now, Jimmy, tell me what this meeting is all about."

He knew that he could speak with her and share with her all his questions and that she alone would understand. "Miss Idy, I have come to a crucial point in my life. It is so serious that I am bordering on panic trying to decide what I should do next. I have a scholarship to go to college, and I have that money from the sale of my dog."

She could see the pain in his face as he remembered Goliath.

"I can go into business here in Paw Paw or in Whippoorwill. I think I would do good wherever."

Suddenly, he got up and began pacing the floor with his

long strides while he ran his hands through his tousled hair. "Miss Idy, what do I do? Tell me please, you are the only one I can rely on as I bare my heart and soul to you."

He laughed nervously and looked embarrassed, as he continued without giving her time to speak. "You know, I don't remember when I planned to be a rich man, but it has always been with me. It has been my goal, my whole goal. I don't know why, maybe because of the humbleness of our little town and its people. Maybe I wanted to someday flaunt my riches before everyone in Paw Paw. Then you appeared in my life, upsetting me every way I turned and, little by little, you would bring me down to earth.

"You accomplished that! I remember one time I was playing marbles with some other boys and I spoke up and said, 'Let's play for keepies.' You had warned me that that was a form of gambling. Well, I won all the marbles. There they lay in my hand, but my victory wasn't sweet, as I knew there was the specter of Miss Idy frowning down at me."

Suddenly, he stopped pacing the floor. She looked at him and felt a heartwarming, stirring emotion coming from him as he struggled to speak. "Thank you, Miss Idy, for being who you are and doing the things you believed right. Miss Idy, you tutored me in spite of myself," he chuckled. "Oh, I was an unruly, headstrong, impetuous young man, wasn't I?"

She arose and went to her bedroom and returned carrying a small black velvet box with gold leaves on its lid. She sat it on the table and told Jimmy to open it.

With trembling but gentle hands, he lifted out the newspaper clippings. They were from the Paw Paw Times and the Whippoorwill Gazette, and they were all about him, Jimmy C. Simpson. He noticed the one about Goliath, the dog he had sold for five hundred dollars, and felt that old tinge of pain. She had saved everything that had been written about him, and he could tell these clipping were precious treasures to her. He felt hot tears forming in his eyes; there was no way to hold them back. He bowed his head, and their tears blended as one on Miss Idy's little kitchen table.

Jimmy wept for the son this wonderful woman never had. He was going to see to it that she had him. He made a covenant with himself and God that he would be there for her if she ever needed him.

She got up, walked behind him, and kissed the top of his head. Then she abruptly said, "Now Jimmy, it's time to stop this nonsense and get on with dealing with your problems."

He knew love was behind her brusque words.

"Okay, Miss Idy. Well, there was a lawyer there at the graduation ceremonies tonight. He practices in Whippoorwill, and his name is Daniel Peterson. He brought a friend from Washington, D.C., with him named Warren Bishop. Mr. Peterson told me that Mr. Bishop is a politician, a big go-getter, and he's looking for some future candidates he can school for high positions in politics. He's looking with the governor's mansion in view, or a congressional or maybe even a senator's seat."

"Well, it seems they came and looked us over. Mr. Bishop appeared to be pleased and excited with everything he saw—the General Store, the men on the porch, Doctor Allen's office, the telephone exchange, the library, and the paper. And he liked me. Oh yes, he thought this was the kind of background that would get the voter's blood stirring.

"The problem is he told me I would have to go back to Washington, D.C., with him and go to college there. He said he would see to it that I would be groomed and would meet all the bigwigs."

Jimmy again started pacing the floor. "Miss Idy, I think this would be a way to help turn this state around for the common folks. What do you think? Do you think this is all a pipe dream? It sounds a little far-fetched to me."

As she listened and watched, she wondered if this tall, stalwart person before her was a boy or a man. She decided he was a man; he might even become a man among men. "Jimmy C.

Simpson, never doubt that you are qualified to be what you want to be. God said without a vision, the people perish. You alone can make this decision, my dear."

All of a sudden, Jimmy stopped pacing and sat down at the table. He poured a cup of tea, ate another cookie, and looked at her with a sparkling twinkle in his black eyes. "Miss Idy, tell me, please tell me, how you can read my thoughts? Tell me, my mentor, my teacher, the one that long ago put a leash around my body, soul, and spirit. Tell me how you captured this rebellious radical youth who strained against his bondage. It seems like you already know the things that I have only discussed with my soul.

"Miss Idy what if I became a teacher? I could get some school buses and bring children in from far and wide. I could teach them and even raise up teachers out of our own students. You and I together could build schools and teach using the latest methods. I'm sure I could convince the people to pay more taxes to help us build them. What do you think?"

Before she could even answer, he began again. "Then in the back of my mind, I have always yearned to be a journalist. I like the idea of writing for newspapers and reporting. Maybe not here, but you know our town is going to grow after this Depression and drought is over.

"Then again, I could go to college and maybe become a doctor. In the vision of things, I see a small hospital, and Miss Idy, I can see myself being a sympathizing, compassionate doctor. I could heal the outward man, and you could be the healing voice for the inward man. You can light the candle of the Lord! Oh yes, can you see? Think about that Miss Idy. If a man's soul and spirit is healed, most often the outward man has also been healed. You know Malachi wrote: 'The son of righteousness will arise with the healing in his wings.'

"Miss Idy, I see a big new Baptist church with rooms for Sunday school for the children. I see a small Christian college where our youth can prepare for the ministry. I see a youth center. I see a place to school missionaries where they cannot only hear the pleading cries from the heart of man, but also go everywhere they are needed in the world. Jesus said, just before He left, 'Go ye and teach all nations, and I will go with you.'

"Miss Idy," he said with a sigh, "I can't deny it anymore. I have a calling, a summons, a mission from God." Jimmy carried her along with his eagerness and high expectations. "I just had to talk with you first. But you know, in truth, I think I have already made a covenant with God. It's as if I have a fire in my bones. I must tell His story, take it to the lost, to the ones that are in the dregs of despair. King David cried to the Lord, 'As the heart panteth after the brooks of water, so panteth my soul after thee.'

"Miss Idy, this had become an obsession. The Old Testament prophets told in the eleventh chapter of Hebrews, 'They always moved on, they all sought for that city which hath foundations whose builder and maker was God.' The apostle Paul wrote that he always pressed for the mark, the prize of the high calling of Christ Jesus.

"Miss Idy, this calling awakens me in the night. There is a wonderful feeling of warmth I feel spreading over me, the chosen vessel, Jimmy C. Simpson. Sometimes it happens in the daytime when I see someone who needs help.

"But, Miss Idy, I don't feel qualified. Therefore, I must search out a Christian college or a school of divinity. I want to be taught. I need to learn so much. I want to be a leader of the spiritual movement, which I think will encircle the world. I want to discover how God wants to use me." Jimmy suddenly stopped and raised his arms up, and she saw the look of the Divine on his face. She remembered the passage about Moses: 'And it came to pass when Moses came down from Mount Sinai, he wist not that the skin of his face show and Israel put a veil over his face.'"

As she sat and listened to this anointed plea to his God, she remembered her own calling which she received so long ago. She should have had a little training herself. Maybe then she would have been more helpful to people instead of just their judge and jury.

Jimmy was still, tranquil in this most holy moment, as he drank of spiritual waters that didn't come from any well.

Jimmy C. sat down at the table after giving this highly emotional speech. She knew that it was time for her to speak and that all was in order, ordained by the Holy Spirit. Her tone and manner bordered on the celestial and loving; yet sitting apart from anything that was earthly. "My son, are you going to be able to be a servant, not only of God, but a servant of the masses who will come to your cathedral of learning? It won't be the richest, most affluent that will beat a path to your door, you know. It will be the poor, the sick, the troubled, those from the highways and byways of life. Can you bid them to come in?

"You must remember nothing touches us that has not passed through the hands of our Father. Everything we endure is designed to prepare us for serving others more effectively. Everything. Our heavenly Father is committed to shaping us into the image of His Son, Jesus Christ. We should only be satisfied when we awaken in God's likeness."

"Miss Idy, where is the will of God? How can a mere man obtain it?"

"Jimmy, the will of God dwells in that place where your will does not dwell. There, and there alone, you find it.

"My son, I think you are right. You should go to a Bible school for at least a couple of years. You need to study and depend upon the Spirit of God to lead you into deeper depths and higher heights. I would like to think this little quotation came from the Bible, but it doesn't. Shakespeare wrote that 'knowledge is the wings wherewith we fly to heaven.'" She smiled at the thought.

"Oh, Miss Idy, do you realize I have kept you up the entire night? Please forgive me."

Jimmy started to walk over to her chair, then impulsively he knelt before her. She began stroking his tousled hair and said, "My son, you are going to fulfill your dreams of riches that you've wanted all your life. You will, indeed, be rich, rich with the blessings of God."

As Jimmy went out the door into the night, Miss Idy whispered to herself, "Yes, he has gone forth, my heavenly Father, but I think You and I should watch him closely, as I think he might just set Your world on fire." She smiled and murmured, "You said a little child would lead them."

I will greatly rejoice in the LORD,
my soul shall be joyful in my God;
for he hath clothed me with the garments of salvation,
he hath covered me with the robe of righteousness,
as a bridegroom decketh himself with ornaments,
and as a bride adorneth herself with her jewels.

ISAIAH 61:10

Chapter 69

The Wedding

The whole town filled the little church to overflowing because a wedding like this had never happened before in Paw Paw. It was scheduled to begin at 2:00 P.M., but Miss Idy had arrived at the Baptist Church at noon. If anything were out of kilter, she would have time to correct it, although she had worked all day yesterday and felt everything was perfect. She opened the door and caught her breath at the beauty of the little church. The ladies from the Sewing Circle had helped her scrub the old board floors and wash the windows inside and out until they shined.

It had been almost three years since there had been rain, so there were no fresh flowers to decorate the church. To solve that problem, Miss Idy bought crepe paper in pink, blue, and white and made paper flowers. They decorated the edges of the altar, the podium, and the ends of the seats with pink and blue paper flowers and satin ribbon bows.

Miss Idy sat down on a back seat to rest until it was time to ring the bell. She remembered another wedding, so elegant, so elaborate, in another town and long ago. But now the memory carried no sting of shame or bitterness. Now she only saw how that trial by fire had led to her salvation, her calling. She realized she was chosen by God to serve Him by serving others, but with love and compassion instead of the "holier than thou," sanctimonious, self-righteousness.

"Oh yes, Chessy, you and your babies have taught me that and taught me well." Those sweet little children had led her to peace, just like the Scriptures say.

Miss Idy awakened from her reverie. "Oh, merciful heaven, it's time to ring the bell!"

As she pulled the rope, the ringing of the silvery bell sounded like a pastoral hymn being sung as it drifted over hills and valleys and echoed back to the bell ringer. The wives in their kitchens, the men on the porch, and the little children at play stopped at this signal. The peal of the bell marked a new beginning in Paw Paw.

Doctor Allen and Chessy decided to have just one attendant in their wedding. Since Reverend Peabody was the minister, it appeared logical to choose Lizzy. She was excited about it, especially when Doctor Allen told her he would pay for all of her wedding finery, as she knew Reverend Peabody would be happy about that.

Reverend Peabody nodded to Miss Rose Anderson to begin playing the wedding march. Jimmy C. Simpson opened the door and down the aisle came Lizzy, dressed in a blue chiffon gown. Everyone, including Miss Idy, gasped and gazed ogle-eyed as Lizzy smiled and fairly flaunted her blossoming body. Reverend Peabody's face blanched with astonishment. One could see the reverend had known nothing of his wife's condition. The men on the porch commented later that this blessed event probably went unnoticed by him because she had been in the family way so often in recent years. People were just pulling themselves together when Chessy Lou Darnell and Doctor Allen came in the door.

She wore a dusty pink gown of lace and satin, and her bountiful curly hair was caught up and held by glittering jeweled combs. Everyone caught their breath at her beauty and another surprise as well. Chessy carried her baby boy, and Doctor Allen carried the baby girl. This caused a bit of a twitter, and then the hearts of the people softened.

The ceremony proceeded without a hitch until Reverend Peabody said, "Doctor Allen, do you take Chessy as your lawful wedded wife?"

Miss Idy felt the blood drain from her face. Her heart cried, "Stop! He loved me first!" She thought of the night the colts were born and felt his arms around her.

Yes, this last year had been bittersweet for her. She had let her lover go and then walked through the pain of seeing him turn his special affection from her to another. Dear Chessy. She looked so beautiful today!

Reverend Peabody droned on, "Is there anyone gathered here that would object to this marriage? If not, forever hold thy peace."

Miss Idy looked at the congregation. No one knew how she had been loved. And with her secret knowing she was suddenly content. She looked at Doctor Allen. He was like the dear brother she had never had, beaming from ear to ear with his newfound happiness. God had given him the love and family he had longed for since he had been a child.

Her heart whispered, "Good-bye my love, good-bye." Again, God reached down from heaven and touched an aching heart, and from that moment her joy was free and unfettered. As Doctor Allen and Chessy turned around holding their babies, she stood up. Her enchanting voice rang out in the final song as Doctor and Mrs. Allen marched down the aisle, arm in arm, babies in tow.

Miss Idy glowed in her black silk taffeta gown and matching black hat. Only Jimmy Simpson noticed the big paper pink rose on the brim.

He hath made every thing beautiful in his time.

ECCLESIASTES 3:11

Chapter 1

The Divine Prophecy of Miss Idy

Miss Idy walked through the dried leaves, grasses, and weeds. They made a crackling, splintering sound under her feet. Here and there were patches of bare whitish dust that her shoes sank into. She walked up the slight hill to the edge of the ten acres of vegetables and small fruit the town had planted. Without this food, the people would have starved. She felt humbled as she realized that she had only sowed the seed; it was God who brought the harvest.

She looked with love where Jimmy C. had constructed a crude irrigation system for getting Mr. Plenty's water to the ten-acre field. When Morgan Creek went dry, they pumped from Plenty's Well. The residents of Paw Paw were not surprised at Jimmy's contraption. Who else could have done it? It came to her that one of the men on the porch had remarked that God lost the pattern when he created Jimmy, and there wouldn't be anymore like him. Miss Idy forced a smile again. Talking to herself, she said, "The Bible agrees with them. 'For what can a man do that cometh after the king, even that which hath been already done?'"

There was still a lot of hand-watering to do. The children did that, and they complained every day that they were going to die from this cruel torture. Their job erupted occasionally into water fights. Since Miss Idy began overseeing the hand-watering operation, she found that by day's end she had lost the power of speech from scolding the children.

Miss Idy was contented and satisfied. From these dark weary years of want, old feuds, strife, and hard feelings had come to a halt as families helped one another in the struggle to keep their children fed and maybe a pair of shoes on their feet in the winter. The town of Paw Paw became famous and even prospered a little during these terrifying years. City fathers from other small towns came to Paw Paw and were flabbergasted, as the men on the porch liked to say. These officials went back to their own little towns and tried to pattern themselves after it.

Men from the big city had come searching out the best place for a five and ten cent store and a ladies' apparel shop. She had already discussed with others about starting a cheese factory, a shoe store, and a garment factory. She thought a new courthouse for the town's circle square was a good idea.

As Miss Idy stood looking out over the town, she saw the future. She saw a high school built in Paw Paw, so the children wouldn't have to travel to Whippoorwill to finish their schooling. She knew Jimmy would build a new and bigger Baptist Church—its attendance had doubled during the Depression and drought. She knew without a doubt he would also build his Christian Bible college, a place for missionaries, evangelists, pastors, teachers—anyone who felt the "spiritual call"—to study and prepare themselves.

She knew she would soon see a big truck unloading building supplies beside Doctor Allen's office, as he planned to build a big house for Chessy and their babies. He also wanted to build a small hospital in town where nurses and students would come and learn the healing arts. Her heart was healed of its pain when she saw him. The old adage was true, it was better to have loved and lost than never to have loved at all.

Clara and Jacob would be building a new porch for the General Store, as the men who sat there were complaining that the current one was a mite dangerous for man and beast—the beasts, naturally, were their hound dogs. Miss Idy smiled to herself as she thought of the new banister. She guessed it wouldn't take long before it mysteriously became wobbly, so the men could continue their evaluation of the health of everyone who came to the store.

Dear Jacob and Clara moved some merchandise to the back of the store and put one of his pianos and an organ near the front window. Clara called it "Jacob's Music Corner." There he taught the endless line of children that were eager to learn the playing and singing from Jacob. He also began to teach several Paw-Pawites how to build the magnificent instruments. She had to smile as the men on the porch complained that Clara was his most enthusiastic pupil and her lessons ended up in various ways of kissing. The men called it "lolly-gagging" and they declared to Miss Idy, "We're afraid this kind of conduct will contaminate the children!" So one day in a discreet and loving way, she told Clara she ought to pull the curtain down when Jacob was teaching her.

Beloved Jeremiah and his lovely Priscilla were starting to build their new house; for sure their material was very scarce and rough because of the lack of money in this Depression. Miss Idy's eyes were misting as she thought of the way the men on the porch agreed to use the big pile of lumber at the mill to help Jeremiah with his house and were donating their labor of love a few hours each day.

Jimmy C. said, "This is indeed one of the Lord's miracles in Paw Paw."

Miss Idy looked down at the vegetable acres. She had almost forgotten the wildflowers that once grew in this field. She vowed they would soon start growing again and thought she might as well stop at the General Store and order the seeds on her way home. She could also tell the men on the porch they had another task—sowing those seeds.

A soft tender smile played around her lips. "Yes, it will rain again when God makes up His mind. Let patience have her perfect work," she murmured.

Miss Idy came out of her delightful reverie as she saw Jimmy C. coming up the hill to join her. How did he always know where she was? She answered her own question by asking another. How did she always know where he was?

When he stood beside her, she said, "Jimmy, my dear son, a portion of God is housed in everyone's body. Therefore, we must be careful in our associations with others, whether at work or play, that we do nothing to quench the Spirit that is within us. God's love is timeless. It is like an ever-flowing stream that bears its sons and daughters away, yet each deciding which way to go. In God's eternal love, there is no where and no when. When we are able to grasp this, it causes us to step a little higher.

"Jimmy," she murmured, "I have learned the hard way, even to the suffering of my own body, the cost of judging one's fellow man. Sometimes we judge someone as if we were looking at a tapestry on the wrong side. We see a figure distinguishable, yet there are so many ends and knotted threads that the beauty and exactness of the work is obscured. We look at the outward appearance of a man, but God looks at his heart."

Miss Idy smiled and said, "Jimmy, I'm sure the Lord is looking down on our lovely tapestry from the right side this morning."

"Miss Idy, you must not be too hard on yourself. You have taught me it is important to forgive others, but it is also important to forgive ourselves. I knew from the day I first saw you many years ago as you came tripping down the dusty road to Paw Paw and threw that big pink flower in the ditch that you were special."

Miss Idy gasped, "Why, Jimmy, I didn't know anyone saw me that day. You never told me."

"No, Miss Idy, I never told anyone. But I must tell you now that every good thing that has happened in Paw Paw is because of you." Then in a loving voice, he whispered, "Who knoweth whether thou art come to the kingdom, for such a time as this," Esther, Chapter 4.

Dear reader, I know I have left you perplexed and befuddled about the no vote that was in Jeremiah's hat at Paw Paw's elections. Yes, you knew it was Miss Idy. Instead of leaving the men on the porch at the General Store laughing, she left them a mystery to solve when they had exhausted the subject of the day.

Rise up, my love, my fair one, and come away.
For, lo, the winter is past, the rain is over and gone;
the flowers appear on the earth;
the time of the singing of birds is come,
and the voice of the turtle is heard in our land;
the fig tree putteth forth her green figs,
and the vines with the tender grape give a good smell.
Arise, my love, my fair one, and come away.

Song of Solomon 2:10-13

Epilogue

Thank You, my heavenly Father, for giving to me the sweet pleasure of writing my beautiful book.

LaVonne Snowden

THE END